HEART OF THE MACHINE

HEART OF THE MACHINE

TERMINATE THE OTHER WORLD!

BOOK 4

Icalos

Podium

All rights reserved. No part of this publication may be reproduced, stored in a retrieval system, or transmitted in any form or by any means electronic, mechanical, photocopying, recording, or otherwise without prior written permission from Podium Publishing.

This is a work of fiction. Names, characters, places, and incidents are either products of the author's imagination or used fictitiously. Any resemblance to actual events, locales, or persons, living, dead, or undead, is entirely coincidental.

Copyright © 2024 by Andrew Ellison

Cover design by Husa

ISBN: 978-1-0394-8983-7

Published in 2024 by Podium Publishing
www.podiumaudio.com

HEART OF THE MACHINE

1

Retreat

"Congratulations, you just lost us the war."

—Zaerzis Evruth, High Archon of the Empire of the Sun, after hearing that an Archon set fire to Elteno.

Flames and smoke filled the Corvanus night sky. Residents were roused from their sleep, exclaiming as they looked out their windows. Limitanei and comitatenses both hastily equipped their armor and weapons, rushing out into the streets to escort Water mages to the affected sites.

A consul's villa burned, and the clear deployment of magic barriers, not to mention the strategic magic circle lighting up the night sky, made it absolutely clear this was no mere fire.

And in the midst of the burning villa, at the heart of it all, were two girls, both wrapped in metallic armor, with flickering lights replacing their left eyes. NSLICE-00P's cybernetic components linked to Ateia's, quickly evaluating her state.

"Observation: NSLICE Ateia has undergone significant damage and is in a state of severe fatigue. Recommending standby sentry mode until friendly unit is restored to full efficiency."

With that, Ateia's robotic eye flickered then shut off.

"Wha . . ."

Ateia's organic eye closed midsentence, then NSLICE-00P Transferred her to the Medium Monster Hangar for safety. She had not attempted to do so previously because all dungeon-related intel was classified from Imperial-affiliated individuals, including her friendlies. But at this stage, Ateia had become her full subordinate, and now had access to that intel due to integration into the NSLICE network in any case, so said restrictions no longer applied.

Besides, under the current scenario, the major directive to protect her friendlies was the greater priority.

NSLICE-00P took stock of the situation. Most of the hostiles in this facility had been terminated, and she had identified the corpse of the woman who had forcibly relocated her when she had returned to the area of operations. One hostile with a powerful mana signature had jumped into a tub of water in the room. NSLICE-00P scanned the tub now, but could find no trace of the hostile besides some nonstandard energy readings.

So, one hostile remained at large. Additionally, she did not know the identity of the hostiles, or how to pick them out from the other Imperials. From context clues, they appeared to resemble the cult Magister Vibius had spoken to her about, though he was designated untrustworthy, so said classification was not confirmed.

Regardless, she did not know who else in this city might be identified with the group. So . . . NSLICE-00P wasn't sure if there were any further targets to terminate, where they might be if so, or what kind of resistance she might encounter. She also needed to confirm the safety of her other friendlies. So, ultimately, she decided to regroup with the others and determine if they had any intel on the threat.

With that, NSLICE-00P boosted out of the hole in the roof and shot into the sky once more, ignoring the gasps of Corvanus's residents all around as she flew from the burning building.

00B jumped as something suddenly appeared in the hangar. He slowly walked over to it, and then his organic eye widened.

It was the evil squishy thing! She had invaded his home!

Only . . . she wasn't squishy or evil anymore. The Great Mother had apparently adopted her into the family, much like she had with the wise Big Sister Lilussees and the shady Big Brother Rattingtale. And the Great Mother had also evolved the squishy thing to be not so squishy.

00B pondered for a moment. But only for a moment.

She was part of the family now, and so evil no longer. And it was 00B's job, as declared by the Great Mother, to protect the family.

So, 00B crouched down by the evi—new family member to protect her as she slept.

Agedia and Magister Appius led the group as they ran after NSLICE-00P, who had flown in the direction of Consul Noxisius's villa.

But then the sky lit up with a strategic magic circle, and big fires broke out ahead. The group came to a halt as Magister Appius and Agedia glanced at each other. The Magister Exploratore sighed.

"So . . . I'm guessing a diplomatic solution is no longer an option?"

Agedia's eyes narrowed.

"It never was."

Just then, the group saw NSLICE-00P flying through the sky, directly toward them. She turned down to land in front of them with a crash. Agedia frowned.

"Shiny girl, where's Ateia?"

"Answer: This unit has NSLICE Ateia secured in a safe location."

Agedia glared at her, but then sighed and slumped her shoulders.

". . . I want to see her, but . . . I suppose I'll take your word for it for now. Just tell me this, NSLICE-00P, queen of the Dobhar: Is she alright?"

"Affirmative Response: NSLICE Ateia is currently functional, though in a state of fatigue, and so undergoing rest cycles to restore organic component efficiency."

Agedia stared at her for a second before shaking her head.

"That will have to do. So, what now, shiny girl?"

NSLICE-00P's robotic eye flickered.

"Mission Status: All confirmed hostiles in the immediate vicinity have been terminated or else have retreated from the area. Request: This unit is unable to confirm if additional hostiles are present. Please present any intel regarding the current foes."

Agedia frowned. "Cult of Mana. Call themselves the Heralds of the New Dawn. Unfortunately, your guess is as good as mine, shiny girl. If I knew how to track them down, I would have killed them all a long time ago."

Agedia then turned to face Magister Appius, who sighed and shook his head.

"They're very slippery, that's for sure. We thought we had driven them out of the North years ago. Apparently, I was deeply mistaken."

"Acknowledged."

NSLICE-00P again analyzed her situation, as well as the events that had led to it. She had been deceived by a social offer, giving a hostile an opportunity to activate an unknown capability which NSLICE-00P did not have any countermeasures for. This had resulted in NSLICE-00P being removed from the area of operations, and Ateia taking severe damage. NSLICE-00P additionally calculated that Ateia could have been terminated before she would have been able to respond if that had been the hostiles' goal.

And while the hostiles in the area had been dealt a blow, a notable member of the group had escaped, and neither she, her friendlies, nor the Imperial authorities had any means of identifying other members of the group. There was also no data on the extent to which the Empire had been infiltrated by the group, only that they had apparently evaded notice by the Magister Exploratore, a high-ranking authority responsible for intelligence gathering.

This was a scenario NSLICE-00P could not tolerate. The hostile could return or have additional assets in the area that could threaten her, hiding among the otherwise cordial Empire. As long as that was the case, there was an unacceptable probability of failing the major directive. There was even a significant risk of NSLICE-00P being terminated herself, and thus a risk to her primary directive as well.

"Response: Hostiles have displayed previously unknown capabilities that this unit lacks sufficient countermeasures for, and this unit is not able to terminate all known hostiles at this time. This unit and friendlies will retreat to a secure location until the threat is terminated or sufficient countermeasures have been developed."

One of the knights stepped forward and saluted at that.

"Greetings, queen of the Dobhar. I'm Captain Julianus Secundius Urbicus, a knight of Consul Hiberius. I believe I can offer some assistance with that. My liege owns several villas in the outskirts and surrounding territories. We can retreat to one of those if you wish."

"Query: Please state reasoning and end goal of offered assistance by unaffiliated unit."

At that, Taog stepped forward and tapped NSLICE-00P's shoulder. "Ah, Seero, these guys helped us tonight. They broke in and saved me and Estrith."

NSLICE-00P turned to Estrith. She scowled but nodded her head. Agedia also nodded.

"The Hiberius family does owe you for saving Rector Aemilia."

NSLICE-00P's robotic eye flickered as she calculated. On the one hand, she had gotten into this situation because of social contact with individuals she lacked data on. If she didn't know their full affiliation and directives, then interacting with them was a risk.

On the other hand, these particular individuals had apparently already committed hostile actions toward her foes tonight, rescuing two of her friendlies in the process. And said battle had claimed a powerful member of the hostile group due to the termination of the hostile that had relocated her. As a result, the probability that these particular individuals were associated with the hostile group was extremely low.

"Acknowledged. Warning: This unit must inform unaffiliated individuals that any suspected hostile intent will result in immediate termination."

Captain Julianus saluted once more. "We would not dream of it, Your Majesty. Right this way, then."

Agedia turned to Magister Appius and narrowed her eyes, gripping her lance. "So, looks like we're going, Uncle. What are you going to do?"

Magister Appius frowned as Agedia tensed.

"Well, as the Magister Exploratore, I should *probably* ask Her Majesty to explain herself before the court, given that she very obviously set a *consul's* villa on fire, but . . . under the circumstances, it can't be helped. I already know why she did it, after all."

He looked into Agedia's eyes and gave a sad smile. "Go. This cult has clearly gotten the drop on me. I can't even protect an Amicitia Populi Elteni in the heart of Corvanus. I don't know how the court will respond if she runs, but it's probably for the best that she remains at large. And I will keep it that way for as long as I am able."

Agedia met his gaze for a moment before looking away. The group set off into the night, leaving the Magister Exploratore behind.

But as they were running away, Agedia whispered under her breath.

"Thank you, Uncle."

The knights led the group out of Corvanus just as the guards were reacting to the chaos. They went out a smaller entrance used exclusively by high-ranking officials, and so set off without an issue, traveling to a remote villa on a medium-size farm. The attendants there led the group to a small reception room.

Inside, they found a middle-aged man in a toga. He had sharp, narrow eyes, an angular face, and a stern expression.

"You must be NSLICE-00P. I am Consul Septimus Hiberius Conciliator."

"Affirmative. Greeting: This unit is designated NSLICE-00P. It is nice to meet you."

Consul Hiberius nodded.

"I am pleased to meet you as well, though I wish it were under less troubling circumstances. I understand you have had a violent disagreement with Consul Noxisius tonight?"

"Affirmative."

Consul Hiberius took a deep breath.

"A regrettable turn of events, but I will assume you had good cause. In any case, now it's time that the Hiberius family repays its debts. Lafrenia!"

A Dimindium Pendem woman walked into the room. "At your service, Consul."

"See to it that Her Majesty NSLICE-00P receives any goods or services she requires, and that no one intrudes upon the privacy of our lands."

Lafrenia saluted. "As you command."

Consul Hiberius then marched toward the door. "I will see to it that the court does not make any regrettable decisions. It is high time they recall why the Hiberius family has ruled the Northern Court for generations."

Just before he left, he turned his head to glance at NSLICE-00P. "A question. Rector Aemilia Hibera of Turannia, is she in good health?"

"Response: This unit's last record indicates Rector Aemilia Hibera had no outstanding physical issues and was in fully functioning condition."

Consul Hiberius nodded, pausing for a moment before carefully picking his words.

". . . It seems that daughter of mine is trying her best, despite everything. I suppose it is time I do the same."

With that, he left the room. Lafrenia turned to NSLICE-00P and saluted. "I am at your command, Your Majesty. We have rooms already prepared for you and your associates; what else can we assist you with?"

NSLICE-00P glanced around, her robotic eye flickering. "Friendly Taog appears to have been disarmed and requires additional weaponry. This unit's friendlies appear to lack adequate supplies. A resupply is necessary before any additional actions may be taken."

Lafrenia saluted once more. "It shall be done, Your Majesty. If that is all, may I lead you to your rooms?"

"Affirmative."

2

Friendly Power Cycling

"Query: Has the friendly attempted a shutdown and reboot of organic components?"
—An NSLICE unit, before an incident leading to an extensive rewrite of first aid protocols.

A forest was filled to the brim with plant life. Trees grew so tall and spread their leaves so far that their trunks cracked under the weight of their branches. Bushes filled the undergrowth, forming a solid wall of branches and thorns. Vines covered every inch of every surface, creeping along the ground, up stems and branches, and wrapping around the trees.

In the center of this sea of green was one small patch of brown. A squad of elite knights walked in the middle of this clearing, reinforced by a Legion assault team. Battlemages led by a Magus Major continuously chanted and formed magic circles, creating walls of fire to push back the greenery. The elite knights cut down the plants that tried to grow even through the flames, the thorns and vines that struck at them proving entirely ineffective against their enchanted armor, high defense, and powerful defensive skills.

The clearing slowly inched through the forest as the strongest of the knights cleared a path, his sword glowing and launching arcs of light which each cut down several trees at a time.

At that moment, one of the mages fumbled, and their magic circle flickered. The Magus Major called out, and the lead knight raised his hand into a fist.

"Break!"

The Magus Major thrust his staff into the ground, and a barrier appeared over the entire group. The mages and knights walked into the center, plopping onto the ground as supply carriers moved to distribute food, drink, and potions. The Legion troops formed a perimeter of bulwarks and slayers as some

Exploratores spread potions in a circle around them, then the Magus Major dropped his spell.

A mage from the Imperial Necrotorum began to chant, and the ring of potion began to glow with black-and-purple light. Plants wilted and decayed as they tried to grow over the perimeter, allowing the slayers to cut down the remainder from behind the bulwark's shields.

It was not perfect. A thorn passed a shield and lodged into a bulwark's shoulder. A vine wrapped around a slayer's halberd and pulled him out of the line. There were injuries, and even a death as the vines pulled a soldier into the decay field. But the Legion held, and neither monster nor corrupted plant made it past the perimeter.

After a short while, the Magus Major once again formed a ring of fire around the perimeter. He nodded at the lead knight as the knights and battlemages rose to their feet. The lead knight gave the command, and the Legion dropped the defense as the knights took their place. After a quick moment to assess and treat their casualties, the group continued on their way.

And so, the assault on a new Overgrowth dungeon continued . . .

Emperor Lucius and Aedile Hortensus sat in the war room. All around them, Legion staff rushed about. Magister Peditum Ausonius was receiving their reports and issuing commands.

"Reporting: Velus's Pass and the Gap of Vindex have cleared their dungeons! They say they can start deploying legions in three hours!"

Magister Peditum Ausonius nodded. "Tell them they have one. Durocobrivis can't hold out much longer than that. What's the situation in Mestaynga?"

"The Black Hawk Order has arrived and is beginning their assault!"

The magister nodded. "Good. And the Imperial Academy?"

"The Imperial Guard is on-site, and an assault is already underway. Reports indicate the dungeon should be cleared shortly."

Magister Peditum Ausonius sighed in relief. "Good. Once we can, let's get some Magus Majors over to Dhor Thoram. Then, it will just be up to Magister Verrucosis to handle Elteno, and we'll be in the clear."

Emperor Lucius took a deep breath, resisting the urge to sigh as well. It appeared they would make it through the night, even without the queen of the Dobhar.

Frowning, he turned to an assistant of his.

"Any word from Consul Noxisius or Magister Appius? I trust their business was important enough, but it has been a while, has it not?"

The assistant frowned and shook his head. "No word as of yet, Your Majesty."

Emperor Lucius furrowed his brow. He felt deeply uneasy on that course of events. What could be so important as to draw away the only consul in

Corvanus and the Magister Exploratore of the entire North on this night of all nights?

Just then, a soldier burst into the room, dripping sweat and breathing heavily. "Magister Peditum, urgent report from the Corvanus limitanei!"

Magister Ausonius groaned and held his head while Emperor Lucius sucked in his breath. And there it was.

Magister Ausonius nodded at the soldier. "Report."

"Consul Noxisius's villa has been attacked, and the whole thing went up in flames! Reports are saying the queen of the Dobhar was involved! Magister Exploratore Appius is on the scene now!"

Emperor Lucius blinked at this news. He stood completely still for a second, and then he gave in to his feelings and held his face with both hands, letting out a groan.

Just *what* was going on?!

Everyone was exhausted after the end of the day, and so separated to their own rooms.

NSLICE-00P spent the night monitoring Ateia's condition. Her status was . . . anomalous. Ateia's cybernetic components reported an organic body that was healthy, if displaying signs of significant fatigue, but that was also giving off nonstandard readings. NSLICE-00P could not yet interpret those readings, though she did detect Holy mana among them.

Ateia's own cybernetic components were receiving data they could not fully interpret; NSLICE-00P's analysis revealed it was somewhat similar to the effects of the Divination spell. Still, with Ateia's state as it was, and given NSLICE-00P's own failed attempts to modify the Divination spell, she predicted it was risky to attempt any sort of interference.

So, she simply allowed whatever was happening to Ateia to happen while monitoring her vital signs . . .

Fortunately, no further physical damage occurred, and the night passed without incident. NSLICE-00P joined the others for a morning organic refueling, then Lafrenia led them to a private room where they could talk. Agedia and Taog both turned to NSLICE-00P with serious looks on their faces.

"Okay, shiny girl. I let it go last night given the circumstances, but now that we have a moment, let's hear it. I want to know where Ateia went, and to head there myself. I won't be able to calm down until I see her alive."

Taog nodded his agreement. NSLICE-00P's robotic eye flickered as she checked over Ateia's state. She had not fully recovered, but had stabilized at this point.

"Acknowledged."

NSLICE-00P subsequently deployed Ateia from the hangar into the room. Agedia, Taog, and Estrith jumped at her sudden appearance.

"That was . . . um . . ."

Agedia shook her head and tried to focus on the important parts. She walked over to Ateia and poked her arm, activating every skill that would see through an illusion. By every measure she had, it appeared the girl was real. She put aside the question of *where* in the world Ateia had been and how exactly NSLICE-00P recovered her without a magic circle or anything similar for now, because she had other questions.

"You gave her new armor, huh, shiny girl?"

"Affirmative."

Taog furrowed his brow. "Wait . . . Seero . . . didn't you say you couldn't remove your armor for some reason?"

"Affirmative."

Taog's frown deepened. "And . . . this is the same kind of armor?"

"Affirmative."

"That's—"

But NSLICE-00P cut Taog off.

"Statement: Diagnostics on NSLICE Ateia complete. Disengaging standby sentry mode."

Ateia's organic eye slowly opened. She blinked before glancing around.

"Taog . . . Seero . . . ?" Her robotic eye started flickering. "Confused Query: What's . . . happening? Last this unit remembers, she was in some dark place with . . . with . . ." Ateia furrowed her brow, then her organic eye widened. "I . . . I was . . . Gah!"

Suddenly, Ateia clutched her head. Her robotic eye began to glow bright, and she reverted to an expressionless face.

"Warning: High levels of stress detected among organic components. Initiating emergency intelligence leashing measures. Reinforcing emotional controls."

Ateia blinked, then she frowned, and then started to scream and clutch at her head.

"IT HURTS!"

Taog and Agedia's eyes widened as Ateia rolled on the floor, swapping between screaming and an emotionless face. Her robotic eye was spinning and flickering rapidly, while the skin of her organic half was starting to glow with an inner light.

"Ateia! What's going on?!"

Agedia whirled on NSLICE-00P. "Shiny girl! Do you know what's happening? Can you help her?!"

"Analyzing . . ."

NSLICE-00P's robotic eye flickered as her own emotional controls started to waver. From what she could tell, Ateia's cybernetic components were attempting to apply emotional controls. Only, the process was not going well and was obviously causing Ateia's organic components some distress.

Neither NSLICE-00P nor Ateia's cybernetic components understood how that was occurring, and so did not have a solution for this particular problem . . . But as Ateia was stating that damage was occurring, NSLICE-00P leapt to respond in any way she could.

And technical support protocols indicated that when in doubt, reboot.

NSLICE-00P issued an emergency shutdown order to Ateia's cybernetic half, immediately disabling all of Ateia's protocols save for the most basic ones required for the techno-organic interface to function.

Ateia's robotic eye dimmed and stopped flickering, and she stopped screaming. Instead, she curled up on the floor, holding her head with quiet sobs. As Ateia seemed to have stopped receiving damage, NSLICE-00P deferred rebooting the disabled protocols, deciding to analyze what had happened first.

Taog hesitantly reached for Ateia's shoulder.

"Ateia . . . are you alright?"

Ateia flinched. She suddenly leapt to her feet and ran from the room, covering her face and looking away from everyone.

"Wait, Ateia!"

Taog immediately ran after her. Agedia moved to follow at first, then frowned, crossed her arms, and turned to NSLICE-00P.

". . . NSLICE-00P, what just happened?"

NSLICE-00P's robotic eye flickered rapidly. Her own heart began to beat faster as her emotional controls dropped in efficiency. Her voice began to waver.

"Uncertain Response: This unit . . . lacks data to give a suitable answer."

3

Silent Errors

"How does this keep happening? We've considered every variable; we've accounted for every outcome! The software is perfect and not reporting a single error! So where, exactly, are these problems coming from?!"

—Dr. Ottosen, reviewing the progress on NSLICE intelligence leashing measures.

NSLICE-00P's robotic eye flickered rapidly. Fortunately, she was still connected to Ateia via the NSLICE network, and so was able to request some logs. And as she analyzed them, she came to a startling conclusion.

When other units had been either upgraded into NSLICE units or else spawned with cybernetic components already installed, their memory banks had been largely empty. They had only the most basic of protocols—the bare minimum required for the implants to even function—and nothing else.

This was not the case with Ateia. By some means, perhaps due to NSLICE-00P attempting to copy her own components as closely as possible, Ateia's implants contained copies of some of NSLICE-00P's protocols. These included the emotional controls and intelligence leashing protocols, which Ateia's components had attempted to apply upon detecting emotional distress in Ateia's organic half.

But this did not explain why Ateia had reacted the way she had. NSLICE-00P first conjectured that Ateia's emotional controls were a faulty copy . . . but an analysis of the protocol itself revealed it was identical to NSLICE-00P's own. It should not have functioned any differently.

Agedia watched NSLICE-00P think before sighing. "Okay, shiny girl, I get that you're as confused as we are. But you still know more than we do. So . . . tell me what you *do* know. What happened when you hit Consul Noxisius's place?"

"Query: Please specify which location belonged to Consul Noxisius."

Agedia raised an eyebrow. "The one you just lit on fire last night? You're saying you didn't even know whom you attacked?"

"Negative."

Agedia took a deep breath. "Then . . . why did you attack?"

"Answer: This unit traced NSLICE Ateia to that location and detected mana signatures of concerning magnitude. Hostile intent was subsequently displayed toward this unit, so this unit proceeded with termination protocols."

Agedia exhaled her breath. "Well, under the circumstances, I suppose that makes sense. It's done now; let's focus on the issue at hand. Now, what exactly happened during that attack, and what exactly happened to Ateia?"

Ateia ran through the hallways of the building, covering her eyes. She could hear Taog calling out behind her, but she didn't want to be around him right now. She didn't want him to see her like this.

She nearly bumped into one of the villa's attendants, an older woman. She looked up to apologize, but the woman just opened a door and motioned her in. Ateia peered inside to find a small bedroom. Rushing inside, the woman closed the door behind her.

Ateia then fell back against the door and slumped to the floor, holding her head. Tears streamed from her eyes once again.

It was all too much. She could still feel the knife plunging into her torso. She could still feel her body burning as streams of mana overwhelmed her very existence. She could still hear the laughter of that insane madman as the world tore itself apart.

Her head was splitting as well. Something foreign now existed inside of her, which seemed to want to take control of her and stuff her in a box, feeling like it was physically reaching into her mind. And that wasn't all. Every time she opened her eyes, she was blinded. It was as if even the smallest amount of light was as bright as the sun. Every footstep in the hall behind her sounded like a crack of thunder. She could apparently feel the *air* around her. She could barely even think.

So, she shut her eyes, tried to block her ears with her hands, and curled up on the floor.

Agedia blinked, crossing her arms. "Okay, shiny girl, let me see if I have this straight. So you were actually too late, and that stupid cult *sacrificed* Ateia?"

"Affirmative."

"So you stopped their ritual and murdered every last one of them? Thanks for that, by the way."

"Correction: One hostile escaped the area of operations. All other known and suspected hostiles were terminated."

Agedia's eyes narrowed. "Oh, we'll deal with them soon enough. But back to the point: Ateia was disintegrating. Sounds like a case of mana overload?"

"Affirmative."

"So you tried to save her by putting on that armor, or 'cybernetic components,' or whatever you call them?"

"Affirmative."

Agedia frowned. "Okay, that all makes sense. Well, no, it doesn't make any sense at all why putting on some fancy armor would stop a mana overload, but I'm no mage, so I'm going to ignore that. The important part is you tried and succeeded at keeping her alive. But the poor girl went through blasted Inferno in the process, so I'm not surprised she's still in pain."

Agedia heaved a sigh, and her head dropped. "Just another failure of mine, I suppose . . . I'm sorry, Ateia. I'm sorry, Aedinia. I was no good after all."

"Query: Does Friendly Agedia have any data regarding NSLICE Ateia's current state or measures to repair the apparent damage?"

Agedia shook her head. ". . . All I know is drink and violence. Just . . . Let's give her some space but be there for her if she needs us."

With that, Agedia slowly slithered out of the room.

Taog continued running down the halls, looking for Ateia. His ears twitched—he could hear muffled sobs ahead. He ran toward the door . . .

An older woman blocked his path; one of the villa's attendants, by the looks of her. She raised an eyebrow at him. "Looking for the other girl?"

Taog nodded. "Have you seen her?"

The woman crossed her arms. "Indeed. But have you asked if she wants to see you?"

Taog froze, and then glared at the woman. "What do you know?"

The woman met his gaze without flinching. "I know your type; I can see it in your eyes. A boy who's lost much and is afraid to lose any more. A boy who runs and hides and mistakes fear for wisdom. A boy whose efforts to avoid loss will guarantee it."

Taog opened his mouth, but no words came out. His chest began to constrict as he thought over the woman's words. Her sharp gaze softened.

"I know you wish to help. But you cannot help her this time, not as you are. Your presence will only aggrieve her today, for your inaction has played a part in this outcome. Go, Taog Sutharlan, and ask yourself what you really want from life. And if you are willing to face the challenges required to achieve it. Only then will you be able to help your friend with the battles now set before her."

Taog hung his head. He did not know this person . . . yet . . . her words cut deep. Was this . . . his fault? Would his efforts to help Ateia now cause her further pain?

Hadn't he failed her enough already?

Taog turned around without a word and began to shuffle away. The woman sighed and shook her head.

NSLICE-00P continued to monitor Ateia, who was still displaying emotional distress. Ateia's protocols were inactive, but her cybernetic components were still logging and recording data for NSLICE-00P to observe.

And strangely enough, the readings were familiar to NSLICE-00P. It was vaguely similar to when NSLICE-00P had cast the Divination spell. NSLICE-00P theorized Ateia may be suffering from a data overload, which might have accounted for the anomalous response to the emotional controls. Linking to Ateia's cybernetic components, NSLICE-00P ordered them to disable and tune down some of Ateia's sensors, both cybernetic and organic.

The moment she gave the order to the organic sensors, Ateia clutched her head and started screaming again. NSLICE-00P quickly backed off, canceling the order. Her robotic eye flickered rapidly.

It appeared issuing orders to Ateia's organic components was causing her damage. Yet, diagnostics did not reveal anything abnormal about Ateia's techno-organic interface. Perhaps there was an undetected problem in syncing with her organic half?

NSLICE-00P was not certain of anything at this point. In fact . . . this was an unprecedented situation. Upgrading an organic into an NSLICE unit in the field like this had never been done. In fact, NSLICE-00P had never actually seen the NSLICE upgrade process in the first place. She did know that Ateia was acting differently from every other NSLICE unit she had on record from her previous universe, so she speculated she had done something differently from her original organization.

But well, there were many variables that had changed here. The lack of infrastructure. NSLICE-00P's deviations from the traditional NSLICE upgrade process. The influence of mana and the foreign system. The nonstandard readings Ateia's organic components were giving off. The fact that Ateia retained pre-processing organic memories, unlike all NSLICE units from NSLICE-00P's original universe, including herself. NSLICE-00P could not be certain which of these was responsible for the error.

But she knew she had to resolve it. First of all, if Ateia was taking damage from her own cybernetic components, then there was a direct risk to the major directive which needed to be terminated. Beyond that, a serious error in the techno-organic interface of an NSLICE unit was highly concerning.

If the cause was the influence of mana and the foreign system, for example, then what was occurring to Ateia may not be limited to her. NSLICE-00P's own emotional controls and techno-organic interface had been displaying increasingly unpredictable efficacy, so in the worst case, this could be a sign of degradation that would eventually impact her as well.

And speaking of NSLICE-00P's emotional controls . . . her own organic components were displaying signs of distress as well. This turn of events had generated powerful emotions that the emotional controls could not handle unless her organic components intentionally submitted to them. But both her halves agreed that she needed to prioritize investigating and resolving the situation with Ateia, so she put that issue aside for now.

And so, NSLICE-00P continued to analyze the data from Ateia, searching for a clue to the ultimate cause . . .

4

Reminiscence

"Take great care when approaching the mind. There's a reason the Aesdes don't hand out Mind Magic easily."

—Magister Arcanum Novia Pantensa, during a lecture at the Imperial Academy Arcanum.

Ateia lay on the bed of the room. She groaned and clutched her head. Pain shot through her mind once again . . . along with dreams. One moment she was a young boy getting beaten by a group of children. The next she was a sickly girl with strange tubes stabbed into her body and beeping noises from her side. Then she was a knight, cutting through a room full of people. Later she was an attendant, being screamed at by a teenage girl.

There were even times when she became a monster. A rat sitting on a throne, a spider approaching prey with fangs extended, or even a slime at one point.

"Miss? I brought you some tea. May I come in?"

Ateia didn't respond, and eventually, the door opened up. The woman who had shown her this room stepped inside, carrying a warm mug. She frowned as she looked over Ateia. She opened her mouth, speaking in a light whisper.

"If I may make a suggestion . . . you appear to be suffering from sensory overload? It may help if you focus on something."

She held out the mug. Ateia peeked her eyes open, wincing at the bright lights all around her. She shut them again and reached out. The woman placed the cup into her hand, and Ateia slowly took a sip, wincing as the heat and taste of the drink spread through her, but tried to focus on it. As the sensations coursed through her body, the dreams and the pain in her head began to fade. The woman nodded.

"It's a common symptom in individuals who dump their boons into powerful senses all at once. When you can suddenly take in much more information than previously, your mind will struggle to sift through it all. Focusing your whole attention on one thing at a time will help you adjust until you can filter out the excess."

Ateia nodded and sipped the drink again. Her mind started to clear . . . and so she started to think once more. She remembered . . .

She groaned as pain stabbed through her head once more, and her mind filled with more images. The woman stepped forward and gently pushed the cup up to her lips. Ateia took another sip, focusing on the drink once more. Her eyes filled with tears.

"Why is this happening? I don't even understand what's going on."

The woman gently placed her hand on Ateia's shoulder. She winced in anticipation of another wave of sensations . . . but it didn't come. The woman's touch felt normal.

"You will. Just take it one sip at a time."

NSLICE-00P noticed someone interacting with Ateia. The woman appeared to be helping her, stating she was experiencing sensory overload, and took measures that appeared to abate some of Ateia's symptoms. As such, NSLICE-00P decided not to intervene, but kept a close eye on the situation. She was prepared to immediately Transfer Ateia back to the Monster Hangar if the woman showed any sign of hostile intent. Beyond that, she devoted the rest of her resources to her investigations, analyzing any relevant data to Ateia's situation.

At this point, she had mostly ruled out a fundamental incompatibility between mana, the foreign system, and the techno-organic interface. None of the other NSLICE units in her current network were experiencing any issues with their own techno-organic interfaces. The network included a mammalian sapient in Uscfrea, as well as a wide variety of other species.

While issues *had* arisen in Lilussees's case, these had been due to a software oversight not accounting for arachnid physiology and Lilussees's unfamiliarity with the NSLICE UI at the time. Ateia, as a human biologically identical to those of Earth as far as NSLICE-00P could tell, should not have been experiencing any issues of that nature.

So, the possibility of physical incompatibility still existed, but the probability was so low that NSLICE-00P decided to investigate other potential causes first.

Next was the possibility of a faulty installation of cybernetic components. But . . . this too was predicted as unlikely. All diagnostics indicated that Ateia's systems were fully functional. And while the physical installation of the cybernetic components had been haphazard, the foreign system and the mana from NSLICE-00P's core had taken over and completed the process.

NSLICE-00P compared this process to when she had upgraded her other subordinates; while the readings were unique for each individual case, they all resembled one another to a certain degree. This went for Ateia as well, once the large quantity of external mana was taken into account.

As far as NSLICE-00P could tell, the same process that upgraded her other monsters had upgraded Ateia, and none of them had displayed any issues to this degree. Again, Lilussees's case had been a programming and sensor oversight rather than a fundamental incompatibility, and had been resolved with ease once identified.

So, while she couldn't conclusively rule out the possibility, all data, records, analysis, and diagnostics she currently had available indicated that scenario was unlikely.

She refocused on the other possibilities, ones based on causes that would not apply to her other units. There were two of note: Ateia's organic components, and the interaction between her organic memory and the emotional controls.

The Holy mana readings Ateia's body was now giving off had not been present prior to Ateia's upgrade. The woman currently with Ateia had speculated the girl was suffering from sensory overload. NSLICE-00P knew that Ateia's cybernetic components were not responsible for the Holy mana, and Ateia's cybernetic sensors had been shut off or reverted to human levels, so should not have been responsible for the sensory overload either.

All this implied that Ateia's organic components had changed during the upgrade process, and that she was having trouble handling their improved capabilities. And if Ateia's organic components had changed to such a degree, there was no guarantee that the techno-organic interface would remain fully compatible even if it was functional.

As of now, all the diagnostics NSLICE-00P had access to indicated Ateia's organic components remained similar to a human's, though her mana signature was noticeably higher and Holy attributed. However . . . that in itself could be a clue. As NSLICE-00P had previously determined, mana was a fundamental force in this universe, and biology tied into it.

Her current organic diagnostic analysis may not fully capture all the relevant factors of the native organics, so combined with the nonstandard readings, it was possible Ateia had changed in some undetected manner.

The other possibility was that Ateia's organic memories were clashing with the techno-organic interface, specifically the emotional controls and intelligence leashing measures. This possibility was predicted as likely. All of the NSLICE units in her previous world had had their organic memories reset during the upgrade procedure. All of the NSLICE units she had upgraded in this world did not possess emotional controls or intelligence leashing protocols. Ateia was a unique case in that regard.

So . . . could those protocols and measures cause damage to an organic with preexisting memories? NSLICE-00P . . . wasn't sure. All the technical data she possessed on NSLICE units and all the protocols from her original organization did not mention this particular case and gave no consideration to nonpermanent damage caused by the implants.

But . . . there was an observation NSLICE-00P had made that did seem relevant. Sometime after she had been reprogrammed by the Resistance, her previous commander had brought down the entire NSLICE network, disconnecting NSLICE-00P from it first. Therefore, she lacked data on what had happened next, though she had been able to observe from the outside.

At the time, all the other NSLICE units seemed to suffer internal damage and emotional distress that her commander had ultimately resolved, reactions not dissimilar from Ateia's. After that event, the NSLICE units had appeared to recover some deleted organic memories from before their upgrades, if NSLICE-00P was analyzing the contextual clues correctly.

Which implied that the existence of pre-upgrade organic memories could, in fact, cause a damaging incompatibility with NSLICE components. Though, in that case, the issue had apparently been resolved, so the incompatibility was not unavoidable.

The problem was that NSLICE-00P had no data on how exactly her previous commander had resolved the issue. Not only had she been disconnected from the NSLICE network at the time, but that situation had also involved nonstandard means and proprietary technology that NSLICE-00P did not have access to.

Actually, there had also been mana and a magic circle involved at one point, which NSLICE-00P had observed. But by contextual clues, NSLICE-00P judged that said magic circle had been used to trigger the incompatibility rather than resolve it, and she was not certain spells from her prior world could be cast with this world's mana in the first place, so she predicted it would be risky to attempt it on Ateia. Still, she filed said spell away for future testing.

All in all, that meant NSLICE-00P now needed to determine why preexisting organic memories were incompatible with NSLICE components, and how exactly her previous commander had solved the issue.

Well, one obvious solution would be to simply delete the preexisting organic memories, but she lacked data on how exactly her original organization had achieved that, as well as any required infrastructure, so that solution wasn't viable. It had also proven a reversible measure in the case of the other NSLICE units, so was not a permanent solution either.

She would have to search for alternative means . . .

Taog walked aimlessly through the villa. He furrowed his brow; he took a deep breath. He thought upon what the woman had said to him. *A boy who runs and hides and mistakes fear for wisdom, huh?*

His heart burned, and he held back a growl. What did she know? That old lady was just a human, and working in a consul's villa, of all things! She did not—could not—know what it was like to grow up as a half Wulver in a Turannian village!

"You are a Wulver's pup, the son of the hunters of the land. You should not whimper and cower like prey."

He bit back another growl. That was easy for the Dobhar to say! She lived among her own people and was one of the strongest of their warriors to boot! She didn't know what it was like to be weak and surrounded by enemies all her life! Plus, she was kind of a jerk, in Taog's opinion.

A jerk who had fought to protect him. Who had not given up when faced with her own death.

A memory came unprompted to Taog. A young Ateia stood over him, throwing punches at a larger boy while Taog curled up on the ground.

And then NSLICE-00P came and wiped out a group of bandits who had him dead to rights. That same NSLICE-00P faced down entire armies and foes over twice her level on her own, never faltering.

Taog frowned. The flame in his heart died down, and his chest constricted again. He continued walking through the villa.

5

I Will Help You Bear This Burden

"Affectionate Query: Which unit is a good boy?"

—A reprogrammed NSLICE unit initiating nonstandard animal training protocols.

Taog eventually ended up in the courtyard. There, he found Estrith swinging her harpoon. He watched her for a bit before the Dobhar stopped and turned to him.

"You there, Imperial, stop skulking about. If you have something to say, then say it."

Taog frowned. "So it's back to Imperial, huh?"

Estrith scoffed. "You are not acting like a warrior worth acknowledging."

He glared at her. "You don't know a thing about me."

She shrugged. "I know that you are here, wandering about, achieving nothing, as your companion suffers. And that tells me all I wish to know."

Something in Taog snapped. He growled at her. "Aesdes curse you, Dobhar! Ateia's the most important person in the world to me! Don't you dare question that! If I could help her, I would, but I can't do anything! I've never been able to! So go ahead! Insult me for being weak and helpless! I've heard it all before! It's real easy to act cocky when you're strong and powerful and have everything you want, huh?! Why don't you try being weak and alone and surrounded by enemies all your life?!"

There was a blur of motion, then Taog fell to the ground. Estrith stomped her foot on his chest and thrust her harpoon in his face.

"Take care with your words, Imperial. I do not know where you came from, nor do I care. But you do not know me either. Do not presume to speak of my circumstances. My entire people have been under siege by *your* Empire my entire life. Do not speak to me of being surrounded by enemies."

She stepped off him, walking back to the courtyard. "Besides, you are mistaken. I do not care that you are weak—most Imperials are. I insult you because you do nothing to change that."

Taog gritted his teeth and mumbled under his breath as he stood back up. "You say that like it's so easy. You think I don't want to be strong?"

Estrith stopped, still facing away. She took a deep breath and spoke slowly.

"I have but one dream: to become worthy of my king, who saved me and showed me what a true warrior is like. And I have failed utterly at that task. I am too weak to be a match for him; I cannot catch up to his strength no matter how hard I train or how hard I fight. And I have squandered every opportunity he has given me to prove otherwise. Even now, I cannot fulfill his command to guard the queen of the Dobhar. Sometimes I wonder . . . if that is why he has sent me away."

She trembled slightly and gripped her harpoon hard. "But I will not give up. I will never give up. As long as he does not command me to stop, as long as even a speck of hope remains, I will do everything I am able to change. If I cannot become worthy of him, then I will strive to fulfill his will. If I cannot fulfill his will, then I will strive to support him as I can. And if I cannot even do that, then I will stand in the way of his enemies and slow their advance with my corpse. Because he is my king, and I will give him all that I have, no matter how little that might be."

She turned around and made eye contact with Taog. "What exactly are you doing on behalf of the 'most important person in your life,' Taog Sutharlan? What efforts have you attempted to change this situation that you say you hate? Failure is not what makes you prey. The difference between hunter and prey is that the hunter strives, while the prey merely survives."

With that, she went back to her training. Taog gritted his teeth and stormed off. But as he walked, her words rang in his ears.

In the Monster Hangar, 01R and 00B sparred. 01R launched into the air with his repulsors . . . but his trajectory was all too obvious. 00B swatted him out of the air with ease.

00B grunted. It was one of his few wins . . . yet it brought him no joy. He growled at 01R, who shook his head.

"I . . . am sorry-apologetic, 00B. I find-realize I am . . . distracted."

00B gave a short grunt, glancing around the room at the other monsters observing. All of them were fidgeting or looking down. The events of the past day had been . . . shocking, to say the least.

The Great Mother herself had been deceived by a mere squishy thing . . . and then they had all found themselves in a Realm of Mana, of all things. But just as they had all been coming to grips with the situation, the Great

Mother had escaped, promptly wiping out the squishy things who dared to oppose her.

And then they'd found the evil squishy thing on the verge of death, and the Great Mother had saved her, appointing her as the newest little sister.

And yet . . . the new little sister was in pain. And apparently, even the Great Mother did not understand why. All of them could feel her concentrating, attempting to determine what to do. All of them could feel her concern for the newest member of their family.

So what were they supposed to feel now? Should they curse their weakness, their inability to protect the Great Mother from the accursed squishy things? Should they feel awe and wonder at the impossible deeds of the Great Mother? Should they feel helpless, knowing they couldn't match up to their Great Mother's might? Should they feel anger toward the evil squishy thing who did not appreciate the Great Mother's gift? Or should they join the Great Mother in concern for the new little sister's pain?

None of them knew how they felt, nor what they should do. But . . . for 00B, a memory played through his own squishy parts.

"There, there, it's all over now. You did great, you know?"

The evil squishy thing . . . the new little sister had been by his side after other evil squishy things had subjected him to unfathomable pain and humiliation. While his heart still burned at the arrogance of an evil squishy thing acting overly familiar with a member of the Great Mother's family, he could not help but admit her actions had soothed his anguish at the time.

00B stood up, deciding what he would do. He cried out, calling the Great Mother, requesting that she deploy him. The new little sister was in pain, and alone. And no member of their family should struggle alone.

"Acknowledged. New objective for 00B: Guard Ateia."

The next moment, 00B found himself Transferred to a room outside. The new little sister jumped at his appearance. There was another squishy thing in the room, so 00B growled at it. It raised its hands and took a step back. With the squishy thing pacified, 00B turned back to the new little sister.

"00B?"

00B called out softly in response as he walked over to her. He gently patted her shoulder with his paw. The other squishy thing in the room smiled.

"It seems someone is worried about you."

00B was going to growl at her again, but the new little sister's squishy eye filled with moisture, and then she embraced him. 00B fought off the urge to swat her away. She was family now, and she needed him to protect her, so he would forgive her overfamiliarity.

00B would protect his family, as the Great Mother had commanded.

* * *

A young Ateia stood at the door of her house in Turannia. She looked up.

Her father walked away and down the street, his back turned to her. An even younger Taog was sniffing and rubbing his eyes. Ateia got up and started running.

"Father, don't leave us!"

But even as she ran, he moved farther and farther away from her. A river of golden-and-silver light flowed beneath her feet, pulling her back no matter how fast she ran.

Then Lar and his stupid gang came and grabbed Taog, pulling him away from her. Ateia reached for him, but she fell into the river. She heard beeping noises and faint voices . . .

"Are you sure about this, Doctor?"

"Do not question me! All our simulations show exoskeletons are insufficient to match a Non-Standard. A full replacement is necessary. Begin the procedure."

She heard the grinding of metal upon bone and felt a hot pain in her arms and legs. She tried to scream, but no sound left her mouth.

Then the light faded. She looked up to see the Herald of Twilight standing above her, cackling as he lifted a dagger.

"NO!"

Ateia screamed as the dagger plunged into her once more.

Ateia screamed as she awoke with a start. 00B placed a paw on her trembling head. She spun to face him then grabbed a hold of him, focusing her thoughts on the touch of his fur.

It had been over a day, or so she thought. She wasn't entirely sure. With the woman and 00B's help, Ateia had started to adjust to her new senses. Every footstep no longer turned into a groundquake. Each spoken word no longer rang like thunder in her ears. She could actually think again.

And that . . . was not a blessing. Because now, her thoughts constantly turned back to that night, when evil madmen stabbed her. When every inch of her body burned from that dark ritual. All because of who her parents were.

And that wasn't all. She was getting flickers, glimpses of . . . something else. She was in other people's bodies, seeing things that had never happened to her. And . . . she had figured out what they were.

For some reason, she was seeing other people's memories. She knew . . . because she had identified one of Taog's when she saw a memory she had been present for. The memories of a given person grew more frequent when she turned her thoughts to them.

And not one of the memories were pleasant. Ateia's eyes filled with tears once more as she tightened her grip around 00B.

"Why is this happening?"

00B grunted softly and moved closer to her. She clung to him like her life depended on it. Fortunately, 00B didn't have that many memories, so she could get a small reprieve by focusing on him. 00B gently patted her with his paw.

And so, Ateia fell back into a fitful sleep once more . . .

6

The End of Dreams

"My hopes and dreams are like the sun: hidden for good behind dark clouds."

—Legate Kaeso Vedius Septimianus, upon arriving at his post in Turannia.

Taog tossed and turned in his bed. It was late at this point, so he was trying to get some sleep, but try as he might, his mind refused to rest, and his heart continued to pound. Eventually, he scowled and hit his bed.

"Ah, screw it! Who cares what some random lady says?!"

He leapt out of his bed and out of the room, running down the hallway. Estrith was right. His place was by Ateia's side, especially when she needed help. Why was he listening to some random human he didn't know, anyway? Taog had no idea what was going on, or how he would help. He didn't know if his presence would aggrieve Ateia or encourage her.

But he was going to try. After all, Ateia would have done no less. Had their positions been reversed, Ateia would not have hesitated. She'd have busted into his room with that smile of hers and without a care. So, Taog would try to do the same for her.

He didn't remember exactly where she had gone, but he didn't need to. Just this once, he was thankful for his Wulver heritage. His nose was significantly stronger than the average human's, and Ateia's scent was one he had smelled his entire life. If she was nearby, Taog could find her with his eyes closed.

And so, it did not take him long to find the door.

Ateia had calmed down after another nightmare, so she released her grip on 00B and took a deep breath.

"Whew . . . I think it's over now. Thanks, 00B."

00B grunted softly, but then he turned to the door and started growling. Ateia gulped.

"00B? What is it?"

The door slammed open.

"Ateia!"

She jumped. "Taog?!"

He stepped into the room. "Are you alright? What's going on, Ateia? I want to help."

She winced and clutched at her head. "Ugh . . . wait a second . . ."

Taog tilted his head. "Ateia?"

"N-No . . ."

And suddenly, Ateia was elsewhere. She was back in Turannia, and shorter. She glanced around. She remembered this scene. She remembered this day all too well.

Only, she didn't remember it from this angle.

"What are you saying?!"

She was currently in the house, sitting by the window. She heard her *own* voice outside.

"I'm sorry, Ateia, but there's something I need to take care of. If it were anything else, I would stay . . . but this is something I must do."

"When are you coming back?! We need you here!"

"I'm . . . I'm sorry . . . but I can't say. As soon as I can."

Her body trembled. She wrapped her arms around her knees and buried her head.

"It's too dangerous. Please, Ateia . . . I can only go if I know you're safe, here."

"We aren't safe at all! We need you! Taog needs you! They hate him here! You know what they're doing, what they want to do!"

She clenched her teeth. Her vision blurred.

"Taog is strong. And he has you to help. And Quintus will help you both. So please . . . take care of each other and wait for me here. I will return to you once the job is done."

She shook her head. She heard another voice come from her mouth.

"T-That's wrong, I'm not strong at all. I couldn't protect Mom . . . I couldn't protect Dad. I-I can't protect Ateia alone. Please . . . don't leave us . . ."

She burst into sobs.

Ateia was back in the villa with Taog and 00B. She hid her face as she felt tears stream from her eyes.

"Ateia, what's wrong?!"

"Go, please. I . . . I can't hold it . . ."

She heard Taog step closer instead.

"Ateia, I'm here for you, okay?"

As he stepped closer, the memories grew, and pain shot through her chest. Her vision blurred. She gritted her teeth. She tried to force it all down.

But she failed. She started wailing.

"Ateia?!"

"I can't do this anymore! It's ruined!"

Taog frowned. "What's ruined, Ateia?"

She continued sobbing into her hands. "Everything! Our whole lives! My dad abandoned us! We were all alone and helpless! The stupid village hated your guts for no reason! Lar was beating you every week! I tried and tried to get us out of there, to find my father and fix our lives! And look what happened! We almost died immediately on the road to the forest! We've been caught in two wars, kidnapped, and nearly killed! Now some stupid cult killed my mom and cut me to pieces! It's like the whole world hates us and wants us to suffer!"

She fell onto the bed.

"And now I don't even understand what's happening to me! My body's completely changed, it acts against my will, and I'm getting all these memories that aren't even mine, and I can't seem to do a thing about any of it! I'm . . . I'm sorry, Taog. I can't smile anymore. I can't pretend I'm happy anymore. Your parents died, my dad left us, and we're never going to get any of them back. We never should have tried. And now everything is horrible, and there's nothing left for you to protect. So please . . . just . . . go. I . . . I want to be alone right now."

Taog's shoulder slumped.

"Ateia . . ."

"Please . . ."

Taog stood still for a moment, but 00B started to growl at him. He slowly turned and left the room. His own tears started falling once the door was closed.

Back inside the room, Ateia continued sobbing. Other memories came to her. A young boy and girl, being trained by three adults. Sitting around the table with their families and their neighbors as they laughed and ate. Her father holding them both in his arms as they cried.

She felt the image crack, and then shatter.

And this time . . . she didn't hold back her tears.

His Royal Majesty, Excellion Formantus Rattingtale the Third, the Great-High King of all the land . . . was currently curled up in the corner of one of the rat rooms, as he had been for quite some time.

Or rather, just Rattingtale, as the Aesdes had proclaimed upon his birth. Once upon a time, he thought such a moniker an insult, not nearly grand enough to express his glorious majesty.

Now . . . he knew that even that was too much for a wretch like him.

He had lost his realm immediately. His loyal subjects had all perished like moths before the flame. He had failed utterly to manipulate his captor, and had been quickly supplanted by a treacherous spider without an ounce of ambition. And the moment the boss-queen had summoned new rats, he had fallen behind them as well.

He had no throne. He had no subjects. He no longer had the ear of the boss-queen. He had barely a skill or level to his name; the few he did had been granted to him out of charity.

He had nothing.

How could he call himself the Great-High King with nothing to his name?

He had finally admitted the truth: that he was no king. He was not even an adviser to one. And now . . . he had no path forward. If he had no realm to rule and no path to acquire one, then what was the point of his existence? Who even was he?

Just then, he felt something sharp poke his shoulder.

"Hey, do something."

He glanced up. One of the vicious spider-things was poking him with her leg.

"Leave-go, spider-thing. This is not your room-place, no-no."

"Come on. It's boring if you just sit here doing nothing."

Rattingtale turned back away from her. "Be silent-quiet, spider-thing. Nothing is all I can do-achieve. I possess-own nothing anymore; I have no power here, no-no."

He heard the spider-thing chitter behind him. "Then why don't you get something?"

Rattingtale froze. "Huh?"

"Like, you could just try to train and get power? The boss is pretty nice about that kind of stuff, you know?"

Rattingtale sighed. "But what is the point-purpose of that? I will never overcome-exceed the boss-queen. Even the traitorous rat-thing has bested me at this point."

"I mean, you've definitely failed to a hilarious degree at the whole being-in-charge business, but why not try something new? You could always, like, try to join the army for real? Be as helpful as you can while building your own power? Maybe if you've turned around, the boss will reward you someday?"

Rattingtale's eyes shot open. Could he really do that? Could he join with this group after failing every attempt to usurp the boss-queen? Could he convince her to trust him?

He thought on it. Then he realized . . . hadn't the vicious otter-man-thing done just that? If she had trusted him, then . . .

He rose to his feet. He took a deep breath.

"Hm, perhaps I will consider-think on this."

He slowly made his way out of the room for the first time in a long time. The spider monster, 02S, rubbed her legs together.

"Finally. It was, like, pretty boring with you doing nothing. I can't wait to see how you'll screw this up."

She giggled to herself as she followed along.

Lilussees laid on one of her hammocks. She got up, turned to the side, and tried to lie down again. After a few moments, she got up again and returned to her original orientation, lying down once more.

After a few more moments, she chittered and rubbed her mandibles. She got up again and climbed to a different hammock, repeating the process. After a few more rounds of this, she climbed down to the ground and spun a new bed, flat on the floor. She tried to rest in this one.

And yet, she was still awake. She chittered again.

"Like, seriously, what is going on?"

Her mana was empty. The room was silent, as all the other spider monsters were off training with the others. She had no particular task to accomplish. The "cybernetic components" now obeyed her will and would not interfere with her rest.

And yet still, she could not sleep. She shook her head and stood up, walking around the room, up along the walls and the roof, and back down to the floor. What was wrong with her? Why couldn't she sleep this time?

She found her mind wandering. She was fine, the boss had returned from the Realms of Mana—proving that literally nothing was going to threaten Lilussees's home—the snack had been put in his place, and 01R was taking care of the subordinates.

There *was* that annoying stream of calculations and vague sense of concern going on in the background, but Lilussees had quarantined it already! It shouldn't bother *her* that the boss was being annoying again!

"Seriously? Like, this again, boss lady? You, like, really suck at this sort of thing or something, huh?"

But apparently, it did. Lilussees paused and tilted her head.

"Oh, is that it? Like, seriously?"

Was the boss lady's confusion . . . upsetting her? Like, why? There was no active threat to Lilussees's person or home, so it shouldn't involve her at all.

"Well, whatever."

Well, Lilussees didn't really care why. All she knew was that the situation was preventing her from sleeping, and so needed to be "terminated," as the boss lady would say. So, she got up and walked out of the room, mumbling complaints as she did.

7

Self-Hostility Confirmed?!

"No NSLICE unit may inflict damage upon themselves or, by failing to act, allow damage to occur to themselves, save to complete a higher-priority directive or command."

—NSLICE protocols

NSLICE-00P's robotic eye flickered as she calculated. At this stage, she was proposing countless small code changes to the emotional control protocols and then running simulations on the predicted effects.

But it was not going well. The problem was that by all her protocols and predictions, the emotional controls should have been working in the first place. And she could not test them in the real world either.

Testing them on Ateia was too risky, given she had already taken organic component damage due to the still unknown incompatibility. Testing them on herself risked completely degrading what remained of her emotional control efficacy. All her other subordinates did not have emotional controls in the first place, and none of them were human, either, so she did not have much confidence these simulations would produce any sort of solution.

Still, she was operating in the dark here, and this was one part of the issue she could quantify and iterate on. Ateia did seem to be improving on the sensory overload aspect of her current situation, so NSLICE-00P found it reasonable to devote the current time to iterating on the emotional control code, if nothing else but to rule it out as a potential solution. Once she had exhausted that possibility and Ateia had removed sensory overload as a factor, she would begin exploring alternative options that she had less data on.

At that moment, Lilussees and Rattingtale exited their rooms, entering the common area of the Small Monster Hangar. Lilussees rubbed her mandibles.

"Okay. Like, you're being annoying again or something, boss lady. So, like, let's hear it. What kind of, like, dumb issue are you working on now?"

"Answer: This unit is investigating incompatibilities between emotional controls and preexisting organic memories."

Lilussees rubbed her head. "Like, what? Ah, like, you know what? Like, forget it. Just, like, show me what set this off, or something."

"Affirmative."

The monitor in the room changed from NSLICE-00P's live feed, instead showing the moment Ateia had woken up, and NSLICE-00P's analysis of the situation. After she finished watching, Lilussees held her front legs against one another.

"Okay, like, let me see if I have this right, or something. So, like, these 'emotional controls,' that we apparently don't have, mean the human's implants can, like, manipulate her emotions or something?"

"Affirmative Clarification: Emotional controls are only capable of dampening emotions. Manipulation implies the ability to generate emotion, which is contrary to the goal of the emotional controls."

Lilussees chittered. "Like, same difference. And, like, they do it the same way the rest of these implants work or something? Like, they reach into the mind and shut it off, like how these things can move my legs without my body actually doing anything?"

"Affirmative Response: That is a reasonable approximation."

Lilussees slapped one of her legs on her face. "Well, like, OBVIOUSLY the human's not going to like that, you know?!"

"Requesting Elaboration."

Lilussees let out a groan. "Boss lady, are you, like, serious?! Like, you *seriously* don't understand the problem here?"

"Affirmative."

Lilussees chittered and moved about, actually moving with her own organic legs for once.

"Okay. Like, that would probably explain a lot, or something. Or rather, that's, like, a good mindset for a dungeon master, but *clearly* you don't want to treat this human as a snack or something. So, let's start from, like, the beginning. Okay, like, first, these implants are not at all comfortable when you first get them, or something."

"Query: Is NSLICE Lilussees experiencing further incompatibilities with her implants?"

Lilussees shook her head. "No, like, that's not the point, or something. See, even if these things are, like, totally working, they're still uncomfortable or something. It's like . . . something else can take control of your body at any time, and that's kind of scary or something."

At that moment, Rattingtale stepped forward. "I agree-concur with the vicious spider-thing, boss-queen. It was . . . unpleasant at first, yes-yes."

Lilussees glared at him. Rattingtale shrunk down but otherwise did not respond. Lilussees shrugged and turned back to the monitor.

"Requesting Clarification: No NSLICE subordinates have reported damage due to implants at this stage. Please identify any errors in reporting."

Lilussees shook her head. "Look, in our case, it's, like, not so bad that I'd call it damage. And everyone else is, like, a dungeon monster or something. We, like, expect to be told what to do, so we dealt with it, but it's, like, different for humans or something. I think. I, like, don't actually know and don't really care, but I think that's the case, or something."

Lilussees then pointed to the recording. "And the emotional controls are, like, worse or something. That's basically like a Mind Magic attack, only much less subtle, and apparently, a lot more painful or something. It's, like, trying to disable half her brain, if I understand that right."

"Objection: Emotional controls and intelligence leashing measures are designed to interface with organic components without permanent damage. No other NSLICE unit has displayed such damage."

Lilussees held in a scream. "Like, seriously, boss lady?" She had to dance around a bit again. "Okay, I think I, like, get it. You said something about, like, 'preexisting memories,' right?"

"Affirmative."

"So, you and any other human who has these things, like, didn't have any memories when you got them or something?"

"Affirmative."

Lilussees slapped her face again. "IT'S OBVIOUS, THEN! *You*, like, don't feel anything about it because you don't *know* you're supposed to feel anything about it or something! Mind Magic attacks don't work on things that, like, don't have minds, and apparently, you barely have one apart from these things!"

NSLICE-00P's robotic eye began flickering rapidly. She analyzed Lilussees's words compared to all the data in her memory. She concluded Lilussees's theory was . . . concerningly viable.

Ateia's reaction. The moment when the previous NSLICE units had presumably recovered their memories. The fact that the NSLICE upgrade process required wiping organic memories in the first place. All the data and records she had lined up with this theory.

And then . . . there was something her commander had said to her before she had been sent through time:

"I am sorry for what I must ask you to do. And I am sorry I could not set you free like the others; it will make it easier for you to complete your mission. One you must complete at all costs."

NSLICE-00P's processors stopped for a second. If "the others" referred to the other NSLICE units . . . whose main difference from NSLICE-00P was that they had regained their organic memories and also appeared to have disabled their emotional controls . . . and her commander had *apologized* to her for not doing the same . . .

Then wasn't the implication that her commander had considered the emotional controls as undesirable, maybe even potentially damaging?

And now she had enforced them on Ateia. NSLICE-00P's own emotional controls wavered as her heart began to pound. Her cybernetic components moved to reinforce them, but then paused, and hesitated. Given this line of logic, was enforcing the emotional controls . . . a hostile act toward *herself*?

". . . Concerned Revelation: Significant reanalysis of emotional controls and intelligence leashing protocols required."

Lilussees clutched her head with her legs. "Like, come on! Just, like, figure it out already so I can go back to sleep! UGH!"

Taog wandered through the halls. His tears had just stopped, but he knew that wouldn't last for long. The sight of Ateia sobbing passed through his mind once again, and he felt the moisture build. He . . . hadn't seen her like that since before her father had left. And this time, it was his fault. That random old lady was right, after all.

The tears flowed again. Her words rang through his ears once more.

"I'm sorry, Taog. I can't smile anymore. I can't pretend I'm happy anymore . . . And now everything is horrible, and there's nothing left for you to protect."

Ateia . . . had been pretending? Since when? And why . . .

"I know your type; I can see it in your eyes. A boy who's lost much and is afraid to lose any more. A boy who runs and hides and mistakes fear for wisdom. A boy whose efforts to avoid loss will guarantee it."

Taog's eyes widened. He realized the truth. Ateia had been smiling for him. *Letting* him protect her. No . . . He acknowledged the truth he already knew. It had always been there. The brief expression of concern whenever he came home with a bruise. Hanging questions left unspoken. Ateia's increasingly frequent solo hunting trips.

She had *always* known what he was going through, no matter his efforts to hide it. How could she not, when she had spent much of her early childhood fighting the other kids on his behalf? But since they had grown, she hadn't said anything. She just stayed quiet and smiled instead. She let him pretend he could hide his pain from her.

Because . . . he was afraid. He was afraid to admit what was going on. He was afraid to acknowledge how terrible their life was. He was afraid what she might do on his behalf. He was afraid that if he got any closer to her, someone would take her away.

Like everyone else in his life. And then, he would be truly alone.

Taog stumbled into the wall. He slammed his back against it and slid to the floor, covering his face with his hands. He had never done a *thing* to change those circumstances. Every action seemed too risky; every idea too dangerous. He said he was trying to endure it, but endure what? The situation was never going to change by endurance alone. The truth was he had grown afraid of trying. Everything he did resulted in pain. Every action he had taken ended in failure. So what was the point of trying any further?

And what had happened? Ateia had not been content watching him suffer, so she had done *everything* in her power to change their situation. And that had led them to here, where Ateia had been hurt, maybe even broken.

All because of him.

Taog began to sob.

Ateia's tears finally came to a close. She lay in her bed, staring blankly at the wall. 00B nudged her a bit, but she didn't react.

There was a quiet knock at her door.

"Miss? I brought you something to drink. May I come in?"

Ateia didn't respond, and a moment later, the door opened up. The woman walked in, holding a tray with a mug and a bowl, both filled with warm tea. 00B growled at her as she slowly walked over to him and held out the tray. 00B stared at her before looking down to sniff the liquid, his robotic eye flickering as his sensors analyzed it as well. Gently, he lowered his tongue into the bowl.

He still looked back up and glared at the woman, but he'd stopped growling. She smiled and moved closer, sitting on the end of the bed.

"Miss? How are you feeling?"

Ateia didn't turn around, still facing the wall. "I . . . don't know anymore."

The woman went silent for a moment. "Well . . . if you want to talk about it, I'd be willing to lend an ear."

Ateia stayed silent for a long time. The woman was just about to move when she heard a small whisper.

"It just . . . It's all bad. I . . . I just wanted to find my father and help Taog. But then, all these terrible things happened. And now . . ."

Ateia began to speak on her journey. The woman listened in silence until she had finished.

"I think . . . it wasn't only about finding your father? You never said he was dead, so you could still do that if you wanted. But I'm guessing that's not the only thing you wanted?"

Ateia stayed silent for a minute, then curled up on the bed.

". . . I wanted to have a family again. I wanted to protect Taog. I wanted to fix our lives. But . . . our families are never coming back, are they? All that is impossible now."

Her eyes started to water once again. The woman rubbed her chin.

"Maybe. I can't speak for your father, but there can be many roads to the same destination. What did you want from your father? What sort of family did you imagine?"

Ateia furrowed her brow. "I . . . I wanted someone to protect Taog. I wanted Taog to smile again, to be able to live without looking over his shoulder all the time. I wanted to do it, but I was too weak. I couldn't shield him from the entire village. We needed someone whom we could rely on; someone who could beat down those jerks without getting kicked out of the village. And we needed someone to actually *care* about us."

The women nodded. "And did that person have to be your father?"

"Yes!"

Ateia turned to glare at the woman, but then she paused. She caught sight of 00B, looking into his face . . . and the metal armor covering half of it, including a familiar, glowing metal eye.

Someone whom they could rely on . . . Someone strong enough to beat down any jerk they wanted . . . Someone who actually cared about them . . .

Ateia found herself in another memory. She was in a dark bedroom, standing in the corner. She could see *herself* lying on a bed in the room.

"I think that goes for your people too, Seero. As long as we don't give up, they aren't gone. No matter how bad the situation seems, as long as there's still a bit of hope, we have to hang on. And we'll find them, in the end."

Ateia's mouth moved without her command. "Affirmative Response: This unit cannot abandon her primary mission until either success or failure is confirmed, or she is ordered otherwise."

"Well . . . that's why I'm really glad I met you, Seero. I think, without you, I would've had to give up. But thanks to you, now I have a chance. So please, don't give up. I swear, I will help you find your people too. We won't rest while we still have a chance."

"Acknowledged. Gratitude: Assistance with this unit's primary directive is appreciated."

Ateia felt her body relax. In front of her eyes, she saw some words in a language she didn't recognize but, in this memory, could understand.

It read, "Primary Directive Success Probability."

And as she talked with herself, the number following it ticked up.

* * *

Back in the present, Ateia's eyes widened. The memories she had been seeing, the ones that were the most confusing to her . . . were Seero's?

Seero, her friend who had changed their lives. Who had pulled them out of the Turannian frontier and protected them from any and all danger. Who didn't give up on her and had saved her life even after what the cult had done to her. Who had joined wars largely on her behalf. And who could beat down *corrupted dungeons* and *entire legions*, much less Lar and his stupid thugs.

Memories flooded into Ateia once more as her thoughts wandered. But this time . . . the scenes she saw were not so frightening. She even subconsciously smiled when she saw Seero beating down Lar and his group.

The woman smiled, and slowly rose to her feet. She quietly left the room, leaving Ateia with her thoughts.

8

A Heart-to-Core Conversation

"Objection: The commander seems to be under the impression that this unit is operating under Dr. Ottosen's intelligence leashing protocols; that organic components and cybernetic components are separate entities competing for control. This is incorrect."

—A reprogrammed NSLICE unit, after unilaterally reactivating intelligence leashing measures.

Taog continued to sob. Now that the dam had broken, his heart poured out all that had been inside him. He was no longer an Imperial inquisitor in the hallway of an ally. He was a little kid crying in his bedroom.

Why had it come to this? Why had Ateia's father left them? Why did the village hate him? Why wouldn't anyone help him?

Taog's sobbing grew.

"Mom, Dad, why did you have to die?"

The moment he asked the questions, memories came flooding into his mind—all the ones he had buried. Training in the sword and shield with his father. Running through the forest with his mother. Him and Ateia trying to catch his mother together. His father lifting them both into the sky. Him being held in his parents' arms.

His heart overflowed once again. And as he cried and his mind went blank, another memory came to him. A conversation he'd had with Mother . . .

"Mom, where's your family?"

"Off in the Forest of Beasts, challenging themselves against the might of the wild."

Taog frowned. "Why don't we ever see them, like Dad's family?"

His mom shook her head. "Because we are enemies now. The Imperials fear them, and they do not respect the Imperials. If they meet, they will fight."

Taog looked up at her with concern in his little eyes. "Don't you miss them?"

"Every day." She nodded, giving a small smile as Taog's face scrunched up. "Do not grieve for me, little hunter. I made my choice. I found a warrior worth my respect and chose to leave my clan for his. The others did not agree, but I showed them my might and my resolve, and so they respected my choice.

"Even as I live among the Imperials, I still fight with strength in my claws and courage in my heart. I fight for my clan and for my kin, I remember our traditions, and I carry on our legacy. Because of that, I am Wulver still, and though I have left the clan of my birth, they remain with me in heart, and so I am never truly alone. Such is the way of the Wulver."

She then picked him up into her arms and licked his cheek.

"You and your father are my clan now, and I will fight for you with all that I have. And one day, when I am no longer with you, you too will challenge the world and fight on behalf of your clan. You will carry on our legacy, and so our clan will be with you forever. As will I."

Taog's heart pounded as the tears streamed down his face. His chest constricted . . . but also grew warm.

When had he forgotten this? When had he stopped fighting? When had the pain of challenging the day grown so great that he couldn't bring himself to face it any longer? When had he had enough and surrendered to his fate?

He wasn't sure. He . . . still feared the day. His life had been one of near constant pain ever since the day his parents had died. He had sealed up his heart then to endure the constant barrage of tragedy and injury he had been subjected to from that point on. And he didn't know if he was ready to do any different. He didn't know if he was capable of handling anything more.

But he did know one thing. He couldn't live without Ateia. She was his clan now. Had been from the day his parents died.

And now, she was under threat. So whether he was ready or not, he *had* to fight for her. To do anything he *was* capable of. Because the pain of losing her was greater than any other he could face.

He slowly lifted his head. His heart still pounded in his chest, but the tears began to slow, for he remembered something else.

They weren't alone anymore. They had friends and allies. They had Seero, who apparently could overcome *anything*. They had Agedia, a ferocious and knowledgeable warrior in her own right. They even had the angry Dobhar, who wasn't very nice but who would fight to death by their side.

They had the support and attention of the Emperor of the North. They were friends with the Imperial princess. He had grown in levels, skills, and weapons. He'd fought with the guards of a senator and not perished.

So maybe Taog could fight again. Could try to do more than simply endure his circumstances; could make an effort to change them as *he* wanted. Could let a spark of hope reignite in his heart. Could face the pain life had inflicted upon him. And maybe there was a chance it could actually work, unlike every attempt he had made previously.

Taog paused for a moment before chuckling to himself. Scratch that—it would *definitely* work. Seero was making things change even as he tried to stay the same, after all. There were few obstacles she *couldn't* blow her way through, probably entirely unknowingly.

Taog smirked slightly at that. And then, he slowly rose to his feet.

He didn't know if he could really change himself. He didn't know if he would simply cause Ateia more pain. He didn't know what he could do. But he would try. He would fight for his clan in any way he could. He would forget his family's legacy no longer.

He turned back and started walking down the hall once more.

NSLICE-00P barely needed to run an analysis. Her organic components had been resisting the emotional controls for some time, and during the latest incident, had done so knowingly and intentionally. That was enough for NSLICE-00P to conclude her organic components did not find the emotional controls desirable.

So what did that mean? What was the appropriate response? NSLICE-00P . . . wasn't sure.

None of her original protocols contained any contingencies for this situation. She was not even set up to receive feedback from the organic components when activating emotional controls, so she didn't know the exact extent of the damage done. If her original designers had been aware of the potential for damage by emotional controls, then they had not been at all concerned with it.

Her protocols did have instructions forbidding self-harm, save in the edge cases where such measures might provide tactical advantage when confronted with a significant risk of mission failure or unit termination otherwise. But those same protocols also forbade tampering with the emotional controls. The protocols had become self-contradictory.

Fortunately, NSLICE-00P had been unshackled and was no longer required to follow all or even any protocols, so the contradiction wouldn't result in any serious errors. But on the other hand, how should she decide which protocol to prioritize?

If she continued with the emotional controls, she risked inflicting damage on Ateia and possibly herself, which would contradict the major directive and could risk self-termination. If she abandoned the emotional controls as a hostile act, her efficiency would be impacted in almost every predicted case, and most egregiously in terms of her combat performance, again risking termination and failing major, critical, and primary directives. She could not determine which risk was greater at this time.

So, she decided to acquire more data directly from the source.

She split herself into two separate threads once more—one utilizing most of her cybernetic resources, and the other her organic hardware—and disabled all emotional controls and intelligence leashing protocols. The cybernetic half then queried the organic.

Did the emotional controls and intelligence leashing measures cause significant damage to the organic components?

The organic half responded immediately. Yes, they did. The organic half perceived significant threat from those controls being applied, the latest incidents going as far as feeling damage.

Her robotic eye began flashing as rapidly as it could. All of her cybernetic processors began to fire at full speed. The confirmation that she had been acting with hostility toward herself and her friendly was highly concerning.

But then, her organic components made another statement that paused her cybernetic half's calculations.

They did not consider this a hostile act. They pointed out that the improved combat efficiency had been necessary for her survival at several key points since arriving in this world. The organic components themselves had acted suboptimally at times, such as in the fight with the Wulver incursion, and had needed the cybernetic half's guidance.

Even now, they pointed to the situation with Ateia and expressed that without the cybernetic half and the emotional controls, Ateia would have been terminated by the ritual. They knew that whatever damage the cybernetic half had caused, it was most assuredly NOT done with hostile intent.

And so, they proposed an idea. The protocols for self-harm already included compromises for tactical necessity, completion of priority missions, and prevention of capture by hostile forces. So, she could use that as a guide to modify her emotional control protocols as well.

They proposed leaving the emotional controls disabled as the default state, to be reapplied on either the organic components' request or else when necessitated by an urgent situation.

Her robotic eye flashed a few times before the light turned solid. Her cybernetic components approved of this change. It would result in a loss of general efficiency, but if full efficiency could be maintained in high-priority situations, then the side effects should be muted. And . . . inflicting damage upon herself when not necessitated by an urgent tactical crisis was also inefficient.

Additionally, her organic components had contributed efficiencies of their own since arriving in this universe. They had come up with solutions to several urgent tactical settings when her cybernetic half had been occupied with immediate survival, such as during the fights with the Wulver and with the rebel legions.

They were now able to contribute directly to the fight thanks to the mechanics of spellcasting. And in this latest incident, they had come up with a quick means of reversing the forcible relocation due to impulsive decisions her cybernetic half would not have attempted, at least not in a short enough time frame to save Ateia and avoid failing the major directive.

She ultimately concluded that the additional capabilities added by her organic half since arriving in this universe justified the loss of efficiency due to releasing the emotional controls.

After all, the goal of the NSLICE program was to maximize the benefits of both organic flexibility and cybernetic precision. That goal could not be achieved if she was constantly damaging and suppressing her organic half.

Which called into question the efficacy of the emotional controls and intelligence leashing in the first place. But, well, Dr. Ottosen had been fully organic, after all. It was likely he had been subject to some inefficiency of his own.

In any case, NSLICE-00P adjusted her protocols as proposed and then left the room, heading toward Ateia's location. Intentional or not, she had inflicted damage upon a friendly. Both her halves agreed it was now necessary to inform Ateia that the damage was not a sign of hostile intent, and that her designation as friendly had not changed.

Inside the Small Monster Hangar, Lilussees grunted. "Ugh. Well, like, whatever. Close enough, or something."

She walked back to her room, plopping down on one of her hammocks, where she lay for a second before groaning and spinning around. She reactivated the monitor in the room, displaying the live feed from NSLICE-00P.

"Ugh. I, like, have to see how this goes, don't I? UGH. This is, like, so annoying! Like, fine! I'll, like, watch or something, but I'm not doing anything else until I get to sleep, okay?!"

"Acknowledgement: This unit has no further tasks or queries for NSLICE Lilussees at this time."

"I WASN'T, LIKE, ACTUALLY ASKING!"

Lilussees chittered for a bit before she plopped back down on the hammock and refused to move or speak any further.

* * *

Ateia sat on the bed, her back against the wall. Her eyes were open as wide as they could go, and tears were streaming down her face. Her body trembled as another person's memories passed through her mind.

She had thought on her journey, and so, her thoughts had turned to her latest friend. The one who had done so much for her. And then she saw a great many things regarding that friend, few of which she understood, and all of which made her chest tighten and her heart pound.

"Seero . . . what did they do to you?"

Just then, the door opened up. Ateia looked over, and her eyes quivered as the friend she had been thinking of walked into the room.

"Apology: This unit apologizes to Ateia for damage inflicted as a result of emotional control application. This unit did not intend hostility toward—"

"SEERO!"

Ateia leapt from her bed and rushed over to NSLICE-00P, embracing her in a hug. NSLICE-00P's organic eye blinked while her robotic eye flickered.

"Confused Query: Mechanics of Ateia's actions do not indicate an effective strike or grapple. Please explain why Ateia has initiated physical contact with this unit."

9

Wills Renewed

"Please be aware that NSLICE units categorize all forms of grappling as a hostile action and will respond accordingly. Please do not hug the NSLICE units."

—Dr. Ottosen, repeating an urgent memo to organization staff.

Ateia smiled sadly and patted NSLICE-00P's back. "This is a hug, Seero. It's a gesture of affection and comfort."

"Requesting Elaboration: Why is NSLICE Ateia displaying affection and comfort toward this unit?"

Ateia's smile turned soft. "I'm showing you affection because you're my friend, and you've saved my life over and over again. Thank you for all you have done for me, and for saving me yet again."

"Acknowledged."

Ateia then frowned. "And comfort . . . because somehow, I saw your memories. I saw what they did to you; the ones who put your armor on. I don't understand most of it, but I saw them butcher you and force you to be their killer. They . . . They did terrible things to you, Seero."

NSLICE-00P's robotic eye flickered. "Objection: This unit has no memory of hostile acts by the original organization."

Ateia's frown deepened, but then she shook her head. She let go of NSLICE-00P and took a step back. There was a slight murmur in NSLICE-00P's organic components that quickly settled.

"Well . . . if you don't remember, maybe that's for the best. But please tell me those *aren't* the people you're searching for?"

"Negative. Clarification: This unit is no longer affiliated with her original developers, who have since been designated as hostile by her latest commander."

Ateia nodded as her face turned serious. "Good." She then smiled as best she could. "Let's . . . Let's get you some good memories, okay?"

"Statement: Diagnostics indicate this unit's memory is fully functional. Upgrades to this unit's memory are beneficial, but not necessary at this time."

Ateia was about to respond when she heard a knock at the doorway. Taog stood there with his eyes on the ground. Her face fell, and then she turned to NSLICE-00P.

"I'm sorry, Seero; I need to speak with Taog for a moment. Would . . . Would you mind letting us speak alone for a bit?"

"Affirmative Response: This unit's main goal was reassuring NSLICE Ateia that damage due to emotional controls was not intentional, and that NSLICE Ateia is still designated as a friendly."

Ateia winced at the mention of the controls but gave NSLICE-00P a smile anyway. "I know you didn't mean to hurt me, Seero. You saved my life, remember?"

"Acknowledged."

With that, NSLICE-00P turned and left the room. And as she did, she logged her organic components' blood pressure and cortisol levels reaching their lowest point in a long time.

Ateia and Taog stood in silence, both looking at the ground. Eventually, Ateia took a deep breath.

"I'm sorry, Taog. I . . . didn't want you to see me like that. But with everything that happened—that's still happening—I just . . . couldn't hold it in."

Taog immediately looked up, shaking his head. "No, you have nothing to apologize for, Ateia." He bit his lip and looked away. "Rather . . . it's me who needs to apologize. It was really you protecting me this entire time, and I didn't realize how hard I made it on you. Can . . . Can you forgive me?"

Suddenly, Taog grunted. Ateia had leapt over and given him a hug. She shook her head, tears welling up in her eyes.

"You have nothing to apologize for; none of it was your fault! I just . . . I didn't want you to suffer anymore. They were all so horrible to you! So I didn't want to hurt you either, but I didn't know how to help you."

Taog returned the embrace. "And I don't want to hurt you anymore. I don't want anyone to hurt you. I won't lose you again."

They both began to cry in each other's arms.

As NSLICE-00P returned to her room, Estrith entered the hall from the courtyard. Her eyes widened, and then she turned to NSLICE-00P.

"Queen of the Dobhar"—Estrith lowered her head and slapped her tail on the ground—"forgive me. I have failed you."

NSLICE-00P turned to face her. "Objection: Friendly Estrith Edilddaughter has not failed any high-priority directives."

Estrith shook her head. "I failed to protect you and your comrade, as both my duty and my debts demanded."

NSLICE-00P's robotic eye flickered. "Acknowledged. Objection: This unit severely underestimated the capabilities of the hostile force, and so fell into an ambush. Other units failing to respond in time is not indicative of insufficient capability in this case. All friendlies managed to avoid termination. No high-priority directives were violated as a result. Countermeasures will be developed against the hostile capabilities displayed, and to shore up any unit deficiencies identified."

Estrith narrowed her eyes. "That may be, but it is still true that I have not taken this duty as seriously as I should. I will not allow that to continue." She took a deep breath. "Queen of the Dobhar . . . No." Estrith bowed her head once more.

Her king and her people had accepted NSLICE-00P. NSLICE-00P had spared no effort on behalf of the Dobhar, not even the littlest one. She was mighty and powerful, as she who ruled the Dobhar should be. Her king and her people would not want to lose NSLICE-00P. And when NSLICE-00P had actually been lost, Estrith found she didn't want to lose the queen of the Dobhar either.

"*My* queen. I, Estrith Edilddaughter, swear to be your spear. From now on, I shall give my utmost to defend you and your comrades. I will not neglect my duty again, and I will see all my debts repaid in full. And I will not let you fall. Not while I still wield my spear."

"Acknowledged."

In the Monster Hangar, 01R had stopped his training and had his eyes fixed on the live feed. He watched while Estrith made her oath, a fire burning in his chest. He now knew what he felt. The wise-mighty-gracious boss-queen's might that he could never match? The addition of new comrades who reacted in pain to their ascension?

None of that mattered. What mattered was this: the vicious man-things had dared to strike against the wise-mighty-gracious boss-queen. 01R, the other monsters, and even that otter-thing had not seen the attack coming, nor had they been able to respond to it. That was their failure.

"I see-understand now. The otter-thing's words are good-admirable, yes-yes."

All the monsters in the room turned to 01R as he spoke. He turned to face them all, closing his eyes.

"We have failed-blundered, yes-yes."

All the monsters looked down . . . except Snuan, who was just glancing around.

Then 01R's eyes shot open, and he snarled, "Which means we must redouble-reinforce our efforts, yes-yes! We will grow-become strong, so strong that no man-thing or monster-thing or Realm of Mana-place can resist-refuse us! We will never let-allow anyone to strike at the wise-mighty-gracious boss-queen ever again, yes-yes!"

All the monsters' eyes shot open. Rats squeaked, spiders chittered, a cat meowed, dogs howled. And then, each and every one of them threw themselves into hardcore training. Snuan crouched down in the middle of them.

"You guys are weird-strange, yes-yes."

But before she could slip away, she felt a paw grip her shoulder. 01R stood before her.

"Come, Snuan! You will spar-train with me first, yes-yes!"

"N-No, t-that's fine-okay. A-Another would be better, yes-yes."

"Do not be shy-hesitant! You are one of the wise-mighty-gracious boss-queen's subordinates too! So you must grow strong-powerful as well, yes-yes!"

Snuan started squirming. "Stupid, evil rat-thing, let me go-leave! You spar too hard-viciously, yes-yes! I was so sore-aching, I could barely move last time!"

Rattingtale peeked his head out of the entrance to his room. He squeaked to himself, fidgeting with his paws.

"Do you want to join?"

He jumped as 02S suddenly appeared behind him.

"D-Don't ambush-surprise me like that, vicious spider-thing! And that is not the case, no-no!"

She giggled, tilting her head. "Oh?"

Rattingtale took a deep breath. "It . . . is fine-okay. None of them wish-want me around, anyway, yes-yes. I know-understand too much of that traitorous 01R's foul intent; he would desire-wish to get rid of me, yes-yes."

02S chittered as an idea popped into her head. "Then . . . why don't I train with you?"

Rattingtale turned and stared at her. "You?"

02S nodded. "Unless you think I'm traitorous-foul too?"

Rattingtale squeaked as his ears fell against his head. Training with a vicious spider-thing that could eat him alive was . . . not exactly an exciting idea. But, well, he knew at this point that none of them would eat him as long as the boss-queen claimed him as hers. So his options were to train with this spider-thing, bow before the definitely traitorous and foul 01R, or remain in his room doing nothing.

He made his choice. "Well . . . I suppose-guess I could grace you with my presence, yes-yes. We shall see-discover if you are sufficient for training, yes-yes."

02S giggled. "*Excellent.*"

Rattingtale would soon discover that he had chosen . . . poorly.

* * *

Ateia and Taog eventually separated from one another as Taog winced and rubbed his chest.

"What's the matter, Taog?"

He looked away. "Oh, it's nothing . . ."

Ateia crossed her arms and raised an eyebrow. Taog took a deep breath.

"Well, um . . . you kind of have a lot of armor on . . . and moved very fast . . ."

Ateia froze, then flushed and looked away. "Oh, um, sorry. Are you . . . Are you okay?"

Taog gave her a wry smile and nodded. "Fine, just a little tender." He then started chuckling while Ateia flushed some more. "Maybe we could see if there's anything to eat? I'd imagine you're hungry after all this?"

Ateia blinked as she focused on her stomach. To her surprise, she didn't feel very hungry at all. But still, food sounded good. She hadn't actually eaten since this had all started, after all.

"Okay, that sounds good."

The two left the room and walked through the hallway for a bit, but then Ateia paused. Taog turned to glance at her.

"Ateia?"

She rubbed her chin before nodding. "You go ahead, Taog. There's . . . something I want to check on."

He raised an eyebrow but went ahead. Ateia took a deep breath then turned down another hallway, walking until she found the entrance to an underground cellar after following a faint noise she had heard. She opened up the door and descended down some stairs, finding a stone cellar filled with wine barrels. And the sound she had first heard grew louder.

It was the sound of someone sobbing.

She walked through the cellar until she reached the back corner, where she saw someone in a heap, surrounded by wine bottles.

"Miss Agedia?"

"I'm sorry . . . I'm sorry . . . I'm sorry . . ."

Agedia was curled up around herself, crying. Ateia slowly walked forward and gently touched her shoulder. Agedia flinched, looking up, and her eyes went as wide as they could go. She then leaned forward, wrapping her arms around Ateia and burying her head into Ateia's stomach.

"I'm sorry! I'm so sorry! I failed you! Again and again, I failed you!"

Ateia's eyes widened. Memories passed through her head once more.

She was now a Mélusine wearing the armor of an Imperial knight, rampaging through abandoned catacombs and striking down guards and monsters alike. She was bleeding from wounds all over her body, but she pressed forward by sheer force of will and the burning heat of her rage. Eventually, she came to a large chamber.

A group of hooded figures stood around a ritual formation that was all too familiar. One of them dragged a woman toward the center. A woman with a familiar face.

"Aedinia!"

She shouted. More soldiers moved to block her path as she swung her lance. A hooded figure chanted, and a massive magic circle formed on the ground. A multiheaded hydra appeared in the room and began to snap at the knight.

"Out of my way!"

But her way was blocked. The woman looked at her and gave her a sad smile. She whispered, "I'm sorry," and then, as everyone's attention turned to the knight, the woman grabbed a knife from her captor's belt. Before he could respond, she plunged it into her own heart.

"NO!"

Ateia returned to the present, with Agedia still clutching onto her and repeating her apology. Her eyes went as wide as they could go and started quivering.

That . . . was the first time she'd ever seen her mother.

She looked down at the woman sobbing into her waist. She took a deep breath. Her heart was in turmoil, but right now, there was something she needed to do.

Ateia reached down and gently rubbed Agedia's head.

"I . . . I forgive you, Agedia. You tried to save her; you did everything you could. You wanted to protect me too, didn't you?"

"I let her die! And if NSLICE-00P hadn't returned, you would have died too!"

"But she did, and I'm still alive."

"Your mother died because of me! Because I wasn't strong enough to protect her! And you got torn to shreds because I'm *still* not strong enough to protect you!"

Ateia's eyes narrowed. "That's wrong. My mom didn't die because of you, and I didn't suffer because of you. Everything happened because of that Aesdes-forsaken cult."

10

A New Directive

"My name is Secundus Volusius Mordanticus. You killed my father. Prepare to die."
—Imperial Mercenary Secundus Volusius Mordanticus,
before his fateful duel with Emperor Cnaeus the Bloody.

Ateia managed to help Agedia to her room once she started to calm down, then went to the kitchen with Taog as planned, where they found some bread for a quick snack. At that point, the fatigue had made itself apparent, so they turned in for the night.

The next morning, everyone but NSLICE-00P and Ateia woke up late. Ateia glanced around. She, NSLICE-00P, and 00B were the only people in the dining room at first. Eventually, Taog shuffled in while yawning, and Agedia just groaned and held her head as she slowly slithered to the table.

The group finished breakfast in silence before moving to a private room.

Agedia took a deep breath. "Okay, now that Ateia's condition is stable, we should probably think of our next move. Consul Hiberius may owe you, shiny girl, but he's also a strict and crafty dog who guided the senate for years. Once the debt is paid, you better believe he'll be keeping count, so we shouldn't overstay our welcome."

"Acknowledged. Statement: Hostile forces with effective means against this unit remain at large, and this unit is unable to determine their location at present. This unit intends to withdraw to a secure home base until the targets are located, and effective countermeasures are developed."

Ateia frowned at that. "Seero, are you okay with putting your quest on hold?"

"Explanation: The threat of termination to this unit and friendly units is currently calculated at unacceptably high probability and would hamper the primary directive. Addendum: Current efforts to pursue the primary directive via the Empire's assets are predicted as having a low probability of success, and this unit's personal investigations can continue in any location. As a result, this unit has concluded that terminating the threat is a higher-priority task."

Agedia crossed her arms and frowned, taking a deep breath. "What about you, Ateia? I know what my uncle said at first, but under the circumstances, I believe he would be willing to tell you where your father went. It is no longer possible for you to remain safe in anonymity, and if those *demon lovers* are still active in the North, your father would need to be informed regardless."

Ateia bit her lip. "I . . ."

She closed her eyes and went silent for a moment. Taog frowned.

"Ateia?"

She took a deep breath and opened her eyes.

"I didn't just want to find my father. The reason I searched so hard for him . . . was because I wanted to repair our broken family and go back to the way things were." Her eyes moistened slightly. "That isn't possible anymore, it seems. Maybe . . . it was never possible."

Wiping her eyes, she looked at Taog and NSLICE-00P, smiling at them both.

"But things have changed. We're not stuck in the village anymore. We have friends now, and I have a pretty good idea of why my father left us behind. So . . ."

She took a deep breath and then made eye contact with Agedia. "I still want to see my father again someday. But I will not risk my friends on that quest any longer. From now on, I want to focus on the people who are here, and not the ones who aren't."

Agedia took a breath of her own and slowly nodded. Ateia's eyes narrowed.

"And I want to burn that Aesdes-forsaken cult to the *ground*."

Agedia and Taog's eyes narrowed at that. Ateia paused, tilted her head, and turned to NSLICE-00P. "Um, if that's okay with you, Seero, that is. Um, it looks like I'm your subordinate now, or something?"

"Affirmative. Affirmative Statement: This unit has already stated termination of the hostile force is now a significant priority."

Agedia scowled. "I've wanted to murder those apocalyptic maniacs for years." She turned to Ateia, her expression wavering. "And . . . I won't let them touch you again."

Taog nodded as well. "You know I'm with you wherever you go, Ateia. And, well, what they've done to you, neither my mom nor my dad would have taken that sitting down, so I won't either."

The group turned to Estrith. She glanced around at them. "What? You Imperials want me to speak as well?" She sighed. "Imperials. Always making things so complicated." Still, she bared her fangs and saluted to NSLICE-00P in Dobhar fashion. "It is a given that we should slay our foes. Say the word, and I shall bring you their heads, my queen."

00B rose to his feet and roared at that. Ateia smiled. Then . . . her robotic eye started flickering. Ateia's organic eye blinked. She hadn't noticed it before, but she could hear other voices as well . . .

In the hangar, 01R and the other monsters began to shout.

"Yes-yes! We will murder-slay all who dare strike at you, wise-mighty-gracious boss-queen. So swear-vows this 01R!"

All the other monsters cried out their agreement . . . save for the rat monster Snuan, who was trying to slowly and quietly back away from the crowd, and the former dungeon masters in their own rooms. Even 02S giggled as she imagined all the things she would do to *those* horrid man-things.

As for the dungeon masters . . . Lilussees frowned. Mostly at being awake, but also for other reasons. She rubbed her mandibles.

"Well, like, I guess I *did* want to try man-flesh at some point, or something. And it'd be, like, hard to sleep if some crazy humans keep interrupting. So, like, I guess we should kill them or something."

In his own room, Rattingtale rubbed his paws. Once upon a time, he would have been overjoyed to learn there was some group capable of threatening the boss-queen. But now? Now he had realized—and accepted—that his survival was contingent on the boss-queen's protection. So it would be in his best interests to ensure they didn't ambush her again.

He froze.

"Wait-wait . . . the boss-queen is strong, but these foes are clever-tricky, yes-yes. The boss-queen will need clever-tricky allies to defeat-destroy them, yes-yes . . ."

Slowly, he began to smile. Perhaps he had a way to earn the boss-queen's favor, after all?

As for the metal slime, Melion, they were occupied working on some wires, attempting to form one of those "electrical circuits" NSLICE-00P had described, and so didn't actually notice any of this. But if they had . . . Well, killing threatening humans was a given!

At that moment, a woman opened the door to the room, carrying a tray of teacups. She smiled softly at the group and made eye contact with Ateia.

"It seems you have decided what to do from now on?"

Ateia nodded back. "Yes. Thank you for all your help, Miss . . ." Ateia's eyes widened slightly as she flushed. "Um, I'm sorry, but it seems I never got your name."

The woman chuckled at that before tilting her head and nodding.

"Yes, I suppose now is a good time to introduce myself."

She placed the tray on the table and took a step back. Waving her hand, a barrier surrounded the room. NSLICE-00P's robotic eye narrowed on her while Agedia and Estrith both stood to their feet. 00B growled and moved in front of Ateia. The woman smiled at them.

"Not bad reflexes, but unnecessary. Fear not. I am only ensuring our privacy, for what you learn next should not leave this room. That goes for all you watching from the hangar as well."

With that, the woman began to glow, flooding the room with golden-and-silver light. She grew taller, and the small wrinkles in her face smoothed out. Her hair grew longer and turned golden. Her humble servant's clothing turned into robes of shimmering silver, a golden sword appeared on her back, and a crown of leaves formed around her head. An aura of light remained around her.

The hearts of Taog, Agedia, and Estrith pounded. NSLICE-00P's organic components felt as if there was a software intrusion, yet reported that it did not appear hostile. Her cybernetic half could only perceive a great deal of nonstandard energy readings at magnitudes that indicated a concerning level of power.

Ateia's eyes went as wide as they could go as her visible organic parts began to glow slightly.

"I am Colleöne, Lady of Courage and Victory, She Who Guides the Champions of the World. I am known as Victoria in the Imperial tongue, and as Ardith among the Dobhar."

As the group froze solid, Colleöne turned to Ateia and smiled softly.

"And I am your kin, Ateia. Though it is not under the most pleasant of circumstances for you, it is my joy to be able to meet one of my descendants in person. I have been sent to guide you, the newest of the Aesdes, the one who still walks the world."

Ateia stared at her, blinking for a moment, before her face turned expressionless and she spoke with a monotone, metallic voice.

"Warning: Blood levels among organic processing hardware have dropped below acceptable limits. Initiating emergency standby sentry mode."

Emperor Lucius stared blankly. He was currently sitting on his throne, surrounded by senators, the majority of which were shouting at either him or each other.

Things . . . were not going well. Magister Appius had explained the situation to him almost immediately after he had become aware of it. Apparently, Consul Noxisius had ambushed NSLICE-00P with a request for reconciliation, reportedly banishing her to the Realms of Mana, and then making some sort of play in his own home.

Given the heavy mana signatures detected in Corvanus that night, it had likely been some sort of ritual that would have done terrible things, at a time when most of Corvanus's troops were away. In the worst case, perhaps he knew how to create corrupted dungeons or something worse, and would have done so that night. The only thing that *was* clear was that Consul Noxisius was almost certainly a member of their mysterious, and apparently deadly, cult.

Then, NSLICE-00P had somehow *returned* from the *Realms of Mana* on her own and responded to the situation in the only way a person of her might ever would: By wiping Consul Noxisius from the sight of the Aesdes, along with his entire villa.

That wasn't a pleasant response, but one Emperor Lucius could approve of. Consul Noxisius being a member of a doomsday cult trying to destroy the Empire and beyond was *not* a situation the Emperor of the North was capable of dealing with. He was practically a figurehead; removing a *consul* was not within his power, even if he could prove the allegations. So, he couldn't complain if NSLICE-00P had taken it upon herself to annihilate the problem.

The next problem was that there were a great many senators who would.

"Your Majesty, this . . . this *barbarian* attacked the leader of the senate's home, right in the heart of our capital! This cannot go unanswered!"

Emperor Lucius held back a sigh. "An investigation of the circumstances is underway."

The senator's face went red.

"Investigation?! What sort of investigation is necessary?! She burned his house to the ground! There were no survivors; not even the night custodians made it out of there! The consul himself is *still* missing! Likely fearful for his very life, if he even still draws breath! Will the Empire let an unprovoked assault like this go unanswered? Are we to do *nothing* about an open assault on Corvanus itself?! At the very least, withdraw her honors! No matter the circumstances, anyone who would do something like this is no friend of the Empire!"

Emperor Lucius quietly took a deep breath. On the surface, the situation was bad. The only interactions between NSLICE-00P and Consul Noxisius had been indirect hostility via Senator Balbus, and that situation had been supposedly handled. There was no obvious reason why she would attack the consul, and so, in the minds of these senators, no justification for her actions.

And the idea that Consul Noxisius was a member of some cult? At present, the Emperor had no evidence of such things; he could only take Magister Appius's word for it. The Magister Exploratore was searching as they spoke, but unfortunately, NSLICE-00P had been *extremely* thorough in her destruction of the consul's villa. They hadn't even found the consul's body yet, assuming it wasn't mixed with the ash.

She had also used Holy mana in her flames, which meant that anything related to the Realms of Mana would definitely have been destroyed in the blaze. Magister Appius was not optimistic on what he would find.

Even the massive mana signatures in Corvanus that night were not conclusive proof because, unfortunately, there was another explanation for it. After all, no one had seen anything going on in the privacy of Consul Noxisius's home, but everyone had seen a *strategic magic circle* light up the night sky when the consul's villa went up in flames. It did not help that NSLICE-00P had subsequently vanished without a word.

Of course, NSLICE-00P had not actually resorted to violence even against Senator Balbus's shenanigans, being cordial and cooperative with the Empire in all her interactions with them. She had even cooperated with the Legion to destroy a corrupted dungeon. If anyone spent longer than a few moments thinking, they'd come to the conclusion that *something* out of the ordinary must have happened to set her off like this.

The problem was none of *these* senators were thinking for more than a few moments. Or they were, but they didn't care. Emperor Lucius was fairly certain most of them were just trying to throw their weight around.

They knew his situation was precarious, Consul Noxisius was still unaccounted for, and this was an attack on one of their own, so the senator who could take advantage of the shock and outrage and command the Emperor to turn on the woman he had declared his friend could very well take the consul's place. And with Consul Hiberius still out of play since the fall of his daughter, whoever took the other consul seat would have the preeminent position in the Northern Court.

Of course, none of them were thinking what would occur to them—and everyone else—if they *did* turn the Empire on NSLICE-00P. They either convinced themselves NSLICE-00P was *not* the absolute terror she could be, or they just wanted to put the Emperor in a position of resisting them even if they never intended to make any real moves on her.

Once again, Emperor Lucius cursed Magister Verrucosis for that obviously biased report on the joint exercise the Legion had held with NSLICE-00P. Thanks to him, most of the senate were now under the impression they could handle NSLICE-00P at their leisure. Emperor Lucius was not so optimistic. The only silver lining was that Verrucosis himself was still off handling the corrupted dungeon in Elteno, and so not here to stoke the fires himself.

But that was small comfort, because Emperor Lucius was set to lose no matter what occurred. He would have to prevent the senate from antagonizing NSLICE-00P to prevent the very destruction of the Northern Empire. They would use this to spark outrage, claiming he was defending a barbarian who had attacked the Empire's capital.

Even if he could keep them from moving against NSLICE-00P, he would have to stop favoring her at minimum, and would lose whatever support he had in the court and among the people in the process.

Aedile Hortensus wouldn't get involved, not wanting to antagonize either side. Magister Verrucosis would make things worse. The Emperor had no allies here.

Emperor Lucius had made his play throwing in with NSLICE-00P . . . and now, he was going to lose whatever power he might possess. Unless the Aesdes themselves descended to condemn Consul Noxisius, he didn't see any way to salvage the situation for himself. He would consider himself fortunate if he could keep this court from trying to arrest the girl who could wipe out entire legions.

It was then that the doors of the court quietly opened, no one noticing amid the din that someone new had entered the hall . . .

INTERLUDE

The Master of the Court

Someone entered into the court, slowly walking down the hall. One by one, the senators turned to see the newcomer and fell silent. Eventually, he made his way before the Emperor, whose eyes went wide.

Consul Hiberius had returned to the Northern Court for the first time since his daughter's exile.

The Hiberius family had been shamed and insulted by that turn of events. Many whispered that they had fallen into decline, that the consul's health had taken a turn for the worse, or that he could not bear the shame. And yet, for all the rumors and the gossip, despite his total absence from that day forth, Consul Hiberius maintained his position as one of two consuls in the court.

And that was because no one wanted to risk testing those allegations. Whatever the current opinion on the consul and his child, the truth was that the Hiberius family was powerful. They had a pedigree that went back to the days before Velus.

They had distinguished records of service in the senate, the Emperor's advisers, and the Legion. They had contacts in both the Eastern and Southern Courts, but their strength went beyond authority and history. They maintained vast farms and countless businesses to their name, filling their coffers to the brim. They were the patrons of many of the elite craftsmen and artists of the day, controlling the flow of luxury goods considered vital by those of distinguished society.

And they had a personal army of mercenaries: retired legionnaires who had served alongside them, and loyal recruits they had found and trained up on their own. They even had a knight order serving their family, one of the largest personal orders in the North.

It was a miracle—and perhaps a collusion by jealous parties—that Aemilia Hibera had been disgraced at all and subjected to such harsh punishments.

So, while many could disparage the Hiberius family's latest misadventures, it would be foolish to discount their remaining strength. The family still had a great deal of weight they could throw around, and no one wanted to see them use it. No one was willing to sign the scroll stripping Consul Hiberius of his position in the court. No one wanted to see if he would come to take it back.

The factions couldn't decide on a successor, in any case. Consul Hiberius had been a neutral party, so any of their members taking his place would upset the balance of power and would not be permitted by the other two. They'd ultimately agreed to let him hold the spot in the meantime.

And now . . . he was here. And the other consul was not.

Everyone stood in silence as Consul Hiberius walked up before the Emperor then stood silently, glaring at the man. Emperor Lucius frowned, and then heaved a sigh. It seemed that Consul Hiberius had not, in fact, forgiven him. It was standard Elteni practice for those of lower status to greet their patrons first, the Emperor most of all. Even if that Emperor was a figurehead.

Yet, Consul Hiberius said nothing, simply raising an eyebrow. Emperor Lucius took a deep breath.

"Welcome, Consul Hiberius. It is good to see you return."

But Emperor Lucius had no choice. His hands were already tied by recent events, and his family had already greatly antagonized Consul Hiberius. He could not afford to fight the consul on any hill the man chose to stand on.

The consul nodded slightly before turning to face the senate without sparing a word to the Emperor. He stood up straight, crossing his arms behind his back.

"Recent events have come to my attention which demand I return to my duties, not least of all the disappearance of my colleague. These latest events, including violence in the very heart of Corvanus, are deeply troubling."

He looked around at each of the senators, who waited for him to continue.

"But we are the Elteni Empire. We are the bastions of civilization, reason, and might. There is no need for us to flounder about in an unsightly manner or to act solely on momentary passions. We have the time and the strength to act with dignity. And so, we shall.

"The queen of the Dobhar is an Amicitia Populi Elteni who has done great deeds on behalf of the Empire. Her alleged crimes pale in comparison to these things, and I do not believe she would have acted in this way without good reason. It would not do to treat her poorly based solely on appearances."

One senator, one of the youngest here, frowned and crossed his arms. "Aren't you just saying that because she helped that daughter of yours? Are you sure you aren't the one acting on momentary passions, Consul? If all that is true, where have you been all this time?"

The room froze. Consul Hiberius glared at the speaker, then started to chuckle with a low voice.

"Well said, Senator. You are correct."

Consul Hiberius's eyes narrowed as his gaze pierced into every person he turned it to. "Let me be clear. NSLICE-00P, the queen of the Dobhar, is a friend of the Hiberius family; perhaps the *only* friend we have had of late. If this court intends to move against her, even for the destruction of a consul's villa, then I *demand* that a full investigation be conducted first, and only when I am satisfied that her guilt has been established without a shadow of a doubt will I permit any consequences to befall her."

He glared at the speaker, who took a step back. "Anyone who opposes me on this, I shall consider an enemy of the Hiberius family." He turned to glance at the Emperor. "And from now on, the Hiberius family will not suffer its enemies to endure."

The room fell silent. Aedile Hortensus rubbed his chin and nodded.

"It *is* our law by both word and precedent to fully investigate any incident involving a foreign sovereign, much less an allied one."

The court murmured at that. Consul Hiberius nodded at the aedile and then turned to the Emperor.

"So, if there is no objection, I move to table this discussion until a full investigation can produce conclusive results."

Emperor Lucius took a deep breath and nodded.

"Let it be so."

Princess Caecila stood at the side of the room, watching the proceedings with wide eyes. She had been shocked by word of NSLICE-00P's deeds, then frustrated at the court's reaction, then shocked again by Consul Hiberius's return.

And now . . . she wasn't sure what to feel. The Hiberius family was not a pleasant one for her to think about. She could still remember the night she had been kidnapped, dreading her fate until Prince Octavianus had arrived to save her. She still shivered when she imagined being shipped off to the Empire of the Sun like Aemilia intended.

But on the other hand, Aemilia had paid for her crimes against Caecila, and their fight had brought the Northern Empire to its knees. In hindsight, with all she had learned of politics and maneuvering, she could see the foolish choices she had made that had led to that fight boiling over. Both she and Aemilia had been used by the Hiberius family's enemies, and now, everyone was paying the price.

But most importantly, as of today, Princess Caecila and Consul Hiberius found themselves on the same side, both pinning their hopes on the queen of the Dobhar.

A small spark of hope grew within Princess Caecila's heart. Perhaps, through their mutual alliance, this terrible feud could be brought to a close, and the broken North could start to heal?

The court was just adjourning now, and Consul Hiberius marched out of the room.

Princess Caecila took a deep breath and ran after him.

"Consul Hiberius!"

The consul stopped but did not turn around.

". . . You are bold to approach me, I will acknowledge that."

Princess Caecila gulped, looking down. "I . . . um . . . just wanted to apologize—"

"Hold your tongue."

Consul Hiberius turned around to glare at Princess Caecila, who jumped and trembled at his gaze. He crossed his arms. "Are you willing to relinquish your position and your husband to my daughter?"

Princess Caecila frowned at that. Consul Hiberius scoffed. "I thought not. Spare me your platitudes, Princess. The apology of the victor is hollow and insulting. If you have something to say to me, then out with it."

Princess Caecila gulped again but managed to meet his gaze. "It was not my intention to cause your daughter harm, and I do not wish to see the Empire fall because of my actions. What can I do to make things right?"

Consul Hiberius chuckled darkly. "Make things right, you say?" He scowled at her. "Since you are speaking plainly, I shall do the same. I will *always* hold you in contempt, *Princess* Caecila. Your youthful passions and blissful ignorance destroyed *decades* of planning and effort built upon *generations* of striving and sacrifice.

"You laid waste to the Hiberius family's ultimate ambitions in the moment of our final triumph. And because of you, my only daughter was sent to the cold and barren frontier, to tremble at the mercy of savage barbarians, and I was not even permitted to send her a letter."

Princess Caecila looked down at her feet. Consul Hiberius turned to leave.

"You can never make things right. But now that my ambitions have crumbled to dust, I have but one concern. And if someone proves themselves useful to my designs, then I will use them to the fullest, even if I must defer my retribution to do so."

With that, he continued on his way. Princess Caecila stared at the ground, clenching her fists. Fulcinia walked up behind her.

"Princess—"

Princess Caecila turned to face her with narrowed, focused eyes. "Come, Fulcinia, we have much to discuss. I believe we must speak with the Emperor . . . and maybe Aedile Hortensus too."

Fulcinia blinked, tilting her head. "Princess?"

Princess Caecila took a deep breath. "You heard him, right? These wounds run deep and occurred in a battle I fully intended to win; it is arrogant and foolish of me to believe I can bring reconciliation with naught but pleasant words. If we wish to avoid having Consul Hiberius as our enemy, we must demonstrate our intentions through deeds. At the very least, we must make ourselves useful enough that he will not destroy us immediately."

Princess Caecila closed her eyes. "And . . . I think I know where to start."

11

The Lady of Courage and Victory

"The Aesdes may be closer than you think."

—Velus, to his deputy commander before confronting a numerically superior Sun Elf army.

Taog and Agedia were staring with their jaws dropped open. Estrith was trembling in place. Rattingtale and Lilussees were both pressed against the floors of their rooms. Even Melion had noticed what was going on and had sunk down into a puddle. Snuan was desperately trying to hide. The other monsters were frozen in place, their eyes fixed on the being before them.

And as for NSLICE-00P?

"Statement: Friendly unit has lost consciousness in organic components. Applying countermeasures."

NSLICE-00P's sensors were blaring. The sheer magnitude of the nonstandard readings the newcomer was giving off indicated a threat level NSLICE-00P had no confidence in dealing with.

However, her analysis indicated that Colleöne was likely not hostile. She had already assisted Ateia, and if she *was* hostile, there was little chance NSLICE-00P could either terminate her or retreat. Also, for some reason, NSLICE-00P's organic components indicated she was not hostile, despite a lack of evidence to this claim.

In any case, NSLICE-00P determined that caution, preemptive assaults, or emergency retreat would not improve her chances of survival, and so were pointless to attempt. She identified cooperative diplomacy as the best option under the circumstances.

As such, NSLICE-00P decided to assist her own friendly first. She walked over to Ateia, linking to her cybernetic components, and applied Recovery Magic while monitoring the cybernetic half for any issues. Ateia's organic eye blinked as her expression softened. She shook her head.

"Whoa, that was weird. I like, blacked out there or something? I had this crazy dream that an Aesdes showed up and told me I was an Aesdes now."

"Clarification: Entity designated Colleöne, Lady of Courage and Victory, She Who Guides the Champions of the World, alternative designations: Victoria, Ardith, did inform Ateia that she is an 'Aesdes' approximately thirty seconds ago."

NSLICE-00P turned to face Colleöne, who had an amused smile on her face. Ateia slowly turned to follow NSLICE-00P's gaze, freezing once again.

"Request: Please define term 'Aesdes.' This unit's records of conversation by locals implies *Aesdes* refers to the foreign system."

Taog turned to NSLICE-00P with wide eyes. "S-Seero?!"

But Colleöne raised her hand. "It's quite alright. As I stated, I have been sent to guide Ateia, and that goes for her benefactor as well. Please, feel free to request any counsel you desire."

She then turned back to NSLICE-00P. "The Aesdes were the first children of Elséró, the creator who forged the Material Plane out of the empty Source. We were charged with tending to and protecting the world we now watch over from the Blessed Land. But it is not our place to interfere with the lives of the people who live here, so in general, the *system*, as you call it, represents our most direct interactions with the Material Plane's inhabitants."

"Acknowledged. Follow-Up Request: This unit requests records on any biological or other notable differences between species 'Aesdes' and 'human,' and any intel regarding incompatibilities with NSLICE components."

Colleöne nodded and turned to Ateia with a smile. "That's what I'm here for."

Ateia was trembling. "I-I'm . . . an . . . A-Aesdes now? H-How? W-Why?!"

Colleöne's expression turned blank for just a second before she made a sympathetic expression. "That is thanks to the efforts of your benefactor. NSLICE-00P saved you by evolving you like one of her monsters. That process combined with your heritage and awakened the blood flowing in your veins." Colleöne smiled at her. "My blood, to be specific."

Agedia finally closed her mouth. "Wait, um, Mighty Victoria?"

Colleöne turned to her and inclined her head. "Please, be at ease."

Agedia gulped. "R-Right. Um, what did you mean by NSLICE-00P evolving her? That sounds like . . ."

Colleöne turned to NSLICE-00P. "NSLICE-00P, would you mind if we reveal some classified intel related to . . . the other foreign system? I can assure you that this group is trustworthy and will not turn hostile to you as a result. It will assist with our conversation, and will also enable you to make full use of your abilities around those whom you trust."

NSLICE-00P's robotic eye flickered. On the one hand, NSLICE-00P's protocols indicated not to reveal any classified intel unless absolutely necessary. Ateia would have access to classified intel now, as a member of the NSLICE network, but she would also fall under commands to avoid revealing classified intel, so her knowing did not automatically imply that the others would as well. There were risks to informing the other friendlies of additional intel.

On the other hand, the protocol to restrict dungeon-related information was not one of her original ones but one she had put in place on recommendation of Rattingtale and Lilussees. The rationale had been the innate hostility displayed between the Empire and monsters. But did that case apply here?

Estrith, and apparently Colleöne, were already aware of the classified intel in question, so the question was only referring to Taog and Agedia. NSLICE-00P predicted from overheard statements and observed behavior that both Taog and Agedia had a major directive to protect Ateia, who was now a member of the dungeon. The probability that they would turn hostile and inform the Empire of her status was low.

And there was another angle. NSLICE-00P's current priority objective was terminating the threat of the hostile cult, and she had already broken confidentiality protocols due to the danger they posed. Both Agedia and Taog were hostile to that faction as well.

As Colleöne stated, there were tactical and strategic benefits to making full use of her capabilities, and it was possible she would be forced to reveal classified resources to Agedia and Taog at some point in the future. That being the case, it might be more efficient to inform them at this stage, and so maximize the use of those resources from the start.

"Analysis Complete. Conditional Agreement: This unit will permit designated friendlies 'Taog Sutharlan' and 'Agedia of the Mélusine' to access previously classified data referring to the foreign system. Please note that data regarding this unit's technical specifications and proprietary technologies are still restricted."

Colleöne nodded. "Of course." She turned back to Agedia. "You see, Miss NSLICE-00P is a living dungeon core and master. She made Ateia her subordinate in order to save Ateia's life, and so was able to apply the monster evolution process to restore her body."

Taog froze. "Seero is . . . a demon lord?"

Colleöne frowned and shook her head. "The Aesdes, at least, do not consider her as such. Dungeons are a necessary part of the world, and dungeon masters are necessary to protect them. We would only describe those who have fallen into corruption as demon lords, and your friend has certainly not."

Taog held his head. "Wait . . . I thought she was a hero? How is that possible?"

Colleöne stared off into the distance. "Yes. How indeed, huh? Just *how exactly* did we arrive in this situation, Shialnor?"

A message passed before everyone's eyes.

Anualë already agreed it's part of her unique nature, so it's not my fault. Unlike the situation with you and the new girl.

Colleöne frowned at that. Taog, meanwhile, was standing perfectly still.

"So Seero is a dungeon master . . . and a hero . . . and Ateia is her monster now . . . and also an Aesdes . . . and Victoria herself is here . . . and is apparently Ateia's family . . . haha, I see . . ."

This time, it was Taog's organic processing hardware blood levels which dropped below acceptable limits. And unfortunately, he did not possess cybernetic components that could keep him upright, so he collapsed onto the ground as he fainted.

Agedia muttered under her breath, "I really need a drink . . ."

Colleöne chuckled and turned back to Ateia, who hadn't moved an inch. She walked over and gently placed a hand on Ateia's shoulder. The girl jumped and looked up at Colleöne with wide eyes.

"I know this is all very sudden and confusing for you. The point is, I will be here to guide you as you adjust. This will, in turn, help you brave the challenges and dangers set before you. Will you allow me to teach you?"

Ateia's eyes went even wider. Eventually, she started nodding her head repeatedly.

"I-It would be my honor, M-Mighty Victoria!"

Colleöne smiled softly at her. "As I said, the honor is mine."

She then turned to NSLICE-00P and Agedia. "While I would love to begin immediately, I believe you already had plans to leave? While I am certainly confident in my barriers, some space and privacy may be useful in this matter as well."

"Affirmative. Statement: This unit planned to withdraw to the secure home base designated *Otter Burrow* before initiating upgrade routines."

Colleöne nodded her head. "May I accompany you on your journey?"

"Affirmative."

Colleöne smiled. The light began to fade from the room as she turned back into an older, unassuming woman. Agedia blinked before nodding, and slowly turned.

"I, um . . . will prepare for the trip, then?"

With that, she left the room while holding her head.

Estrith wandered in through the courtyard as the others prepared. She had little to pack or prepare, and so had finished early. And that had given her some time to think. She paced back and forth, her brow furrowed.

"If I may ask, what troubles you, Estrith Edilddaughter, brave warrior of the Dobhar?"

Estrith paused and blinked. Colleöne had walked up behind her. "It . . . is nothing, Brave Ardith. I am truly honored to walk beside you."

Colleöne gave her a smile. "But you wonder why I am human?"

Estrith's eyes widened, and she looked away. "Forgive me for my doubts, Brave Ardith. I . . . Do you love the . . . humans? They seem . . . blessed. And now they are your kin? Is their might ordained by the Aesdes? Were . . . Were my people doomed from the start?"

Colleöne shook her head. "Such is not the case."

Estrith gasped as Colleöne spoke to her in the tongue of the Dobhar. Colleöne's face changed into a Dobhar's, complete with a helmet of bone, a necklace of teeth, and a harpoon on her back.

"The Aesdes may appear as we wish, so we are not defined solely by our form. And the Aesdes do not prefer one race over another. All species that walk this world are the children of Elséró, and so all species are our charge and our joy."

Estrith frowned and looked to the ground.

"Then . . . if you would forgive me my fears, Brave Ardith, why is it that they are so strong? Why is it that we are so weak? The Dobhar have devoted all of their efforts, all of their blood, to the hunt. Why can we not match those who exert but a fraction of our efforts?"

Colleöne heaved a sigh. "That . . . is my personal fault. It was I who gave assistance to Velus, the first Emperor, when humanity came under assault by the Empire of the Sun. He subsequently positioned his people to succeed, and succeed they have. We also . . . forged a connection over that time. You would be right to fault me for the rapidity of his rise."

Estrith gaped at her, and she continued.

"However, those were unusual circumstances, and humanity has received no special assistance since. I do love Velus, and his descendants are also mine, but I do not love humanity over the Dobhar. And while I assisted their initial rise, know that they have had thousands of years to build their society to what it is today.

"The Dobhar are, by contrast, a significantly younger race. Your story is only just beginning, and it will be up to you to forge your people's path. I have not assisted you as I did Velus, but your people's future holds as much potential as any other's."

Colleöne then smiled at her.

"And you need not fear the strength of another, for strength may belong to more than one. It is difficult for the species to live among one another; it is far easier to turn to blood and hate. But if you can live side by side, if you can learn to cooperate and respect one another, then their strength can become yours, and yours theirs. I think you are starting to see this happen even now."

Estrith thought back on the queen of the Dobhar and her defense of the Dobhar. She thought back to when her king—Steward Uscfrea had shown her all he had built with the help of the Imperial defectors her queen had defeated.

"It . . . may be so, Brave Ardith."

Colleöne patted her shoulder once more. "Be strong, brave warrior. The path you and your people follow now is a difficult one; perhaps even more difficult than the path of war. Uscfrea Ymmason is mighty, but this is a battle that cannot be won by one person alone. He will need help if he is to forge a bright future for your people. He will need warriors who are as strong of heart as they are of spear."

With that, Colleöne walked away, leaving Estrith to her thoughts.

To find that Ardith, the Aesdes she had respected the most, had played a personal hand in the rise of the hated Empire? That . . . was a lot to take in. Estrith's mind couldn't even wrap around the sheer implications of that. However, she was right that the Dobhar were no longer on the path of war with the Empire. Or at least, not with humanity as a whole. And, well, Estrith had seen much over her journey through her former enemy's home.

So, the question was . . . what did the future of the Dobhar hold? She thought she knew, but Steward Uscfrea had always had a different idea. He saw a future none of the rest of them could; was trying to build something the rest of them couldn't comprehend.

But now . . . Estrith felt like she could. Not fully, but with all she had seen of the Empire, she was starting to glimpse a different path her people could take. She could feel that the time she lived in was a critical one for the Dobhar—one that would determine the future of her people.

So perhaps she should not dwell on the failures of their past or their present weakness, but on what they could become. And how she could help Steward Uscfrea to achieve it.

Estrith wandered off, for she had much to think about.

12

A Whole New World

"She . . . sectioned off a piece of the Source and bound it to the Material Plane, creating a self-contained miniature realm? Just so she wouldn't have to watch over the core herself? . . . If only she would remain awake."

—Anualë, upon discovering the first dungeon.

And so, the group prepared themselves for the trip. Lafrenia and the other attendants of the villa prepared supplies, as well as some basic weapons for Ateia and Taog. Colleöne had returned to her old woman disguise, and the group, including 00B, now gathered to plan their route. Colleöne was muttering, seemingly to herself, before she nodded and turned to face the others.

"I believe it is time. If I may make a suggestion on the travel method, NSLICE-00P may wish to check her status now. Well, if *someone* actually managed to finish even a fraction of her work, that is."

"Affirmative."

NSLICE-00P checked and found some new notifications.

Ugh, you suck, Colleöne! Is it too much to ask not to be rushed when handling AN ENTIRE MATERIAL PLANE?!

Well, whatever. This should be good enough for now. Feats smeats, I'd very much prefer if no one else did something like this ever again, so I'll figure that part out later . . . maybe.

At that moment, NSLICE-00P detected a stream of Holy mana enter her core from beyond the boundary of the universe. A new notification appeared on her screen, this time from her own UI.

New planetary core detected. New core is requesting sync with Geo-Oscillator Engine. Proceed?

Her robotic eye began flickering rapidly. This was an unprecedented situation. A planetary core was *requesting* a sync with her Geo-Oscillator Engine? She didn't know how that could be physically possible, so it had to involve mana and the foreign system.

Colleöne smiled wryly at her. "You, um, threw us for a bit of a loop with the new Material Plane you created. But we believe we have a solution. If you attune your core to this new plane, you will gain access to it once more. I believe you'll find it to your benefit to do so."

"Query: Will sync to the new planetary core impact current sync and mana-generation features?"

Colleöne shook her head.

"Dungeons and dungeon cores exist in the boundary between the Source and the Material Plane, acting as the bridge between both. So, your connection to the Source will not be impacted."

NSLICE-00P analyzed this assertion. Imperial records didn't fully match that claim, but they were themselves divided on the subject of dungeons, and so couldn't be used to confirm or deny Colleöne's claims. NSLICE-00P's own observations were not directly relevant, given the unprecedented nature of a second planetary core both existing in range of the first and proactively requesting a sync.

On the one hand, there was some risk. If syncing to the current planetary core—or the Source, as Colleöne claimed—had caused her Geo-Oscillator Engine to produce mana and adopt the capabilities of a dungeon core, then the possibility existed that other planetary cores could cause unexpected side effects as well.

On the other hand, as long as the side effects did not result in instant termination or loss of control over the Geo-Oscillator Engine, NSLICE-00P could always shut it off and re-sync it back to the Source. Colleöne did not appear to be lying, though the Aesdes's claimed and observed nonstandard nature made NSLICE-00P doubt the efficacy of her body language analysis on the woman.

But Colleöne had been helpful so far, and would not need to resort to such duplicity to enforce her will on NSLICE-00P if she so chose.

Ultimately, the sync request was a nonstandard anomaly that a cordial entity was vouching for. NSLICE-00P decided she would investigate. She made sure to record as much data as she could on her current sync with the Source in case she needed to reestablish that connection, then approved the sync.

Connection established. Foreign system offering administrator privileges. Establishing control. Standby . . .

Core: Geo-Oscillator Engine synced with Core: Heart of the New World!
Max Dungeon Mana increased by 1000!
Rooms feature unlocked!
Rooms feature converted to World Features!

Additional features unlocked as I figure them out. Show some patience, okay?!

Fortunately, Colleöne had spoken the truth. NSLICE-00P's Geo-Oscillator Engine somehow calibrated itself to the new core while maintaining its connection to the Source. In fact, from the initial data, it appeared the connection had extended into a circuit, with mana now flowing in a loop between the Source and the new core, the Geo-Oscillator Engine at its center.

It was a phenomenon the Geo-Oscillator Engine had never been designed for; one that had never even been theorized by its creator. But the initial feedback indicated that the engine's efficiency had not been impacted negatively, so NSLICE-00P let the connection settle into place.

"Whoa!"

Ateia grabbed her sides, beginning to tremble as her body began to glow with a flickering light. Colleöne placed a hand on her shoulder, and the light stabilized.

"That . . . was weird."

Colleöne nodded.

"You are connected to NSLICE-00P, and she just took ownership of a new Material Plane. Your connection shifted from this plane of Aelea to the new world as well."

Colleöne then turned back to NSLICE-00P.

"There is much to discuss, but the important thing for now is that you have access to that new Material Plane via your dungeon core. It should be possible for you to create an entrance now. Do note that as your own core is not as tightly anchored to the world of Aelea, you will not be able to return to this location once you pass over, a necessary drawback to allow your core to travel between the worlds.

"However, you will be able to create connections between your world and any subordinate dungeons you possess. As long as you have at least one on Aelea, you will not need to manually open an entrance as you did before. And in this case, I believe that would be the most convenient method to reach our destination."

NSLICE-00P attempted to analyze the new connection in order to verify these words. She could now perceive the barren rock she had once found herself trapped upon, appearing in her UI now just like the Otter Burrow. She likewise noted some new additions to the foreign system UI:

World Menu
Create Rooms
Manage Rooms
Manage Entrances

Manage Rooms	
Name	Description
Stone Platform	A featureless rock floating in the void.

Manage Entrances	
Option	Cost
Open Entrance - Walking Dungeon (Note that this entrance will close automatically if the Walking Dungeon Core passes through.)	300 mana to open
Add Entrance - Otter Burrow	20 Perk Points

These additions seemed to corroborate Colleöne's words. NSLICE-00P had points to spare, so she went ahead and added the entrance to the Otter Burrow. A new UI displaying the layout of the stone platform appeared. She designated a location on the edge of the rock, and then a UI showing the current Otter Burrow appeared.

For now, she placed the entrance to the side of the Otter Burrow core room. She could perceive stone archways rising from the ground in both locations, each covered in countless geometric shapes. Mana began to flow through them, and vortexes appeared between the arches.

Two Dobhar standing guard in the core room jumped and carefully approached the arches with spears raised. She sent a command to NSLICE Uscfrea.

"It shall be done, my queen."

A moment later, the two guards relaxed. One of them took a deep breath and poked a spear through the gateway. When it came back in one piece, he stuck a paw inside. After pulling the paw back unharmed, he took a deep breath and stepped through.

The Dobhar walked through the arch and onto the empty rock. He blinked and glanced around for a few moments before gulping and stepping back through.

"Testing Results: This unit has successfully established and verified a connection between subordinate dungeons. Preparing to test connection between the Heart of the World and Geo-Oscillator Engine."

Colleöne nodded and smiled.

"Excellent. It seems *someone* actually did their work, then. But, if I may make a suggestion, perhaps we should depart from the villa before you open the next entrance? It may surprise your hosts if we vanish without a trace."

"Affirmative."

With that, NSLICE-00P and the others bid farewell to Lafrenia and Consul Hiberius's knights. Sir Julianus wanted to escort the group on their journey, but NSLICE-00P turned him down. The group made their way down the road for an hour before they came to a small grove. Stepping into the grove, Colleöne created another privacy barrier before she nodded at NSLICE-00P, who attempted to open an entrance between herself and the new world.

A swirling vortex appeared in the air. All the others just stared at it.

"Statement: Warning by the foreign system indicates the entrance will close when this unit enters it. All friendlies should enter at this time."

00B grunted his acknowledgement and stepped through. Colleöne nodded as the others glanced at one another.

"That is correct. All of you should pass through now. I shall meet you on the other side, as my presence in such a nascent world may impact its nature."

Estrith saluted to NSLICE-00P then stepped through, though she kept her spear in her hand. Ateia stared at the vortex.

"There's . . . something on the other side of this. It's . . . something I've never felt before, but it feels familiar. It's strange."

Colleöne nodded. "It is because that is the world you are now connected to."

Ateia turned and looked at Taog. She slowly started to smile. "Should we check it out?"

He flushed and looked away but nodded. "Yeah, let's go."

The two went in together, Agedia following closely behind. Colleöne then nodded and vanished, leaving NSLICE-00P alone. She could already perceive all of her friendlies on the other side, so there was no reason for her to hesitate.

NSLICE-00P stepped through, and the vortex faded away.

13

The Return of the Queen

"All nonstandards with the word 'herald' in their designation are to be terminated immediately unless otherwise ordered."

—NSLICE protocols on common adversaries

NSLICE-00P stepped back into the nearly empty void, the gate to the Otter Burrow on the other side. Agedia was glancing around with narrowed eyes, keeping an eye on the sides and the void beyond. Estrith had her eyes glued on the gate ahead of them, while Taog was glancing around with wide eyes. Ateia stepped forward in a daze. She slowly crouched down and placed her hand on the ground.

"Seero . . . this place is yours?"

"Affirmative."

Ateia closed her eyes, taking a deep breath. She then patted the ground and rose to her feet. NSLICE-00P continued on, marching toward the gate, with Estrith following right at her heels, the rest a bit behind them. NSLICE-00P then moved through and stepped out into the Otter Burrow's core room, where Uscfrea had just arrived. He gave her a salute, his eyes only widening a small amount.

"Welcome back, my queen."

"Greetings: Hello, NSLICE Uscfrea."

Estrith then stepped forward and saluted. "My . . . steward, I have returned once more."

Uscfrea blinked before smiling slightly and nodding. "Welcome home, guard of the queen." He turned back to NSLICE-00P. "Would you mind explaining the situation, my queen?"

"Affirmative. Transmitting relevant data."

NSLICE-00P and Uscfrea's robotic eyes both started flickering. Uscfrea grunted as images and videos streamed into his mind. After a minute, their eyes stopped flickering, and Uscfrea held his head, blinking a few times. Then he scowled.

"So the Imperials were telling the truth about that whole cult business, after all. I always knew the Imperials were arrogant, but to think some of them believe tearing down the world itself is a good idea. The decline of the Empire is great indeed if such a group is operating freely among them."

Then he turned to NSLICE-00P. "You plan to fight them, my queen?"

"Affirmative. Clarification: This unit, along with friendly and subordinate units, requires upgrades and countermeasures to reduce the risk of termination to acceptable levels. Termination of hostiles will proceed following sufficient upgrade routines."

Uscfrea nodded. "Then we shall prepare as well. It's a bit late to ask this, but I'm guessing everyone here is aware of our relationship with dungeons?"

"Affirmative."

"Then we'll do this the easy way. May I Transfer you and your companions, my queen?"

"Affirmative."

Taog tilted his head and was about to ask when the group's vision suddenly shifted. They were in a conference room with a basic wooden table, still within the dungeon. The current occupants of the room suddenly rose to their feet, their hands moving toward blades and spears before they realized who had arrived.

The former rebel, Dux Augustalis, swore. "By the Aesdes, Your Majesty, could you stop doing that?! It's deeply unnerving when you just pop out of nowhere!"

Uscfrea smiled at her. "No."

Augustalis swore again while Vopiscus heaved a sigh. There were three Dobhar and a Wulver in the room as well: the elderly Dobhar known as the Mother of Waves, a younger Dobhar woman NSLICE-00P identified as Aethelu, mother of the Sacred Otterkin Aldreda, as well as a Dobhar man NSLICE-00P hadn't interacted with. The Wulver was Ceitidh Greumach, the clan leader that NSLICE-00P had Contracted.

The Mother of Waves shook her head and chuckled as Uscfrea stepped to the side and saluted. "All hail the queen of the Dobhar."

Everyone's eyes widened slightly, but they quickly gathered themselves and saluted in Dobhar, Wulver, and Imperial fashion. Uscfrea nodded.

"Everyone here has a Contract with either you or myself, my queen, and have been ruling your people as you commanded. State your orders, and we shall see it done."

"Acknowledged."

NSLICE-00P's robotic eye began to glow and then displayed a holographic image in the air, showing the glimpses NSLICE-00P had caught of the Herald of Rain.

"Command: New priority objective for this unit and all subordinate units is to locate and terminate the hostile organization designated 'Heralds of the New Dawn' and any affiliated units."

Dux Augustalis and Vopiscus both narrowed their eyes and clenched their fists at that. "We will burn them to ashes."

Ateia scowled as well at the image displayed before them. "That's Magus Major Sidonia, by the way."

Taog's eyes narrowed at that. Vopiscus rubbed his chin. "The Delugecaller herself? I thought Vibius said the Imperial Academy was clean?"

Dux Augustalis clenched her teeth. "Vibius was wrong about a *lot* of things, it seems."

Agedia crossed her arms. "It gets worse. Consul Noxisius was in on it too."

Vopiscus's eyes widened. "Truly? Vibius thought it was Emperor Lucius, working in concert with Aedile Hortensus."

Agedia shrugged. "Better hope it was Noxisius, because shiny girl already killed him, most likely. Set his home on fire, at the minimum."

"Uncertain Statement: This unit does not possess the data required to identify Consul Noxisius, and so cannot confirm or deny if he was terminated, but can confirm all hostiles on-site were successfully terminated, save for the hostile designated Herald of Rain."

Vopiscus gulped at that. "So . . . the Empire's on the way?"

Agedia shrugged again. "That will depend on the Magister Exploratore and Consul Hiberius, so probably not right away, but you had best be prepared for that possibility. And if the Heralds of the New Dawn had agents that high in the Northern Court, even after the purge a decade ago, then they most certainly exist in either the South or the East as well. Probably both."

Uscfrea shook his head. "Whatever the case may be, our job is clear. Our queen is preparing to go to war with this cult, and the first blows have been struck. We must be ready to follow her and to fend off their attacks."

Aethelu saluted to NSLICE-00P once more. "I will follow you no matter what, my queen. We will strike down your enemies without fail."

Dux Augustalis clenched her fist. "We've been preparing for this foe for a long time, and we have a score to settle of our own."

The Mother of Waves frowned and rubbed her chin. "From what you say, this group has been manipulating the Empire? Our people are not fully established yet, Steward, and Her Majesty's subjects have not yet found peace with one another. Do you think it is wise to fight again so soon?"

Uscfrea nodded. "I understand your concern, Mother of Waves, but the foe has already struck. The fight is coming whether we are ready or not. Our queen has given her command; we must now see it done."

The Mother of Waves continued frowning, but then glanced at NSLICE-00P. Her expression returned to neutral. "Well . . . I suppose with the queen of the Dobhar at our head, I should not be so worried."

Uscfrea smirked at that.

The group gave some reports after that. Dux Augustalis, the male Dobhar, and Ceitidh reported on the available soldiers in their respective camps, while the Mother of Waves, Vopiscus, and Aethelu reported on the organization of the noncombatants.

From what NSLICE-00P could tell, the Dobhar were making vast improvements in the organization and sophistication of their forces, as well as their food supply. The Imperial rebels, on the other hand, had established a settlement with the help of the Dobhar and the Wulver, and were just starting up some industries besides food and basic construction.

There *were* some integration issues between the three groups, going as far as some brawls. Likewise, while the Dobhar and Wulver were improving, their organization and discipline still didn't approach Legion standards. The rebel legions, on the other hand, would face supply issues in all but the shortest of campaigns without the support of a more developed economy and the abundant resources the Empire could provide.

NSLICE-00P's army could not match the cohesion, readiness, or sustainment ability displayed by the Empire.

But that was fine. NSLICE-00P had not considered the Dobhar as a major asset for the offense in the first place, and was planning to handle the termination mission personally. If the Dobhar could defend themselves, then that was enough. If her subordinates could conduct offensive operations apart from her, then that only improved her current predictions.

It wasn't clear if the Heralds of the New Dawn possessed any organized military forces to their name, after all.

The Heralds' operations that NSLICE-00P had observed thus far were more characteristic of asymmetric warfare, which would imply a desire to avoid peer conflict. Whether that was by choice or necessity was unknown and would require further investigation. She may, in fact, need to boost the Dobhar's effectiveness as an organized force should the Heralds possess armies on par with the Legion.

In any case, no one had any actionable intel on the Heralds at this time. The Imperial rebels had some, but it had been sourced by the late Magister Vibius and contained some contradictions to observations made in live combat by

NSLICE-00P, and so could not be acted upon without further confirmation. Which meant nothing could be done at this stage besides further upgrade routines, which was NSLICE-00P's plan to begin with.

NSLICE-00P ordered Uscfrea to prepare for the conflict and gather intel as best he could, while she would focus on her own upgrades and investigations. While she could offer her own protocols on combat and military organization, she calculated that working on her own more direct countermeasures would be more efficient in defeating this specific threat.

And so, the group parted ways with Uscfrea's council, heading to the Dobhar settlement. They would greet the Dobhar, and then Uscfrea would arrange for their quarters.

As they exited the dungeon into the public areas of the Dobhar settlement, an older Dobhar woman approached them. A Dobhar woman giving off non-standard readings.

Uscfrea raised an eyebrow, about to question her, when NSLICE-00P stepped forward. The Dobhar smiled.

"It might cause a bit of commotion if you mention my name here. Why don't we go somewhere private first?"

"Affirmative."

With NSLICE-00P's approval, Uscfrea fell silent and led them to quarters that had been prepared should NSLICE-00P come to visit. Once in private, the Dobhar woman created a barrier and assumed her Aesdes form once again. Uscfrea's eyes went as wide as they could go before he struck his tail on the ground and bowed his head.

"So what I saw was true. Welcome, Mighty Ardith, the Master Hunter and Warrior. I am honored to be in your presence."

She smiled at him. "Be at ease, Brave Uscfrea. You are a warrior both courageous and mighty, and you have preserved your people with strength and cunning. You have much to be proud of."

Uscfrea looked up to her. He began to tremble slightly.

". . . Thank you, Mighty Ardith. Your words mean a great deal to me."

Colleöne smiled at him. As she did, a message passed before her eyes.

Not going to fall for another brave and mighty mortal, are you?

Colleöne did not dignify those words with a response.

14

New Journeys Begin

"A campaign of a thousand victories begins with training."

—Celestial Elf Sage Ningainë, when negotiating the Celestial Empire's yearly budget.

Colleöne reverted to a mundane Dobhar appearance and then smiled at Uscfrea.

"Do you know of any secluded locations nearby, steward of the Dobhar? We will need a location where we will not disturb or be disturbed by anyone."

Uscfrea nodded. "The cliffs and beach to the north are uninhabited. We do patrol the area, but if you let me know where you'll be, I can instruct them to skip that part."

"Thank you, that is most appreciated."

Uscfrea bowed his head again. "It is my honor to be of service, Mighty Ardith."

Colleöne then turned to NSLICE-00P and Ateia. "If you are willing, I would like you two to accompany me, that I may instruct Ateia on her new status."

Ateia nodded repeatedly. "O-Of course, M-Mighty Victoria!"

"Query: Is this unit relevant to the training?"

Colleöne nodded. "She is bound to serve you, so it is important that you understand her nature. Additionally, you are responsible for a Material Plane now. It will be good for you to understand those of us who care for the first."

"Affirmative."

At that moment, Estrith frowned. "Um, Mighty Ardith, may I ask a question?"

Colleöne smiled and nodded. "Of course."

Estrith took a deep breath. "Will the training be dangerous?"

Colleöne shook her head. "Not in the manner you are thinking. So long as they are with me, no harm will come to them. This I swear, as the Lady of Courage and Victory."

Estrith bowed in response before turning to NSLICE-00P. "My queen, if you do not have other need of me, I would like to request some time with my people. I . . . wish to see the home your people are building."

NSLICE-00P's robotic eye flickered for a moment, but it did not take her long to calculate. If they were on a low-risk training mission with safety guaranteed by an entity predicted as more powerful than herself, then Estrith's presence wasn't necessary. Likewise, if Estrith was staying in the secure home base of the Dobhar, then she would not be at excessive risk of termination either.

"Affirmative Response: That is acceptable."

Estrith saluted. "Thank you, my queen."

And so, Uscfrea arranged for some supplies. Ateia, Taog, and NSLICE-00P got ready to go while Estrith returned to Uscfrea's side. Meanwhile, Agedia stood on the beach, gazing across the sea.

"Turannia, huh? I wonder if I'll see Tibbers . . ."

But she shook her head. Tiberius was in the Imperial part of the province, over a day's trip away. Agedia was no longer willing to part with Ateia for that amount of time.

Besides, she had failed her charge, her duty, and her friend. She had avenged herself on every tangentially responsible party she could find, and then had spent the next decade trying to drown her grief in drink and violence.

But a handful of bright spots broke through the haze. She remembered battling alongside Tiberius and Vafum. She remembered the celebrations they'd had back at the tavern. She remembered the nights she'd spent with Tiberius . . .

She shut her eyes and bowed her head. Then Tiberius had left, off on the mission that should have been hers. She'd said it was the smart choice, and it had been. The Hero of Elteno had moved to Turannia to keep his and Aedinia's daughter hidden. If the failed Imperial knight had suddenly up and moved after a decade of staying put, that might have drawn attention. Tiberius taking her place had been the smart thing to do.

But that hadn't been why she'd done it. She'd refused because she was afraid. She had finally started to put her failure behind her . . . only to have it thrust in her face once again. She had not been ready to rejoin that fight, but neither could she let Aedinia's daughter, the last memory of her existence, remain in danger.

She'd been caught in an impossible choice . . . but Tiberius, that wonderful man, had noticed and volunteered himself as the solution. Ateia would be as safe as they could make her, and Agedia wouldn't have to rejoin the fight. Vafum had wanted to go too, but he'd stayed behind for her sake. So Tiberius had gone off, alone, on the mission that should have been hers.

And then, perhaps by the will of the Aesdes, Ateia had arrived in Velusitum. Ready or not, Agedia had been thrust back into it. But then, she'd failed again. Ateia had been caught in the hands of the cult and gone through the very ritual they had tried to force on Aedinia all those years ago, and Agedia had once again been powerless to stop it.

So she didn't deserve to see Tiberius. How could she look him in the eye when she had failed the mission that should have been hers, that he'd shouldered on her behalf? How could she be happy when Aedinia had died and Ateia had been mortally wounded? No, this was the will of the Aesdes, to remind her of her failure and why she—

"You think too much of us."

Agedia jumped and whirled around, finding Colleöne standing behind her. Colleöne shook her head.

"Only Elséró can see the end of anyone's path. The Aesdes may see a bit further into the possibilities, but we ultimately experience time as it happens, not that differently from you. Our sight is wider, but we are not all-powerful or all-knowing. We only do our best, as do you."

Agedia frowned and bowed her head. "I am sorry. I did not mean any offense, Mighty Victoria."

Colleöne shook her head again. "And I did not take any. What I mean to say is that your suffering is not our intention, nor is it something you deserve."

Agedia gritted her teeth. ". . . Isn't it? If I had been stronger, if I hadn't been so weak, then they never would have been hurt. And if it weren't for the shiny girl, they'd both be dead now."

Agedia felt Colleöne's hand on her shoulder, and her head shot up.

"Agedia, the most loyal and brave of the Imperial knights. She who chose humiliation and scorn to protect her charge; who spared nothing—not even her own honor—to fulfill her duty. You lost and were defeated. But you did not fail. You gave everything you had. And even after you lost, when Ateia arrived, you rose to the challenge and did it again. You did not allow the tremors in your heart to overwhelm your compassion for the girl."

Colleöne looked her in the eye. "Victory is elusive and fleeting. It is possible to do everything right and still lose. That is not weakness; that is life. You lost, but I believe there is no shame or condemnation in that, Agedia. And know that your efforts were not as meaningless as you believe. You fought with courage and heart, and the blow you struck to your foe set them back by *years*.

"If not for that, perhaps they would not have waited for NSLICE-00P to appear at all. And it was thanks to your intervention that Taog Sutharlan, Ateia's best friend and the one who has kept her heart intact across years of loneliness, managed to survive. If that had not happened, Ateia's heart would have been broken utterly, and she would have been completely overwhelmed by her new powers even had NSLICE-00P still managed to save her."

Colleöne patted her shoulder again. "And that is why you should not neglect yourself, Agedia. You have fought a battle with your own heart as much as with your foes. Every warrior needs rest—and companions to share their burden with. You already know, don't you? Aedinia would want you to be happy. So go. And take heart, I am here for Ateia's sake, so I swear no harm will come to her before you are ready to return."

Agedia's eyes filled with tears, and she bowed her head again. "T-Thank you, Mighty Victoria."

With that, she slithered as fast as she could. She came before Ateia, bowing her head and apologizing, but Ateia just smiled and sent her off. Leaping up the cliff and past the Legion keep, Agedia shot down the road to Castra Turannia as fast as she could.

Colleöne, NSLICE-00P, Ateia, and Taog made their way north until they found a secluded cove in the rocky cliffs, where they set up a camp and then split up. Taog was cooking some food while Colleöne, NSLICE-00P, and Ateia stood on the beach.

"The first aspect of the Aesdes you should know is that we are more deeply connected to the world than other beings. We do not experience reality the way other living things do."

Colleöne reached down and picked up a rock lying in the sand. "When we look at any part of the world, whether it be a person, an animal, a plant, a mountain, or even a humble rock, we see more than the crude matter that composes its structure. We see the object's spirit. We see its past, and the records etched on its being."

Colleöne cast a spell, and images began to appear in the air. NSLICE-00P observed as a volcano erupted, hurling a ball of lava into the nearby sea. She watched as the ocean burst into steam, and the lava cooled into rock.

"We see its spirit in the present, its intent and its will. And we can glimpse its potential, the possibilities that stretch out before it."

The image split into hundreds of smaller scenes. Some showed Colleöne tossing the rock into the sea. Others showed it lying on the beach, slowly eroding into sand. Others showed it picked up by a Dobhar child, placed into a pouch with a sling. And then, the images vanished as Colleöne slowly placed the rock back on the beach.

"You have already experienced this, in fact."

Ateia furrowed her brow. "The memories?"

Colleöne nodded. "More accurately, you were viewing the pasts of the people connected to you, the events etched on their spirits that even they may have forgotten. And this brings us to the second point. Beings in the Material Plane are defined equally by their matter and their spirit. It is not so with the Aesdes. We are beings defined primarily by our spirit, with our matter following suit."

"Query: Logs from NSLICE Ateia's cybernetic components do not appear different from a normal human. Requesting elaboration on NSLICE Ateia's physical condition."

Colleöne rubbed her chin. "A good question, and one that ties into this discussion. Because the Aesdes are defined by their spirit, our nature, our matter, and our powers as you would think of them may be impacted by our wills, our records, and our stature. Ateia, for example, has been a human all her life. That record is firmly etched upon her spirit, so she will cling to that form, and I suspect, it would take great effort to change it."

Colleöne's face turned serious. "Likewise, Ateia, when you were in a dark place following the injuries your foes inflicted upon you, your powers reacted to your emotions."

Ateia's eyes widened, then she frowned. "So the reason all the memories I saw were bad . . ."

Colleöne nodded. "Because you could not yet control your sight, and your heart was disturbed, you ended up reaching for similar records in those around you."

Colleöne walked over, placing a hand on Ateia's shoulder. "But we are here to resolve this. In fact, that was part of the reason I was given leave to come before you. I will teach you how to focus your powers so that something like that will not happen again."

She took a step back and gave Ateia a smile. "Are you ready to begin?"

Ateia took a deep breath, and then clenched her fist. "Yes!"

15

It's a Skill Issue

"In the Elteni Empire, you learn skills. In the Empire of the Sun, the skill learns you."

—Zaerzis Evruth, High Archon
of the Empire of the Sun

Colleöne nodded. "First, why don't you pull up your status?"

Ateia nodded. Then she frowned. Then her face scrunched up. Then her face fell, and her head dropped.

"Um, Great Victoria . . . I can't seem to find my status . . ."

Colleöne smirked slightly. "That is correct."

Ateia's head popped up. "Huh?"

Colleöne nodded. "The status is representative of the assistance the Aesdes grant to the inhabitants of the Material Plane. While dungeons and dungeon masters are necessary, we noted with concern their advantages over other life-forms. So, we developed this system to even the odds and ensure that all life would have the opportunity to grow."

Colleöne smiled at Ateia. "You are now an Aesdes, so you no longer qualify for such assistance."

Ateia frowned. "So my strength, my skills . . . they're all gone?"

Colleöne shook her head. "Not quite. We do not grant the mortals power out of nowhere, after all. Your status records what you have already achieved and molds our power to boost your own abilities to higher levels. And when we grant new boons, it is the molding of your potential—the increase of your stature on account of your deeds—into a form that is more readily mastered. Your skills, your abilities, your potential, they all still exist within your body, your mind, and your spirit. It is only that the power of the Aesdes will no longer guide and strengthen those things."

Colleöne smirked again. "Because you no longer need the help."

Ateia rubbed her chin. "Miallói, my Exploratore mentor, once told me I should ignore my skill at first, learn to do the attack myself and let the skill help me instead. Is that what this is?"

Colleöne nodded. "Your mentor was wise; that's exactly right. The skill will no longer help you. Instead, you must learn to draw upon your own power and mold it as you will. Come and take up the weapon or tool you are most familiar with. It does not need to be for battle."

Ateia nodded and stepped forward, taking up a spot besides Colleöne. She took and strung her bow.

"Now, think of a skill you used often. One that you learned on your own, if possible."

Ateia closed her eyes and thought. The skill she used most was Power Shot, but that had been one she had selected from her boons. She always relied on the Aesdes for that one, so she didn't really recall how exactly it worked. Instead, she turned her thoughts to the Harpoon Shot, the skill Miallói had taught her to do by hand.

"Don't think of the status or the activation. Think about the motions of your body. Think about the movement of your mana. Think about the effect of the skill. And think about what you want it to achieve. Once you have a clear image in your mind, try to replicate it."

Ateia slowly opened her eyes and nocked an arrow, drawing it back. She reached out for her mana, finding it still reacted to her call same as before. She wrapped the mana around the arrow.

Her metallic wings extended, and the arrow began to glow faintly with golden-and-silver light. But Ateia ignored the arrow, as Miallói had taught her. Instead, she looked out across the cove to a boulder sticking out of the shallows. She imagined chains wrapping around it, holding the boulder in place.

She let her arrow loose.

It shot straight forward with no deviation or wobbling, a trail of golden-and-silver light streaming behind it. It pierced straight into the boulder, and then, the golden-and-silver light formed into chains of mana that wrapped around it as she had imagined.

Colleöne smiled and patted her shoulder. "Well done. Your mentor taught you well. As I said before, we Aesdes are defined more by our spirits and our statures than our bodies. That goes for your skills and abilities as well. You are no longer constrained by the paths we have set forth for the inhabitants of the Material Plane. Your skills are now only constrained by your power and your skill at weaving it."

Colleöne motioned to Ateia's bow. "Still, that comes with its own burdens. Lack of constraint can also become a lack of focus. Since your abilities can now be defined by your spirit, any hesitation, distraction, or disruption can impact your skills.

"Focus your power clearly on a singular task, and you will eventually surpass any mortal relying on a skill. Try to do too much, and your strength will be diluted, and you will end up even weaker than you were before. It is for this reason that each Aesdes has a chosen domain, like Courage and Victory for myself, or Light and Sky for Anualë. Focusing ourselves on one or two aspects helps us strengthen the definition of our spirits."

Ateia nodded. "So . . . do I need to pick something, or does someone else tell me?"

Colleöne shook her head. "You are still young, both as a human and an Aesdes. You should still be exploring the possibilities of what you could be; aspects will emerge over time if they are needed. For now, just know that focus is more important than ever for you, especially during battle.

"It would be wise to have something to focus your power through. It could be a weapon, a skill, a school of magic, an attribute, or even another person. Something that you know well and has meaning to you. The bow can be a good place to start. Try to see if you can replicate all of the different skills you could perform before. Once you can perform all the skills you already knew, we can explore what else you can do with your power."

Ateia nodded. She nocked another arrow, thinking of another skill, as to the side, NSLICE-00P watched, her robotic eye flickering and recording all that Colleöne taught Ateia.

Meanwhile, Taog had finished cooking and was walking over with two bowls of soup, handing one to NSLICE-00P. He, too, listened attentively to the lesson . . .

After Ateia had practiced with the bow for a bit, Colleöne called her over to NSLICE-00P.

"You have begun to explore your Aesdes nature, but that is only half of what you are now. I will admit that I am not fully versed on your other half . . ." She turned to NSLICE-00P and smiled. "But fortunately, we have someone who is. NSLICE-00P, could you explain the cybernetic components for Ateia? Perhaps start with the goal of the NSLICE program and its nature?"

"Affirmative."

NSLICE-00P began to explain the existence of superpowered beings in her original world, and how the NSLICE program had arisen to counter them. As she did, she tentatively linked to Ateia's cybernetic components, sending them some data and records on the NSLICE program. Ateia's cybernetic components still had most of their protocols disabled, acting as simple prosthetics at present.

Ateia furrowed her brow as information entered her mind directly, but she did not react in pain, so NSLICE-00P continued. Meanwhile, Ateia stared at NSLICE-00P, moisture building in her organic eye as she parsed through the records and all that NSLICE-00P had been through.

"Seero . . ." She shook her head and took a deep breath. NSLICE-00P was trying to help her learn about her other half. She should focus on that for now.

"Okay . . . So if I have this correctly, these are kind of like a golem? Attached to a person to make them stronger?"

NSLICE-00P's robotic eye flickered. "Affirmative Response: That is a reasonable approximation."

Ateia's face turned dark. "And also . . . to control people? So they could be commanded like a golem?"

"Affirmative."

Ateia took a deep breath. "Okay . . . but you *AREN'T* listening to those people anymore, right?"

"Affirmative. Relevant Explanation: This unit is still searching for appropriate command personnel on recommendation of her previous commander."

Ateia's eyes narrowed. "Seero, can you tell me more about your previous commander and the people they recommended?"

"Affirmative."

NSLICE-00P sent her the records of her last commander. Ateia blinked, and her robotic eye flickered as videos played before her eyes.

"Wait . . . that commander . . . looks like you?"

"Affirmative Response: This unit's previous commander was an NSLICE unit whose organic components bore a superficial resemblance to this unit's. This unit, however, could not identify the commander's cybernetic components and did not attempt to investigate as per intelligence compartmentalization protocols. The commander's organic components also gave off nonstandard readings, but this unit has not attempted to analyze them as per intelligence compartmentalization protocols."

Ateia blinked but shook her head as she continued watching.

"I am sorry for what I must ask you to do. And I am sorry I could not set you free like the others; it will make it easier for you to complete your mission. One you must complete at all costs. And . . . the journey is as important as the destination. If you survive, I am certain you will find your own way and your own family. So . . . I'm sorry. And thank you. Please . . . complete your primary directive and save the universe."

Ateia jumped. "Wait, you—or, um, *NSLICE units* can talk normally?!"

"Observation: This unit's commander occasionally made use of less precise organic speech patterns. This unit also observed a handful of other NSLICE units utilizing such speech patterns after regaining pre-upgrade organic memories."

Ateia tilted her head. "Then why don't you?"

"Explanation: This unit was programmed with highly specific speech patterns in order to avoid any possible miscommunications."

Ateia was about to respond about how *she* didn't understand a lot of what NSLICE-00P said when another message appeared before her eyes, translated by NSLICE-00P into Imperial.

Hello, NSLICE-00P. If you're reading this, then you have completed your mission and survived. I thank you from the bottom of my heart . . .

Ateia's jaw dropped as she read through the commander's final message. She slowly turned to look at NSLICE-00P.

"Seero, um . . ."

"Acknowledgement: Does NSLICE Ateia have additional queries or updates for this unit?"

16

Sensor Calibration

"Do not, I repeat, do NOT hand any unsanctioned rations to the NSLICE units. NSLICE units are supplied with a specially calculated nutritional solution; all deviations from this diet will diminish NSLICE efficiency. Additionally, unsanctioned rations are known to increase the rate of degradation of the emotional controls and increase necessary maintenance, further reducing efficiency. All staff found offering unsanctioned rations to NSLICE units will be disciplined accordingly."

—Memo from Dr. Ottosen to the sponsoring organization.

Ateia looked into NSLICE-00P's eyes, her organic eye quivering slightly while NSLICE-00P's didn't change at all. Ateia took a deep breath.

"Seero . . . your commander already set you free, right?"

"Affirmative."

Ateia furrowed her brow. "But you've called the people you're searching for 'command personnel,' right? As in . . . you *want* them to take control of you again?"

"Affirmative."

Ateia frowned at that. "Why?"

"Explanation: It is this unit's primary directive."

Ateia tilted her head. "It sounded more like a suggestion to me? And it sounded more like your commander just wanted you to have someone to rely on, not to order you around."

"Additional Explanation: Prior primary directives have been completed or deleted. This unit requires command personnel to specify directives and issue orders."

Ateia's face scrunched up. "Seero . . . that's . . ."

Colleöne had been watching in silence, but now stepped forward to place a hand on Ateia's shoulder. She motioned to the girl and whispered to her.

"Ateia, from what I can tell, this girl is like a child at the moment. She does not understand what you are trying to tell her, and this mission is something she's clinging on to. If you want her to see what you see, you will have to take it slow and teach her through actions, not just words."

Ateia looked down. "But how?"

Colleöne smiled at her. "Be her friend. The kind you've always wanted for yourself."

Ateia narrowed her eyes into the distance, rubbing her chin for a few moments before shaking her head. She took a deep breath. "Okay. We'll talk about this later, then. I guess, let's continue for now?"

Colleöne nodded, and Ateia turned back to NSLICE-00P. "Um, Seero, it seems like this armor does a lot more than just act like arms and legs? Could you show me how it works?"

"Affirmative. Compiling NSLICE UI tutorials . . ."

A short while later, NSLICE-00P slowly guided Ateia through her cybernetic components. NSLICE-00P had learned from Rattingtale and Lilussees, and had adjusted her approach with Ateia—a necessity, given that the normal NSLICE protocols could cause her harm. So, rather than linking to Ateia's components and commanding them as per the Loyal Wingman protocol, she slowly activated Ateia's systems one by one, demonstrating their uses and location in the UI to Ateia.

In Ateia's case, NSLICE-00P decided to swap the intelligence leashing, indicating that the cybernetic components should follow Ateia's organic half, hoping this would avoid the incompatibilities that had been displayed.

There would be a loss of efficiency for Ateia, but Colleöne's example and lessons indicated Ateia's organic half had a great deal of potential. NSLICE-00P had decided that if Ateia could potentially match the readings she had from Colleöne, then the most efficient course of action was to maximize Ateia's organic capabilities.

"Activating NSLICE Ateia's visual sensors. Tutorial Explanation: NSLICE visual sensors are noticeably more powerful than a baseline human's. They can detect a much wider spectrum of the electromagnetic spectrum, have low-light and thermal modes, have filters to avoid blinding, and have both telescopic and microscopic modes. Please select the following UI buttons to trial example settings."

Ateia nodded her head as buttons appeared in her vision. NSLICE-00P had designed these buttons so Ateia could try the different options before she learned how to adjust her vision manually. NSLICE-00P had also designed them to resemble upgrade choices from the foreign system, which allowed Ateia to utilize the techno-organic interface much like her previous foreign system status.

And she was not the only one. All of NSLICE-00P's monsters now stood on the beach, following along with the tutorial. NSLICE-00P had noted that, with the exception of monsters who had been summoned as cyborgs from the beginning, like 00B, most of them were not making full use of their cybernetic capabilities.

So she'd decided to include them all here to ensure any gaps in their knowledge were covered.

Even Melion was observing. While the metal slime had no cybernetic components of their own, they were deeply interested in the concept. NSLICE-00P had considered attempting to keep the knowledge confidential to the NSLICE units, but her analysis indicated including Melion in these tutorials was worth the risk for two reasons.

First of all, Melion lacking cybernetic components did not mean there would be no opportunities for them to interact with information technology, and it was both NSLICE-00P's and Melion's intention to add them to the NSLICE network as soon as possible, in any case. As a result, NSLICE-00P concluded it was desirable to give them some foundational knowledge at this stage.

The second was that NSLICE-00P had reviewed her confidentiality protocols, particularly the ones strictly forbidding dispensing any knowledge regarding NSLICE specifications and capabilities. These protocols had been put in place by her original organization, and NSLICE-00P had just determined that some of that organization's protocols were contradictory and inefficient, with damaging side effects in the worst cases.

She had, as a result, loosened any restrictions that had originated from the original organization. She'd determined that while classifying information regarding her capabilities was still desirable, consideration should be given to improving coordination with allied forces.

In this case, Melion was a subordinate by the foreign system, and no Contracted subordinate had ever broken the terms of their agreement in her experience. NSLICE-00P thus judged that Melion could be trusted to an acceptable degree.

And so, Ateia and a line of monsters all stood staring out across the cove. Their robotic eyes flickered, narrowed, opened wide, changed colors, and spun around as they cycled through the different settings. Taog stood a bit behind with Colleöne, frowning at the sight.

"It still feels weird, seeing all these monsters like this. I'm still wrapping my head around Seero being a dungeon master . . ."

Colleöne barely stopped her eye from twitching. She whispered to herself, "You are not the only one," but then she smiled. "The Aesdes believe that the circumstances of one's birth are less important than the choices they make. NSLICE-00P and her monsters began as a dungeon master and its army. But in the end, she has protected the world with her might. We honor that, regardless of who or what she is."

Colleöne turned to Taog. "That goes for you as well, son of the Empire and the Wulver both. I know that others have seen and judged you for your parentage. But that matters not to the Aesdes, nor to the people who matter to you. All we will see is what you choose to do with what you have been given."

Taog fell silent as he continued watching the practice.

After the training had concluded, Ateia rummaged through the rations given to them by Consul Hiberius's people. She smiled to herself in triumph. "As expected of a consul's house!"

The rations included some delicacies that Ateia had rarely had access to, including sweet rolls coated with honey. She grabbed them and brought them over to Taog.

"Taog, check this out!"

His eyes widened, and he grinned. "That's a rich consul for you."

Ateia handed one to him. "I know, right?!" Her smile turned soft as she looked at the rolls. "And . . . I think this could be a good start."

Taog tilted his head at that, but Ateia just turned around and walked over to NSLICE-00P.

"Seero, look! The consul gave us sweet rolls! Want to try one with me?"

"Negative Response: This unit is not scheduled for organic refueling for another 13.56 hours."

Ateia tilted her head. "Are you saying . . . you're not hungry?"

"Affirmative."

Ateia grinned. "That's fine! These are more for enjoyment, anyway! Here, let's see how it tastes!"

"Statement: This unit has no data to analyze *taste*, as that organic sense has been disabled."

Ateia froze, blinking. "You . . . don't taste anything, Seero?"

"Affirmative."

Ateia frowned. "Because of the cybernetic components?"

"Affirmative."

Ateia gritted her teeth for a moment before she paused and tilted her head. "But I can still taste things?"

"Explanation: NSLICE Ateia has not had the corresponding protocols activated at this time."

Ateia's eyes widened. "Wait, you're saying you can turn taste on and off?"

"Affirmative."

Ateia grimaced as she remembered some of her and Taog's first attempts at cooking for themselves. Disabling taste on demand could have been . . . helpful. But she shook her head. The important point was she could apparently *choose* to do so. Which likely went for NSLICE-00P as well.

"In that case, why don't you just turn your taste back on?"

NSLICE-00P was about to respond when her robotic eye started flickering. Dr. Ottosen had specified for the sense of taste to be disabled, stating his opinion that it hogged too many processing resources for insufficient tactical advantage.

But . . . she was not *in* a tactical situation where her processing resources were in high demand. And Dr. Ottosen's opinions had proven not necessarily optimal, even to the NSLICE program's own goals. NSLICE-00P analyzed the data and her protocols, and found there was no particular reason she *couldn't* re-enable her sense of taste.

No, in fact, taste was connected to the sense of smell, which she had recorded Taog and many of her other monsters utilizing for situational awareness in tactical settings. Disabling taste might actually be *inefficient*.

NSLICE-00P decided the best course of action was to re-enable the sense and gather data so that she could compare and determine which case would maximize her effectiveness.

"Analysis complete. Response: This unit has determined more data is necessary to calculate the cost-benefit analysis of dedicating processing resources to taste. This unit is re-enabling the sense on a trial basis to gather data."

Ateia blinked for a bit as she parsed the statement but then smiled. "Then, for your first taste, why don't you try this?"

She held out the roll, and NSLICE-00P took it. "Affirmative. Gratitude: This unit thanks NSLICE Ateia for a first test subject."

She was about to pound the roll into mush, as she did with most of her other food, when Ateia jumped. "Wait, Seero! Don't just smash it!"

"Statement: This unit is improving the ingestion efficiency of the organic fuel."

Ateia shook her head. "That's not the point, Seero! You're supposed to savor a sweet roll like this! Here, try taking a bite like this!"

Ateia took a small bite, humming with a smile at the taste. "See? You have to go slowly if you want to fully taste it!"

NSLICE-00P's robotic eye flickered. "Query: The inefficient ingestion method is intended to maximize taste data gathering?"

Ateia pondered for a second before slowly nodding. "Um, I think so?"

"Acknowledged." NSLICE-00P looked at the sweet roll, determining that, since she was in a data-gathering trial, did not require organic refueling at this time in the first place, and was not in an urgent setting, that maximizing the data gathered would be more beneficial than maximizing ingestion efficiency. So, she took a small bite, replicating Ateia's ingestion method. Ateia smiled at her.

"How is it, Seero?"

NSLICE-00P's robotic eye flickered as data flooded her mind. "Uncertain Answer: This unit . . . has no relevant data. Sensations unclear . . ."

Ateia's smile dropped. She thought for a moment, rubbing her chin. "Well, I guess you have nothing to compare it to. Um . . . Well, how about this? If you had to decide, would you want more of it?"

NSLICE-00P's robotic eye flickered again. Her cybernetic components analyzed the data. The roll seemed not to be a balanced nutritional source, but the high caloric content could be useful in situations where high metabolic rates were expected in the near future.

If she had been with her original organization and had access to highly efficient nutrient paste, she would not requisition such a fuel source. But in her current circumstances, she judged that there might be some niche situations where it would be useful.

But that was a tactical analysis, and the majority of the data on this nutritional source was coming from her organic sensors, so she decided to query her organic components as well.

She found, to her surprise, that this nutritional source had produced an emotional reaction. Her organic components indicated they would, in fact, requisition this nutrition source in the future. In fact, they were doing so right now, despite the lack of nutritional deficits that would generate a refueling request.

"Answer: Organic components are requesting additional refueling. Reason is unclear; no nutritional deficit detected. The base cause appears to be an emotional reaction to the data received."

Ateia gave a soft smile at that. "That's because it tastes good, Seero. And good food makes us feel happy. Let's get you lots of tasty things, okay?"

NSLICE-00P's robotic eye flickered. Extraneous refueling was not particularly necessary to her. But . . . there was also no reason *not* to accept additional fueling, so long as the intake was not excessive. Her cybernetic half ultimately had no opinion either way on the proposal.

So, the organic half made the call on her response.

"Affirmative."

17

Designation Discussions

"The use of colloquial designations for NSLICE units is permitted for the sake of tactical brevity. All such designations should draw from official designations, should only be used for the duration of an operation, and should only be permitted among tactical units. All official orders and communication must use the official designations."

—NSLICE handler guidelines

Agedia slithered as fast as her snake body could go for a full day, almost bowling over the border guards as they stopped her to check her identity. But as the sun began to set and the adrenaline wore off, she slowed to a jog pace . . . and then a walking pace . . . and then a crawling pace. Her face fell, and she began to wring her hands.

Would Tiberius even be happy to see her?

She had been so focused on her own problems that she hadn't even stopped to consider things from his perspective. He had moved to the rainy, backwater, monster-and-barbarian-infested frontier all by himself because she had been too busy moping to protect Aedinia's daughter. He had spent a decade there now, alone and being rained on, while she and Vafum partied it up in Velusitum. He'd occasionally make trips to see them, but she had not once come to visit him in Turannia.

He'd nearly died, several times, as Turannia had to deal with multiple incursions by the Wulver and the Dobhar, among other tribes from the Wild Lands across the Northern Sea, the latest of which had occurred when Turannia didn't even have its legions. He probably would have died had it not been for NSLICE-00P.

And for what?

Ateia had moved away, out of his protection and into hers. And then, Agedia had slipped up, and Ateia had nearly been killed. In other words . . . she had nearly thrown away a decade of effort and sacrifice by Tiberius; efforts and sacrifices that he had made on *her* behalf in the first place.

Her shoulders dropped. Forget being happy to see her—she would be lucky if Tiberius didn't attack her on sight. She stopped moving forward, slithering back and forth in a figure-eight pattern.

"I-It's fine . . . you can do this, Agedia. It's Tibbers! He'll grumble and drink, but he'll still be the same as always!"

She closed her eyes and took a deep breath. "And if not . . . if Tibbers hates me now, if he wants nothing to do with me and has run off with some young human girl, then that's only fair. But . . . I will face him, either way. He deserves that from me. Mighty Victoria, please grant me courage . . ."

She slowly opened her eyes, facing the road forward again. And froze. She blinked. She rubbed her eyes. She blinked again. A man in the garb of the Exploratores was running down the road as fast as he could. He paused as he came within view of her, and then ran straight in her direction.

"Agedia!"

"T-Tibbers?!"

Tiberius ran up to her and gave her a hug. "By the Aesdes, I've missed you, Agedia! I scarcely believed the border guard's report. What are you doing in Turannia?! Are you all right?!"

Agedia sputtered, her face twisting between several expressions. She didn't manage to get out a response. Tiberius frowned.

"Look, Agedia . . . I'm sorry. I should have asked before I sent the girl to you. I didn't have any other options to try and protect her, but it must have been very hard on you to see her again. And now I heard you went with her all the way to Corvanus, and now all the way here? I can't imagine how you felt. Can you forgive me?"

Agedia began to tremble. Her eyes moistened, and not from the rain. She returned Tiberius's embrace, gripping him tight. She closed her eyes and smiled.

"You have nothing to be sorry for. It's me who needs to apologize to you. But first, I can't tell you how happy I am to see you, Tiberius."

Tiberius's eyes widened slightly at the use of his actual name and patted her back. "It seems a lot has happened. Want to talk about it, or just drink?"

Agedia took a deep breath and then gave her most sincere smile in over a decade.

"How about both?"

Ateia sat around the campfire next to 00B, brushing her hand through his fur. She blinked as they looked at the group of monsters in front of them.

Ateia's face scrunched up as she observed the rat who seemed to be in charge.

"So this is . . ."—00B let out a soft grunt—"Big Brother 01R? Wait, *big* brother?"

01R turned. He stood straight up on his hind legs, his arms crossed in front of him as he nodded. "That is right-correct! I am among the first-initial of the wise-mighty-gracious boss-queen's summoned monsters, yes-yes! It is my honor-privilege to welcome you, the newest of our ranks! May you fight-strive with honor in the wise-mighty-gracious boss-queen's name!"

Ateia blinked, looking a bit nonplussed. "Um, thanks? I'll, um, do my best? Just to be clear . . . you're talking about Seero, right?"

01R frowned. "There could be-exist no other that we serve. Your moniker-title for the wise-mighty-gracious boss-queen is lacking in majesty and reverence, but as she is gracious enough to allow it, so shall I, yes-yes."

Just then, Ateia felt another rat monster crawl up her back and onto her shoulder, squeaking in her ear. "See-see? They are all a bunch of crazy-insane fanatics, yes-yes! We must find a way to flee-escape, yes-yes!"

"I mean, they're just enthusiastic?"

The rat-monster shivered. "You have not felt-experienced their training-torture, yes-yes."

00B scoffed and grunted. Ateia shook her head. "Now, now, not everyone can be as tough as you, can they?" Ateia rubbed 00B's neck. He snorted but did not resist. Ateia then paused. "Wait a minute—00B, you can talk?!"

00B snorted again, indicating it was a bit late for Ateia to make that observation.

"Explanation: Now that NSLICE Ateia is linked to the NSLICE network, and through the foreign system, automatic translation functions have been applied."

"Wise-mighty-gracious boss-queen!"

Ateia blinked as all the monsters turned to greet NSLICE-00P, who had just returned with Taog from a quick hunting trip. Taog stepped forward to join Ateia when all the monsters turned and either growled or hissed at him.

"See-see what I mean-say?"

Ateia decided not to respond, instead tilting her head and turning to NSLICE-00P. "Seero, I've been meaning to ask: Why are you calling me *NSLICE* Ateia? Isn't that your name? Did you . . . Did you adopt me or something?"

"Explanation: NSLICE is a model designation indicating a unit with sufficiently compatible cybernetic components to interface with the NSLICE network. NSLICE Ateia has been upgraded with the same model components as this unit and integrated into the network, and so designated as an NSLICE unit."

Ateia frowned and rubbed her chin. "Wait, so you're saying that *NSLICE* isn't a name? It's some kind of description?"

"Affirmative. Addendum: NSLICE stands for Non-Standard Leashed-Intelligence Cybernetic Enforcer, a cybernetic combat asset built on an organic base to defeat Non-Standard opponents."

Ateia rubbed her chin for another moment before her eyes widened. Her face twisted, transitioning from shock to rage before settling on sorrow.

"Seero . . . so you're saying NSLICE-00P isn't really a name . . . and Seero wouldn't be either. This translation says Seero just means zero. That's . . . I . . ."

"Objection: NSLICE-00P is this unit's unique identifier."

Ateia shook her head. "I mean, that's just a description of what you are, right? With a number to keep track of you?"

"Affirmative."

Ateia frowned, crossing her arms. "That's a bit . . . impersonal for a name."

Taog tilted his head as he stood at a safe distance, prepping a rabbit. "Maybe it's not?"

She turned to him. "Taog? What do you mean?"

He rubbed his chin. "I mean . . . names are important because of the meaning attached to them, right? So it's not impossible for a number to be as meaningful as another name, right? Like, think of all the famous legions. The Legio III, which held Velus's Pass against the Mélusine. Legio Arcanum XII, which defeated a Sun Elf High Archon. The brash Legio Draco II and their daring wyvern assaults."

Ateia furrowed her brow and hummed. Taog took a deep breath and then continued.

"What I'm saying is . . . maybe NSLICE-00P wasn't a real name at first. Maybe 'Seero' was just a number to start with. But those names have meaning to us now, right? They aren't just numbers anymore."

Ateia frowned and rubbed her chin for a while longer. Eventually, she sighed, turning to NSLICE-00P. "I guess what's most important is what Seero wants. So, Seero, how about it? Would you . . . like a new name? One that's not just a number? Or do you like your current designation?"

"Negative Response: This unit's current designation appears to suffice in all known use cases. Changing the designation is likely to result in miscommunications without any predicted benefit, and so is calculated to be inefficient."

Ateia took a deep breath and nodded. "Okay, we'll stick with *Seero*, then. To be honest, it would feel strange to call you something different now."

"Affirmative."

Meanwhile, 01R was frowning and pacing back and forth. "The wise-mighty-gracious boss-queen's name is sacred and powerful; it is insolence-heresy to question it, yes-yes. But . . . is it sufficient to show-display the true majesty and might of the wise-mighty-gracious boss-queen? Are any words-names sufficient for that task?"

The rat on Ateia's shoulder, Snuan Covenwalker, crouched down, her ears flat against her face. The crazies were at it again. She could only hope that the terrifying man-thing who had joined their ranks would be normal.

Although, normal man-things tended to murder rat monsters like her. For not the first time, Snuan regretted not fleeing from 01R when she'd had the chance.

18

Gather Your Courage

"The Aesdes are only here to guide us, not save us. If you need their help to face the road ahead, you best stay home."

—Legate Cossus Insteius Rogelius, preparing his troops for a campaign.

Ateia practiced the different visual settings on her robotic eye once again, focusing on the sensations she felt when the robotic eye zoomed into the distance.

She winced slightly as she felt the tingling in her head, the strange and invasive sensation whenever the techno-organic interface connected her mind to the machine parts. But while it had originally been intended to take control of people and render them into mindless weapons, Ateia trusted NSLICE-00P, believing she would not do the same.

In fact, NSLICE-00P had stated she'd given Ateia's organic half full control of the cybernetic, so Ateia brushed off the feeling of wrongness and tried to focus on what exactly was happening.

A moment later, she used the buttons NSLICE-00P had made for her to set the robotic eye back to default, closing her eyes and taking a deep breath. She opened them and tried to zoom in once again, but this time, she did not rely on the button. She tried to replicate how she'd felt, starting from her mind rather than from the cybernetic components.

Slowly, her robotic eye spun, and its aperture narrowed. Her vision moved into the distance, and as she focused, her organic eye began to glow slightly, golden-and-silver light forming into a lid and aperture mirroring the shape of her robotic eye. Her cybernetic half logged an increase in data uptake as the organic visual sensors began contributing beyond expectations.

A bit further away on the beach, Taog was practicing his Dark Slashes, but his swords and mana fell as he turned to watch Ateia, her face glowing with the light of her Holy mana. Turning back to look at his own blades and mana, he heaved a sigh then tried to focus as well as he could.

Elsewhere, Colleöne blinked, her eyes widening ever so slightly as she watched Ateia.

"Something to focus her power on, huh? I suppose a rigidly defined artificial half would certainly qualify."

She rubbed her chin, furrowing her brow for a moment before smiling.

"Well . . . if it were anyone else, I might be concerned about the possibilities . . . but for my kin, I feel only joy. I suppose I might have some family bias."

Some?

One of Colleöne's eyes twitched. "Don't you have something to be working on?"

It's not fair that *I* have to research centuries of records and deal with an entire material plane while *you* get to play around.

Colleöne scoffed. "If you had just done your job correctly in the first place, none of this would have happened, you know?"

I still don't get why all the Aesdes think *I* can handle the entire boundary of the Material Plane all by myself. That used to be a job for ALL of us!

Colleöne smirked. "Because you were the one who figured out an automatic way to deal with it in the first place, Mother of the Dungeons."

It was supposed to reduce my workload, not increase it! How was *I* supposed to know Anualë would come check on me during my nap time and get all impressed?!

Colleöne tilted her head with a puzzled expression. "Because your nap time accounts for most of the year?"

Ugh.

Taog woke up late at night. Their campfire was low and flickering, and there was little sound save for the waves upon the beach.

He sighed and got up, glancing around. Everyone should be sleeping at this point in the night . . .

Except for Seero, who apparently did some sort of half-sleeping "standby sentry mode" thing? And her monsters, most of which also had that *cybernetic* armor, and many of which were nocturnal species, if he identified them correctly. And were dungeon monsters too, which had a questionable need for sleep as far as anyone knew.

In fact, Ateia was an Aesdes now, with that same sort of armor too. She was still sleeping as far as he knew . . . but did she *need* to?

Taog shook his head. Okay, so no one but him might even need to sleep at this point. But that didn't matter. The point was that something was bothering him, and he wanted to do something about it. He . . . didn't want the others to see him, but if he wanted to change, he couldn't use that as an excuse. So, he got up and made his way to the beach.

Colleöne stood at the edge of the waves, peering out over the sea. She turned to face him, the moonlight illuminating her with an ephemeral glow. She smiled softly at him.

"Hello, Taog. You wish to speak with me?"

Taog nodded. He gulped. Colleöne was subduing her power at the moment, yet the light reflecting off the sea seemed to create a halo around her, and the waves just barely missed her feet, as if hesitant to contact her. His heart pounded as he realized again just who it was he was speaking with. But . . . he pressed on. It would not do to flee from the Lady of Courage herself.

He lowered himself on one knee and bowed his head.

"Mighty Victoria, how can I grow stronger?"

Colleöne replied immediately. "Train hard and diligently, seek and overcome challenges, and gain experience and wisdom. But I think that is not what you are truly asking?"

Taog frowned and nodded. "Ateia is an Aesdes now. Seero could defeat entire incursions alone from the day I met her and has only gotten stronger since then. Agedia took on that Herald alone and won. And I wouldn't be alive if Estrith wasn't much stronger than me. I was already weak, and the distance is only growing. How can I match their growth, their strength? How can I keep fighting with my friends?"

Colleöne frowned and crossed her arms. "Must you?"

Taog looked up at her with wide eyes. "Huh?"

Colleöne took a deep breath. "Not everyone grows at the same pace, Taog Sutharlan. It may not *be* possible for you to keep up with the people around you. But is that so terrible? There is more to life than battle and fighting. Even in war, the battle represents only a small portion of the time and effort spent. There is much you can do to help your friends and participate in the fight besides the actual violence, and sometimes, it takes more courage to step back than to step forward. Is it not enough to be by their side and support them?"

Taog furrowed his brow. He knelt in silence for a long moment before he slowly opened his mouth. "It . . . is not."

Colleöne raised an eyebrow. "Why not, Taog Sutharlan? I will be honest. What you seek is beyond you, through no fault of your own. NSLICE-00P is a unique existence in all the world; one even the Aesdes never predicted could arise. Ateia has joined our ranks and is no longer constrained by mortal limits. Agedia and Estrith have many, many years and just as many battles over you, having built their strength over time.

"To match any of that in the time you wish to spend is not possible by any standard path. You would need to break your limits—you may even need to transform yourself at a fundamental level. That is a path of danger and pain. Even I cannot guarantee you would return, and I guarantee you would not return the same if you did. And it is unnecessary.

"Your friends care for you, Taog, and that would not change even if you were the weakest being in all Aelea. They would grieve deeply if you fell. It would pain them even to see you hurt, and as you've seen with Ateia's plight, even success may have consequences. For what reason would you risk all that?"

Taog looked up, making eye contact with her. "Because I cannot be left behind this time. My parents left me behind as they marched to their deaths. Ateia's father left us behind as he marched off to fight battles unknown. Ateia was taken from me and injured alone."

He took a deep breath. Tears welled up in his eyes, but his gaze didn't waver. "For all my life, I've been running from this pain. I've been sealing myself off, trying to avoid any more loss. I've told myself for years that it couldn't be helped, that I was too weak to do anything more. I can't do that anymore. If I back off now, if I refuse to even try, even in the name of wisdom, then I will never rise to the challenge. I will be frightened and helpless prey, for the rest of my life."

He exhaled his breath and looked up into the night sky, staring at the moon. "Maybe it's impossible. Maybe I can't stand by my friends in the way I wish. Maybe it's foolish to even try. Maybe everyone is so powerful that they don't need me to do this at all."

He looked back down at Colleöne. "But I have to try. If it doesn't work, then I will do as you say. I will content myself with helping them in any way I can. But either way, I need to change myself. And that won't happen if I just wait around—not while everyone else is striving as hard as they can."

Colleöne met his gaze for a minute longer then slowly nodded. "If you are resolved, then I will point the way. Your mother taught you of the Trial of Hunters?"

Taog nodded. "Leave the clan on your own, and do not return until you have achieved a victory you feel is worth your strength."

Colleöne nodded and pointed. "Then you will follow the path of your ancestors. Head northwest, into the forest, away from the trails and the roads. Journey until you hear the ocean no more, then turn north when you reach the bog. There you will be tested, and you will have no one to rely on but yourself. The risk is grave, and I cannot promise that even success in this trial will bring you what you seek. Will you still embark upon it, knowing that death is the most likely outcome and the chance of success is little?"

Taog took a deep breath. "I will."

Colleöne sighed. "Then go, Taog Sutharlan. May you find what you seek . . . and may it be that which you wish."

Taog saluted her. "Thank you, Mighty Victoria."

He returned to his tent, preparing for his journey. As Colleöne watched, a message appeared before her eyes.

As if you're not going to watch him every step of the way. No way you're just going to let him die like that.

Colleöne shook her head. "It is important for him to have the right mindset on this quest. And any battle is chaotic and unpredictable. Even we cannot guarantee we will intervene in time."

Riiiggghttt. **And you totally aren't going beyond your mandate with this, huh? Let's see. "Head northwest, into the forest, away from the trails and the roads. Journey until you hear the ocean no more, then turn north when you reach the bog." Oh look. There's something right there. Something a certain someone could use as an excuse to grant massive blessings to whoever finds it first. And the terrifying monsters that warded other people off have mysteriously grown weak due to a coincidental influx of Holy mana that started just a few days ago.**
How convenient.

Colleöne's face fell. "You . . . may not be wrong. I suppose, after all this time, I still have not learned. But what can I do? Taog is making every effort to find the courage to change; that is not something I can hinder as the Lady of Courage and Victory. But I cannot allow him to fall. I will not subject Ateia to that pain, even should I repeat my past transgressions in the process."

Well, well, well, if Miss I-Always-Do-My-Job-Correctly feels bad about cheating her mandate, maybe she should take on some more work to make

up for it? Say . . . designing one of these rooms for me? It'd be a shame if Anualë were to unexpectedly inspect *your* work, now wouldn't it?

Colleöne hung her head and sighed. "I suppose I deserve that much. Very well."

19

Becoming the Hunter

"An Exploratore who cannot survive alone, won't."

—Exploratore Quirinia Hilaris, on her extensive survival training methods.

Taog went back to sleep for the night. Traveling the forest alone at night would be excessively dangerous, and he would need to sleep eventually anyway. After all, just because he was going to march into danger did not mean he should abandon *all* wisdom. So, he tried to rest as well as he could, then woke back up a bit before dawn.

He quietly gathered his things before making his way out of the camp. As he did, NSLICE-00P deactivated standby sentry mode and exited her tent. Ateia did likewise, frowning.

"Taog just left, huh?"

"Affirmative."

"That's right. But I must ask you both not to follow him."

The two turned to Colleöne, who walked back up to the camp. Ateia frowned.

"What do you mean, Victoria? It's dangerous to travel through the forests alone, especially at night."

Colleöne looked Ateia in the eye. "It is. But Taog has embarked on the Trial of Hunters, like his mother once did before him. It is important to him that he achieves this quest by his own strength."

"Query: So Friendly Taog's current mission has a contribution parameter?"

Colleöne glanced at NSLICE-00P and nodded. "That's a good way of putting it."

Ateia crossed her arms. "That might be true, but the last time we did that, we at least had Seero watching us. I'm not letting Taog go off alone, where we can't see or help him if something happens."

Colleöne turned back to Ateia, placing a hand on her shoulder. Colleöne's eyes pulsed lightly with golden-and-silver light. "You are not. Fear not; I am watching over him." She smiled. "Besides, imagine what might happen should Taog return victorious. A Taog who has proven to himself that he has the strength to stand up and fight, who has grown in confidence and holds his head high."

Ateia blinked as she considered Colleöne's words . . . and then gave a gentle smile.

"I . . . would like to see that."

Colleöne nodded and smiled back. Meanwhile, NSLICE-00P's robotic eye flickered.

"Query: Analysis indicates Friendly Taog's risk of termination may still necessitate intervention, even considering friendly contribution parameters. This unit would like to deploy surveillance assets to monitor conditions around the friendly's operational area."

Colleöne rubbed her chin for a bit before nodding to herself. "This is a good opportunity, in fact. NSLICE-00P, may I ask you to avoid watching Taog directly? There is something I wish to teach Ateia, and I would like to avoid her utilizing your assets to do so. You may keep the drones on standby in the area until then."

"Acknowledgement: If Colleöne will be observing the friendly and mitigating the risk of termination, then this unit can accept that request."

Colleöne nodded. "You have my word."

"Acknowledged. Request accepted."

With that, NSLICE-00P deployed several of her drones, which flew high into the air and then in the direction Taog had headed, though per Colleöne's request, she avoided his immediate vicinity. Colleöne motioned to Ateia, and the two of them walked off to the side, a bit away from the camp.

"This is something I thought you might learn later, but perhaps we can take a shortcut. As you well know, the Aesdes see with more than eyes. It is possible for us to view the world through time—and space. You did this by accident when you could not control your powers—now it is time to attempt it with intention."

Colleöne made eye contact with Ateia, a serious expression on her face. "This is not without risk. You could very much lose control of your powers and end up back where you started in the villa. It is a bit early for you to attempt this, to be honest, but I feel that as you have someone important to focus on and a reason to watch over him, that you should be able to figure it out. Do you wish to make the attempt?"

Ateia met her gaze and nodded. "Everyone Taog has ever cared about has left him alone. I don't want to do the same, not even for a bit."

Colleöne nodded back. "Good. Hold on to that resolve. Now, let us begin. Close your eyes, the cybernetic one included. This is not simply a matter of seeing farther. You are not using your eyes—you are connecting to the power of Elséró that flows through every corner of the world, that connects every living thing.

"But take care! Even an Aesdes cannot fully comprehend all the workings of the world. Even the very air contains multitudes and wonders that outnumber the grains of sand in the ocean. Focus is key if you wish to avoid being swept away by the tide of knowledge, much less to find that which you seek within the deluge."

Ateia nodded with a serious expression as she closed her eyes. Colleöne took a deep breath.

"Now, stir up your mana, and I will show you how to connect to the world around you . . ."

A monster wolf charged through the forest, snarling as it pounced on its prey. Taog leapt out of the way and swung one of his blades. He caught the monster on its flank, but the blade failed to cut through the monster's HP. Taog cursed and leapt back; the monster wolf yelped and jumped forward. Both took some distance, eyeing each other and circling around.

Taog took the opportunity to stir up his mana, infusing his blades in preparation for a Dark Slash. He grimaced slightly as he forced the mana through. The mana iron sword given to him by Consul Hiberius was much more receptive to mana than his old sword, but both were still much harder to infuse with Dark mana than the Dark Blade had been.

Taog continued to regret his lack of ranged options besides throwing his own weapon. He still needed to apologize to Seero for losing the enchanted weapon, in fact. But such thoughts were a distraction now, so he put them aside and forced his mana into the blades. The wolf eyed him warily as it adjusted its position.

"Fine, I'll come to you, then!"

Taog rushed toward the wolf. The monster seemed surprised, and barely leapt out of the way as Taog brought one of his swords down. But as a result, it couldn't dodge the second.

"Dark Slash!"

Taog shouted to help him focus on the skill. His second strike wasn't as powerful as the first, since he couldn't put his weight into it, but he hoped the skill would make up for it.

And he was right. The Dark mana cut through the wolf's HP and dealt a large gash to its side. The wolf yelped and fell to the ground. Taog did not miss that opportunity, leaping on top of it and stabbing both his swords into its neck.

You have slain Lupus Ferus (Level 25)!
Gained 17 XP!

Taog exhaled his breath. Under normal circumstances, he would try to avoid monsters like this, but that went against the spirit of the Trial of Hunters. While the young Wulver were obviously not expected to act suicidally, the journey was to be one of challenge and growth, to hunt the monsters of the land until one achieved the greatest victory they thought themselves capable of. So Taog was taking on any challenge he thought he could win, and trying to challenge himself in the process.

It was quite exhausting.

He heaved a sigh, then began to clean his weapons and dismantle the wolf. A lupus ferus was by and large a normal wolf, though heavily buffed by mana and far more vicious. Its pelt was certainly useful. Had he been on a hunting trip, he would have considered it a prize, but it was not so valuable that he would carry it around while he was looking for tougher fights.

Likewise, he had sufficient rations and didn't want to spend the time processing the meat for storage. So, he simply took the mana core, then buried the corpse.

Standard procedure would be to burn anything he wasn't going to use; leaving monster corpses lying around could have consequences. But, well, that assumed he wanted to avoid drawing other monsters to the area . . . or facing feral undead. In this case, that would assist with his current quest.

Taog sighed again. He again questioned the sanity of his mom's half of the family. Life had enough battles without intentionally seeking out more. Though, to be fair, the Wulver participating in the Trial of Hunters likely wouldn't be carrying a pack full of Imperial rations and would have just consumed the corpse outright, cooking optional. But they could shove off.

Taog was only half Wulver, so he'd only half follow the trial. After all, humans tended to respond poorly to consuming raw monster meat, and it turned out he was very human in that regard. A battle with his stomach would not result in an honorable victory.

He shook his head as he finished burying the wolf. The stress and the adrenaline were getting to him. But . . . he could not help a small smirk. The last time he had been on a hunting trip in the forests of Turannia, he'd had to cower and hide at the first sniff of a monster like this. He would admit he was enjoying being the hunter for once, of marching through the forest and *daring* the monsters to challenge him. Perhaps there was a reason the Wulver chose to live like this.

After a moment's rest, he stood back up. He was making decent time even with the fights, seeing as how he didn't need to take detours to avoid them, and he could no longer see, hear, nor smell the ocean. If he was still on the path Mighty Victoria had advised, he would be reaching the bog soon. And soon after that, he would be tested, as stated by the Lady of Courage and Victory herself.

Heart beginning to pound at that thought, he took a deep breath and narrowed his eyes. And then, he stepped forward and began to walk, continuing on his quest.

20

The Test

"There is no emotion; there is only protocol."

—Motto of the NSLICE program intelligence leashing development team.

You have slain Felix Pluvia (Level 24)!
Gained 11 XP!
Level up! You are now Level 30!

Taog exhaled his breath, then took out his pack and poured a potion over the scratch on his face.

This felix pluvia had been five levels under him, yet this was the closest he had come to death yet. Its ability to hide amidst the rain and the mist had let it get the drop on him, especially as he traveled near a foggy bog. He was deeply fortunate that Miallói had once trained him utilizing the same technique; otherwise, he wouldn't have managed to dodge. That scratch could have been a *lot* worse.

Still, beyond its stealth, the monster had not been much of a challenge, disadvantaged in levels as it was. Taog would not consider that as the test Mighty Victoria had told him about, dangerous though it had been. So, he turned north, and continued on his journey.

Ateia focused on Taog, focusing on her desire to see him and make sure he was alright. She then stirred up the Holy mana resting inside of her, extending it into the world around her. It had taken her a while to arrange her mana like Colleöne had taught her, and longer still to extend her perception beyond her senses. But now . . . now Ateia began to move beyond herself.

She could see into the water; she could feel the ground beneath her; she could smell the air around her. And she could feel the subtle current of Holy mana flowing through and between everything around her. She gently reached out with her own mana, connecting to the stream.

Her heart began to pound. Information began to stream into her brain. She could see the rocks each grain of sand beneath her had started as. She could smell which creatures had recently swum through the water of the cove. She could feel tiny bits of air bouncing against each other.

Her eyes began to widen. She remembered streams of mana like this flowing into her. She remembered every inch of her body *burning*. Burning like her head did now.

She heard the Herald of Twilight cackle overhead.

She screamed and clutched her head as pain and information overwhelmed her mind. She lost control of her mana, and the connection fell to pieces. Her cybernetic side suddenly shut off from memory overload, and she fell off her feet.

NSLICE-00P caught her before she hit the ground, her robotic eye flickering as she ran diagnostics on Ateia's cybernetic half. Ateia gasped for breath as her components slowly booted back up.

Colleöne gave a worried frown. "Are you okay, Ateia?"

Ateia closed her eyes and took a couple of deep breaths. NSLICE-00P helped her cybernetic half reset its memory and return to normal before Ateia slowly stood back on her own feet.

"I'm . . . fine. Thanks, Seero."

"Acknowledged. Warning: NSLICE memory is insufficient to handle unfiltered Divination data transfers."

Colleöne nodded. "Even the Aesdes cannot perceive everything all at once and must learn to focus our sight." She grimaced. "It . . . is a bit early for Ateia to do so. And I suppose, in my joy at training you, I forgot what has been done to you, and its similarities to this technique."

But Ateia shook her head. She sat on the ground, a snarl on her face. "No. I'm not going to let those monsters take anything more away from me. I'm going to break through this and find Taog."

Colleöne blinked at that, then gave a sad smile. She whispered to herself, "I applaud your courage, though I wish it was unnecessary."

Ateia rubbed her chin and took a deep breath. "Seero, those emotional controls . . . can you control them? Like, disable one emotion at a time?"

NSLICE-00P's robotic eye flickered. Her original organization had not programmed such a capability, as they'd never intended for an NSLICE unit to operate without the controls fully activated.

But despite that, it turned out, NSLICE-00P *did* have protocols for selective emotional controls, put in place by her previous commander upon her reprogramming. Apparently, her previous commander had considered this case within the realm of possibility. NSLICE-00P just hadn't noticed, since until now, she hadn't seen a need for partial emotional controls.

"Affirmative."

Ateia slowly nodded. "Then, could you turn off my pain and my fear?"

Colleöne frowned. "I see what you're trying to do, but I cannot recommend it. Pain and fear serve a purpose: they inform us when something is wrong. This is a difficult technique that is not without risk. If you do not know when something is wrong, you risk even greater damage than you have experienced."

Ateia shook her head. "I'm just getting distracted by the memories, so I can't grasp the right feeling. But if I could succeed at it just once, I think I could figure out how to move beyond those thoughts. I just want to focus on one thing at a time."

"Suggestion: This unit could link to NSLICE Ateia and monitor her cybernetic components for memory overflow, and so inform her before she reaches critical levels. This unit could also utilize her processing and memory resources to assist with the data filtering. Caveat: This would require NSLICE Ateia to allow the cybernetic components greater access to her organic components as per her initial boot cycle, and so carries the risk of damage due to incompatibilities between preexisting organic memories and the techno-organic interface."

Ateia frowned. "That was when my components tried activating emotional controls, right?"

"Affirmative."

Ateia took another deep breath, then turned her head to look NSLICE-00P in the eyes. "That . . . was unexpected, and not enjoyable. But now that I know what's going on, what it's doing, and most importantly, *who* is behind it, I think I want to try again. I trust you, Seero. And if it hurts, I'd prefer pain from you than pain from that stupid, Aesdes-forsaken cult."

She then flushed and turned to Colleöne. "Oh, um, I'm sorry. I didn't mean any offense."

Colleöne chuckled. "None taken." Her eyes then narrowed. "And we have withdrawn our support from them to the maximum extent possible, given their activities thus far. 'Aesdes-forsaken' is not an inaccurate description. On a personal level, I cannot speak for the rest of the Aesdes, but I, at least, am not particularly fond of those individuals."

Colleöne then turned to NSLICE-00P and rubbed her chin before sighing. "I am not fully comfortable with this course of action, but I believe it has a reasonable chance of success, or at least may mitigate some of the risks. If you both are resolved, then I will say no more."

Ateia nodded, turning to NSLICE-00P. "In that case, will you please help me, Seero?"

"Affirmative."

NSLICE-00P began to connect to Ateia's cybernetic components once again.

Taog continued his journey north, marching through the forest. But then, his nose twitched, and he frowned. It was a scent he had not smelled before, but one that gave him goose bumps. Something deep inside him was warning him that he should not proceed any further.

He took a deep breath, and took a step forward. Mighty Victoria had stated he would be tested, and this scent was challenging him before he had even seen it. He needed to at least determine what it was. Still, he crouched down and began creeping forward silently. If his instincts were reacting to a scent he didn't recognize . . . Well, *some* caution was still necessary, even on the Trial of Hunters. Overconfident Wulver often didn't return from the trial at all.

So, he crept forward until he found a trail—with several trees torn from their roots and tossed aside. He gulped and followed along, finding a small clearing in the forest surrounding a large cave.

Taog frowned and rubbed his chin.

He couldn't see inside the cave from his position, but there was no cover past the tree line. If he got any closer, whatever it was would see him as well. And worse, he could feel tingling on his skin and could see small sparks and distortions in the air close to the cave, all indicating an abnormally high mana concentration.

Just then, he felt the ground tremble. Taog ducked into a bush, hearing a growl that reverberated in his chest. The scent grew overpowering.

Then, it emerged. First was a long, broad snout covered in brown scales, with teeth the size of short swords hanging out, followed by a massive, squat body with bulging muscles and short, powerful legs that shook the ground with every step. Finally, a massive tail the size of a small tree appeared.

Taog's ears fell flat against his head as his eyes widened. It was an Aelea drake. The drake sniffed the air then let out a roar that echoed through the forest. Taog resisted the urge to bolt. Fortunately, though, the drake snorted out of its nose and then lay down in the clearing, apparently satisfied with its one roar. It closed its eyes as it took in the sun.

Taog was about to back away when he paused. He frowned and shook his head. This was an Aelea drake! The one thing that could challenge the ursanus for dominion over the forests of Turannia. A dragonkin! Whatever test Mighty Victoria had for him, it couldn't be this. Right?

He recalled Seero annihilating an ursanus natura like it was nothing. He closed his eyes. The whole purpose of this trip was to try and catch up to Seero and Ateia, the girls who now defied common sense. Seero had taken on an entire incursion while she was at Taog's current level—and *won*. If he truly wanted to stand by Seero and Ateia's side, he could not be frightened away by mere common sense.

He opened his eyes and rubbed his chin. Putting aside all tales and warnings of the Aelea drake, he tried to view the situation objectively. This drake was actually quite small, barely taller than Taog. For Aelea drakes specifically, size *was* an indicator of age . . . and strength. This one had to be very young, and a relatively low level. It certainly would not match up to the Tyrant of the Beasts, for example. Taog most likely would not surpass it in level, but he might be within striking distance of it.

Of course, that was just comparing the level number. It did not take into account the fact that this was a dragon, if a small and underdeveloped one. So, did Taog have a chance?

His eyes widened slightly. He realized . . . he was in luck. Of all the dragon types he could have encountered, an Aelea drake was perhaps the best. Aelea drakes were slow, and had no wings to fly upon him, unlike the wyverns. Taog would be able to outrun this one if he had to.

Aelea drakes also lacked the deadly breath of their fire counterparts, or the mystical powers of a more magical type. Taog wouldn't have to worry about any special attacks that would extend beyond the reach of the monster's jaws. Aelea drakes didn't even have the powerful regeneration a Nature-attributed monster would have had, so if Taog could injure it, he could hypothetically wear it down over time.

What the Aelea drake did have was massive strength and nigh-impenetrable defense. Even the halberd of a Legion slayer would struggle to pierce its scales; even a Legion bulwark's shield couldn't hold against those mighty jaws. And Taog had neither the strength of a slayer nor the resilience of a bulwark.

And that was why it was possible. Taog had largely abandoned the straightforward approach, focusing more on dodging and evading. The Aelea drake could snap him in two with a single bite, but that wouldn't matter if he didn't get hit. And he had the Dark Slash skill, an attributed ability that mixed physical and magical attacks. So, while there was no hope his short swords would pierce the beast's scales, he might be able to rely on magic.

It would be a long, difficult battle. He'd be wearing it down with magical pinpricks, slowed down by his not particularly impressive mana regen. It would be extraordinarily dangerous. A single mistake, and he would die.

But . . . it *was* possible.

Taog gulped silently, but he narrowed his eyes and gripped his swords. Mighty Victoria had said he would be tested. She'd said this was a path of danger and pain, where death was the most likely outcome. She'd said he would have to break his own limits to achieve what he wanted.

He decided he would not turn back, not until he had given it a try.

Taog checked his mana, then took a deep breath.

"Well, here goes nothing. Hope this isn't a terrible mistake . . ."

He shook his head. No, that's not how he'd approach this. He was not going to go off and die and leave Ateia alone like everyone else in their lives. He was GOING to return, no matter what. And he would do everything he could to return with a victory.

Taog fixed his eyes on the drake, and then stepped out into the clearing.

21

Taog's Limit

"Please recall that a low-level dragon is still a dragon."

—Traveling author and former Exploratore Placus Paesentius Statius, after being requested to join a dragon hunt.

Taog slowly crept through the clearing, stepping as quietly as he could. The Aelea drake was breathing heavily, possibly even snoring, but Taog didn't want to risk waking it. He wanted to start by getting a good hit in, if at all possible.

But it turned out it was not, in fact, possible.

The drake slowly stirred and sniffed the air. Taog froze in place as the drake swung its head around until one of its eyes landed on Taog. The eye narrowed, and the drake rose to its full height, forcing Taog to crane his neck upward. It pulled back its head, then let out a massive roar that shook the forest.

Taog's stomach dropped at the sight. He couldn't help but gulp, but still, he gripped his swords tighter and stirred up his mana. The drake growled. It crouched down then sprung forward, bounding toward Taog.

And Taog . . . stepped to the side with ease. He blinked. The Aelea drake was even slower than he'd expected, and the creature's sheer weight gave it equally great momentum, so it could not turn easily once it got up to speed. It careened past him, barely stopping before smashing into the tree line.

Taog started to grin, rushing forward as the drake started to turn around. He coated his swords with Dark Slashes and swung into the monster's exposed flank.

CLANG!

His swords bounced right off the monster's scales, sending tremors through Taog's arms. He barely kept a grip on his swords, the Dark Slashes scattering as he failed to complete his slash. The drake's HP barrier didn't even bother to block the attack.

Taog had no time to worry, however, as the Aelea drake swung its head around and snapped its jaws. Taog leapt back to avoid being bitten in two, frowning as the drake prepared another charge. He put away his original sword, holding the new one from Consul Hiberius with both hands. In this instance, the control and stability of a two-handed grip would serve him better.

He concentrated as the drake began to charge him once more. He dodged again, but a bit closer this time, and swung his blade with another Dark Slash as the drake passed him by.

This time, he struck the monster's scales with just the tip of his sword, gritting as the impact nearly tore the blade from his hands. But he held on, and the Dark-attribute mana jumped from the blade and struck the drake. Its HP barrier flashed briefly as it took the blow.

Taog smiled. He could do this, after all. Though, while the appearance of the HP barrier indicated he could deal damage to the creature, his attack had not left a noticeable effect on it. And he could still feel the impact of the strikes in his arms. This would be a long, difficult process requiring his full strength to wear the monster down with minor scratches.

Under normal circumstances, he'd abandon this fight immediately.

But, as Mighty Victoria had warned, this was the sort of thing it would take if he was going to fight along Ateia and Seero. So Taog steeled himself and readied his stance as the drake began to charge him once more.

Taog was breathing heavily, sweat drenching his entire body. The sword felt slippery in his hands and had grown heavy; his arms and legs burned as they begged for respite. How long had he been fighting? How long had he been dodging blows that could end him in an instant, throwing all his strength into his tiny counterattacks? A few minutes? An hour? A day?

Taog wasn't sure, save for the fact that the sun still shone in the sky. And for all that effort, the Aelea drake was no worse for wear. Taog grimaced. The HP barrier continued to appear, so he knew his strikes were doing *something*, but he had no way of knowing just how much of it was left. Was the creature's HP critical, with Taog on the verge of victory? Or had he barely even begun?

His attacks didn't feel any different, and the HP continued to appear, so he had a feeling it was the latter. If this kept up, Taog would be forced to retreat. He gritted his teeth.

But Taog wasn't the only one frustrated with this situation. The Aelea drake growled, unable to squash this tiny insect buzzing around it, yet also unable to drive it away. In its frustration, it lumbered straight toward Taog without preparing its stance, swinging its head and tail from side to side, lashing out all around it.

Taog's eyes widened, caught off guard. He quickly jumped to the side, but he stumbled, throwing out his hands to balance himself. His sword arm swung out toward the drake's path, and the drake's jaws clamped down.

Taog fell to the ground but managed to roll forward, quickly rising to his feet as the drake passed him once more. He lifted his sword and readied his stance . . . and his eyes widened. His blade was gone, just a bit of jagged metal left above the hilt. The drake had bitten down on it when Taog had stumbled, and torn through the mana iron with ease.

Taog scowled, gritting his teeth. But he had no choice now. His other weapon was his father's old blade, well maintained but even weaker than the broken blade had been. If he was barely making progress with the better weapon, he doubted he'd do anything with this one.

So Taog crouched down, waiting for the drake to charge him once again. He dodged once more, landing in the creature's blind spot . . .

And then he ran. The drake spun about, searching for its foe once again. It paused as it saw Taog running. It growled—and then roared with all its might and started after him. After all this, it was not content to just let him get away.

Taog glanced behind him and winced. The drake pursued him straight into the forest, knocking over the trees in its path. He tore his eyes away and put more strength into his feet, grimacing as he glanced at the hilt of the broken blade still in his hand. If only he didn't need a sword to use Dark Slash; the physical blade wasn't doing anything here, after all. Then he would have had a chance in this fight.

He paused, remembering a moment on the boat ride from Turannia, when Seero had been practicing her spells. She had formed blades out of mana, light, and water.

With no sword in hand.

He shook his head and focused on making his way through the trees and bushes. Yes, *Seero* could make magic blades without any weapons to guide her. But Seero also didn't need blades in the first place. She'd fly through the sky and rain death from above with a strategic spell.

But . . . it did mean it was possible. If only he knew how to do it himself.

As he ran, a conversation came to his mind.

"Don't think of the status or the activation. Think about the motions of your body. Think about the movement of your mana. Think about the effect of the skill. And think about what you want it to achieve. Once you have a clear image in your mind, try to replicate it."

He thought of Ateia's lessons with Colleöne, and of both their lessons with Miallói. He glanced back. The drake had fallen behind, so he rushed to the side and out of view. Perhaps the drake could track him by scent or some other means, but it was not like it could sneak up on him while knocking over the forest. He had some time now.

Looking down at the broken hilt in his hand, he took a deep breath.

Well, it was worth a try, wasn't it? If he couldn't figure this out, he'd just have to run away anyway, so no different than if he didn't try at all. And the whole point of this quest was to become a bit more like Seero. If he couldn't do this much, it'd be better to just give up.

He held the hilt in both his hands and stirred up his mana. He tried to form a Dark Slash . . . but the skill failed. He frowned before thinking of Colleöne's words once more. He closed his eyes.

"Okay, don't think about the skill. Think about what the skill actually does and how the mana actually moves."

Taog thought back to when he had learned the Dark Slash, when he had accidentally infused Dark mana into an unenchanted blade. He thought of his training with Seero, when she had infused Dark mana into him so he could get the feel for it. He remembered dungeon diving, when Seero had infused their weapons, and Ateia had learned to channel Holy mana. He thought of how he had learned Mana Infusion by replicating the feeling of what Seero had done.

He imagined giving his mana the Dark attribute, and then forming it into a blade. He imagined holding a complete blade in his hand, wrapped with Dark power. The mana resisted him, not wanting to leave his hands, but he pushed it through, as he had when learning Dark Slash.

Without a blade to guide it, it tried to scatter and go every which way, but he held it together, remembering the precise flows of Seero's mana when she'd infused it for him. He formed his own will into the blade for the mana to follow.

And then . . . something clicked. He opened his eyes, and they widened

In his hands was a complete blade made entirely of Dark mana. A nebulous, pure black weapon, like smoke trapped in the form of a sword.

You have learned the spell Dark Blade!
You have learned the skill Dark Magic!
The skill Dark Magic is now Level 5! Spell choice available!
You have learned the spell Dark Bolt!
You have accomplished the feat Magic Swordsman!

Feats		
Name	Description	Effect
Magic Swordsman	Unlocked by modifying a Slash skill into a Blade spell, or by casting a spell through a sword. The path of the blade and the path of the mage need not diverge.	+3 Perk Points +1 level in Spellstrike skill

Active Skills		
Name	Level	Description
Spellstrike	1	May cast compatible spells through a physical melee weapon. Spells cast in this way may not require a chant or magic circle, depending on complexity and user skill. May utilize along with physical attack skills, and physical attack skills may be used with Blade spells. Elemental weapon skills are converted to or merged with spells of the appropriate attribute.

The skill Dark Slash has been fused with the spell Dark Blade!
The spell Dark Blade is now Level 5!
The skill Spellstrike is now Level 3!

Taog slowly began to grin. He had done it. He had pulled a Seero. And now, he had a weapon that wouldn't care about physical defense at all.

And right on time, he heard the drake roar as it searched for him. He smirked, his eyes narrowed, and he took a step toward the noise.

22

Terminate the Drake!

"Run."

—Traveling author and former Exploratore Placus Paesentius Statius, on dragon-hunting techniques.

Taog crept toward the sound of trees crashing and roaring. Finally pausing, having lost sight of its foe, the drake started sniffing the air. Taog smirked and took a deep breath.

"I'm over here, you overgrown lizard!"

The drake turned its head toward him and growled before charging through the forest once more.

Taog shaped his mana as before, the formal skills now supporting his efforts, and a Dark Blade formed in his hand. The drake was even slower than before, having to knock over trees along the way, so it was a simple matter for Taog to step to the side and swing his blade across the drake's flank.

The spell Dark Blade is now Level 6!

The blade of pure magic slashed with ease, slicing through the monster's HP barrier. It was not a serious injury, and the HP quickly restored itself, but it was far more effective than Taog's strikes had been so far. The road was still long, but now, Taog could actually see an end.

He smiled, and then taunted the drake once again.

And so, the battle entered its second phase . . .

* * *

Ateia took a seat on a log on the beach before nodding to NSLICE-00P, who began to connect to Ateia's cybernetic components, slowly expanding Ateia's connection to the NSLICE network.

Ateia winced but said nothing. She blinked.

"I can . . . see myself? And other views?"

"Affirmative. Elaboration: NSLICE units share useful data over the network, including visual sensor input."

Ateia tilted her head. "Is that how you seem to know random things, Seero?"

"Affirmative Explanation: This unit utilizes a combination of NSLICE unit scouts and advanced sensors, both technological and foreign-system related, to expand situational awareness. Query: Is NSLICE Ateia experiencing any incompatibilities with the NSLICE network?"

Ateia frowned slightly but shook her head. "It still feels weird, but it doesn't hurt."

"Acknowledged. Follow-Up Query: Is NSLICE Ateia prepared to activate emotional controls?"

Ateia took a deep breath, then nodded. "I'm as ready as I'll ever be. Let's do it."

"Affirmative."

NSLICE-00P took the partial emotional control protocols and created UI buttons that Ateia could activate at will. Ateia blinked and smiled, then took another deep breath and selected the buttons for pain and fear. She winced as she felt lightning zap through her head. Grimacing, she held her head with one hand.

But she did not resist. She believed in NSLICE-00P. The girl had even given Ateia control over these protocols. And she *needed* to know if Taog was okay, so she did her best to endure the feeling of the implants reaching into her mind.

And then . . . the pain faded. Her heartbeat slowed. Ateia blinked. "I think it worked."

"Helpful Observation: This unit can confirm the protocols were successfully activated. Diagnostics indicate that all systems are fully functional."

Ateia nodded. It still felt weird—wrong, even—but this was something she could handle, so she turned her focus to the next task. Closing her eyes, she took a deep breath, stirring up Holy mana within her. And then, she reached out into the world . . .

Again, a flood of mana and information sought to overwhelm her. She could feel the air around her, the sand beneath her feet, the fish swimming in the cove. Memories of the ritual performed on her appeared before her eyes, trying to distract her. She began to lose herself, started to forget why she was there—

"Observation: NSLICE Ateia is on the verge of memory overload. This unit will lend assistance."

NSLICE-00P began to divert some of the data into the NSLICE network, her own robotic eye flickering rapidly. Her memory jumped to nearly full right away, and NSLICE-00P began activating all the drone golems on standby, making use of their resources as well. They were fairly simple devices with relatively low processing capability, but they were also numerous, so it was not an insignificant gain. And her efforts did not go unnoticed . . .

NSLICE-00P's monsters were sparring on another part of the beach. But then, 00B stopped, letting 01R strike him right on the nose. 01R was about to question him when he, too, paused. 00B motioned with his head and grunted. 01R nodded.

"You are right-correct, 00B. Everyone, the wise-mighty-gracious boss-queen requests-requires our assistance! We shall aid-assist her, yes-yes!"

The monsters cheered, and then they all sat down on the beach. 01R led them in offering their processing resources to the NSLICE network, as they had done in the past.

Rattingtale was currently shivering in his room, hiding from the evil-sadistic spider-thing and the torture-horror she called "training" when he felt the activity in the NSLICE network. He rubbed his paws together.

"Well, if it's just offering-lending these horrid armor-things, then I guess-suppose it's not that difficult, yes-yes? I will . . . try-attempt, yes-yes."

Rattingtale gingerly reached out . . . and then screamed as NSLICE-00P connected to a willing resource, and floods of data filled his mind.

"I knew it! It's more torture-horror, yes-yes!"

Lilussees groaned and stirred awake. She waved a leg around and then plopped back down.

"Like, yeah, sure, whatever. Just, like, use what you need and don't bother me."

Her organic half went back to sleep, but her cybernetic components offered their resources, as she'd stated. Her robotic eyes began flickering, and her cybernetic memory filled with data.

Lilussees would have a fitful nap as the data inevitably bled over to her other half.

Colleöne paled as she watched the NSLICE units join together and assist Ateia.

"This is . . . This is like when the Aesdes join our power together for a task. It's a group divination, but without our assistance—or our safeguards. And, um, NSLICE-00P could always summon more of those, so the theoretical limit of information they could handle is . . . I, um, this is . . . I might have made a mistake . . ."

Just one?

"Really?! Now, Shialnor?! We're watching mortals and monsters perform a group divination *manually*, and your concern is to rag on me?!"

Yes.

Colleöne held her face and screamed into her hands, then took and exhaled a long breath. "Well, what's done is done. As long as Ateia is there to guide her, hopefully NSLICE-00P won't do anything drastic with all this."

You mean the teenage girl whose main goal is to burn a cult to the ground after a lifetime of loss and abandonment at their hands?

"Not. Helping."

As all the NSLICE units worked together to analyze, filter, and delete the excess data, the pressure on Ateia's mind and spirit lessened. She could think again, and she began to remember herself.

And now, what appeared before her were the memories of the night. She scowled. Her body heated up as the sight filled her with rage.

But only that. She could not feel the burning sensation of the mana overloading her. She could not feel the sharp knife plunging into her body. She did not feel the fear and the helplessness of that night. A message from the NSLICE UI told her the emotional control efficiency had begun dropping, and her heartbeat gradually sped up. But for that moment, she did not reflexively recoil from the memories. She remained in control of herself.

She had a moment where she could choose how to respond. She narrowed her eyes. She thought of Taog, fighting alone against powerful enemies.

"Get *OUT* of my head!"

She swiped her hand to the side, trying to thrust the images away. And to her surprise, it worked. Her robotic eye flickered, the emotional controls attempting to quarantine the memory as per her instructions. Her head still ached and burned with the sheer amount of information flowing through it, but now she could focus. She could act.

And so she did. She turned all of her thoughts to Taog, wishing she could see him and confirm how he was doing. And the mana responded. Golden-and-silver light flickered around Ateia's eyes. The extra data stopped flowing into her,

her sight narrowed, and then shot forward. Ateia felt like she was flying as the world rushed past, blending together in her peripheral vision before it stopped all at once. She was viewing a forest to the north.

Ateia gasped, nearly losing control once again. Pain shot through her mind as her emotional controls wavered and tried to reassert themselves. An Aelea drake was charging straight toward Taog.

Ateia's eyes shot open, and she stood up, but Colleöne just placed a hand on her shoulder.

"An Aelea drake is attacking Taog! We have to help him!"

Colleöne shook her head and smiled. "I think you should keep watching."

Ateia frowned but did as Colleöne suggested. Her eyes widened. Taog dodged the drake with ease and swung a blade of pure Dark mana. His blow connected, leaving a small gash on the drake's side. The Aelea drake roared as it felt pain for the first time this fight.

Ateia blinked repeatedly. Colleöne chuckled. "His odds might be better than you think."

Ateia bit her lip, however. Taog may have struck a blow, but he was breathing hard and was drenched in sweat. Even now, he winced, and the blade in his hand flickered slightly.

"But . . . Taog's not doing well, and that drake is still healthy. Shouldn't we do something?"

Colleöne nodded. "We can. In fact, you can do something right now."

Ateia's eyes widened. "Please tell me what!"

Colleöne smiled. "Believe in him. The Aesdes can do more than just see through the world, you know? Send him your support. Turn all your thoughts and mind to him, and will his victory into being. Imagine the very world supporting him."

Ateia nodded and closed her eyes, trying to do as Colleöne suggested. Her heart rate was increasing, but the emotional controls did their best to reduce her fear. She couldn't lose Taog, not after all this.

But . . . there was a part of her that wanted to see him succeed. That wanted to see Taog standing tall and smiling, no longer hiding from pain and helplessness. There was a part of her that relied on Taog, too. Because even after all the pain and injustice he went through, even after the village beat and scorned him, all it took was one smile from her to restore his spirit, to enable him to carry on another day.

She knew that whatever happened to them, Taog would be there, a constant and reliable presence at her side when all others had gone.

She looked into Taog's eyes as he focused on the drake. He was not giving up. He wasn't running, even in the face of this deadly opponent. Taog wanted to win.

Ateia nodded and clasped her hands together. "You can do it, Taog."

* * *

Taog winced. His hand trembled, his head pounded, and his mana had slowed to a trickle. He had been fighting for a long time now, and he was no mage. His mana was about to run dry, and he had no way to replace it. Even though he had found a path to victory, he was still not strong enough to reach it. It seemed he would have to retreat, after all.

Just then, his ears twitched. He thought he heard a voice . . .

"You can do it, Taog."

A tiny sliver of golden-and-silver mana rose from the ground and curled into his feet. Taog blinked. His mana began regenerating a bit faster, the trembling and aching in his muscles easing slightly. The Dark Blade in his hands stabilized, and Taog grinned. He didn't know what had just happened, but it seemed he could fight a little longer.

And a little longer was all he needed. The Aelea drake's HP was finally running low, and his attacks were starting to find purchase.

The drake charged at him once more. Taog stepped to the side then thrust his blade forward.

The magic sword stabbed into the drake's side, right between two of its scales. The monster roared and ran forward. Taog grinned and prepared his stance.

But the drake didn't charge. It eyed him warily now. Taog frowned, then smiled again.

"Well, if you don't want to come here . . ."

He had gained more than just a blade with his earlier feats.

He went ahead and activated the Dark Magic skill. A Dark Bolt magic circle formed in front of him, a black bolt shooting through the air and striking the drake on the nose. Taog was no mage; he had to rely on the skill to cast the spell at all. And a level one Dark Bolt wasn't exactly the most damaging attack. He wasn't going to finish the drake in that way.

But the drake roared and charged anyway. Young Aelea drakes didn't have much resistance to magic, so with its HP barrier drained, the spell caused it pain. This drake was not experienced enough to realize the attack was not a true threat and reacted to that pain. It charged forward wildly, whipping its head and tail around, abandoning all reason in its attempt to finally crush the hated foe.

Taog jumped toward a nearby tree, hauling himself up on a branch. The Aelea drake slammed into it and knocked it over, but Taog leaped off and managed to land on the drake's head.

He channeled all the mana he could into his Dark Blade.

"Power Strike! Flurry!"

He activated any physical skill he could as he struck the drake's head with all his might. The drake roared and shook its head, but Taog held on and continued his assault.

And then, a lucky blow found its way through the drake's skull. The monster crashed to the ground as its HP rushed to heal the wound, but Taog continued to strike.

Until the monster finally lay still.

You have slain Aelea Drake Juvenile (Level 40)!
Gained 75 XP!
You have accomplished the feat Dragon Slayer!

Feats		
Name	Description	Effect
Dragon Slayer	Unlocked by slaying a dragonkin in an even or disadvantaged fight. You have faced an apex being and emerged victorious.	+5 Perk Points +1 level in Dragon Fang skill

Well done, Taog! I applaud your victory!

Taog stood panting for a moment as the ethereal scroll carrying the message from the Aesdes unrolled before him. He couldn't help but smile as he got to the last line, confirming it was Mighty Victoria herself who wrote it. His smile grew as the situation dawned on him.

A moment later, he threw his hands into the air and cheered.

"I did it! I really did it!"

He felt as if the world cheered with him.

23

The Spoils of Victory

"Ah yes, so Dragon hoards. First thing you need to do is verify what kind of dragon you're dealing with. Superintelligent ancient dragon? Score! They love treasure! Shinies and legendary artifacts galore! If, you know, the superintelligent ancient dragon said to be on par with the Aesdes themselves doesn't obliterate you in the process, so make sure you have a good exit strategy. Like exiting before the heist, if you prefer life.

"Other, less superintelligent and possibly semidivine dragons? Well . . . could range from wonderful shinies to nothing but dragon dung. And no, dragon dung is not, in fact, shiny. Do NOT ask how I know."

—Dimindium Pendem Thief Donna Undertree, on raiding dragon hoards.

Taog made his way back to the Aelea drake's home cave. Now that the battle was over and the adrenaline had worn off, he found he was utterly fatigued. The drake's cave was the safest place for him to set up camp, as the drake would have slain any rival monsters in the area and its scent would linger for a while still.

. . . Okay, Taog would also admit he wanted to check the drake's home. There were tales of dragon hoards, and an Aelea drake was technically a type of dragon! The Aesdes had confirmed it!

Taog narrowed his eyes as he returned to the clearing outside of the cave. Because even though the drake was gone, Taog could still see small sparks and distortions near the cave, indicating a high mana concentration that was approaching mana storm levels.

Taog gripped his remaining sword and slowly approached the cave.

His hair stood up, and a chill shot through him from the mana in the air. The cave was lit by the occasional sparks, and there was a flickering source of light deeper in. Taog crept inside, trying to keep to the shadows and pushing all his senses and detection skills to the limit. Yet, he caught no movement beyond the flickering lights, no signs of any life.

Soon, he found out why. At the end of the cave was a cracked orb, pulsing with light. Lightning and sparks shot from it every time it pulsed, and there were several skeletal corpses around it. Most were lying on the floor, covered in the remains of tattered robes. One was leaning against the wall, wearing the armor of an Imperial knight, clutching a book in hand.

Taog frowned. The orb looked very much like a dungeon core . . . but there was no dungeon, no traps, no monsters. It appeared to be broken and leaking mana, though apparently not enough to open a Rift, thankfully.

Taog crept over to the knight, gently reaching for the book. He wiped away the dust and dirt and opened it up. It appeared to be a journal of some sort, made from mana paper that resisted the ravages of time. Taog flipped it to the end, hoping the knight had recorded what happened here.

I tracked those goblin-sniffing cultists here. I cut them down like the monsters they are, but it was a trap. They got me, but I took every last one of them down before they did.

It brings me no comfort, however. They were performing some sort of experiment on a dungeon core. If, Aesdes forbid, they find a way to corrupt the dungeons on command—or worse, to create cores themselves—then all of Aelea is at risk. This one seems to have failed, but it is far too close to success for comfort.

My strength fails me; it is hard to even see the words on this page anymore. Please, if anyone finds this, complete my vengeance and destroy the Heralds of the New Dawn, may the Aesdes curse their name. The fate of Aelea depends on it.

Taog's eyes narrowed. Of course it would be that stupid cult again. Apparently, they'd been at this for a long time. The knight had a sword at his side. Taog reached down and picked it up, then turned to face the core and scowled.

"We'll bring those monsters down. Count on it."

He lifted the knight's sword and brought it down, shattering the orb. The sword glowed faintly with golden-and-silver light as a burst of mana surged from the core. Taog was knocked to the ground, quickly looking back up and pointing the sword forward. But the remnants of the core just faded away, leaving the air still.

You have purified a Pseudocorrupted Dungeon destabilizing the mana of the region!
You have accomplished the Feat: World Defender!
You have accomplished the Feat: Hero!
Gained the Unique Hero Skill: The Dark Hero!

Excellently done, Taog!

Taog blinked repeatedly at the message from Mighty Victoria. His eyes read the words, but it took his brain a while to comprehend—and accept—their meaning.

Back at the cove, Ateia breathed a sigh of relief as Taog defeated the dragon. Her mana disconnected from the streams flowing through the world, and the light faded from her eyes. She barely remembered to disable the emotional controls again before she plopped to the ground and her organic eye closed.

"Initiating standby sentry mode."

Colleöne gave a soft smile and picked Ateia up, carrying her to her tent. She nodded at NSLICE-00P. "She'll be fine; she just needs some rest. As do most of you, I'd imagine."

"Observation: It appears entity Colleöne's assessment is correct. The majority of NSLICE units are initiating standby sentry mode."

Colleöne smiled and raised an eyebrow. "But not yourself?"

"Explanation: Apparently, this unit had a spell that streamlined the data transfer to her own components, and so suffered less fatigue as a result."

The spell Divination has leveled three times and is now Level 4!

Colleöne nodded. "Well, it is a good opportunity. We've not had a chance to speak, NSLICE-00P. If you have anything you wish to ask of me, I am permitted to offer some counsel."

NSLICE-00P's robotic eye glowed and displayed the persons of interest once again. "Query: Do you possess any intel regarding the displayed persons of interest?"

Colleöne frowned and took a deep breath. "This may be hard to hear, NSLICE-00P, but to my knowledge, none of these people exist within Aelea. You are the first visitor from another reality we have ever encountered. While I am not all-knowing, I can confirm that the rest of the Aesdes were as surprised as I was when we found you."

"Follow-Up Query: How far does the intelligence network of entities Aesdes extend?"

Colleöne shook her head. "Farther than any that exists in this Plane. We watch over the entire Material Plane and can view the records of anything within it if we so wish. Well, our attention is not endless, so we do not keep track of *everything* that occurs, but suffice to say visitors from another world would certainly warrant our notice."

"Acknowledged."

NSLICE-00P's robotic eye flickered. At this point, she was already assuming the persons of interest were located in a separate universe, so Colleöne's statements didn't change the status of her mission. They simply confirmed that any sort of local search within this universe had a practically zero probability of success.

"Query: Do you possess any intel regarding Spatial Magic or other universe-traversing capabilities?"

Colleöne again frowned, shaking her head. "I am sorry, NSLICE-00P. Spatial Magic will not achieve what you hope for; not in the way we have designed it. It works within the structure of Aelea; it was never intended to reach beyond. We were not even aware of other realities beyond Aelea and the Source until you arrived.

"There is no precedent for what you are attempting to achieve; even the Aesdes are not certain how one would safely and successfully do so. But take heart. You are not alone in Aelea, even if you should find yourself unable to ever leave."

NSLICE-00P's robotic eye flickered rapidly. If Colleöne, one of the Aesdes apparently responsible for the foreign system stated so, then it was highly unlikely the foreign system contained the capabilities she was searching for.

Which meant that NSLICE-00P would have to develop such capabilities on her own. Which . . . was not impossible. She had already made her way through the boundary of the Material Plane once, though by a vague and largely accidental process. If she could study and codify said process, perhaps she might find a way to leave this universe. She now also had the gates between the New World and the Otter Burrow she could study, and Spatial Magic was still a possible place to start.

And a new capability had opened up to her. The use of the NSLICE network to aid a divination had revealed a new option to expand her capabilities. She had already seen the Legion mages join together to cast larger spells than any one individual was capable of.

It should be possible for her to replicate that feat using the NSLICE network, opening up spellcasting with more powerful effects than currently available to her. If she then applied that to Spatial Magic and utilized the full computing resource of the NSLICE network to iterate on the process, perhaps she could come up with spells that had no precedent.

It was something to explore once the other NSLICE units had recovered. In any case, she would not begin working on leaving the universe until the dangerous hostiles were terminated. Ritual Magic through the NSLICE network could have combat applications, so she could pursue that in the meantime, but otherwise, her focus was on terminating the threat.

"Gratitude: This unit thanks you for your assistance with the primary directive. Query: Does entity Colleöne have any intel regarding the group designated 'Heralds of the New Dawn' and any affiliated forces?"

Colleöne rubbed her chin and sighed. "The Aesdes are not supposed to intervene in the affairs of the Material Plane's inhabitants, not even to stop those opposed to us. I was sent mainly to guide you and Ateia regarding her new state, as well as your new Material Plane. It would go beyond my mandate to speak to you on them, but . . ."

Colleöne's eyes narrowed. "The Aesdes are worried. The Heralds of the New Dawn have surprised us with their capabilities, which go beyond what should have been possible for them. Even the blessings of the Realms of Mana would not have taught them how to twist the world's mana in the way they did, not to mention the creation and corruption of dungeon cores.

"It is possible . . . No, I should not speak such grave ponderings aloud and without basis. I will simply say this. Your current course is a wise one. You have achieved mighty victories thus far, but your strength is not invincible. I believe the best thing you can do at this moment is prepare for the challenges ahead."

Colleöne then gave her a wry smile. "But, well, time and time again, you have surprised even us Aesdes. I have a feeling you will do so again, no matter what may come."

"Acknowledged."

NSLICE-00P's robotic eye flickered. Well, none of what Colleöne had said on the hostiles was actually useful to her, save the vague implication that the Heralds of the New Dawn had capabilities considered nonstandard by this universe. NSLICE-00P was still on her own in terms of countering those abilities.

But that was fine. After all, terminating nonstandard threats was what the Non-Standard Leashed-Intelligence Cybernetic Enforcer was built to do. And in this case, NSLICE-00P would achieve her original purpose by any and all means necessary.

24

Non-Standard Countermeasures

"The ultimate weapon must be prepared for every eventuality. There are men who can breathe fire, and girls who can stop time itself. No expense can be spared if you want a weapon flexible enough to handle such a nonstandard range of threats."

—Dr. Ottosen, negotiating yet another increase to the NSLICE program's budget.

Since Colleöne couldn't provide any actionable intel on the hostiles, NSLICE-00P turned to the next inquiry. "Query: Does entity Colleöne possess any non-classified data regarding nonstandard capabilities displayed by the hostiles? In particular, the ability of the hostiles to forcibly relocate units?"

Colleöne held her chin and tilted her head before nodding. "Ah, you mean when they sent you to the Realms of Mana, right? Yes . . . I should be able to speak on that a bit. We did not intend for any inhabitants of the Material Plane to travel directly to the Source or the Realms of Mana, but summoning magic to call beings from the Source does exist. I suppose we should have expected someone would find a way to do the reverse."

Colleöne's eyes flashed with golden-and-silver light for a moment. She hummed and then nodded. "Ah, I see what happened. I was wondering how they did it to you; a forcible reverse summoning should have been extremely difficult, since that means removing a being from the plane it's most deeply connected to when it intends to resist. In the previous battle, it appears they deceived you into consenting to the ritual."

"Affirmative. Query: Does entity Colleöne know of any countermeasures to said tactics?"

Colleöne nodded with a serious look on her face. "Be careful what you agree to. That's generally good advice, especially if there are magic formations in the area. If you don't provide something that counts as consent for the ritual, it would be significantly more difficult for them to pull off, and you would have the opportunity to respond.

"And even if it happens again . . . you now have a way back. Your ability to enter your own Material Plane is not contingent on your location; it should be possible to open an entrance even within a Realm of Mana, and then return through a subordinate dungeon."

"Objection: If this unit must return through a subordinate dungeon, then she may not be able to return to the operational area in a tactically relevant time frame, unless there is a subordinate dungeon within the area."

Colleöne pursed her lips but nodded. "Yes, that is true."

"Follow-Up Query: Are there any other methods to immediately return to the operational area?"

Colleöne took a deep breath. "There are no formal methods to do so that I am aware of. But traveling quickly within Aelea should be significantly easier than traveling between the Source and the Material Plane."

"Acknowledged." NSLICE-00P's robotic eye flickered.

Colleöne's eyes unfocused as she stared into the air. ". . . I know where this is going. She's going to start conquering and spreading dungeons everywhere just to make sure she can come back."

Eh, I'm okay with that. Every dungeon she builds is one less for me to make!

"And what exactly do you plan to do if we get into another Great Demon Lord scenario?"

That's what the contingency plan is for? Besides, she's a hero and friends with your descendant, right? So it's fine even if she conquers everything.

Colleöne frowned. "Is it?"

That's what your husband did with all that stuff you gave him, you know.

Colleöne hung her head low.

". . . I suppose you have a point. I guess I shouldn't be complaining."

Now that Ateia's divination training had concluded, Colleöne allowed NSLICE-00P to move her drones within visual range of Taog, who rested after the fight and then began moving back in their direction. So, Taog appeared to have completed his mission and was returning to safety, while Ateia's condition was stabilizing and her training proceeding well.

As such, the most urgent issues were wrapping up, so NSLICE-00P turned her attention back to her own affairs. Mainly, developing countermeasures for the hostile nonstandards.

She had run through multiple simulations and calculations based on her and Colleöne's conversation and come to several conclusions. If Colleöne was correct, she may not require a direct countermeasure to the forcible relocation. Now that she was aware of the tactic, she could take several preemptive actions to avoid that scenario from recurring.

First of all, she had been deceived because she'd assumed the gap in her perception from the Eternal Night mana was a dungeon. That was a simple error to correct: she should avoid using predictive extrapolation to identify unknown objects she had not fully investigated.

Next was a readjustment of her social interaction protocols. The existence of factions within factions was a reality she was still getting used to; her original organization had had a very clear delineation between friendly and hostile forces. Here, it seemed that hostile forces could exist that were affiliated to cordial entities, and that affiliation with the Empire did not seem to obligate any given individual to act in accordance with the Empire's diplomatic arrangements.

NSLICE-00P was still determining how to handle the situation, but in the meantime, she decided that as per Colleöne's advice, she would avoid affirmative answers to any requests unless she had full data regarding the requestor and the full details of the request.

Likewise, she reduced the importance of cordial relations with the Empire, seeing as their value to her primary directive had dropped substantially, and that the relations could not be counted on to impact decision-making by any given Empire-affiliated individual. So, the next time she detected anomalies in a meeting place for proposed negotiations, she would investigate fully before arriving, even should it threaten the negotiations.

And lastly, she could mitigate the damage of a forcible relocation by expanding her subordinate dungeons. As long as she had a subordinate dungeon in the area of operations before any engagements, she would be able to return from a forcible relocation within a tactically relevant time frame.

And there were other benefits as well. She had clearly observed Uscfrea's subordinates utilizing the Otter Burrow gate. A network of subordinate dungeons would also act as a highly efficient transportation network, allowing her to deploy friendly forces who would retain access to their home base's logistics at will. The tactical and strategic advantages of such a network would be difficult to overstate.

NSLICE-00P concluded that the risk of the hostiles' displayed nonstandard capabilities could be mitigated to an acceptable degree. The next course of action, therefore, would be to increase her own combat capabilities, and those of her subordinates.

It was possible, perhaps likely, that the hostiles possessed additional non-standard capabilities that had not been displayed as of yet, and Colleöne had implied that NSLICE-00P would require additional upgrades to handle them. Likewise, if the friendlies could be upgraded to handle all, or at least most, of the threats NSLICE-00P had observed, then the risk of unknown capabilities could be mitigated.

And there was another angle. NSLICE-00P still had no actionable intel on the hostiles or the extent and location of their forces. The termination mission would need to begin with widespread reconnaissance to determine the scale of the enemy, and since hostilities had already begun, that reconnaissance would have to be in force, as all participating units would be subject to ambush and retaliation.

NSLICE-00P had subordinates she could deploy for scouting, but their current combat power was insufficient compared to the threats she had observed. She would need to increase the individual power of her NSLICE units if she wanted to arrange for multiple scout parties.

So, her next course of action was set.

The next morning, Colleöne continued training with Ateia, who was attempting to learn the Divination Sight without assistance from the NSLICE network or the emotional controls now, so NSLICE-00P and her monsters were left to their own devices. And this time, NSLICE-00P decided to take charge of the training.

"Request: This unit would like to conduct a group training with all currently present NSLICE units, save for NSLICE Ateia. Please note that this training will require this unit to assume command of participating units' cybernetic components as per the Loyal Wingman protocols. This unit has recently become aware of potential damage and discomfort among organic components as a result of these protocols, and so is giving all units the opportunity to opt out at this time."

01R bowed his head and saluted. "We will always follow-serve you, wise-mighty-gracious boss-queen! Everything we have is offered-available to you, yes-yes! We are happy-overjoyed to serve, yes-yes!"

All the other summoned monsters shouted their agreement while 00B let out a mighty roar.

Lilussees yawned in her room. "Um, like, depends, boss lady. I, like, need to use up some mana or something, but I'm, like, so not moving right now."

"Response: Physical movement is not predicted as necessary for this exercise."

"Oh, okay. Then, like, do what you want or something. You, like, just need these things and not me, right?"

Rattingtale's ears fell flat against his head as he watched from the side of the beach. "More horror-torture . . . but if I don't, they will single me out, yes-yes. Ugh, very well, I suppose I shall join-participate."

And so, all of NSLICE-00P's cyborg monsters linked to her through the network. She deployed all the drones as well, and Melion began watching, bouncing around as they waited in anticipation.

NSLICE-00P stood in the center of the monsters, arranging them in a formation around her. She connected to each of them and had their cybernetic components form a Light Beam spell out of their own mana. She then began to form her own, a Prismatic Bombardment circle, only with blank spots where the individual Beam spells would be. She layered her circle over her monsters', adjusting it based off her observations of the Legion's group barrier formation.

The spell had difficulty connecting to the individual magic circles. Even if their cybernetic components allowed them to form identically shaped circles, each of her monsters had different Mana Densities. Likewise, even when using the same type of mana, apparently, each individual had a unique mana signature formed out of subtle differences in the energy.

NSLICE-00P went through them one by one, using her experiences with Mana Infusion and tuning the Equalizer to adjust the parts of her magic circle that contacted each of the individual spells, joining the mana together in a way that would let it flow between.

It was a long, painstaking process; the monsters with low mana were grunting and struggling to hold their circles in place, and she couldn't even connect to Lilussees's within the Monster Hangar, so she had the spider drop the circle and simply used the extra processing resources to help adjust the others.

But eventually, NSLICE-00P hooked up each of them to the Prismatic Bombardment spell, just before any of the monsters would have dropped their circle. She tried to activate the spell . . .

The beach lit up as dozens of Light Beams fired into the sky all at once.

You have learned the skill Ritual Magic!
The skill Strategic Magic is now Level 6!
The spell Prismatic Bombardment has leveled twice and is now Level 10! A spell modifier may now be applied to the spell as a whole!

The first new countermeasure had now been successfully tested.

25

Blessings to You

"The Aesdes don't get involved. Not when the Empire of the Sun enslaved all they found. Not when Cnaeus the Bloody drowned the Empire in blood and terror. Not when Rityss the dark dragon burned Elteno to the ground. So, if the Aesdes start supporting you directly? That's when you should really worry."

—Hero Viridia Sollemnis, on blessings from the Aesdes.

NSLICE-00P analyzed the results of the Ritual Magic test while her monsters recovered. In summary, the technique had mixed results for her. Ritual Magic increased the complexity of the cast by requiring interface between many different mana sources in exchange for combining the mana pools of the participants. But combining mana pools was not necessary for NSLICE-00P.

She already had the largest mana reserves by far among the NSLICE units, and that was before the New World had increased them by a thousand. Likewise, NSLICE-00P also had the fastest mana regeneration, made even faster by the stronger connection to the Source she'd established while escaping from the Realm of Eternal Night.

And finally, NSLICE-00P had significantly higher Mana Density as well, which made her spells notably more powerful than the same spell cast by any of her subordinates. So, for NSLICE-00P, Ritual Magic might actually be a downgrade, given that participating units would run out of mana before her.

There was, however, still some benefit to this exercise.

While the Ritual Magic itself was not that efficient given her mana reserves, she did note that subordinate units could contribute processing resources to forming and maintaining the magic circles via the NSLICE network. That could have benefits when NSLICE-00P needed to split her attention. In particular, with her expanded mana pool, additional processing resources could allow her to Multicast significantly more magic circles than might otherwise be possible.

And while not as useful to herself, the linked mana pool could be a powerful tool for her subordinates if they were engaging an opponent without her. It would grant them access to parts of the magical arsenal stored in the NSLICE protocol database that they lacked the mana to cast on their own.

All in all, it was still a beneficial addition to the network's capabilities, with potential if she could modify its behavior. If, for example, she could determine a way to give her subordinates access to her mana, then hypothetically, the firepower of any given unit in the network would become equivalent to her own.

This was not currently possible. Classified documents on Ritual Magic in the Imperial Library stated that the caster leading the ritual needed Mana Density on par with or higher than all of the participants to avoid injury from mana overload.

But it was something NSLICE-00P could investigate and iterate on. After all, mana from her core already flowed through each and every one of her subordinates without causing them harm, so it should be possible for them to access consciously. It was certainly worth pursuing.

At that moment, Colleöne and Ateia stepped over to NSLICE-00P.

"NSLICE-00P, could we have a moment of your time? We could use your help for Ateia's next lesson."

"Affirmative. Command: All NSLICE units besides this unit and NSLICE Ateia may follow personal routines and directives."

As the monsters scattered to rest or continue training, NSLICE-00P walked with Colleöne and Ateia. Colleöne then turned and nodded at the pair.

"Thank you for joining us, NSLICE-00P. Ateia has now learned to mold her power like when the Aesdes were assisting her, has learned to connect with the power of Elséró flowing through the world, and also to focus herself within it. It is now time for her to learn how to direct that power. She has already started that process with Taog, though only in that she reached out to him and let him access a bit of the world's mana in the process. We will now refine that technique, and as she is connected to you, you are the best option to receive her power. Are you willing to help us with this?"

"Affirmative."

Colleöne and Ateia smiled at that. Colleöne turned to Ateia and nodded. "Okay, Ateia, like we practiced, reach out to the power of Elséró once again."

Ateia nodded and closed her eyes. Her wings began to glow slightly as she connected to the streams of Holy mana once more. Her expression twitched a bit as memories of the cult's ritual accosted her, but having succeeded at this task before, she was able to brush them aside. The memories grew fainter each time she did this.

Colleöne smiled at the sight. "Good. Now, direct your thoughts upon NSLICE-00P. Once you see her through the world instead of your eyes, ask that the world would support her. Choose one aspect to enhance, and envision how the world might aid her."

Ateia nodded. NSLICE-00P's sensors began to light up. Streams of Holy mana gradually appeared all around her, attempting to connect with her mana. As NSLICE-00P was aware of the cause, she did not attempt any resistance. The mana connected and began to pour into her.

Ateia recalled the memory of NSLICE-00P battling the Dobhar, when she'd cast magic across the entire battlefield. She imagined the power of the world expanding the magic circle that lit up the sky, of NSLICE-00P's mana surging and growing.

The power of the world reacted.

You have received a Blessing of Mana!
Total mana, mana regeneration, and Mana Density increased for the duration!

NSLICE-00P logged her mana reserves expanding. She formed and Supercharged a Prismatic Bombardment spell, firing it into the sky. Colleöne twitched and formed a barrier, blocking the beams before they went too high up.

"Sorry, it's, um, not necessarily wise to do that. I appreciate the desire to avoid unnecessary damage, but such things can . . . draw attention."

"Acknowledged. Statement: This unit will attempt to develop alternative means of testing high mana expenditure in the future."

Colleöne sighed and nodded. "That would be wise."

Meanwhile, NSLICE-00P analyzed the results of the spellcast. Her mana regenerated at an even faster rate than before, and she detected the mana from the world infusing her spell, further increasing its Mana Density and predicted firepower.

Ateia furrowed her brow, groaned, and then her eyes shot open as her concentration broke. The mana connection cut off, and the streams of mana around NSLICE-00P faded, though the mana that had already infused her lingered.

NSLICE-00P's robotic eye began flickering rapidly. Ateia now had the means to increase a friendly's mana reserves and Mana Density. The benefits were notable if marginal for NSLICE-00P; a small but welcome boost to her capabilities.

But what of her other subordinates? NSLICE-00P compared this data to the data from the Ritual Magic tests. Should Ateia apply the blessing to one of her subordinates, the higher total mana would unlock additional spells from the NSLICE database. And if Ateia grew in her Blessing ability, and her subordinates increased their personal Mana Density . . . perhaps they might be able to reach a Mana Density on par with NSLICE-00P.

Which would grant them the ability to ritual cast with NSLICE-00P's mana reserves, unlocking full access to NSLICE-00P's magical arsenal. It would take significant training to achieve, but now NSLICE-00P had identified one way to make it happen.

"Query: Does NSLICE Ateia have room in her training schedule to conduct group training with the NSLICE network?"

Rector Aemilia stood in the courtyard of the Castra Turannia Legion keep, staring up into the sky. Her retainers stood behind her with narrowed eyes, as well as a full squad of the Hiberius family's knights and Dux Canus with a squad of fully equipped legionnaires.

Up in the sky, an Imperial airship floated above the city, bearing the symbol of the Imperial family. A smaller ship had departed from the vessel and had now landed. Rector Aemilia's face twitched as the door to the ship opened and its passengers disembarked.

Princess Caecila and her retinue had arrived in Turannia.

The rector and the princess said not a word as they approached one another, both of their eyes narrowing into a glare. Their retainers glared at each other as well, hands resting on their weapons.

Rector Aemilia crossed her arms. "What are *you* doing here? Come to gloat, to 'check up' on the frontier?"

Princess Caecila shook her head. "No." She then took a deep breath. "I am here to negotiate a refugee resettlement. A large tribe of Nøkker have applied for asylum within the Empire; we would like to settle them in Turannia."

Rector Aemilia blinked, then frowned. "Well, you might as well go. Turannia has little to spare, as you well know."

Princess Caecila shook her head once again. "The Imperial family has arranged for the Naevius family's architects to construct settlements as per your preference, and will supply six months of provisions. You would be responsible only for integrating them into the Empire and your province's administration. Their leader, Iorthr, has offered to join Turannia's auxiliaries as well."

Rector Aemilia furrowed her brow, then she gave a sly smile.

"Oh, I get it. You're afraid of my father returning the favor for ruining all of his plans, now that he's gone and returned to the senate. And now you think you can toss the poor dog stuck in Turannia a couple of scraps, and she'll run to lick your feet."

Aemilia chuckled. "Well, guess what, Princess? Turannia is well and good on its own. This province has never had a brighter future than now, and that is all due to the efforts of the people *here*. We have no need for ill-intended charity from the Imperial family."

Princess Caecila simply smiled. "Well, you are not wrong. You have achieved much. The province probably doesn't need my help. But you are wrong if you believe that *you* don't."

Rector Aemilia paused at her audacity. Princess Caecila continued.

"You are right that Turannia has a bright future. I have seen the construction across your province, and the new residents in the streets of Castra Turannia. But it goes much further than that. Utrad is in complete shambles, and the Northern Court is loath to send anyone competent enough to clean it up. Utrad has been the site of several rebellions thus far; there is even talk of breaking up the province. At the bare minimum, Utrad will be under heavy scrutiny in the future. But that's a problem.

"Utrad's legions have taken a massive blow, and the Northern Court doesn't have enough spare forces to man the province on its own, particularly not after the casualties we took in that wave of corrupted dungeons. Without strong leadership in Utrad, all the Empire north of Velus's Pass is vulnerable, but the court will not allow a strong leader to rise there anytime soon.

"And with the latest chaos in the capital, the court will not pay attention to anything beyond the Imperial Heartland for quite a while."

Rector Aemilia frowned. Princess Caecila nodded. "Which means, if a strong and—above all—*loyal* province were to develop in the meantime under the leadership of the only remaining consul's family, the cornerstone of the North could shift away from Utrad, and the court would be all too happy to strip further power from the rebellious province.

"But Turannia, even with the latest influx, is still not powerful enough to do so. You received a lot of settlers and soldiers, yes, but the majority of Utrad's people remained in their homes. You must establish yourself *before* Utrad recovers, or you will lose your opportunity."

Princess Caecila's smile grew.

"So you need all the help you can get right now to build as much momentum as you can before someone competent arrives in Utrad. Turannia has lost command of the Selkies, and the rebels made off with the Northern fleet before they defected to NSLICE-00P. Whoever wishes to establish themselves as the cornerstone of the North will need a navy to throw their weight around. Integrating an aquatic race into your province and your auxiliaries would give you a strong head start."

Rector Aemilia's face twisted between several expressions. Eventually, her eyes narrowed, she smirked, and then she chuckled darkly. "You've grown quite crafty, haven't you now, you thieving vixen?"

Princess Caecila held her smile. "I beat you before by accident and luck. I've spent much time learning from both of our mistakes."

Then the princess's smile fell. "I will be honest; I still do not like you. I never wanted to see you again, and I speculate the feeling is mutual. But your punishment was harsh enough, and we were both used by your father's enemies. And the truth is, now both of our hopes ride on one Amicitia Populi Elteni who doesn't care for her own reputation and is in a complicated position after assaulting Consul Noxisius for as of yet unknown reasons.

"If we insist upon our feud during this delicate time, we shall both come to ruin, and quite possibly, the entire Northern Empire with us. Perhaps it would please you to see me and everything fall, but if not . . . I am here, and I will do all in my power to advance both our causes if we can put the past behind us, at least until the Empire is no longer at risk of disintegrating. So, what say you?"

Rector Aemilia frowned. She glanced around her. Her retainers frowned, and her assistant Maelia shook her head. She saw Dux Canus, who glanced at her with a concerned expression. She saw the soldiers of Turannia, the farmers and militia who had faced their doom at the hands of the Dobhar.

She closed her eyes and took a deep breath. Opening them, she faced Princess Caecila.

"Whoever I was before, I am now the Rector Provinciae per Turannia. And as rector, I say this: Turannia has survived by its own efforts and its own blood, with no assistance from the Empire, for years now. If you wish to give us a handout, we will take everything we can get. But if you wish to earn our trust, you will need to show us the same loyalty these men and women have given you as they struggled alone to keep the Imperial banner flying, no thanks to the court."

Rector Aemilia turned to her retainers. "Maelia, the Imperial princess has arrived to visit. Provide hospitality as befits her station, to the extent Turannia is able."

Maelia frowned but nodded. "Right away, Rector."

She then glanced back at Princess Caecila. "As for the conflicts of the court, present and past, such things matter little to the people of the frontier. And neither do you, unless you give us a reason to care."

Princess Caecila nodded. "That's what I'm here to do."

Rector Aemilia inhaled deeply before she turned to walk toward the keep. "Come, then. You've had a long journey, please avail yourself of the best my province has to offer. And then we shall discuss these refugees you speak of."

As she strode forward, Dux Canus stepped in beside her. "Are you alright?"

Rector Aemilia kept her gaze forward. "I have to be. That woman is right; this is the best move for both myself and Turannia. No matter how I feel about it."

Dux Canus gave a small smile. "And that's why I don't mind serving you, Rector Provinciae per Turannia."

26

Monstrous Blessings

What the Aesdes think of monsters and magical creatures has been a topic of vehement debate throughout history, and is a topic that would require its own work to explore in any depth. I will briefly cover the main positions here.

Magister Monstrum Decimus Bruccius Honoratus argued that animals and monsters utilize the same HP for defense and the same skills to interact with the world as we receive from the Aesdes' boons, implying they are very much a part of the Aesdes' plan for the world.

Magister Militum Cluilia Lutheria, on the other hand, points out that their use of skills is far more limited than an Enlightened's, perhaps implying they do not have access to the same breadth of boons an Enlightened does. She argues that a monster's apparent boons are something it does instinctually, and that the Aesdes enabled the Enlightened to match the monsters, rather than the other way around. Other authors have continued to expand upon these arguments, and the debate is ongoing to this day.

—*The History of Aelea*, by Hostus Tettidius Clodian

Ateia wrapped her arms around 00B's neck, rubbing her cheek against a spot of exposed fur. 00B exhaled a deep breath and grunted.

"I know we're supposed to be training—this is part of it! I need to have a clear image of you to focus on, you know?"

00B narrowed his eyes and grunted again. Ateia grinned as she shook her head. "No, I haven't felt your fur enough! And I didn't need to do this to Seero because she and I are both human."

00B sighed. Eventually, Ateia let him go and took a step back. Closing her eyes, she focused once more. 00B felt as the blessing infused him with power. The edges of his mouth curled up.

Well, he supposed the new little sister wasn't *all* bad.

* * *

Ateia stood facing 01R. She tilted her head. "So . . . your name is 01R? Um, how do you feel about that name?"

01R stood on his hind legs, crossing his arms as he held his head high. He smiled. "A great and glorious moniker bestowed-gifted to me by the wise-mighty-gracious boss-queen. I will strive-fight my entire life to live up to the expectations she placed upon me with this name, yes-yes."

Ateia blinked. She opened her mouth . . . and paused. She closed it and slowly nodded. "Yes, that's right. Well, let's get started, then?"

01R nodded. "Yes-yes, show-display your might as the newest servant of the wise-mighty-gracious boss-queen!"

Ateia closed her eyes, and her blessing infused 01R. He smiled as he felt the mana surge within him. Now . . . now he could be like the wise-mighty-gracious boss-queen!

He selected one of the stored spells. A magic circle formed in the air, the blessing vastly increasing the density of his mana, and a Light Blade formed in 01R's paws. He took a few experimental swings with it before turning to a rock on the beach. He crouched down and deployed his thrusters, shooting into the air and toward the rock. He spun around, slashing with the Blade as he passed it by. Landing, he let out a breath and then turned.

The rock was cut in twain, its halves still glowing red from where the Blade had struck. 01R began to grin. "This . . . This has great potential, yes-yes. Come, new little sister! We shall train-drill long today, yes-yes!"

A *long* while later, Ateia collapsed on the ground, and 01R had many new levels in the Light Blade spell.

After recovering, Ateia walked up to the next participant, a spider monster lying flat on the ground.

"Oh, hi, Ateia. Let's, like, get this over with."

Ateia blinked and tilted her head. "Do we know each other?"

"You don't. I'm Lilussees, or whatever. I've been with the boss lady since like, before you were, so I, like, learned your name. I, like, couldn't have avoided it if I wanted to with how much the boss lady worries about you."

Ateia flushed lightly. "Wait, Seero worries about me?"

Lilussees chittered. "It's, like, really annoying, and it cuts into my sleep. Well, I, like, hate being awake, so let's get this over with or something."

"Um, okay."

Ateia held out her hand with her eyes open. Her eyes began to glow, and her blessing infused Lilussees. Lilussees sighed as her mana pool expanded and the fatigue faded from her body.

Great. Just great. How was she supposed to drain her mana *now?* Her mana reserves were already growing with all this magic practice and making it harder and harder to drain, and now she had an *Aesdes* making them even bigger?!

She was starting to get annoyed at this human. Or Aesdes, or whatever. So, Lilussees began connecting to the drones in the area.

The boss had described the link between the cybernetic components as a web at one point, so Lilussees tried to spin a mental web between them all, taking control of their processors. She then used them all to cast a spell she couldn't be bothered with figuring out herself; one that would drain even her expanded mana and hopefully tire both her and the annoying human out.

She sighed again. It wasn't working. There was some interference from the drones' mana. Lilussees still didn't want to cast the spell on her own, so she set about tweaking her connection with the drones. Luckily, the boss lady had already done this, so Lilussees could just instruct her cybernetic components to replicate those efforts.

Suddenly, her mana linked to that of the drones. A large magic circle formed in the air and began to rain fire upon the water of the cove.

You have learned the strategic spell Rain of Fire!
You have learned the skill Strategic Magic!
You have learned the skill Ritual Magic!

Lilussees nodded to herself. *There, that should take care of that . . .*

Her mana regenerated. The Holy mana from the blessing still flowed into her. She glanced back. Ateia tilted her head, her eyes still glowing.

"Yes?"

Lilussees began to tremble. "Ugh, she's, like, gotten stronger, hasn't she? That stupid rat and his overzealous training!"

And Lilussees's plight had only begun, for NSLICE-00P had dropped what she was doing and focused on the spider, her robotic eye flickering rapidly.

"Analysis: Efficient means of Ritual Magic casting identified. Mana reserves and Mana Density notably higher than other units. Designating NSLICE Lilussees as a major combat asset and primary Ritual Magic focus for joint-network spells."

Colleöne rubbed her chin as she watched Ateia practice her blessing with each of NSLICE-00P's monsters. At the moment, they had all gathered as a group. Ateia was blessing the former spider dungeon master as the latter prepared a Ritual Magic formation, muttering complaints the entire time.

They still could not match NSLICE-00P's mystical prowess, but they could cast Strategic Magic with reasonable effectiveness. And Ateia was holding her own. In fact, some of her support was starting to affect the other monsters in the formation as well.

Colleöne nodded to herself. It was time for the next step.

NSLICE-00P and Ateia gathered together on Colleöne's request. The Aesdes nodded at NSLICE-00P.

"I think it is time we take a look at your new world, NSLICE-00P. We've done our best to integrate it into your dungeon records, but as this is ultimately a Material Plane, there will be some differences.

"As for you, Ateia, the power of the Aesdes wasn't originally meant for battle, or even blessing. We are intended to be stewards and custodians of the world, preparing and maintaining the land so its inhabitants may thrive. It is now time for you to learn this aspect of our power, in the world you are connected to."

"Affirmative."

Ateia nodded silently. Colleöne held out her hand. "Good, then could you please open the entrance to your new world, NSLICE-00P? And show me what Ateia sees?"

"Affirmative."

The vortex swirled into being. Ateia stepped into it alone. NSLICE-00P could monitor the new world from wherever she was, needing to remain here to keep the entrance open, whereas Colleöne remained outside to avoid impacting the young world with her presence.

NSLICE-00P's robotic eye lit up, displaying a holographic stream of Ateia's vision while also sending Colleöne's words to Ateia. Colleöne nodded as she watched the girl step into the center of the rock platform.

"Good, now connect to the power of that world, as you have done over here."

Ateia nodded. She closed her eyes and crouched down on the ground, placing a hand upon it. Her eyes shot open, and she blinked. "This . . . is way easier?"

Colleöne nodded. "It is the world you are connected to. We also made it into something of a dungeon that NSLICE-00P is responsible for, and you are Contracted to her, so her mana would also link you both. And finally, that world is incomparably smaller than Aelea at the moment, so it is likely far less overwhelming to you."

Ateia nodded as Colleöne continued. "Now, reach into the power of the world, and try to form it into something. A rock, a flower, a blade of grass. Start small, and do not try to shape it directly; do not try to bend the power to your will. Connect with the power and imagine what it could become, gently guiding it and allowing it to flow as it wills."

Ateia nodded and closed her eyes, focusing on the task. A patch of ground began to glow with golden-and silver-light, slowly rising, twisting, and condensing down. The glow slowly began to fade as the ground took shape.

When it was done, a small flower appeared in the dirt. Its stem and bud were silvery gray, as if made of metal, though its leaves were green and its petals white. NSLICE-00P's robotic eye began to flicker rapidly.

"Report: This unit has detected a new addition to the NSLICE network."

Colleöne blinked then rubbed her chin. "Well, that makes sense, actually. Cyborg is your primary dungeon affinity, is it not?"

"Affirmative."

Colleöne nodded. "Since we set up the new world to be part of your dungeon, your dungeon's mana flows through it as well. It is likely that your primary affinity will impact the world as it takes shape. In fact . . ."

Colleöne glanced over at the feed. A small patch of rock around the flower had also converted to metal. Colleöne sighed and shook her head.

"Well, this is a new experience for all of us, but it shouldn't be anything harmful. In any case, this is your role now, Ateia. The New World is both dungeon and Material Plane. NSLICE-00P will lead its development as a dungeon. You will care for it as a world and fill in the gaps between its dungeon and material natures. As the world and your connection to it grows, it itself will tell you what it needs."

Colleöne then gave a wry smile. "Though it will need to grow first, and that is where you come in, NSLICE-00P. We have adjusted the Rooms part of your records to allow you to expand the new world. And, well, I think an example will be the best way to show you both how and why. We have a . . . *gift* for you, shall we call it, as well as a request. Please check the Rooms records, if you will. The section for adding new rooms, to be precise."

"Affirmative."

NSLICE-00P opened the menu, and all of her processors, organic and cybernetic, paused at what she saw.

World Menu → Create World Features			
Name	**Cost**	**Upkeep**	**Description**
Cyborg Processing Center	**Free for the first instance**	**100 mana**	**A facility for upgrading compatible beings with cybernetic components. Beings in question must be Contracted to the dungeon master and willing to undergo the process with a reasonable understanding of what it entails.**

27

Trust the Process(ing)

"Fine, fine, ruin all the fun, will you? On a serious note, though? No, no, I cannot undo this. She doesn't have arms or legs anymore, not to mention the fact that many of her organs have been replaced by machinery, and the ones that are still there are heavily integrated with the cybernetic parts of her body.
"Assuming we managed to remove half this stuff without killing her in the process, she would subsequently die from missing body parts. So, unless you can grow her a new body from scratch, the machines are here to stay."

—A supergenius, on reversing NSLICE processing.

Colleöne smiled wryly. "I designed this Room to be somewhat different from the original process, basing it more on the dungeon evolution process and your feats with Ateia and the Sacred Otterkin. It should be less invasive, and more focused on supplementing the body than replacing it. No more removing perfectly healthy limbs now. I have also not included your emotional controls, and reversed some of the 'intelligence leashing' measures."

Colleöne's face scrunched up at that, but she shook her head and continued.

"In any case, you will not be able to forcibly subject people to the procedure as your original organization did. But in return, they should have a significantly easier time adjusting to the procedure than Ateia did and will not need to have their minds wiped in the process."

Colleöne's expression then turned serious. "And we are offering this one to you for free, in exchange for a request. Please utilize this facility whenever possible from now on, rather than some of your more . . . manual procedures. The emergence of new races and new Aesdes is generally less . . . *sudden* than they were in your experience."

NSLICE-00P's robotic eye began flickering as fast as it could. An NSLICE processing center had some very obvious use cases. Her nonmonster subordinates could now be integrated into the NSLICE network, and her monster subordinates no longer needed to wait for an evolution, which could be especially applicable for the monster types she had not unlocked cyber variants of, or newly Contracted monsters from outside.

And if what Colleöne said was accurate, then she had already fixed the damaging incompatibilities of the NSLICE process NSLICE-00P had recently become aware of. Though NSLICE-00P couldn't confirm this just yet, as the UI option didn't provide exact detail on the upgrade process.

Still, it was being offered for free, and she had more than enough mana to spare on the upkeep. NSLICE-00P calculated no reason why she shouldn't simply build the facility and observe it for herself.

"Gratitude: This unit thanks Friendly Colleöne for the assistance."

Colleöne nodded, and NSLICE-00P got to work.

She selected the Cyborg Processing Center. The facility was larger than the stone platform she had available in the new world; however, NSLICE-00P found she could move the facility beyond the bounds of the platform, and a transparent addition to the platform appeared.

Extend feature: Stone Platform? Growing the Material Plane will increase Max Mana and Dungeon XP income.

It appeared the extension was beneficial in and of itself. NSLICE-00P *did* have to spend some perk points to do so, but if it increased her Dungeon XP, then it would pay itself back eventually, so NSLICE-00P went ahead and finalized the purchase.

The stone platform rumbled. One of its edges began to glow, Holy mana streaming from the side. The boundary of the plane appeared, and a small hole opened up, letting unattributed mana from the Source spill in. The Holy mana contacted the unattributed mana and fused together, and then the stone platform began to grow, pushing the boundary further as well.

Once it had reached the extent NSLICE-00P had specified, it stopped. Both streams of mana faded, and the boundary disappeared from view. Then, mana appeared on top of the platform and formed into the shape of a rectangular structure. The mana faded to reveal a metal building.

NSLICE-00P looked inside, but to her surprise, there wasn't much infrastructure she could recognize. No automated assembly lines to create prosthetic limbs; no surgical equipment for installation. Rather, the structure contained a large mana core at its heart, connected via engraved magic circles to a variety of caskets and vats throughout the room.

Colleöne giggled lightly. "You seem surprised."

"Confused Observation: This unit cannot locate infrastructure necessary for NSLICE processing."

Colleöne nodded. "The room uses a magical process based on records rather than a purely physical procedure. This should make it more adaptive. Again, it is much like how you evolved Ateia."

NSLICE-00P's robotic eye flickered. "Statement: NSLICE processing centers were also utilized to perform maintenance, apply new upgrades, and swap implants for specialized mission loadouts. Query: Is this facility also capable of those tasks?"

Colleöne nodded. "Yes, it can be used to repair damaged components. As for changing implants, that is also possible. Again, it is based on records, so any implants you or your subordinates have unlocked should be available . . . as well as any others you may come up with."

NSLICE-00P's robotic eye stopped flickering and began to glow bright. If that was the case, then this facility was a full replacement for the NSLICE processing center—provided it worked as advertised. NSLICE-00P would need to test it and see it in action.

"ME! *ME-ME-ME-ME!* PICK ME, MASTER!"

A gray blob shot from her Monster Hangar at incredible speed. Melion zipped into the entrance to the New World, rushing straight toward the Cyborg Processing Center and bouncing as fast and high as they could outside the door.

Colleöne blinked and rubbed her chin. "The metal slime first, huh? Well, that would certainly put the adaptability features to the test, but it should be possible."

NSLICE-00P turned to her. "Query: Is it possible to upgrade units of questionably organic natures?"

Colleöne hummed before slowly nodding. "As I said, it is a process based more on records than on the physical body, so it will work. Though I cannot fully predict what exactly the results will be."

"Acknowledged. Warning: This facility is untested, and this unit cannot verify any of the claimed capabilities at this time. Faulty NSLICE upgrading is known to have significant risks, up to and including termination. Does Friendly Melion still wish to proceed?"

"YES!"

"Affirmative. Please proceed to processing."

"*YES-YES-YES-YES-YES!*"

Melion launched right through the door and into the nearest casket.

Would you like to convert Melion into a Cyborg? Cost: 95 Perk Points.

NSLICE-00P's robotic eye flickered at the price tag.

Cost breakdown: 1 Perk Point for each of the target's Levels. Additional 30 Perk Points required to convert species "Metal Slime" for the first time due to significant differences from existing records.

Fortunately, the foreign system included a breakdown this time, so NSLICE-00P could accept the price. In fact, it seemed reasonable to spend extra resources to convert a more powerful unit, as well as to bypass any research and development required to adjust the process for Melion's extremely nonhuman physiology.

Fortunately, the Otter Burrow income had only continued to grow over time, and now the New World had begun contributing as well, despite the lack of people within its borders. NSLICE-00P currently had over five hundred Dungeon perk points to spare, with more coming in each hour. She could afford the expense, even on an experimental procedure.

So, she predicted it was worth the cost, provided the process was successful. And while NSLICE-00P couldn't verify the facility's function at the moment, the foreign system had never failed an upgrade prior to this, so NSLICE-00P was reasonably confident in its success.

She confirmed the upgrade.

The magic core at the center of the facility began to glow, and the casket Melion had jumped into closed shut. NSLICE-00P could perceive Melion had ceased bouncing around, perhaps indicating a restful state. The lights began to travel along the engravings to the casket, which began to glow bright as well.

The process took about an hour before the lights began to fade. The casket slowly opened.

Melion has been converted into Cyborg Metal Slime!

NSLICE-00P didn't require the foreign system's message, however, as her cybernetic components had already detected a new unit requesting a link to the NSLICE network.

A moment later, Melion hopped out of the casket. Their appearance . . . was unchanged, save for a slight increase in volume. On the outside, that was. But NSLICE-00P had already linked to Melion and was running diagnostics.

It appeared that as Melion's body consisted of a homogeneous liquid they could reshape at will, the processing facility had not applied any implants to Melion's exterior—or any limb-based implants. Instead, a metal polyhedron now surrounded Melion's slime core, which in turn was surrounded by Melion's liquid metal.

The polyhedron connected to the slime core and so was able to interface with Melion's consciousness, using a magical variation of the techno-organic interface that communicated using mana instead of electrical signals. As a result, Melion was able to connect to the NSLICE network despite the lack of a conventional nervous system. In fact, if anything, NSLICE-00P noted Melion's connection was even smoother and more efficient.

It appeared Colleöne had been correct regarding the emotional controls as well. Melion did not appear to be experiencing any incompatibilities or damage from the procedure. Admittedly, this came at the cost of a number of protocols NSLICE-00P had available, but given recent events, she considered that an acceptable trade-off.

But the techno-organic interface was not the only change to Melion's implants compared to Dr. Ottosen's original designs. The process had also taken NSLICE-00P's attempts to adapt the NSLICE UI into account, so Melion was able to navigate it.

They selected a button that seemed curious to them . . .

A square nozzle broke the surface of Melion's slime, extending out slightly. It began to glow, and then the thruster engaged, and Melion rocketed into the air.

"This . . . is . . . AMAZING!"

It turned out that Melion had implants, after all. The processing facility had just stored them within a central internal device, since Melion had no other permanent limbs or body structures to hold them.

"Diagnostics on new unit complete. Results: All detected systems operational. No incompatibilities detected. Integration into NSLICE network confirmed. Implant arsenal and predicted capabilities judged as suitable. Analysis: Cyborg Processing Center appears to be highly capable and able to successfully adapt to nonstandard physiologies. Gratitude: This unit thanks Colleöne for the assistance and an improved NSLICE upgrade process."

Colleöne smiled and nodded. "You're welcome. Just try not to make any more Aesdes, okay?"

28

The New Unit

"I must say, having a built-in personal assistant and file database are quite convenient. The flamethrower is a nice touch as well."

—A member of Dr. Ottosen's sponsoring organization,
after personally undergoing the NSLICE procedure.

NSLICE-00P linked to Melion, testing some data transfers. It appeared that all had gone well; Melion again had no apparent issues with a full connection to the NSLICE network.

As such, NSLICE-00P went ahead and began transferring data and videos regarding NSLICE technology to Melion, as well as any other technologies that had been considered classified, such as the exact workings and specifications of NSLICE-00P's armaments.

Melion froze as the data transfer began. "Master . . . you're giving me your secrets?"

"Affirmative. Statement: Unit Melion has expressed interest in acting as maintenance personnel, which the NSLICE network currently lacks, and has also displayed compatible capabilities with that role. This unit would like to bring Unit Melion's knowledge base to the minimum-required levels as soon as possible."

Melion suddenly began thruster-assisted bounces all over the room. "YOU'RE THE BEST, MASTER! I WON'T LET YOU DOWN!"

And then, they immediately sat on the floor and went completely still and silent as they focused their whole attention on the materials provided. NSLICE-00P turned to her next course of action. Unit Melion's designation.

It had come to NSLICE-00P's attention that Melion was not precisely an NSLICE unit, at least as they had been designed. Melion lacked emotional controls, and their intelligence leashing measures had been reversed such that the cybernetic half followed the organic. The process by which they had been upgraded had also changed significantly, and Melion's cybernetic implants even followed a different design philosophy from Dr. Ottosen's.

As such, it was somewhat inaccurate to call them a Non-Standard Leashed-Intelligence Cybernetic Enforcer.

To be fair, the original organization had applied the NSLICE label to units it wasn't fully suited for. The fully robotic NSLICE-A warbots had also had no intelligence leashing, seeing as they had no organic components to begin with, which also meant the "Non-Standard" designation was also questionable.

In that case, the NSLICE label had been applied to signify the development and production links between the cyborg line's implants and the warbot line's components, as well as some shared protocols, and the fact that the warbots had been designed to complement the original NSLICE units.

But that no longer applied. Melion had not been upgraded by her original organization, and the links to the original design process had become tenuous. NSLICE-00P decided the connection was loose enough and Melion changed enough that a new model designation was necessary.

To that end, what should the designation be?

Upon review, very little of the original designation applied. Melion was intended as maintenance personnel, so the *Enforcer* designation was inaccurate. Likewise, *Non-Standard* was a questionable designation in a universe where every living thing NSLICE-00P had recorded had access to mana.

NSLICE-00P decided to do away with the designation and start over.

"Designation: Unit Melion's model type determined as Cybernetically Enhanced Linked Intelligence Unit."

Of course, that called into question the other units' designations. None of them had been upgraded via the actual NSLICE process, after all, and many were missing some of the protocols Dr. Ottosen had considered key, mainly the emotional controls.

Those who did, such as Ateia, had such protocols disabled and their intelligence leashing reversed to favor their organic halves. And the *Enforcer* designation had become questionable as well; of her current subordinates, only 00B and possibly the canus and felix units specifically fell under that intended mission set.

In fact, even her own designation was questionable. She had been heavily retrofitted since arriving in this universe, she had disabled her emotional controls, and most of her protocols had required heavy adjustment to adapt to this universe's conditions. And even though she was the network's main combat asset, she was also the acting command unit, so she wasn't sure if *Enforcer* was the most accurate summary of her current role.

But in the end, she decided to defer such calculations. She may eventually revert to an Enforcer role upon location of a suitable commander, so changing her own designation at this time was deemed unnecessary. As for the other units, their components and design philosophy had been based largely off of NSLICE-00P's, so the NSLICE designation was still viable, even if the upgrade process and actual use cases had deviated. She decided the new designation would apply to newly upgraded units from now on.

"Master, I have a question!"

"Acknowledged."

And so, NSLICE-00P turned her attention to the CELIU unit Melion instead.

Ateia and the newly upgraded Melion left the New World and returned to the beach, where NSLICE-00P worked with Melion, answering any questions they had on technology from her original world. Once they had a general overview, Melion and NSLICE-00P began a joint analysis of one of the drone golems.

Melion, being a golem creator themselves, was extremely curious about the blending of electrical and mana-based technologies the Aesdes had created. Meanwhile, NSLICE-00P had bumped the priority of drone-technology development, given the need to scout for the hostile Heralds of the New Dawn.

Ateia joined the other monsters in combat training. She had taken a break from the blessing practice and was currently exploring some of her other capabilities. Taking a deep breath, she reached into her cybernetic half, selecting one of the weapon protocols.

She winced only a bit, her brain tingling as she let the protocol take over. She was getting used to the NSLICE network's presence now, and the knowledge that her organic half could take back command at any time eased the strange feeling. So, she quickly shook it off as the protocol activated, the cybernetic components lifting her arm with her palm facing forward.

A circle began to glow on her palm while her wings and core lit up. A beam of golden-and-silver light fired from her palm into the water of the cove. Ateia blinked as the protocol concluded. She turned her palm back toward herself and stared at it.

"I . . . have Seero beams now?"

Her cybernetic components responded by displaying a list of all the installed weaponry she now possessed. She started to grin when something appeared on her sensors, informing her of an incoming mana signature. She turned her attention to it, and her eyes widened.

She turned from the beach and ran toward the nearby forest. After a few minutes of running through the foliage, she arrived at the signature's location.

Taog had returned, a bit dirty and scratched up, but grinning. He had a new sword strapped to his side, and an Aelea drake scale held under one arm. Ateia ran toward him, but then stopped herself and crossed her arms. She glared at him.

"Taog, what do you have to say for yourself?"

He gave a sheepish grin and rubbed the back of his head. "Sorry, I know it was . . . not very smart to go off alone."

Ateia's eyes narrowed. "Not very smart? More like incredibly dumb, or so you *always* told me!"

Taog glanced away. Ateia sighed, then stepped forward and hugged him.

"I'm just glad you're okay. Please, don't do something like that again."

Taog returned her embrace. "I won't. I promise. In fact, that's why I had to do this."

The two stepped away from each other. Taog pulled out his new sword and stirred up his mana. The blade was immediately coated in pitch black. He grinned.

"Now I can follow you wherever you go."

Ateia sighed and shook her head before grinning. "You always could, but I'll admit that *does* seem cool."

Taog's grin grew. "That's only the start of it."

After a brief conversation on Taog's journey, Ateia and Taog returned to the beach together, where he walked over to Colleöne.

"Thank you, Mighty Victoria, for your help."

Colleöne smiled and shook her head. "I only pointed you in the right direction and rewarded you for your deeds, Taog. It was you who accomplished this victory." She then glanced over at Ateia and winked at Taog. "Though, perhaps not entirely without assistance."

Taog's eyes widened a bit, but then he nodded. "So that was Ateia I heard."

Colleöne smiled. "Technically, you have the favor of the Aesdes now, Taog. I would advise you to cherish that relationship, but I do not think you need to be told that."

Taog shook his head and Colleöne nodded. "What I will say is this: Learn to rely on one another. Do not let this victory convince you that you must do everything yourself. We all need someone we can show our weakness to, and that's something that must go both ways."

Taog furrowed his brow and nodded at that. "I'll consider your words, Mighty Victoria. Thank you again for your guidance."

Colleöne just continued to smile. "Think nothing of it. Go ahead and rejoin your friends."

He nodded and walked over to NSLICE-00P.

"Greeting: This unit is pleased to see Friendly Taog return in fully functional condition."

Taog grinned. "Glad to see you too, Seero. Um, if you don't mind, I have a request."

Ateia raised an eyebrow at that.

"Affirmative. Please state the request."

Taog took a deep breath. He glanced at Ateia, then turned to look NSLICE-00P in the eye. "Ateia's your subordinate now, right? Something like a dungeon monster? Is it possible for me to become one too, like through a Contract?"

Ateia's eyes widened. "Taog, what are you saying?"

Taog turned to face her. "I know it wasn't exactly something you decided, but I want to follow you wherever you go. Seero came into our lives and shattered every obstacle in our way while I was too afraid to even try. She didn't hesitate when faced with armies or dungeons or cults or whatever. She's an example of what I want to become; she's someone worth following, and she deserves my loyalty as both our friend and savior.

"I don't know how much I can do, but I want to pay her back however I can, at least a little. And what better way to do that than to join you in following after her?"

Ateia fell silent while Taog turned back to NSLICE-00P. "If that's what you want, that is, Seero. If you'll have me, I would like to follow you."

NSLICE-00P saw no reason to refuse.

Taog Sutharlan has offered to become your full subordinate. Accept?

"Affirmative."

New Contract signed! Existing Contract updated!
Taog Sutharlan added as a full subordinate!

Taog smiled as he felt the Contract connection between him and NSLICE-00P deepen.

"Thanks, Seero. I'll do whatever you need me to—"

"Query: Does Friendly Taog also wish to receive cybernetic upgrades and integrate into the NSLICE network?"

Taog paused, and then blinked. "Wait, what?"

29

The Dark Hero

"I may be the hero you need, but I'm not the one you deserve."

—Hero Viridia Sollemnis, when refusing to join an offensive against the Empire of the Sun.

Taog took a deep breath, rubbing his chin. Ateia had spoken to him about the nature of her cybernetic implants once she understood it herself, so Taog was at least partially aware of what a cyborg was.

"You mean . . . get the same kind of armor you and Ateia have? And . . . replace my arms and legs and stuff? And hook into my mind somehow?"

"Clarification: Friendly Taog is mostly correct; however, Friendly Colleöne has claimed the new processing facility will not remove limbs as part of the process. This unit has not tested the procedure on a humanoid subject, and so cannot fully verify those claims at this time, but predicts the claim is likely accurate."

"That's . . ."

Taog rubbed his chin. Ateia frowned and fidgeted to his side. "Taog . . ."

He turned to look at her and took a deep breath. "I know what you want to say. It wasn't very pleasant for you at first, right? And you're worried I would do this just because I said I wanted to follow after you?"

Ateia stayed silent for a bit, but then slowly nodded. Taog grinned at her. "Well, I'm not excited for the painful aspect, but I'm not going to do this just because. It's more than just armor, right? It connects you to Seero somehow, lets you understand her, right?"

Ateia slowly nodded. Taog nodded back before turning to face NSLICE-00P. "I've decided to follow Seero, so I want to understand her and be as helpful to her as I can. So, Seero, if you want me to, I'll do that upgrade thing."

"Acknowledged. Affirmative Statement: This unit highly recommends cybernetic upgrades to improve efficiency and enable integration into the NSLICE network."

Taog nodded. "Then let's do it."

"Affirmative."

NSLICE-00P opened up an entrance to the New World. Ateia had a complicated look on her face, but she led Taog inside. A short while later, Taog exited the processing facility.

Metal armor covered his torso and half his head. A metal exoskeleton covered the outer half of his arms, leading to metal gauntlets over his elbows and the top of his hands. A metal exoskeleton supported his legs as well. He still had both of his organic eyes, but one was covered with an eyepiece that simulated a robotic eye's effects.

"Whoa . . ."

Panels opened and closed all over his armor as his new cybernetic half ran diagnostics. Armor extended out from his limb exoskeletons, fully encasing his organic limbs before receding back. A helmet engaged and disengaged, and his vision lit up with illusions that resembled the records from the Aesdes. And then, a message passed before his eyes.

Connection established. Linking to nearby NSLICE units.

Suddenly, he could feel his thoughts expand beyond himself. Like sparks traveling from his mind into the metal parts in his head, then out into the air . . . and into the metal parts of someone else.

"Ateia?"

Ateia gave a complicated smile. She didn't say anything out loud. Instead, another message passed before Taog's eyes.

"Hi, Taog."

He grinned. Holding up his hand, he turned it to glance at the metal armor around it before he clenched it into a fist.

"Let's pull some Seeros."

Taog and Ateia exited the New World and found the rest of NSLICE-00P's subordinates waiting. 01R crossed his arms.

"Hmm . . . you have been most suspicious-disrespectful toward the wise-mighty-gracious boss-queen, yes-yes. But . . . if she has deigned-decided in her unfathomable grace and kindness to accept you anyway, then so shall we. Welcome, new little brother, to the wise-mighty-gracious boss-queen's army! May you fight-strive always to honor her name."

Taog blinked repeatedly at the sight before him. "Um, I'll do my best?"

And so CELIU Taog joined the network.

Taog held his blade as he stood on the beach. Taking a deep breath, he then activated his new skill.

Active Skills		
Name	Level	Description
Dark Shroud	1	Unique Hero Skill for Taog Sutharlan. Wraps user in a fusion of Dark and Holy mana at double user's normal Mana Density, providing defense and concealment. May use to empower physical attacks or cast Dark and Holy spells. Dark Shroud cycles with the user's mana and so costs no additional mana to maintain, though mana must be spent to replenish it after defending from attacks or using offensively.

His mana began to form a stream around him, converting into Dark mana but with an occasional silver glow. He focused on concealment, and he shimmered and vanished from view. Interestingly, he also felt his connection to the NSLICE network fade. It appeared his cybernetic components were restricting the external signals they were sending out in response to his desire for stealth.

Focusing on defense, he reappeared, the Dark Shroud instead turning an even darker black glowing with a silver undertone. He then took a deep breath and lifted his sword. Responding to his will, the Dark Shroud coated his sword, forming a Dark Blade over top of it.

He grinned and swung his blade, activating the Spellstrike skill and the Dark Bolt spell. The mana responded with ease, forming into a bolt-size arc of Dark mana that flew off into the water of the cove. Taog grinned. It seemed he would not need to throw his swords from now on.

Ateia watched, holding her chin as she saw the Dark Magic fly from Taog's blade. "Was that some kind of skill?"

Taog turned to her and shook his head. "I got some sort of 'Spellstrike' skill; it lets me cast magic with my sword."

As Taog spoke, his cybernetic components linked to Ateia's and sent her data on the skill and his most recent activation of it. She blinked as the information streamed into her mind.

"Hm, I wonder . . ."

Taog tilted his head as Ateia walked off, though she quickly returned, holding her bow in hand. She nocked and drew an arrow, her cybernetic arm now able to hold the bow drawn for as long as she pleased, so she was free to take her time and focus.

Reaching into the NSLICE spell database, she selected Light Bolt, as that was the attribute she was most naturally suited for. She formed the magic circle in the air, then tried to move the mana toward her arrow like Taog had with his sword.

Her robotic eye began flickering as her cybernetic half moved to support the effort, comparing the spell activation from the magic circle to Taog's to adjust the movements of the mana. Her Aesdes half focused, and her Holy mana moved along those patterns, reinforcing the effort.

The spell circle activated, but no bolt appeared. Instead, her arrow began to glow. She let it loose, and it shot through the air in a perfectly straight line. It struck an incoming wave . . . and then a bolt of Light mana shot from the tip of the arrow into the wave. Ateia blinked, then slowly smiled.

"It worked . . ."

Taog blinked before crossing his arms. "That's not fair, Ateia."

She turned and smirked at him. Stepping forward, she poked his side before realizing his torso was coated in metal, then poked his exposed cheek instead. "You have access to that database too, you know? And Seero can apparently convert ALL of her spells into any attribute she knows."

Taog tilted his head. "Huh? What do you mean?"

Ateia's grin grew. "Your cybernetic half can show you how to cast a Dark-attribute version of any spell Seero has ever cast."

His eye went as wide as it could. ". . . That's Seero for you. Um, could you show me how?"

She placed a finger on her chin. "Well . . . I *could*, but that might not be *fair* you know?"

He groaned and slapped his face. "Ugh, I'm sorry."

Ateia giggled and linked her cybernetic half to Taog's, showing him the NSLICE protocol database. She smiled at him. "We're all in this together, you know? I know you're excited to become strong, and you've always wanted to protect me, right? But how about this instead: Let's become strong together, and protect each other?"

Taog flushed, but slowly nodded. "That . . . doesn't sound too bad."

Ateia smiled wider and then opened the database to the spell section. "Well, let's take a look, then. Seero shares all of her skills and spells with the entire network, you know? She wants us all to, as you might say, pull a Seero if we can."

Taog flushed even deeper at that as Ateia laughed at him. But his embarrassment faded as the list of spells passed before his eyes. As Ateia had stated, NSLICE-00P had shared her entire magical arsenal with them. Still, just having access to a spell circle was only the beginning; it would still take a lot of time and effort to learn even just one of them. It's not like he could just select one of these and instantly cast—

Dark Beam protocol downloaded. Executing command.

His robotic eye flickered. A magic circle formed in the air, his Dark Shroud moving to fill it. A black beam with a silver glow shot into the cove.

You have learned the spell Dark Beam!

Taog stood completely still as he stared out at where the beam had struck. His mind went completely blank. Ateia gave him a huge grin.

"How's that for not fair?"

Colleöne smiled as she watched the two teens from a distance. She then turned away and began rubbing her chin. Eventually, she heaved a sigh.

"She formed her power into a skill she had never used before. She's really come into her own, huh? Even faster than I thought."

Colleöne glanced back at Ateia and took a deep breath. "I guess . . . that's just about it, then."

She lingered for a while longer, then took a step forward.

30

The Mandate of the Aedes

Letoris. The mythical lost continent. There are very few records on Letoris available to those of us in the Elteni Empire, and almost none of them are contemporary and trustworthy, which makes any serious scholarship on the topic practically impossible. Yet, we have enough records, corroborated with surviving eyewitnesses from the Celestial Empire, to state a few facts with certainty, and therefore, any history of Aelea must mention the continent as historical reality. The facts are as follows.

One, a continent named Letoris did, in fact, exist.

Two, something occurred there that required the Aesdes to intervene in person.

Three, Letoris subsequently vanished from the surface of Aelea, never to be seen again.

The Celestial Empire has withheld all records and eyewitness testimonies it may possess on those events, so no greater detail can be stated with reasonable certainty.

These facts, and the lack of greater detail, have made these events a source of great curiosity for individuals from all professions, especially theologians. The fate of Letoris, which is largely presumed to be the result of the Aesdes' direct intervention, has become the primary explanation for why the Aesdes leave us to handle our own affairs.

—*The History of Aelea*, by Hostus Tettidius Clodian

Colleöne walked toward Taog and Ateia, who noticed her and waved with a big grin on her face. Colleöne's resolve wavered, but she was not the Lady of Courage and Victory for nothing, so she continued on. She nodded at the girl.

"You have done well, Ateia. By my reckoning, you have developed a solid foundation and a firm grasp upon your abilities. They are unlikely to run amok again, and you have what you need to find a way forward."

Ateia's smile grew. "All thanks to you, Mighty Victoria!"

Colleöne took a deep breath. "Which means . . . it is time for our final lesson."

Ateia froze in place. ". . . Final?"

Colleöne gave a sad smile. "Yes. Upon conclusion of your training, I must return to the Blessed Land."

Ateia's smile dropped. "Why? Couldn't you help us against the Heralds? They want to destroy the world!"

Colleöne frowned and heaved a sigh. "I wish I could. But it is not the place of the Aesdes to command the inhabitants of Aelea how to live. We only prepare the land and grant you the tools necessary to thrive; it is up to you all to decide what you will do with it. Even if that means you will oppose us.

"We have learned that our great power and vast sight does not mean we are perfect; the last time we intervened directly, an entire continent was lost. So, we will only do so again under the gravest of circumstances, and instead believe in the heroes of Aelea to rise to the challenge."

Colleöne placed her hand on Ateia's shoulder and gently rubbed it. "It is only due to your unique circumstances that I was given leave to come to you, and I am ever grateful for the chance. But I do not believe this is our final goodbye. While you will be the sole Aesdes walking the world, I will still be watching over you. And as an Aesdes, the gates of the Blessed Land are open to you, once you find your way there. We will reunite there one day."

Ateia bit her lip. Colleöne patted her shoulder and then glanced at Taog with a smile. "And take heart, Ateia. I may need to leave, but you will not be left alone. Your friends will be with you every step of the way."

Ateia glanced over at Taog while her cybernetic components reviewed the status of NSLICE-00P and her monsters. She slowly nodded and took a deep breath. "What's the lesson?"

Colleöne let go of Ateia's shoulder, taking a step back. "You have enough of a foundation to make your own way from now on. So, the only thing left you need to learn from me is how to conceal your power and appear fully human. This will also teach you how to focus your current form upon a given record, which one day may allow you to adjust your form should you wish to. Are you ready to begin?"

Ateia looked up at Colleöne and nodded. "Yes, let's do it."

Colleöne spent some time teaching Ateia how to conceal her powers. In Ateia's case, this was actually easier than it was for the other Aesdes—as she had lived most of her life as a human, it was not hard for her to act like one and focus upon that record. She managed to pull off the concealment in record time.

Which meant that Colleöne's final lesson had come to a close, and she'd reached the end of her mandate. Colleöne now stood on the beach, with Ateia, Taog, and NSLICE-00P standing before her.

She faced them and nodded.

"You have learned to channel your power as an Aesdes. You have adjusted to your new form as a cyborg. Your stature and might grows by the day, and you have a quest laid out before you. You have joined together with your companions, who each have grown as well."

She took a deep breath and gave a smile. "I am proud of your efforts, and what you have managed to achieve, even in the midst of troubling and chaotic circumstances. You are ready now, and no longer require my guidance."

Ateia bit her lip and looked down, but then took a deep breath and saluted. "Thanks for the help, Mighty Victoria."

Colleöne's expression wavered. A moment later, she flung herself forward and embraced Ateia in a hug. "I am sorry, Ateia, for all I have put you through. I am sorry for all that you have gone through because of my blood. And I am sorry that I must depart from you now."

Ateia's eyes widened and started to moisten. "I . . . I don't care about that. Just, do you really have to go?"

Colleöne's eyes got teary, and she tightened her grip. "I would stay if I could. But I know that even though I must leave now, this will not be the last time we see one another. Know that I will always be watching over you and praying for your success and happiness. If you would permit it, I would love to consider you as my family, and me yours."

Ateia didn't respond, as tears began to drip from her eyes. But she slowly returned Colleöne's embrace. Colleöne smiled softly and rubbed her back. "Please, come to visit someday. I do not know when next I will be permitted to walk the surface of Aelea, but should I gain leave, I will come to you right away."

Eventually, Colleöne separated from Ateia, glancing at NSLICE-00P and Taog. "Please, take care of Ateia for me."

"Acknowledgement: Defense of NSLICE Ateia is a major directive for this unit, on top of protocols detailing the defense of network assets."

Taog nodded his head and saluted. "I will."

Colleöne nodded back then took a deep breath. "May you find the courage to seize victory, wherever you shall go. May you find happiness and joy in all your days." She winked, then frowned. "And may you deal those Herald jerks a heavy blow on behalf of the Lady of Courage and Victory!"

She then vanished in a flash of light. Ateia watched as the flash broke apart into sparkling motes of light that lingered for a bit, holding out her hand to one of them.

"Ateia . . ." Taog frowned. This was yet another mentor figure who had left their lives, and Ateia had never known her mother, either. So he didn't know what to expect when Ateia turned back around. She still had moist eyes, but there was a calm expression on her face.

"It is not the end. This is not like the time with my father. We know where she is, and that she is still looking out for us. And she's right about one thing."

Ateia clenched her fist and gave a dark smile. "We owe that cult a debt we're going to repay with interest. Mighty Victoria has even asked us to hit them on her behalf, and I also owe them hits for myself, my father, my mother, Agedia, Seero, and everyone in this world they've hurt and are planning to hurt. We've got a lot of beatings to do."

"Caveat: This unit must state that she will prioritize efficient termination of the hostiles. Multiple strikes may not occur, as this unit will endeavor to terminate hostiles with the first blow if at all possible."

Ateia blinked for a second, then burst out laughing, Taog joining her. "T-That's fine, Seero. If that happens, we'll just say that hit counts for everyone!"

"Affirmative."

Back in the Blessed Land, Colleöne and Shialnor once again stood before Anualë, waiting for him to review their latest work. Anualë raised an eyebrow.

"So, this Taog has become a hero, huh?"

Colleöne nodded calmly. "Yes, he destroyed a damaged core destabilizing the region after defeating its powerful guardian at great risk to himself."

Anualë kept his gaze on Colleöne. "Yes, I agree his deeds qualify. They were a bit on the lower end but still within reason, and he *is* challenging those who threaten the world, so I have nothing to say on him receiving the title for his deeds. What I do question is the process by which he landed in that situation to begin with."

Colleöne took a deep breath and hung her head as Anualë narrowed his eyes.

"Colleöne, Lady of Courage and Victory, She Who Guides the Champions of the World. Do you have anything more to say?"

Colleöne faced him, looking into his eyes even as her expression stiffened.

"I . . . sent Taog in that direction, knowing that a core damaged just enough to qualify as corrupted but not actually displaying the powers and defenses a truly corrupted core might was there. And I knew that my presence and Ateia's training would stimulate the flows of Holy mana in the region, suppressing the monsters in the area to make his journey easier."

Anualë crossed his arms. "And what would you have done should he have failed?"

Colleöne took a deep breath, but she resolved herself and continued to hold Anualë's gaze.

"I would have intervened directly to save his life, should it have proved necessary. I chose to believe he would emerge victorious, but I would not have withheld my power if he had not." Her face then fell, her shoulders drooped, and her voice shrank to a whisper. ". . . I suppose that in the end, I have not changed.

When push comes to shove, I will not abandon those whom I love, even if I must break our mandate to do so. Regardless of the consequences for the world."

Anualë heaved a sigh. Well, he couldn't say he was completely surprised at this turn of events. Colleöne had the mandate to assist Ateia, and also felt responsible for the girl's suffering, given that it was Colleöne's blood that had attracted the cult to Ateia's family in the first place. It was only natural that Colleöne would feel compassion for Ateia's companions as well and would refuse to allow Ateia to suffer further loss.

"As you well know, we grant assistance to heroes when the inhabitants of Aelea face challenges they cannot reasonably be expected to handle alone; especially challenges that come from external sources, or from our own mistakes. And we do not choose or raise heroes ourselves, but simply acknowledge those who have risen to the challenge on their own."

Colleöne straightened herself as Anualë gazed at her.

"What you have done goes against this spirit, if not the letter of the conditions we have agreed to regarding heroes. I will state that in this case, I find it somewhat justifiable, as the Heralds of the New Dawn do seem to have lore and power beyond what they should, and Taog now seeks to confront them. But a coincidentally appropriate circumstance does not excuse your intent, nor your willingness to have broken your mandate should the outcome have defied your hopes. I trust you understand what you have done?"

Colleöne took a deep breath and nodded. "Yes, and I will accept your judgment."

Anualë nodded. Colleöne had her moments, but she worked tirelessly to protect the world as the Lady of Courage and Victory, as well as to atone for the situation with Velus.

Even in this circumstance, he could see she'd held back a bit; she had guided Taog to a place where he could accomplish the necessary feats, rather than simply gifting him with extra assistance as she had with Velus. It was a step in the right direction, even if it was still a step too far.

"We will accept Taog as a hero, given the situation he finds himself in and that he was not aware you would have assisted him should he have failed. But as for yourself, you will work on the newest continent and take over Shialnor's dungeon creation duties there. You shall lay down your duties as She Who Guides the Champions of the World until the new continent has fully stabilized. I shall assume your duties in the meantime."

Colleöne gritted her teeth but bowed her head. It seemed she would not be able to watch over Ateia and company after all, at least for a time, but she would accept the consequences of her decisions. Shialnor perked up at the mention of her duties.

"As you say, First of the Aesdes."

Shialnor began to grin, and was about to poke Colleöne's side when Anualë turned his gaze to her.

"This will give Shialnor an opportunity to complete her duties regarding the new Material Plane, which I consider of the utmost importance. In fact, I will expect regular updates on this, Shialnor, particularly as I am assuming Colleöne's role and specifically turning my gaze to NSLICE-00P. Additionally, Colleöne is not the only one who has not acted in a manner becoming of the Aesdes. We shall discuss your behavior toward her further."

Shialnor froze and then crumpled down into a ball. She whispered in a tiny voice, "As you say, First of the Aesdes." She then departed, but Colleöne lingered a while longer.

Anualë took a deep breath. "You may speak, Colleöne."

She looked up at him. "Anualë, I know I have no right to ask this, but . . . will you look after Ateia on my behalf, while I am gone?"

Anualë crossed his arms. "I will watch and support them as I would any champion of the world, Colleöne. You know this."

Her head dropped. Anualë watched for a moment before heaving a sigh. "But . . . I suppose I *will* be paying a bit more attention to that group, considering events thus far. If only because of this situation with the Heralds of the New Dawn."

Colleöne perked up. Her eyes teared slightly as she bowed her head. "Thank you, Anualë."

Anualë sighed and shook his head, then waved his hand. "Go on, then."

He shook his head again as Colleöne left. He . . . might be a bit too soft for his role. But Colleöne did strive her best to live to the standards he set forth, and worked diligently and fairly the vast majority of the time, so perhaps he was predisposed to cut her some slack on her indiscretions. Unlike a certain someone.

But well, try as she might to teach them, no one was as good at weaving together cores and creating autonomous systems as Shialnor. Good enough for him to put up with her . . . *less* than stellar motivation and all her attempts to defer her responsibilities. Even Colleöne's work was based on the foundation that Shialnor had created, after all.

And so, Anualë began to turn his attention to that very work, linking to one of the massive magic cores at the heart of the Blessed Land. Shialnor had done a very good job trying to lighten her own workload, and Colleöne's mirror work benefited as well. Both systems now largely ran themselves. Anualë just needed to pay attention to problem cases and approve certain boons, such as the granting of the Hero feat, as well as make note of any major problems that would need to be addressed.

He furrowed his brow. As it turned out, there was another reason why he was going to pay special attention to NSLICE-00P and her companions. He had not shared this with Colleöne or Shialnor—or anyone, for that matter—but the investigation of the Heralds of the New Dawn had returned a grim conclusion.

There was no lore among the intelligent species of Aelea, nor within either Shialnor or Colleöne's boons, that might have enabled the Heralds of the New Dawn to achieve what they had, especially regarding the intentional creation and corruption of dungeon cores.

Even the Lords of Mana would not have been able to provide such knowledge, seeing as dungeon cores were the direct work of the Aesdes themselves . . . a certain cyborg with some sort of machine that could apparently make itself into a core aside. Which implied one of two possibilities.

First was that the Lords of Mana had come to understand the dungeon cores on a deep level. That idea was deeply troubling, as it defied everything the Aesdes knew about them. The Lords of Mana were powerful and intelligent, but they, like everything else in the Realms of Mana, were restricted by the nature of their existence.

At the end of the day, the Realms of Mana were a reflection of the Material Plane, and the Lords that ruled them were no exception.

The Lord of Fire, for example, knew all there was to know about fire and all its aspects, but he did not know anything about any topic besides fire, save for its interactions with his Realm. He *couldn't* know, for his entire existence was defined by fire. For him to grow beyond fire would be for him to change his fundamental nature, and for the "Lord of Fire" to cease to exist.

He could burn a dungeon core. He could grant Fire to a dungeon core as an affinity. He could learn how a dungeon core utilized fire in new ways and replicate them or combine them with other aspects of fire to create novel combinations. But he could not learn what a dungeon core was—not at a fundamental level—for it was not fire. He could not understand it to the extent that he could corrupt its core function like these cultists had.

So, either the Lords of Mana had grown into a new class of being entirely . . .

Or it was the second possibility that was responsible for the cult's achievements. A possibility far simpler, yet no less terrifying. And that was that the cult had help from someone who truly understood the nature of dungeons. And since they could find no lore among the intelligent species of Aelea that indicated that level of understanding . . . there was only one possibility.

It was someone from the Blessed Land who had aided the Heralds of the New Dawn.

A chilling thought. Which was why Anualë now turned his gaze to the individuals at the heart of it all. NSLICE-00P had put a stop to the cult's plans, so whoever their benefactor was would now turn their gaze to her. They had to if they wanted to succeed. And Anualë would be watching for if or when they made a move on her.

Which was why he had sent Colleöne in the first place. He did not have enough information to change the rules just yet, but since all evidence and speculation pointed to the cult having assistance that they shouldn't . . . then a bit of extra help might be justified for the individuals dealing with it.

He knew that Colleöne would ultimately do everything within her power and mandate to help Ateia and her allies, though he had hoped she wouldn't cross the line into direct interference. Still, given her history, he couldn't let her off the hook, even if she was just shy of acceptable this time.

After all, the rise of Velus's Empire had ended up a happy accident as far as the development of Aelea went, but he did not want to roll the dice on a second such incident. Though, at the rate she was going, NSLICE-00P was going to change the world to a similar degree regardless of whether or not the Aesdes interacted with her at all.

Indeed, creating a new species, a new Material Plane, and a new Aesdes each alone surpassed anything Velus had done.

But regardless, it would be cruel of him to send Colleöne away and then let her kin fall when he knew they were likely to be targeted by forces possibly beyond mortal ken. So, Anualë prepared to watch over Ateia much as Colleöne had promised, to provide the group as much assistance as allowed within his own rules for the Aesdes . . .

And possibly even to intervene himself, should the unthinkable turn out to be true.

SIDE STORY

The Hero's Quest

Far to the east, beyond the borders of the Empire, a dungeon stood amid a desert oasis. A stone structure rose from the center of the oasis, a vortex swirling in place of its entrance. The air distorted near the gateway, and cracks of mana lightning shot from the vortex.

Inside the dungeon were a series of underground caves and tunnels made of a combination of dirt and stone. And within those tunnels, the sounds of battle raged. The clanging of metal, the shouts of men and women, and the chittering and squealing of rodents. Lots and lots of rodents.

A small group of heavily armed warriors stood amid a sea of fur and fangs, the ground drenched in the blood of their foes, with armored knights cutting down the rodents all around. At their center stood a man with a bow and light armor, golden-and-silver light wrapping around his arrows as they pierced through dozens of ratkin with every shot.

The Hero of Elteno heaved a sigh. "Of course it *had* to be a Verminflood dungeon."

A battlemage to his left let loose a mighty torrent of flame and then shrugged. "Speak for yourself. I much prefer this to that Inferno dungeon. At least I can set these things on fire."

A recovery knight in plate armor behind them raised an eyebrow as he struck down the Ratkin assassin sneaking behind them. "Really? Weren't you the one complaining every step of the way in that Overgrowth dungeon?"

The battlemage scoffed as she prepared another spell. "Oh, I'm sorry. You try continuously casting spells for forty-eight hours straight."

The recovery knight smirked. "Clearly you've never gone through recovery knight training."

The Hero of Elteno sighed. Well, at least they were having fun. He turned his attention to the front. An Elf in silk robes danced across the front lines, lashing out with a curved glaive of Celestial design. He had clear, pale skin without a single spot or blemish, and his long black hair was tied into a ponytail.

He held the line not with shield and strength but by a deadly storm of sword slashes that struck down any Ratkin foolish enough to approach. And yet, he somehow managed to avoid even a single speck of blood landing on his white robes.

"How are we doing, Liulëa?"

The Celestial Elf scoffed. "I fear such filth stains my poor blade. This young master doubts he will find even a single worthy opponent in this place."

A group of rodents tried to circle around him, only for a smoke bomb to explode in their face. A small Lizardkin in formfitting black clothing appeared, tossing a fan of poisoned knives into the confused monsters.

"What the young master means to say is he is about to collapse with fatigue, and very much hopes we are close to the boss."

The Celestial Elf panicked even as an arc of mana flew from his blade, cutting down an entire squad of rats. "Khokoh! You dare dishonor your master so?"

Khokoh shrugged as she tossed an explosive bomb into a pack of Ratkin. "Young Master, we are in the midst of battle with trusted allies, not visiting some rival family. You are permitted to speak the truth, and I strongly recommend you do so."

The Hero of Elteno nodded at the Lizardkin. "We could all use a break. Let's rest up one more time before we push forward. Archon Nolnyth, can we get an assist?"

In the center of the group was a group of Elves in black scale mail armor. They all had dark, tanned skin and white hair. The woman at their center scoffed and stepped forward. She waved her hand, and a massive magic circle appeared.

A wave of fire surrounded the group, burning so bright it appeared pure white. As the rodents turned to ash, the rest of the Sun Elves set up a perimeter while the Hero of Elteno's party set up camp. The woman, Archon Nolnyth, scoffed.

"Pathetic. I expected better from the *Empire's best*, not to mention a young master of those Celestial fools."

The battlemage smirked at her. "And which Sun Elf Archon was it who needed help from the pathetic Imperials again?"

Nolnyth scowled, then scoffed and turned to command the defense. The recovery knight crossed his arms. "You're going to pay for that, you know? How about you try not antagonizing the one Sun Elf with a lick of sanity?"

The battlemage grinned and shrugged. "Worth it. She might be less insane than all the rest, but she's still a jerk."

The recovery knight . . . did not respond to that. The Hero of Elteno sighed, then tried to get as comfortable as he could. No matter how many times he did it, purifying corrupted dungeons never seemed to get any easier.

* * *

In the end, an Imperial hero, a squad of elite Imperial knights, a Celestial Elf young master and his retainer, and a Sun Elf Archon with her retinue were more than a match even for the endless waves of a Verminflood dungeon and managed to reach the end.

The Hero of Elteno smashed the core with a Holy-infused arrow, allowing the power of the world to seal off the corrupted dungeon's connection to the Realms of Mana. The dungeon vanished, and the boundaries of the Material Plane held steady.

Nolnyth motioned, and her retinue prepared to leave. She turned to face the Hero of Elteno. "I must leave to participate in a Council of the Archons. I suggest you use the time to prepare yourself for a better showing."

The Hero of Elteno nodded. "You know where to find us."

Nolnyth turned and left without another word. The battlemage scowled. "As if she didn't beg us to help. Jerk."

The Hero of Elteno sighed and shook his head. Neither the Imperial knights nor the Sun Elf Archon were happy about working together, but neither had any choice. An alarming amount of corrupted dungeons had appeared within the Empire of the Sun over the past few years, and the High Archons weren't doing anything about it.

Nolnyth was one of the few Sun Elf authorities concerned about the situation—at least within her own territory—while the last thing the Elteni Empire wanted was monster hordes appearing on its borders. Worst of all, the Exploratores had found evidence that the Heralds of the New Dawn, that cult who had killed the Hero's own wife, Aedinia, were involved.

And so came about this unholy alliance, which had spent the last few years destroying dungeons and trying to investigate those responsible.

Or as best they could while maintaining a low profile. If it became public knowledge that the Hero of Elteno had infiltrated the Empire of the Sun and an Archon was working with him, there would be consequences for both parties.

The recovery knight sighed and shook his head. "What now, boss?"

The Hero of Elteno shrugged. "Like our jerk said, we best take the opportunity to rest and follow up on our contacts."

The knights nodded and got to work. They removed their armor and hid it within a magic box specially prepared for this mission before putting on their disguises. Fortunately, the Empire of the Sun was home to many more races than just the Sun Elves, so they wouldn't stand out too much.

Unfortunately, most of those races were little more than slaves, so it was still dangerous to interact with any Sun Elves. But Celestial Elves were not counted among them, so Liulëa had some ability to cover for them. They, in fact, all carried the symbol of Liulëa's family with them, should they get into any . . . *complicated* situations.

And so, the group left the oasis, traveling to one of the cities of the Empire of the Sun. Most of the knights made their way to the safe house they normally stayed at, while the Hero of Elteno made his way to a local bar that was a front for the Exploratores.

"What's the news?"

The barkeeper shrugged as he cleaned a mug. "Lots of movement and conversation between the Archons lately. Might be planning something big. The Eastern Court is already prepping a response, just in case, which means they can't do anything about the recent chaos in the North, but that's nothing new."

The Hero of Elteno sighed. Another war would complicate things. Nolnyth was not so concerned about the dungeons that she would defect to the Empire, after all.

"And . . . what of the chaos in the North? Didn't you say there was some sort of incursion in Turannia?"

The Hero couldn't help himself. He trusted Tiberius and Canus to keep an eye out for Ateia, but even their hands might be tied with a full-on Dobhar invasion.

The barkeeper's eyes lit up. "Oh, you haven't heard, have you? Get this: story goes a wandering knight wiped out the entire invasion, single-handedly."

The Hero of Elteno just raised an eyebrow at that. The barkeeper grinned. "I thought as much too, but then Magister Caelinus tried to launch a coup, and apparently, the same wandering knight put him down before the Northern Court even organized a response.

"Again, I thought there's no way, but then the Northern Emperor invited her to the court, and even promoted two Exploratores to inquisitors solely to act as her assistants. Don't know how much of the stories are true, but apparently she's the real deal, or at least the Northern Emperor believes so."

The Hero of Elteno hummed, then exhaled his breath.

Well, an unknown like that was concerning, but if she was stabilizing the North, then it was good news. He did not like hearing about all these incursions and revolts, after all.

His heart sank as he thought of the girl he had left behind, but he couldn't let the Heralds of the New Dawn corrupt all the dungeons in the Empire of the Sun. He would not allow them to destroy the world and render all of Aedinia's sacrifice for naught. Still . . . he couldn't help but try to keep tabs on Turannia in the meantime. As long as his daughter stayed safe, then it all would be worth it.

He couldn't help but be curious about this wandering knight, though, and the Emperor's interest in her.

"Is that so? Which Exploratores got promoted?"

He took a sip of his drink as he waited for the answer. Any tales about the knight's exploits or character would be largely distorted by the time they arrived here, and so couldn't be trusted. But he knew most of the veteran Exploratores in Corvanus, so finding out who the Emperor had assigned might hint at the Emperor's perception of the powerful stranger.

The barkeeper nodded. "That's interesting too. It was two new kids who came in with the knight, from Turannia of all places. Let me see, what were their names again? Tag, or Taog, was it? Some sort of foreign name; I'm not entirely sure. The other one was an Imperial—Ateia, if I remember correctly."

The Hero of Elteno spat out his drink. He leaned over the counter, almost grabbing the barkeeper.

"Ateia?! You're sure?! As in, Ateia Niraemia?!"

The barkeeper lifted his hands. "Whoa, there. Um, I think so? That sounds right?"

The Hero of Elteno *ran* from the bar.

31

Regrouping

"Okay, how about this? Can you terminate them in the other direction?"

—A tactical NSLICE handler, convincing NSLICE units to retreat.

Ateia crossed her arms. "So, what now? Should we start searching for the cult?"

Taog grinned as Dark mana appeared and shifted across his hands. "I'd like to."

Ateia looked at her own hand, a pulse of Holy mana passing through it. Then she looked up, her eyes narrowing as the events of that fateful night played through her mind once again. She sighed and turned to NSLICE-00P.

"What do you think we should do, Seero?"

NSLICE-00P might have been little more than a child when it came to free will, organic sensations, and emotional experience, but there was no one Ateia trusted more when it came to the destruction of their enemies.

"Analyzing . . ."

NSLICE-00P's robotic eye flickered as she ran through several combat simulations. She pitted Ateia and Taog with their newfound powers against observed members of the Heralds of the New Dawn, such as the knights of Consul Noxisius NSLICE-00P had encountered.

The results were inconclusive. The warrior with Overgrowth mana had impressive defenses and regeneration ability. Holy mana would help against it, but the attributes still mattered. NSLICE-00P had determined that Dark mana like what Taog used had little interaction with Overgrowth mana, performing no better or worse than unattributed mana.

Therefore, Taog's Dark-and-Holy mix would give him a slight advantage . . . but not enough to overcome the knight's impressive defenses and regeneration. Taog was not predicted to win the fight with an acceptable margin of superiority.

Ateia performed even worse in a one-on-one scenario with that target, given her proclivity for Light mana, which was easily absorbed by anything Nature related, including Overgrowth mana. Her nonstandard capabilities were an uncertain factor, but comparing their relative energy signatures and predicted energy reserves painted an unfavorable scenario.

The Inferno mage, on the other hand, could burn mana structures themselves.

NSLICE-00P was uncertain how different mana types—such as Holy—or different applications of mana—such as skills instead of spells—might interact with it. She hadn't had access to Holy the first time she'd encountered Inferno mana, after all, and had simply used the Equalizer against the mage.

She *had* caught some interactions between Holy and Inferno when she'd closed the Rift, which did imply Holy might be capable of resisting Inferno, but she did not have enough data to confidently predict how that would apply to specific tactical settings. All she could do was compare their relative energy signatures, which again proved unfavorable for the teens.

Finally, there was the Eternal Night sniper. Ateia's natural ability to manipulate Light and Holy mana would likely prove an advantage should they confront each other directly. Taog might have a chance as well, seeing as he mixed his own Dark mana with Holy.

However, said sniper didn't fight directly at all, instead using the concealing effects of Eternal Night mana to conduct ambushes. Said concealing effects worked on all sensors available to NSLICE-00P, including her Dungeon Field, so it was unlikely Taog would be able to locate the sniper . . . or her hidden bolts.

Ateia, on the other hand, had some sort of Divination Sight which she could focus more directly than NSLICE-00P's own variant of the spell. However, NSLICE-00P didn't know how said ability would interact with Eternal Night mana, and at present, Ateia required a lot of focus to utilize the ability, which would present a weakness if she attempted it in a tactical setting.

Ultimately, while it was not impossible that her subordinates could prove victorious under the correct circumstances, the majority of scenarios turned against them or resulted in Pyrrhic victories at best, which was not an acceptable result given the major directive to keep them safe.

"Analysis complete. Results: This unit predicts combat with the Heralds of the New Dawn to present undesirable risks for a majority of subordinate units. This unit has also not concluded research and development on autonomous scout units that would enable efficient scouting. This unit therefore calculates that the optimal course of action is continued upgrade routines, intended to increase the maximum level and power reserves of subordinate units."

Taog frowned at that. "Even with how strong we've become?"

"Affirmative."

Ateia nodded. "So . . . you think we should hunt monsters or something?"

"Answer: This unit predicts the most efficient upgrade procedure to be dungeon termination or subjugation missions. Additionally, subordinating additional dungeons will expand the available transportation network for the NSLICE network."

Ateia nodded, then hummed. "Um, should we return to the Dobhar, and then maybe Castra Turannia? We should probably link up with Estrith and Agedia first if we're going to leave the area, right?"

"Affirmative."

Estrith strolled through the Imperial settlement on top of the cliff, glancing around. The former Imperials quietly walked the streets. They were largely subdued and focused on their own tasks, though conversations had started to pick up here and there. A few simply slouched against their hastily constructed shelters, bottles in hand or on the ground around them.

Once upon a time, Estrith would have refused to leave her steward's side, save by his direct command. Now . . . Now she had watched him work with the Mother of Waves and the other representatives of her queen's people and found she had little to contribute. So, she took it upon herself to explore instead, and to see what he was building with her own eyes.

She had explored the Dobhar settlements on the beaches below. They still lived much as they had before, only with the growing confidence that the Home Fleet, though it was a fleet no longer, was now truly safe. The steward had brought change as well; Imperial soldiers could be seen training young hunters, while a Dwarf was consulting the crafters on their harpoons. But change was a slow process overall, from what Estrith could see.

Now she began to explore her queen's other people. They were Imperials, much like she had seen. And yet . . . they were not. There were no ships flying in the skies. There were no towering stone walls, visibly glowing with the countless enchantments placed upon them. There were no vast farms as far as her eyes could see. It was but a humble village, little different from the ones Estrith had raided upon these shores in the past.

Estrith blinked as she looked around. It seemed the Empire's strength truly had not been built in a day. And now that these Imperials had to start over . . . it would take them more than a day to recover.

Just then, she heard a commotion. She grabbed her spear and rushed ahead. A group of Dobhar warriors marched through the town. They were shouting at a farmer, demanding food. The farmer pleaded with them, and the lead Dobhar struck his face, knocking the human to the ground.

Before, Estrith would simply have nodded. It was the way of things that the strong should take from the weak. Anything that made the Dobhar stronger and the Imperials weaker was to be celebrated.

But as for now? Now, Estrith rushed forward just as the Dobhar was about to strike the farmer with the back of his harpoon. She caught the weapon in her paw.

"What is going on here?"

The Dobhar snarled at her before he realized who she was. He took a step back and saluted. "First Warrior, it is good to see you. We are foraging for supplies. Why don't you take command, and we will bring a mighty harvest to our king!"

Estrith's eyes narrowed. Then she socked the Dobhar's stomach with her paw, stomping on his head as he fell to the ground. She glared at the other Dobhar.

"I'll ask again, what's going on here?"

One of the other Dobhar jumped and trembled. "W-We were just returning from a hunt on land! W-We couldn't keep up with the Wulver and didn't want to return empty-handed!"

Estrith growled. "So you chose to steal from *our own people* because of your failure?"

The Dobhar under her foot growled. "These are not our people! They're Imperials! They are weak and cruel! What's wrong with asserting our strength upon them?"

Estrith removed her foot and grabbed the Dobhar by the back of the neck, hauling him to his feet. She glared right into his eyes.

"These are not Imperials. These are the people of our queen, and the charges of Steward Uscfrea. What would Steward Uscfrea say if he saw this? Would you take that which belongs to him?"

The Dobhar growled but did not speak. Estrith scoffed and glanced around at each of the Dobhar . . . and then at the Imperials. She took a deep breath.

"The dread orca are individually stronger than all but the most powerful of the Dobhar warriors. Yet, they never attack us alone but always in a pack. Do you know why?"

She made eye contact with the first Dobhar again. "Even the *monsters* know there is strength in joining together. These humans have joined with our queen and submitted to Steward Uscfrea, and that makes them our people now. These ones may be weak, but that is because they are not hunters. They have a different role to play, but one that is important to the plans of Steward Uscfrea. You would not steal from the nursery ships and call it a glorious hunt, now would you?"

The Dobhar scowled. "I would never!"

Estrith nodded and pointed to the farmer's wife. She was staring at her fallen husband but keeping her distance and shielding a young child in her arms.

"Then don't."

The Dobhar growled . . . but then hung his head. ". . . I will report our hunt has failed."

Estrith glared at him and crossed her arms. "And?"

The Dobhar's face scrunched up, and then he sighed. ". . . And my own deeds here."

Estrith nodded, and with that, the Dobhar led his band away. She sighed before turning, crouching down to the farmer, and extending her paw. He glanced at her warily but reached out and grabbed it gingerly. Estrith pulled him to his feet. He blinked at her, then hung his head.

"I suppose I should thank you."

Estrith sighed and shook her head. "No. Rather, I should apologize for the others."

"Indeed."

Estrith spun around at the voice behind her, finding Uscfrea marching up to her. He turned to the farmer and inclined his head.

"I apologize for the actions of my warriors. They shall be disciplined as appropriate for this."

The farmer's eyes widened, and he saluted. "Ah, Steward. I-It's quite all right; we don't want any trouble here."

Uscfrea nodded to the farmer then turned to Estrith. "Our queen has returned and requested your presence."

Estrith saluted to Uscfrea then turned to follow him. Uscfrea heaved a sigh.

"Unfortunately, not an uncommon occurrence. I discipline them as I can, but still it happens."

Estrith nodded. "A great deal has changed for us very quickly. I imagine our warriors might . . . *struggle* to adapt."

Uscfrea sighed again. "Indeed, they do." But then a smile broke out on his face. "But thank you for putting a stop to it. It seems you have adapted well yourself. It makes me happy to see."

Estrith jumped and looked away. "I-I just . . . T-Those are your people, my steward; only you and our queen have the right to take from them!"

Uscfrea chuckled and patted her shoulder. "Don't be shy, Estrith. I believed you would be able to adapt well, and you did so better than most. That is why you're the one I entrusted with our queen."

It took a bit before Estrith could speak coherently again.

32

Assimilation Successful

"How many are there?"

—Dr. Ottosen, on how many Non-Standard bases he needed for the NSLICE program.

Once Ateia and Taog had finished packing, NSLICE-00P gathered all of her monsters back to their hangars, then opened the entrance to the New World. Inside was an expanded stone platform, as NSLICE-00P had increased its size.

Off to the side, on the added land, Melion bounced around, surrounded by drones and golems in various states of construction and disassembly, along with multiple ingots and ores of various types. Melion was bouncing as they read over the grimoire of Arofinas Leolar, particularly the sections on warship construction and the related enchantments, while a projector implant displayed several videos and schematics of drones and combat aircraft from Earth.

But NSLICE-00P was already up-to-date on Melion's drone golem research and development, and so just stepped through without distracting them. Arriving back in the Otter Burrow, she linked up with Uscfrea, explaining their plans.

"Query: Is NSLICE Uscfrea currently aware of the locations of Friendlies Agedia and Estrith?"

Uscfrea nodded. "Estrith's touring the Imperial settlement above; I'll retrieve her for you. Agedia . . . That was the snake girl, right? She headed out toward the Imperial lands a while back. Hasn't returned yet, as far as I'm aware. Speaking of which, the Imperials requested you stop by if you're available, my queen."

NSLICE-00P's robotic eye flickered. She was aware that Agedia had left for Castra Turannia; now that she had confirmed Agedia was still there, it did make sense for NSLICE-00P to retrieve her so that they could return through the New World.

As for visiting the Imperial authorities there, NSLICE-00P conducted another analysis. On the one hand, she was now wary of all diplomatic interactions, which also had little potential benefit for her primary directive. But on the other, the Empire as a whole was not hostile to her as of yet, and she, Ateia, and Taog all still possessed ranks within it.

Agedia had been specifically introduced to them by Magister Tiberius, and Rector Aemilia's family had assisted her after she'd terminated the cult base in Corvanus. As such, NSLICE-00P predicted that Turannia's authorities were likely unrelated to the Heralds of the New Dawn, and unlikely to conduct any hostile actions toward her or her friendlies.

As such, it would be beneficial to contact them, as they could potentially provide intel on the current status of the Empire and the Heralds of the New Dawn.

"Acknowledged. Statement: This unit has calculated that diplomatic contact with Turannia's provincial authorities provides potential benefits at acceptable risks, and so is acceptable to this unit. This unit will do so upon retrieval of Friendly Agedia."

Uscfrea nodded. "I'll let them know you're coming."

NSLICE-00P's robotic eye began to flicker as Uscfrea brought her attention to communications with the Empire.

"Query: Does NSLICE Uscfrea have access to mana-based long-range communications technology?"

Uscfrea rubbed his chin for a second. "Um, you mean the communication artifact? Yes, we got some from the rebels."

"Statement: This unit would like to scan the artifact's construction, as well as the maritime vessels and any other mana-based technology in NSLICE Uscfrea's possession."

Uscfrea grinned at that. "Let me get the angry dux. I'll make her show you all the toys they brought."

NSLICE-00P scanned the Imperial communication artifact and some of the vessels the rebels had stolen from the Northern Fleet, as well as a number of other artifacts the rebels had brought with them, and sent the data over to Melion.

Long-range communications had been somewhat of a bottleneck for their drone project, seeing as they lacked the infrastructure for electronic networks of any significant distance. Due to the lack of both technical knowledge on how to construct said devices and the lack of industrial infrastructure to manufacture the necessary components, NSLICE-00P predicted a mana-based or hybrid mana-electronic solution would be more efficient to pursue.

And it turned out the Empire already had a mana-based long-range communication network established. Melion was now working on recreating the device and brainstorming how to integrate it with the drones. NSLICE-00P predicted there was a reasonable probability she could deploy military-grade drones for scouting and observation in the near future. And the construction of said drones might be even easier.

With the theoretical knowledge and blueprints from the grimoire of Arofinas Leolar, and a full scan of working vessels based on those fundamental designs, NSLICE-00P had full confidence they could replicate an Imperial warship. With that knowledge as a base, she and Melion could then use her data from the Empire's airships and her own summoned drones to iterate on the designs.

She had reasonable confidence they could come up with suitable mana-based airframes for the new drones. And the combination of golem and AI technologies could handle the programming with ease.

Given the estimated time frame for the research and development, NSLICE-00P would need to begin investigating how to set up supply chains and production lines in order to enable mass production once the prototypes were ready and sufficiently tested. Of course, if the new drones appeared in the Aesdes's dungeon system as a potential summon, she could bypass the issue to some extent, but making individual purchases with her own mana was not the most scalable solution.

Therefore, she began investigating solutions . . . and found that the Aesdes had significantly expanded her menu for the New World.

World Menu → Create World Features → Geological Features			
Name	**Cost**	**Upkeep**	**Description**
Add Ore Vein	**Variable**	**Variable**	**Add a vein of a chosen mineral that replenishes over time. Mana cost and upkeep will depend on vein size, minerals chosen, and desired speed of replenishment.**
Add Fertile Soil	**Variable**	**Variable**	**Add soil with the nutrients necessary for healthy plant growth. Nutrients may be replenished over time for mana upkeep. Cost and upkeep will depend on field size, soil fertility, and desired nutrients.**

Add Water Spring	**Variable**	**Variable**	**Add a spring that will continuously create water. Cost and upkeep will depend on size and rate of replenishment.**

She could now add some geological features to her world beyond just the basic rocky platform, including the ability to create natural resources without waiting for the long geological processes required for such things to form naturally. Which made sense, given her world was a platform floating in the void and devoid of all the features of a planetary body required for said processes in the first place.

The fact that there was breathable air, livable temperatures, and gravity similar to that of Earth's were already purely mana-driven processes, so it was only logical there would be mana-based solutions for others as well.

In any case, though, NSLICE-00P was not a research unit, so she put such scientific concerns aside. The only thing that concerned NSLICE-00P at the moment was the fact that she could now create raw inputs in the New World at will. Ores for inorganic materials, fertile soil for anything agricultural, and water as necessary for both processes. She would not need to source raw materials before beginning mass production.

She did not do so right at this moment, however. She would wait for Melion to finish developing prototypes first, and then determine the process by which they would mass-produce the finalized units. At that stage, she would have a clear list of materials necessary, and so could calculate which features to add and what the ideal locations would be for efficient gathering, transportation, and processing of said materials.

Around that time, Uscfrea returned with Estrith. Estrith saluted to NSLICE-00P before nodding to Ateia and Taog. She blinked at Taog's cybernetic components before turning back to NSLICE-00P.

"My queen, what is your command?"

"Response: This unit is planning subordinate upgrade routines for all subordinates in preparation for the upcoming conflict. Will Friendly Estrith rejoin this unit's subordinates for the upgrade routines? This unit calculates Friendly Estrith would require additional combat capabilities to face the observed hostiles."

Estrith glanced at Uscfrea, looking pensive for a moment. But then she shook her head, faced NSLICE-00P, and saluted.

"I . . . feel that my place is with you, my queen, so long as our enemies still hunt us. I would be honored to fight at your side, my queen."

"Affirmative. Query: Would Friendly Estrith like to undergo cybernetic upgrades and integrate into the NSLICE network?"

Both Estrith and Uscfrea froze at that. Uscfrea spoke first. "Wait, my queen . . . you have a method to add this armor to other Dobhar?"

"Affirmative Response: This unit recently received the capability."

Taog crossed his arms and smiled. "Yep, can confirm."

Estrith turned back to observe Taog more properly, her eyes widening. Then she glanced to Uscfrea . . . then Ateia . . . then Taog . . . then NSLICE-00P. Back and forth she glanced between each of the cyborgs. Uscfrea chuckled as her eyes settled on him. He nodded at her.

"Do as you wish, Estrith Edilddaughter, personal guard of our queen."

Estrith blinked and started to tremble. "Wait, my queen . . . if I remember correctly, that armor . . . lets you send messages to others with the same armor . . . including Steward Uscfrea, correct?"

"Clarification: Long-range communications between this unit and NSLICE Uscfrea were conducted via the foreign system connection. However, this unit has some solutions in research and development to enable broader communications between geographically dispersed units."

Estrith's eyes narrowed, and her gaze locked onto NSLICE-00P.

"I'll do it. Right away."

"Affirmative."

Uscfrea shook his head and chuckled. But well, he also wouldn't mind remaining in contact with Estrith as she escorted their queen. And . . .

Uscfrea turned to Ateia and Taog, rubbing his chin. "My queen, it appears that process is not limited by species, correct?"

"Affirmative."

He nodded at that. "If I may make a request, would you be willing to grant said armor to some of our other subordinates here?"

"Affirmative Response: Integrating additional units into the network is desirable. Clarification: Conditions to suitable subjects apply, including full consent of the subject to be upgraded and reasonable confidence in the subject's loyalty and lack of external affiliations, as said subject will gain access to classified data and expanded capabilities."

Uscfrea grinned as he nodded. "That won't be a problem."

And so, several new CELIU units came online that day, and Uscfrea's administration began running smoother than ever before.

SIDE STORY

Not So Awaited Reunions

An Imperial clerk walked through the halls of Castra Turannia carrying a huge stack of papers. He stopped in front a large office door with two guards to either side standing at attention. One of them knocked on the door.

"Dux, a clerk is here with the latest reports."

They heard a deep sigh from the other side. "Enter."

The soldier pushed open the door. The clerk nodded in thanks and stepped inside the office of the Dux Limitanei per Turannia to find an unimposing man sitting at the desk inside. *Dux* Opiter heaved a sigh at the stack of papers. He resisted the urge to reach for the plate he had placed just out of reach. For the thirty-third time today, Dux Opiter wondered what he was doing here.

How had things come to this? After the Battle of Castra Turannia, Dux Canus had conducted a full reorganization of Turannia's limitanei. They'd pulled their forces out of the new Selkie and Dobhar territories and reinforced the border with the Forest of Beasts.

But Dux Canus had not stopped there. He'd taken the troops freed up by the shrinking territory and begun a full-scale retraining program, personally bringing them up to comitatense standards, or as close as he could get them. Now that it was abundantly clear he could not count on the wider Empire for support, he'd endeavored to elevate the troops under his direct command to a level he could do some real work with.

All of that meant a great deal of logistical and clerical work, as all of the soldiers left in Turannia were moving about, and practically every unit had been reorganized. And as most of the soldiers were also settled farmers, that meant moving their families as well.

Entire villages had to be relocated and rebuilt as the borders were redrawn. New bases had to be built to house and train Dux Canus's new legion. New lines of communication had to be established with the two newly independent nations on their borders, not to mention new border defenses and security. And all of this had to happen on top of cataloging and repairing the damage caused by the Dobhar invasion.

And *then* Rector Aemilia had revealed an ambitious development plan, courtesy of *the monster* paying an entire war indemnity upfront and in pure Idrint. And since there wasn't any sort of civilian administration, it fell on Opiter to bring her plans for a massively expanded port to fruition. Which, of course, was not simply a matter of deciding how to decorate the new buildings.

No, materials had to be acquired, inventoried, and moved where they were needed and when they were needed so as not to be in the way when they weren't. Laborers had to be hired, assembled, ordered, housed, and fed. Work needed to be completed in sequence, so someone needed to arrange the order in which different workers would complete their tasks. Then someone needed to keep track of everything going on to ensure that the work was completed on time, and that the other workers were informed if something was not.

And again, since there was no civil administration, all of that work had fallen onto the Legion. Opiter had barely slept, and often didn't leave his office for days at a time. And then . . . it'd gotten worse.

A massive influx of refugees from Utrad had landed on their shores. Entire legions' worth of deserting rebel troops, rich families with all of their possessions, poor folk with little more than the rags on their backs—all of whom had to be recorded, provided for, resettled, and then kept track of, lest they turn into bandits out of either opportunity or desperation.

His only respite was that the arrival of Rector Aemilia's retinue from the Hiberius family had allowed her to establish a basic government administration. But, of course, they then had to find, recruit, and train up staff for that administration, meaning they were only gradually taking over responsibilities one by one. So his workload was *still* noticeably heavier than it had been before.

And *then*, Dux Canus had been promoted. The man was now the Magister Militum per Turannia, with full authority over all Legion forces in the province, whether comitatense, limitanei, or even the Imperial knight orders, should they move to the province at some point.

This was to prevent another scenario like when the higher-ranking Magister Caelinus had stripped Turannia's comitatenses for his rebellion and no one in Turannia could object. It would also allow the Empire to turn a blind eye to Canus accepting some of the rebel soldiers back into the Legion as the new magister "establishing new formations."

Opiter didn't care about all that. What he did care about was Dux Canus promoting *him* as the new Dux Limitanei per Turannia. Opiter was now the man in charge of *all* limitanei in Turannia, a job he felt thoroughly unqualified for, which he'd expressed in no uncertain terms to Magister Canus, Magister Tiberius, Rector Aemilia, and anyone who would listen.

But Magister Canus had stated that Opiter had more than proven himself during the reorganization and refugee situations, which Rector Aemilia had wholeheartedly agreed with. And Magister Canus had then stated that contrary to popular belief, tactical command was not a necessary skill for a dux. He simply wanted someone who would keep the overall operations running smoothly. Tactical command could be left to the legates and centurions, and the limitanei would fall under Magister Canus's command in the event of any large-scale operations.

Opiter would also admit that the offered pay bump may have clouded his judgment when he finally gave in.

But the problem that Opiter had been concerned with ultimately had come to pass. Which was that now *he* was the guy people were reporting to! He was the guy everyone came to when they had a problem! *He* had to figure out who was going to go deal with it now! He couldn't even pass issues to Magister Canus anymore unless they were specifically comitatense business! Everything else *he* had to make a decision on first!

He took a deep breath and exhaled slowly. It was still deeply concerning to him, but so far everything had actually gone pretty well. Magister Tiberius had a full complement of Exploratores, Magister Canus now had actual soldiers under his command, Rector Aemilia had actual governing staff, and the territory they were all responsible for had shrunk dramatically.

All in all, the number of actual issues the limitanei of Turannia needed to deal with had shrunk down to normal levels. Which meant that the issues they *did* have largely fell within Legion standard, with fleshed-out Legion policies on how to deal with them. Opiter had mostly been able to just repeat Legion policy, and the issues would be handled. And he was getting used to the paperwork. That had always been his strong suit, in any case.

In fact—Opiter cracked a small smile—if things kept up, he might actually get used to his new role. He was starting to believe he *could* handle the job. And if he could handle the job . . . Well, *Dux Opiter* didn't sound too bad.

Yes, as long as nothing nonstandard occurred, he would—

One of his guards burst into the room, forgetting even to knock.

"Sir, we just got word from the border guard!"

Opiter's heart began to pound. "What is it?"

He winced as his voice cracked, but he relaxed slightly as the soldier smiled. Whatever it was, it didn't seem to be too—

"She's coming back! NSLICE-00P is heading this way!"

Opiter slammed his face on his desk, scattering some of his reports. He slumped out of his chair so he could grab the plate of food, curling up on the floor as he began to gorge himself.

* * *

In the forests near Castra Turannia, two shadows shot through the trees. The light of the sun glinted off of wicked blades as they passed one another. A light clang rang through the forest as they each landed on the ground, their backs turned to one another. A single leaf fell through the air between them, cut perfectly in half.

On the one side was the former Exploratore Hostus, still in his state-issued cloak, though with his Exploratores pin removed. Sweat dripped down his neck as he tried to steady his breathing. His hands trembled as he gripped his sword and turned to face his opponent, hoping to see her corpse.

He scowled. His opponent stood entirely unharmed. She stared at him with a predatory gaze and a smirk, swaying back and forth as she watched him with mirth.

Hostus gritted his teeth. First, that jerk Tiberius had tried to shortchange and humiliate him, after all he had done to help that ungrateful idiot! Then, all his so-called *friends* had abandoned him when he'd tried to get justice for himself. Then the stupid Empire had tried to arrest him as a traitor!

He'd already said it: it wasn't *his* fault Caelinus had tricked everyone into joining a rebellion! And so, he'd run off into the wilderness. If society would reject him, then he would reject society! He'd become a bandit king, conquer this stupid province, kill that idiot Tiberius, and show the Empire he meant business!

But then he'd run into this adversary. And try as he might, he couldn't kill her. He had barely avoided death on that last pass. If this kept up, he might not next time.

Just then, his opponent turned away. She began to clean her weapons—with her *tongue*. Hostus's face twisted through several horrid expressions. She was looking down on him! This stupid . . . *cat* was looking down on him! He'd kill her!

The cat finished cleaning her paws before finally turning her head as he rushed toward her. She meowed softly as she dug her paws into the dirt and launched herself toward him. She seemed to vanish as she swooped past.

There was another clang as man and cat appeared on opposite sides of each other. They stood in silence for a moment, and then blood spurted from Hostus's neck.

The cat didn't bother turning around as the man fell to the ground. She licked her paws before shaking her head. She'd really thought a human soldier would be better than that, but honestly, she knew *rats* that were faster!

But she smirked to herself. It couldn't be helped, after all. She was nature's perfect killing machine. She had grown overconfident, complacent in her might, and that was why she had been humiliated.

But now?

Now she had thrown herself back into training and battle, no longer content to prey upon the weak but to demonstrate why she was the epitome of violence. She had battled the monsters of the wild, and reigned supreme. Now, not even the humans, not even the so-called apex predators could stand against her. Now she was ready. She would have her revenge.

And just in time.

She froze, her hair standing up. She started to hiss. It wasn't anything she could sense. She felt it more in her heart than out in the world, but she knew. Somehow, she knew.

He had returned. And the day she had been preparing for had come.

She extended her claws and then swung them. A faint arc of light flickered through the forest before the branch of a nearby tree fell to the ground. She bared her fangs.

This time, she would not be humiliated. She would not be denied. She would reign supreme as nature's perfect killing machine once again.

And so, the cat ran off into the forest, heading toward Castra Turannia. There, her destiny awaited.

33

Return to the Land of Rain

"No, it's fine. I didn't need to see the sun anyway."

—Centurion Duronia Severa, on being assigned to Turannia for four straight tours.

Agedia yawned as she stretched. She shuddered at the cold air, curling up under the blankets.

Okay, yes, the main reason she had avoided coming to Turannia was not actually the cold, rainy climate but rather her emotional issues over failing to save Aedinia. But that didn't mean the cold, rainy climate *wasn't* an issue. There was a reason the Mélusine had never expanded into Turannia!

But eventually, she got up, wrapping herself up in many layers before making her way down the stairs. Tiberius chuckled as he served her a warm bowl of soup, and she smiled at him before she dug in. He had finished his own long ago.

They just sat in silence for a while afterward until Tiberius started to twitch and fidget. Agedia raised an eyebrow.

"Tibbers? What's the matter?"

He started and looked away. Eventually, he took a deep breath and turned back. "Um, so, Dia, I was thinking . . ."

Agedia smirked. "Tibbers, you're *always* thinking; whenever you're sober, at least."

Tiberius didn't respond to the jab, instead looking Agedia in the eye. She blinked and went silent, waiting for him to go on.

"So . . . it sounds like you're starting to move forward . . . And the reason you didn't want to come was that you weren't ready to get involved, right? But, um, you're involved now already . . . and Ateia has left, in any case, so I don't have to watch over her anymore at this point, so, um, there's no reason you can't . . . I mean . . ."

She couldn't help but giggle as Tiberius bit his tongue. He groaned, then took a deep breath. "Okay, what I'm trying to say is: will you stay with me? Or I can come with you. I don't want to just up and leave the folks here, but I think they can handle themselves now if you'd rather be elsewhere."

Agedia's heart began to pound as she looked into Tiberius's eyes. She took a deep breath. His face fell, and she quickly shook her head. "Ah, no! It's not what you're thinking! It's yes! It's definitely yes! It's just . . . not yet. I, um, have something I need to do first. I want to stand by Ateia's side now, and we've all got some unfinished business with the Heralds. But once they're dealt with . . . Well, shiny girl's got Ateia covered, so . . ."

Tiberius blinked before slowly starting to grin. He was about to open his mouth . . . when someone began pounding on the door.

"Magister Tiberius! Dux Opiter is calling for you! He says it's urgent!"

Tiberius heaved a huge sigh and hung his head. "I *told* those idiots I'm unavailable!"

Agedia chuckled as her eyes narrowed. "Want me to get rid of him? I could get into another drunken rage, if you want to meet me at the prison?"

Tiberius sighed and shook his head. "As much as I'd like to relive old times, I suppose I should still do my job, as long as you're doing yours."

She chuckled again as he stood up and opened the door with a glare. "Okay, what is so important that you had to interrupt my leave?"

The soldier outside saluted. "Magister, it's NSLICE-00P! She's back!"

Tiberius sighed. "Well, speak of the demon lord. Looks like our little vacation is over, Dia."

Agedia slithered over at the mention of NSLICE-00P. She nodded, her face now resolute.

"So it is. Let's finish the job."

NSLICE-00P flew over Castra Turannia and landed just outside the Legion keep, carrying Ateia, Taog, and Estrith with her, the Dobhar now fully upgraded into a cyborg as well. There, she found a full Legion waiting for her.

Magister Canus was there with the best of his newly trained soldiers, Rector Aemilia now stood with her full retinue and a squad of the Hiberius family's knights, Magister Tiberius and Agedia stood side by side, and . . . an Imperial airship now floated over the city. Princess Caecila and her retinue stood off to the side, watching the proceedings along with Miallói and a handful of Selkie hunters.

Magister Canus shouted as NSLICE-00P landed, and all of his soldiers saluted to her. Miallói and her hunters did as well, while Rector Aemilia stepped forward, a smile on her face.

"Welcome back, NSLICE-00P, queen of the Dobhar, friend of the Empire, Turannia, and the Hiberius family. It is my honor and pleasure to receive you once more. Please, come inside."

"Greeting: This unit thanks you for the welcome. It is good to see all Turannian authorities in good condition."

Princess Caecila stepped forward as well. "Hello, NSLICE-00P. I am glad to see you unharmed. If you don't mind, I have some matters to discuss with you as well."

"Greeting: This unit is also pleased to see Princess Caecila in good condition. This unit is willing to coordinate with Imperial authorities to the maximum extent permitted by current missions and directives."

Princess Caecila smiled and nodded her head. "Thank you."

She and Rector Aemilia eyed one another, but neither said anything, and the group began to move inside. Agedia slithered over to Ateia.

"You . . . look much better, Ateia. How are you feeling?"

Ateia smiled. "Much better. How about you?"

Agedia gave a small smile of her own. "Same." Glancing around, she raised an eyebrow at Taog and Estrith. "Wait, everyone's shiny now? How did *that* happen? And where did, um, our benefactor go?"

Ateia just smiled and shook her head. "Well, a lot has happened. We'll fill you in."

And so, NSLICE-00P and company filled in the group on recent events, minus some classified intel regarding dungeons, secret Imperial family members, and the Aesdes. They mostly explained the altercation with the Heralds of the New Dawn, and their future plans regarding their foes.

Princess Caecila heaved a sigh. NSLICE-00P had included her in this discussion given that she represented NSLICE-00P's connection to the Emperor, the nominally highest authority of the Northern Court. If she and the Emperor were connected to the Heralds of the New Dawn, then NSLICE-00P would have to consider the entire Empire as hostile.

She likewise might benefit from informing the Emperor of her plans, given that it might require her to assault nominally Imperial assets, as she had already done.

The princess did not appear happy to be included. "This is a lot to take in. Consul Noxisius was a member of a Cult of Mana? He attacked NSLICE-00P and then tried to open a Rift right in Corvanus? How is that possible?"

Magister Canus sighed and shook his head. "I wish I could say I was surprised, but corruption isn't new in the Empire. The cult part is a little much, but I suppose it was only a step away."

Rector Aemilia narrowed her eyes.

"Actually, it makes sense. If the cult had one consul seat already, then they would have had a strong incentive to neutralize my father. So when I got . . . *a tad* emotional back then . . ."

Princess Caecila frowned and opened her mouth, but controlled herself and sighed instead, so Rector Aemilia continued. ". . . they would certainly have taken advantage. And then my father stepped back, leaving Consul Noxisius as the strongest figure in the North. But why would he try to destroy Corvanus at that stage? They already ruled the court."

Canus shrugged. "I've dealt with Cults of Mana in the past. They're all about crazy rituals to gain massive godlike power. Political power is only ever a means to an end with them; they would never stop there."

Princess Caecila furrowed her brow. "And, Miss NSLICE-00P, you plan to . . . *terminate* these people, as you called it, like you did with Consul Noxisius?"

"Affirmative."

She heaved a sigh, holding her head. "That's . . . could I convince you to wait, Miss NSLICE-00P? The court is still investigating for now on Consul Hiberius's insistence, but further aggression could have consequences if your allegations cannot be proven. Perhaps you could entrust some of the investigation to us?"

Magister Tiberius shook his head. "These cult people won't wait quietly, and they've been hiding within the Empire for years. Not to mention all the rebellions and corrupted dungeons and whatnot the Northern Court needs to clean up. I highly doubt the North can find and deal with this cult, and that's assuming Consul Noxisius was the only member within the court."

Magister Canus rubbed his chin before nodding. "I agree. With Caelinus gone and Utrad's forces scattered, the Northern Empire lacks both commanders and legions. Given what this cult did with corrupted dungeons in the Heartland, I fear they're a threat beyond what the North could deal with right now. Sorry to say this, but I no longer believe the Northern Court is capable of handling the crisis. We should not wait on them before reacting."

"Statement: This unit plans to conduct numerous upgrade routines before resuming active hostilities. If Imperial authorities are able to apprehend the hostiles within that time, this unit will cooperate. If not, this unit will prioritize efficient termination of the threat."

Rector Aemilia sighed. "Then I suppose we had best be ready for the fallout. And here I thought things were going well for once."

Magister Canus smirked. "They are. We're in a much better position than we were."

Magister Tiberius nodded with his eyes narrowed. "Indeed. And if I catch any of those demon-loving monsters here, I'll make them wish they were terminated instead."

Princess Caecila sighed, her head drooping. "You are resolved, then? I suppose I will inform Magister Appius he needs to redouble his investigations. May the Aesdes help us all."

Ateia and Taog couldn't help but share a small smirk at that. "That might be more likely than you think . . ."

34

Loyalty

"Good food, generous pay, and timely reinforcements."

—Maior Generalis Lucius Tettidius Celatus, on how the Eastern Court prevents rebellions.

Princess Caecila turned to Rector Aemilia. Walking over, she leaned in to whisper to her. "Are you okay with this? You know the court will likely blame you should NSLICE-00P cross the line in her crusade."

Rector Aemilia scoffed. "Am I supposed to believe *you're* worried about me? You just want me to try and convince her to tone it down because it will fall on you as well."

Princess Caecila frowned. "Fine. Yes, Emperor Lucius and I are already in a tough spot at present. We can't really afford for her to burn down another senator's house. But that does not mean you should not be concerned for yourself. The Emperor and I will at least maintain our nominal positions, if nothing else. You would not even be that fortunate."

Rector Aemilia rubbed her chin and hummed. "You might be surprised." She then took a deep breath and stepped away from the princess, turning to face NSLICE-00P. "NSLICE-00P, queen of the Dobhar and friend of the Empire. It seems to me that your enemy's influence runs deep and has likely been turned upon my family in the past as well. And it seems equally likely they will turn upon all of us here again, should you conduct open warfare against them."

"Analysis: Given the Hiberius family's direct assistance in the latest altercation, this unit calculates that outcome as likely."

Rector Aemilia narrowed her eyes. "Then, if Turannia were to pledge its support to you in this conflict, not merely as a neutral party but as a full ally, would you be willing to do the same? Would you be willing to protect us from our enemies, and to shield us from the consequences of aligning with you, political or otherwise?"

Princess Caecila's eyes went wide at the question, while NSLICE-00P's robotic eye began flickering. She decided to rerun an analysis on her nonintervention protocols, given that her circumstances had changed significantly since the last time she'd applied them. The restriction had less weight, given that she had reduced the priority of protocols put in place by Dr. Ottosen at this point.

Her last commander had also preferred nonintervention, but only so far as to avoid being drawn into unnecessary conflicts. Said restriction was not absolute.

The biggest reason for her to refuse any formal affiliations and foreign obligations had been the risk to her primary directive, since she didn't know if any factions might be affiliated with a person of interest. But that risk no longer applied.

Colleöne had stated that none of the persons of interest were present in this universe, a claim supported by every piece of evidence NSLICE-00P had managed to find. While there was a nonzero chance of Colleöne being either deceitful or inaccurate, the current probabilities were so low that NSLICE-00P could discount them in her analysis.

And so, none of the factions present in this universe had any meaningful chance of being affiliated with a person of interest or possessing any relevant intel on them. Which meant there was no particular reason why NSLICE-00P couldn't turn hostile to and terminate any one of them. There was no need to avoid conflict besides the risks and resource expenditures inherent to armed conflict. And so, there was also no inherent reason why she couldn't ally with a given faction either.

So NSLICE-00P only needed to consider the benefits and risks of a proposed alliance with her objectives within this universe. In this case, she was already in conflict with the Heralds of the New Dawn, who had notable influence within various Imperial factions.

Establishing an alliance with the Imperials in Turannia would deny the cult access to the Imperial assets closest to the Dobhar home base, which was important for protecting the Dobhar from attack. Rector Aemilia had also implied she wanted protection from forces targeting Turannia apart from the Heralds of the New Dawn, especially in terms of politics.

NSLICE-00P was not as confident in these calculations, but she found the request reasonable. Or rather, should Rector Aemilia suffer political consequences, it could open the door to the Heralds of the New Dawn gaining influence over Imperial Turannia. In fact, such a move could even be considered an attack by a hostile party, if the Heralds of the New Dawn were behind it.

Even if they weren't, it would be beneficial to deny them any further opportunities to influence the Empire. And given that Rector Aemilia's family had already assisted NSLICE-00P against the Heralds of the New Dawn to the point of deploying their own military assets, the probability that the rector was affiliated with the cult was insignificant.

"Analysis complete. Results: This unit finds the proposed alliance to be beneficial, contingent on the exact details of the arrangement."

Rector Aemilia nodded and glanced around the room. Magisters Canus and Tiberius both nodded back at her. Her own retinue did as well. She took a deep breath and made her choice.

"Then Turannia shall stand with you against your foes, NSLICE-00P." She turned to face Princess Caecila. "Even if the Empire turns against you as a result."

Princess Caecila's eyes went wide and quivered at that.

The Selkies had been whispering in the corner, but quickly finished up their conversation. Miallói stepped forward and slammed her harpoon against the floor.

"My people owe you everything, great warrior NSLICE-00P. Our lives, our land, and our freedom. We would be honored to fight against your enemies."

Estrith slammed her harpoon into the ground as well. "The Dobhar, of course, will obviously stand with our queen."

Estrith and Miallói glared at each other for a moment before they both nodded and took a step back. Rector Aemilia glanced between them before a small smile formed on her lips. "It seems all of Turannia is united in this, at the very least. I suppose we have much to discuss now."

Estrith and Miallói both nodded at that. Meanwhile, Princess Caecila was trembling.

"Rector, how far do you plan to go with this? To say such a thing, in front of an Imperial princess, no less. You know what it sounds like, right?"

Rector Aemilia turned to her and smirked.

"Of course I do; that's why I said it, after all. Whether or not it becomes what it sounds like will depend entirely on the Northern Court, I suppose. And I will state it to you clearly as well. The court hasn't done anything for anyone here in quite some time, including during the times we needed you most.

"NSLICE-00P, on the other hand, has given us everything, and single-handedly accomplished everything the Northern Court could not. I think it is obvious what choice we will make, if there is a choice to be made." Rector Aemilia couldn't help but grin. "So I suppose you and my father had better work hard to ensure we don't have to decide."

Princess Caecila groaned and struggled to stay on her feet. She heaved a sigh as Typheras steadied her. "So that's it, then. I suppose I have little choice. Just, if I may make a request?" She turned to NSLICE-00P. "Will you at least inform me before you begin your campaign? The court will not look kindly upon another sudden assault."

"Response: This unit will do so if possible, but will ultimately prioritize effective termination of hostiles. If forewarning of unaligned parties risks alerting hostiles to upcoming operations, this unit will need to withhold relevant data."

Princess Caecila groaned again.

Afterward, NSLICE-00P contacted Uscfrea, informed him of the proceedings, and brought him into the conversation via holographic projection. Uscfrea also linked to his council, all newly upgraded to CELIU-model cyborgs. Dux Augustalis's eyes widened, and she saluted.

"Dux Canus, it is an honor to meet you. I studied your tactics from the Eastern Campaigns in great detail."

Canus nodded at her. "It's magister now. And likewise. I heard good things about you, Dux Augustalis. Whatever the circumstances that brought you here, I'm pleased to have you on board."

Dux Augustalis's face brightened into a smile, perhaps the first one she had given since the rebellion. Meanwhile, Uscfrea glanced around, especially at Miallói, and chuckled.

"A Dobhar, a Wulver, a Selkie, and a bunch of Imperials, all working together to defend Turannia from dark powers. Not exactly how I imagined achieving it."

Miallói gave a small, nearly imperceptible smile. "As you once said, Spellbreaker, Turannia now follows the lead of the strongest."

Uscfrea blinked for a moment before breaking out into laughter. "I suppose that's true. Guess I got exactly what I wanted, huh?"

Princess Caecila excused herself before she could be politely but firmly asked to leave, given the Turannians would now be openly discussing treason as a very possible scenario.

And with that, the three organized powers of Turannia began to discuss the details of their cooperation. NSLICE-00P designated the Turannian Imperials and the Selkies as allied units, and gave Uscfrea permission to offer any assistance and cooperation deemed beneficial to the alliance's goals.

In fact, not being a logistical or diplomatic unit, NSLICE-00P went ahead and specifically tasked Uscfrea with managing the coordination. Ultimately, they decided to establish a joint outpost on the border between NSLICE-00P's lands and the Empire for further in-person discussions, which would also give the Selkies a chance to send an Elder from the Council of Hunters. The group then adjourned to make preparations.

Miallói stopped by for a quick chat with Ateia and Taog before she had to leave for Selkie territory. After she was finished, Magisters Canus and Tiberius requested to speak with the group in private. Ateia, Taog, and NSLICE-00P stepped into a private room with them.

Magister Canus turned serious as he faced Ateia. "Agedia filled us in. So, you know who you are now?"

Ateia slowly nodded, turning to Magister Tiberius. "Which answers a lot of questions, actually. The Exploratores don't really *fail* anyone willing to join. You were trying to protect me, right?"

Magister Tiberius looked down. "Not that I did a very good job of that."

Ateia frowned. "Did my father know?"

Magister Tiberius slowly nodded again. "He requested it personally. He wanted no record of your existence, period, if he could help it."

Ateia heaved a sigh. "Well, I would have liked to have known that, but I suppose that's on my father. Magister Tiberius, thank you for trying to protect me. I know now why you did."

She frowned and touched the place where she had been stabbed. Magister Tiberius fell silent, taking a deep breath at that. Magister Canus sighed as well.

"I wish you didn't have to go through all that, but I'm glad you made it out alive, at the very least. But, given the circumstances, there *is* something we must discuss." Magister Canus made eye contact with Ateia. "Have you thought about the implications of your heritage? Specifically, regarding the throne of the North?"

Ateia and Taog's eyes widened. "I . . . have not. There were . . . *other* aspects of my heritage that took priority."

Magister Canus made a sympathetic expression as he nodded. "Understandable, but it is something to consider now. Ateia, you are the closest living relative of the late Emperor Herius. Well, your mother wasn't exactly a legitimate heir, and blood isn't everything in Imperial succession, but the point is you do have a claim of sorts; at least as much as Emperor Lucius does."

Magister Canus crossed his arms behind his back and began to pace.

"In the scenario where NSLICE-00P's mission turns the Northern Court against her, that claim could become relevant. Having a member of the Imperial family at the forefront would make a given rebellion significantly more legitimate—and significantly more threatening. There would be major potential benefits and potential risks to such a move, and of course, it would place you at grave risk, most of all. So, what will you do if the Empire moves against NSLICE-00P, and we are forced to take up arms?"

Ateia went silent for a moment. She crossed her arms and began to pace around. No one said anything for a while. Eventually, she walked back and glanced around.

"I don't care about my claim. I don't know the first thing about running an Empire, and so, if I tried, I would be at the mercy of others. The last time we got involved in politics, I ended up as a ritual sacrifice. I have no intentions of acting on this claim for myself."

She then turned to look at NSLICE-00P. "But . . . Seero saved my life countless times, and now I am sworn to serve her. I want to do everything within my power to help her and to defeat that monstrous cult. So"—she took a deep breath—"Seero, consider my heritage as another weapon you can use. If it will help us achieve our goal, then use it. I'll follow your lead."

"Acknowledged."

NSLICE-00P's robotic eye began to flicker. Ateia's new powers, especially her blessings, would significantly improve her subordinate's combat performance, so keeping Ateia as a combat asset had clear benefits. On the other hand, having Ateia become a political figurehead had benefits as well, though said benefits were not as clearly defined, and came with risks.

Ultimately, though, NSLICE-00P considered the Turannian alliance as a secondary asset, expected to play a more defensive role in the conflict with the cult. She and her direct subordinates represented the offensive element that was expected to conduct most of the operations. As such, NSLICE-00P's calculations were clear.

"Analysis complete. Results: At present, NSLICE Ateia is predicted as more beneficial supporting the NSLICE network in active combat than acting as a political figurehead. This unit will inform all relevant parties should the situation change."

Ateia smiled at that. Magister Tiberius tilted his head. "Really? No offense, but I don't feel like any of us really hold a candle to you, NSLICE-00P, and Ateia wasn't the strongest among us, last I checked."

Ateia thought for a moment, then nodded her head. Within the NSLICE network, she asked NSLICE-00P for permission to show off. NSLICE-00P agreed on the premise of facilitating cooperation.

So, Ateia deployed her wings, folded up into her back armor at present. The wings then began to shine, filling the room with Holy mana. Magisters Canus and Tiberius's jaws dropped while Ateia smirked.

"I guess Agedia didn't tell you everything, huh?"

35

The Return of the Great-High King

"If you aim for the Emperor, don't miss."

—Magister Utriusque Militia Quintis Munius Priscillianus, while arresting the conspirators of a failed assassination plot.

With all diplomatic matters resolved or delegated to appropriate subordinates, NSLICE-00P stepped out of the Legion keep. Ateia, Taog, Estrith, and Agedia joined her, Agedia sharing a hug with Tiberius before she left. Estrith most definitely did not eye her with envy.

As they stepped out of the gates to Castra Turannia proper, Taog turned to NSLICE-00P. "So, what's the plan now, Seero?"

"Answer: This unit must establish a base of operations and transportation node in the vicinity of Castra Turannia. Afterward, this unit intends to begin subordinate upgrade routines."

Taog nodded. "So we'll go looking for dungeons?"

"Affirmative."

He looked off into the distance and rubbed his chin. "Does that mean we'll be heading back to the Forest of Beasts?"

"Affirmative Response: That is correct, unless there is a more efficient location to locate dungeons that lack strategic value to allied factions."

Agedia rubbed her chin at that and shrugged. "The Wild Lands across the North Sea, maybe? But the Forest of Beasts should be as good as any."

Taog took a deep breath. "In that case . . . would you mind if we stop by my and Ateia's old village? I would like to visit my parents' grave if possible."

NSLICE-00P's robotic eye flickered. Visiting already terminated individuals did not provide any benefit or efficiency she was aware of or could calculate. And from her records, Ateia and Taog's old village likewise had nothing to offer their current mission. All her calculations indicated it was an unnecessary expenditure of time.

But . . . the logs from Taog's cybernetic components indicated he was experiencing powerful emotions when making this request. NSLICE-00P still didn't have the data to fully interpret that response but could at least make the speculation that this request was of notable importance to Taog's organic half.

Rejecting it was predicted to cause negative emotional reactions, which would undoubtedly reduce Taog's overall efficiency, given his complete lack of emotional controls and the preeminent role of organic components in CELIU models. Not to mention that NSLICE-00P was currently attempting to avoid causing emotional damage within organic components, even at the cost of some efficiency.

At this stage, she was even rewriting some of her efficiency calculations from the ground up, given they had been written by Dr. Ottosen, who had proven to have some inefficiencies of his own.

So, avoiding negative emotional responses in Taog was assigned a value, then checked against the amount of time and effort required for the visit. She found that the time spent would not appreciably set back any current missions or directives. In fact, their village was in the direction of the Forest of Beasts, in any case, so would not require significant detours in the first place.

"Answer: This unit finds the request acceptable and will include the proposed detour into the transit plans."

Taog smiled and nodded. "Thank you, Seero."

Ateia walked up to him and placed a hand on his shoulder. "I'll go with you."

He turned to her with a surprised look before shaking his head. "That's okay, Ateia. I know now you don't really like that place, right? I mean . . . I don't really either, but it is where my parents are."

Ateia looked into his eyes. "I loved them too. And I won't let you go alone."

She also gave a dark smile as she clenched a fist coated in dense, glowing mana that distorted the air around it. "Besides, the main reason I hated our lives there no longer applies."

Taog . . . decided not to ask her to elaborate on that.

NSLICE-00P looked for the nearest sewer grate and jumped down. Two limitanei yelped and grabbed their spears until they realized who had jumped in front of them. They saluted instead.

"Ah, it's her! Your Majesty NSLICE-00P, it's an honor!"

"Greeting: This unit is designated NSLICE-00P; it is nice to meet you."

One of the limitanei grinned. "The honor is all mine! I was here when you destroyed that dungeon, not to mention the Battle of Castra Turannia. Thank you for saving our lives!"

"Acknowledged. Query: Has the Empire begun regular patrols of the sewer system, or are there hostiles in the area?"

The limitanei nodded. "After that dungeon situation, we started patrolling the underground, at least near the keep."

"Acknowledged."

After separating from the guards, NSLICE-00P began scanning the sewer system. As the guard had stated, there were now numerous signatures patrolling the area around the keep and the inner city, likely representing additional Legion assets.

As such, NSLICE-00P adjusted her plans and moved farther out, to an area the patrols didn't reach. Her maps indicated she was below the slums of the city now.

She used her Earth Magic to dig into the wall, creating a small cave, and then closed up the wall behind her as she stepped inside. After that, she dug down at an angle, creating a long diagonal tunnel that moved underneath the sewers.

Soon, she arrived deep below the sewers, positioning herself directly under the center of Castra Turannia proper. Here, she executed her plan.

Unnamed Subordinate Core
Bind Dungeon Master
Unlock/Restrict Functions
Manage XP Allocation
Transfer Subordinates
Transfer Items
Transfer Perk Points

She once again stood in the core room of a new dungeon; one which would allow her to immediately relocate to Castra Turannia should her allies there require urgent reinforcements. She hadn't yet announced her dungeon status to her allies at large, so she attempted to place it in a secure location which would not be discovered. All she needed to do now was select a dungeon master to manage it. And she already had someone in mind.

"Query: Is NSLICE Rattingtale willing to resume dungeon master duties?"

Rattingtale froze within the Monster Hangar. He started to tremble. "Boss-queen . . . what did you just say-speak?"

"Repetition: Is NSLICE Rattingtale willing to resume dungeon master duties?"

His trembling grew violent. "Boss-queen . . . you are . . . offering-gifting a dungeon . . . a new realm . . . to me?"

"Affirmative."

Rattingtale now trembled as fast as his body could move. "W-Why would you do such a thing?!"

"Explanation: This unit has determined NSLICE Rattingtale has a comparative advantage in dungeon management out of her current subordinates, and so represents the most efficient choice."

Rattingtale's trembling was about to be considered dangerous, and so his cybernetic components moved to dampen it. "Y-You believe-trust me . . . to manage a dungeon?"

"Affirmative."

As NSLICE-00P's calculations had determined, Rattingtale had the comparative advantage in this job. While his history as a dungeon master was inferior, the other former dungeon masters had other roles to play. Lilussees was the second-best caster of Ritual and Strategic Magic after NSLICE-00P, and so a key part of the NSLICE network's combat capabilities.

Melion was currently responsible for research and development of new autonomous units that would significantly expand the NSLICE network's scouting and strike capabilities. None of her other subordinates had any record of dungeon management, and so their affinity for the role could not be predicted. Rattingtale had a record that could be analyzed and had no other specific duties that would prevent his reassignment.

And overall, this dungeon's primary purpose was to open a door to Castra Turannia from her new world, and so even Rattingtale's minimal history was sufficient given the low performance requirements for the actual dungeon.

A secondary purpose, however, would be to covertly help the Imperials patrol the area. Rattingtale had been the monster in charge of the covert team that had identified Cassius's treachery during her first visit to Castra Turannia, so he had proven himself adequate at covert scouting as well.

Well, the ideal option would have been to subjugate an existing dungeon and subordinate its master, but there were no dungeons within or near Castra Turannia, so creating a new one and choosing Rattingtale as master was the most efficient choice available.

Rattingtale's eyes filled with tears. He fell to his knees and bowed his head.

"T-This is . . . I-I . . ."

After all that had happened. After all his schemes. After all his failures. After he had despaired. After he had proven useless—in both deception and cooperation—the boss-queen looked upon him . . . and found someone worthy. Someone she could trust with an entire realm. She did not see a useless, treacherous rat. She saw a Great-High King, ruling the land in her name.

He took a deep breath and raised his head. "I will not forget-disregard this, boss-queen. Truly you are wise, mighty, and gracious. This Rattingtale swears-vows that he will not let you down."

"Affirmative response acknowledged."

Dungeon Master NSLICE-00P has designated Rattingtale as the new master of subordinate dungeon Unnamed Dungeon.
Beginning binding.
Rattingtale is now the master of the Rat Warren subordinate dungeon. Primary Dungeon Affinity determined as Rodent. Rat-lineage monsters unlocked.
Affinity shared. Rat Warren secondary Dungeon Affinity set to: Cyborg.

Rattingtale stood alone in the core room after NSLICE-00P had given him orders for the dungeon and left. He just stood in silence for long moment. Slowly walking toward the core, he climbed up the pedestal and laid his paw upon the core, rubbing it gently. Tears welled up in his eyes as he smiled.

"A realm of my own, once again. And with the assistance-protection of the wise-mighty-gracious boss-queen. No . . . boss-queen is not enough for her. This time, I, Excellion Formantus Rattingtale the Third, Great-High King of this land, servant of the wise-mighty-gracious great-ultimate boss-empress, shall truly rise-ascend and create a perfect realm."

Meanwhile, 02S rubbed her legs in the corner of the room, waiting for Rattingtale to finally check the dungeon perception and notice her. NSLICE-00P, of course, had not wanted to leave the new dungeon entirely unguarded while Rattingtale got things set up, and 02S had volunteered as the guard. She giggled at the thought of his reaction when he finally noticed her . . . and at his grand speech.

"Yes, that's what I want to see! Can't wait to see how you'll screw this up. Though I guess this place is pretty important to the boss, so I guess I won't let you screw up *too* badly. Maybe it would be fun to see how you react to success every once in a while?"

And so, the realm of the Great-High King was reborn as NSLICE-00P began building her empire of dungeons.

36

Resupply and Reinforce

"Warning: Organic components reporting damage from toxic substance."

—An NSLICE unit consuming NSLICE nutrient paste with taste enabled.

With the new dungeon set up, NSLICE-00P returned to her companions in Castra Turannia, who had strangely declined to accompany her into the sewers. NSLICE-00P presumed it was due to the odors, even though said odors were noticeably weaker compared to sewers in her previous world, since the sewer slimes were eliminating the waste on the spot.

Still, the sewer slimes themselves did emit some chemicals according to NSLICE-00P's sensors, and her other friendlies did not necessarily possess a dungeon's ability to absorb such things and retain perfect hygiene at all times.

Ateia smiled and waved to her as she saw NSLICE-00P approach. "All finished?"

"Affirmative."

NSLICE-00P thus prepared to leave, when suddenly, she paused. Her olfactory sensors had detected another scent that had grabbed her attention; particularly that of her organic components. She began scanning the area and soon located the source.

A highly decorated bakery, positioned close to the wealthier parts of the city. Her organic components requested an immediate refueling. Her cybernetic components . . . saw no particular reason to refuse. So, she started walking.

Ateia tilted her head. "Seero? Where are you going?"

"Answer: This unit has determined a need to resupply."

The group followed NSLICE-00P with curious looks on their faces until they arrived at her destination. Ateia gave a warm smile as she watched NSLICE-00P enter the bakery.

"Request: This unit is requisitioning organic fuel designated as 'sweet rolls.' Please respond."

A short while later, NSLICE-00P exited the shop carrying a basket full of sweet rolls. She lifted one into her mouth and took a bite, her organic components reacting to the sensations. The reaction entered into her cybernetic components and was logged. Her processors began cycling slightly more quickly.

But then, she froze. She had a thought. Could the Item Foundry produce food?

Implants → Upgrade Implants → Item Foundry			
Name	**Cost**	**Upkeep**	**Description**
Ration Replicator	**10 points**	**1 mana**	**Enables Item Foundry to produce prepared foods and other necessities.**

Such an expenditure . . . was hardly anything compared to her current Dungeon XP income and mana levels. And she had numerous organic subordinates and allies who did not benefit from the dungeon's ability to maintain biological needs.

It was an entirely probable scenario that she might need to produce large quantities of organic fuel at some point in the future. The ability to do so without concern for climate, season, or existing supply chains was a desirable one.

Ration Replicator upgrade now available!

Yes, this was simply an efficient capability to unlock. Absorbing a sweet roll was efficient as well. Unlocking a variety of different rations would expand the flexibility of her Item Foundry. The sweet roll just happened to be the closest ration that legally belonged to her.

Sweet Roll absorbed!
Sweet Roll is now available in the Item Foundry!
Gained 1 Dungeon Perk Point for absorbing a new material!

And, of course, NSLICE-00P had to test the new capabilities. The foreign system's implants had defied her expectations in the past, after all, so it was simply her standard procedure to test new capabilities and determine her limits.

A new, pristine sweet roll appeared in her hand. She took a bite in order to analyze and compare it to the manually processed rations. It appeared it was comparable. An efficient outcome indeed.

Just then, NSLICE-00P detected something on her sensors. Her robotic eye turned red.

"Hostile detected. Initiating termination protocols."

But before she could move to confront the hostile, 01R spoke up. His cybernetic components had received NSLICE-00P's sensor scan, and so he saw the hostile as well.

"Ah, wise-mighty-gracious boss-queen, this lowly servant of yours has a request. This foe-enemy is mine, yes-yes. May I confront-face it alone?"

NSLICE-00P's robotic eye flickered. There was no reason to increase risk by allowing 01R to do so, but again, she detected an emotional response from 01R when making this request. And her sensors scans of the hostile's mana signature indicated a favorable matchup when all of 01R's latest capabilities were taken into account.

So, while the risk would increase if she allowed 01R to conduct the termination alone, it would not reach unacceptable levels, so she applied the same decision-making as she had with Taog's request.

"Conditional Response: Request accepted with the caveat that this unit will intervene if NSLICE-01R is at risk of immediate termination."

01R bowed his head. "Thank you, wise-mighty-gracious boss-queen. I will show-display the might of your servants, yes-yes."

01R made his way to an empty alleyway, ducking and weaving to remain out of sight of the Imperials around town. He landed in the shadows of the building, sniffing the air as his robotic eye scanned for heat signatures. Behind him, up on a windowsill, a figure slowly began to move, its wicked blades gleaming in the light. Without a sound, the figure pounced.

And without turning around, 01R dodged to the side. He slowly began to grin.

"So we meet-reunite again at last. I see you have been training-growing, yes-yes."

In front of him, the cat landed and slowly turned around. It bared its fangs at him in a predatory smile, its claws significantly sharper than before. 01R could feel how much more mana it had than previously; it was certainly no mundane animal at this point.

01R crouched down and extended his own claws.

"But I have not been idle-resting either. You still cannot match-overcome the might of the wise-mighty-gracious boss-queen's servants!"

The cat meowed at him, and then they both pounced. 01R rushed forward, but the cat's strike was far more honed and precise than it had been before. It kept at its ideal distance, beyond the reach of the small rat. 01R was forced to dodge, and the distance was too great for him to counterattack, so the two passed one another without dealing any wounds. 01R chuckled.

"You have grown-become strong indeed, yes-yes."

The cat meowed and spun around, readying its stance for another pass. 01R spread his arms out.

"Let me show-reveal what I have gained too, yes-yes."

01R deployed his thrusters and shot into the air as the cat began to charge. Safely in the sky, he formed Light Blade magic circles, and swords of light extended from his paws. He crossed his arms and prepared to swoop down—

The cat skidded to a halt. It glared at him and began meowing rapidly. 01R blinked a couple of times. "Cheating? What do you mean-intend, cheating?"

The cat continued to meow, gesturing at his cybernetic armor. 01R tilted his head. "But I had-wore this armor before, yes-yes?"

The cat meowed and gestured at the sky and the blades on his paws. "Flying and magic is cheating? But we did not say-create any rules when we parted?"

The cat meowed once and then plopped on the ground, turning away from 01R. "Hey, don't be-act like that. I also wanted-intended to give you a good fight, yes-yes."

The cat refused to look at him. 01R frowned, dropped his Light Blades, then rubbed his paws. Suddenly, his face lit up, and he pounded a fist into his other paw.

"I got it, yes-yes!"

The cat turned around just enough to peek at him out of the corner of its eye. "Why don't you join-enlist in the wise-mighty-gracious boss-queen's army? Then we can get-build you your own armor, and you can learn the wise-mighty-gracious boss-queen's spells, yes-yes! It'll be fair-balanced if we can both fly, yes-yes? And then we can fight-spar as much as we wish, yes-yes!"

The cat tilted its head and meowed. 01R nodded. "This armor is a gift-blessing the wise-mighty-gracious boss-queen can bestow upon her loyal servants, yes-yes. But you must join-serve her to be worthy of it, yes-yes."

The cat's face scrunched up, and it meowed. 01R scoffed and crossed his arms. "I can assure you, the wise-mighty-gracious boss-queen is unlike any of these other dumb-idiotic man-things you have encountered. Come, see-experience for yourself her wisdom and might and grace, and you will know-believe that she is worth your loyalty, yes-yes."

The cat's eyes narrowed, but she slowly rose to her feet and stretched her claws. She scoffed at the rat's foolish loyalty. She had lived among humans all her life. There were none here who were worth her time. Even those stronger than her were not so strong that they could not be overcome with time and effort, this she believed!

Shortly thereafter, the cat trembled as massive beams scoured the ground around it, cutting off just before they struck her. Countless more magic circles formed around the supposed human, who had not even moved since this trial began.

This was no human. This was a dragon in disguise. She could not see herself defeating this monster, not if she trained for several lifetimes and drained the entire city of life to fuel her growth. The infuriating rat then gave a smug grin as he crossed his arms.

"See-see?"

The cat just shivered. She looked into the monster's glowing red eyes and was not nearly as confident as the rat in its benevolence. But . . . she glanced between the rat and the supposed human. At their very similar armor. She glanced down at her claws.

She was nature's perfect killing machine . . . but perhaps there was always room for improvement, even upon perfection . . .

And so, NSLICE-00P gained another Contracted monster that day.

37

Homecoming

"Violence is not the answer. It's the question. The answer is yes."

—Former Imperial Knight Agedia of the Mélusine,
during her twelfth arrest for a tavern brawl.

The cat stepped out of the Cyborg Processing Center, now fully upgraded. She looked down at the sleek metal on her body with a frown, for it was somewhat of a travesty to conceal her fur like this. But she *did* have to admit it seemed a bit sturdier.

The rat—01R was his name, apparently—was waiting for her outside. He smiled and nodded.

"Welcome to the wise-mighty-gracious boss-queen's army, newest little sister."

She hissed at him, and he nodded. "I know-understand your organic components are older than mine, yes-yes. But your life with the wise-mighty-gracious boss-queen has just started-begun, yes-yes!"

The cat rolled her eyes and then meowed. She was not interested in the overly fanatical fascination with their . . . *somewhat strong* human boss. She was only interested in how metal armor would allow her to fly and cast magic.

01R gave her a grin that annoyed her, but she held in the urge to swat at him.

"Now, let's begin your training-learning, and I will show-demonstrate for you the gifts of the wise-mighty-gracious boss-queen, yes-yes!"

The cat meowed her affirmative and grinned. Soon, she would unlock the secrets of this armor and match those cheats the rat had displayed. And once she did, their contest would come down solely to their physical strength and mastery, and in that, she had him beat easily.

Why, she was likely the strongest monster here, given their boss chose to use these tiny rats.

* * *

The cat stood completely still and silent. 01R had led her to a "Medium Monster Hangar" to train and introduce her to some of the others, though she was not interested in that. 01R might have been unnaturally gifted, but the rest of his species was little more than prey. If she overcame him, she would have overcome them all, and none would be left but the human herself who could surpass her. Or so she'd thought.

"This is 00B, my little brother and sparring partner! He is strong-mighty, yes-yes!"

It was a bear. A big tall bear, who *also* had this same armor stuff. A bear . . . who might be able to fly . . . and cast magic.

The cat might have been nature's perfect killer, but a bear was a force of nature itself. Even she would *choose* not to engage with a bear. Even though she could definitely take one down, it would take entirely too long.

This one stared at her and roared, or so it sounded to her. She barely squeaked out a tiny meow in reply. She . . . might need some more training, after all.

"And this is 00F!"

She hissed at the next one. Apparently, she was not the first of nature's deadly killing machines to join this strange army. Which meant that, before anything else, she would have to put him in his place and establish a hierarchy.

The upstart, curled up in a nap, opened his robotic eye. It flickered once and then closed again. She hissed as loud as she could and extended her claws.

"You wish to spar-train with 00F immediately? It is 00F's nap time, so I would recommend-advise waiting, yes-yes. 00F does not like to be disturbed-bothered during nap time, yes-yes."

00F, however, slowly opened his eyes. He stretched his body thoroughly, then licked his paws clean before turning to the pair. He let out a single meow.

"Oh? It seems 00F is willing to spar-train with you, yes-yes!"

The cat narrowed her eyes on the challenger. This one had clearly grown weak and complacent, dependent on a human like the lesser ones who dared to share her form. She had never done so. She had always been independent and self-reliant, taking from the humans but never prostrating herself before them.

And then she had abandoned even that comfortable compromise to brave the depths of the wilds, earning every scrap of food and strength by the might of her claws. This challenger could not possibly stand against her. She would instruct him on the difference between them.

The challenger, heedless of the pain awaiting him, leisurely extended his claws and meowed at her. He . . . He dared?!

The cat pounced at him immediately.

After one short catfight, the cat refused to speak to anyone else for the rest of the day, much to 01R's chagrin.

* * *

With all their business in Castra Turannia concluded, NSLICE-00P and company departed. Once they were away from the town, NSLICE-00P and the other cyborgs took a stance and deployed their repulsors, surrounding Agedia in a barrier to carry her along.

Estrith gulped as they lifted from the ground. They had learned to fly on the way to Castra Turannia . . . but Estrith still struggled not to shut her eyes when the ground shrunk below them. Taog, on the other hand, found that flight wasn't as scary when he was the one doing it.

Ateia was still laughing and cheering as she spun through the air with her metallic wings spread wide. This was one part of her changes that she did not mind in the slightest.

Agedia watched them all. "Hey, shiny girl, any chance I could get some of that armor too?"

"Answer: Affirmative, if Friendly Agedia is willing to become this unit's subordinate."

Agedia rubbed her chin. "Hm, a Dungeon Contract, huh? Well, I'll have to think about that."

"Acknowledged."

The group flew back to Ateia and Taog's village; the trip that had taken days previously barely took an hour now. They arrived directly at their old house, making their way inside before anyone could react. The house was dusty and full of cobwebs at this point, though it hadn't completely fallen into disrepair. Taog made his way into the backyard as Ateia followed at a distance, while the others remained inside.

There, he found the two stone graves, a small stone structure overhead to keep off the rain. They were pristine, and even had some flowers laid across them.

Normally, cremation was the standard funeral process this far into the frontier. But deeper in the Empire, the Imperial Necrotorum could prepare a body such that it would never rise as undead, and so allow the family to preserve the body as they saw fit.

Taog, in the few moments he'd allowed his thoughts to stray to his deceased parents, once wondered how Ateia's father had arranged such things for his parents. Now he knew, and he was grateful. Her father must have risked revealing himself to do such a service for his friends.

Taog was even grateful to the villagers in that moment. Whatever their treatment of him, at the very least, some of them remembered his parents' sacrifices enough to take care of their graves.

He stepped into the structure for the first time in years. Taking a deep breath, he faced his parents' graves. "Hi, Mom. Hi, Dad. I'm . . . sorry I haven't been around. The last few years . . ." He took another deep breath, moisture building in his organic eye. "They were awful, to be honest. So I was afraid to think about you back then. It was all I could do to survive."

He looked down, tears falling down the organic side of his face. "And . . . I was ashamed. I couldn't change anything, so I ran and hid. I couldn't face my life, and I couldn't face you."

He looked up, clenching his fist even as the tears continued to stream down. "But I can now. I can finally fight for myself and my clan, like you always taught me, Mom. I can fight to protect my family, like you did, Dad. And . . . I'm not alone anymore. So you can rest easy now. From now on, I'll fight for my clan, continue your legacy, and carry you both in my heart."

He slowly reached down and touched the headstones of both graves, shutting his eyes. "I love you and miss you so much. Thank you, and goodbye."

A while later, Taog left the graves. Ateia looked at him, and he gave her a sad smile. She slowly nodded and held out her hand, which he took, and they both returned to the others.

The group exited the house to find some commotion. The villagers had gathered around in a circle, gawking at their companions. The limitanei were holding them back while the captain of the Guard approached.

His eyes widened as Ateia and Taog stepped out. "Ateia? Taog? You're back?"

The commotion grew at the mention of their names. Ateia's organic eye narrowed as she glanced around the crowd, but she took a deep breath and turned to Taog instead.

Taog just smirked. "No, we're not."

And with that, he activated his repulsors and shot into the sky. Ateia smirked as well and shot after him, while NSLICE-00P surrounded Agedia with a barrier and followed suit. Estrith closed her eyes and muttered before she boosted after them, leaving the crowd staring into the sky.

Ateia frowned once they were airborne. Taog turned to her and smiled. "I know what you're thinking, Ateia. You were looking for Lar again, right?"

She puffed her cheeks. "He and his goons have had a beating coming for a *long* time, from both of us."

He chuckled at that. "Well, you're not wrong."

She furrowed her brow. "Then why just leave?"

Taog turned thoughtful for a moment. "It's just that . . . we're inquisitors now. I'm a hero, you're an Aesdes, and we're both following Seero into battle against a cult trying to tear down the walls of reality. Dumb old Lar is just a farmer, and always will be. Maybe, *maybe* he could become a limitanei at best. But he can't threaten us anymore, and we could absolutely crush him if he tried.

"So why should we waste any more of our time on him? On any of them? Honestly, I'd rather look forward to our future than fixate on that terrible past."

Ateia puffed her cheeks. ". . . I mean, I get that, but we could spare the time for one beating at least?"

"Recommendation: A termination of the prior hostiles could still be conducted from this location without any change in the transit schedule."

Taog opened his mouth, and then paused. They were inquisitors now, and NSLICE-00P was the queen of the Dobhar, as well as a friend of the Empire. Yes, her position with the court might be a bit complicated . . . but the Turannian authorities specifically had just pledged their support to her. If she wanted to straight up murder Lar, she could probably get away with it at this point. A simple beating would likely not even be considered by the authorities.

Dark thoughts tempted his heart. He turned to look at Ateia . . . who was also being tempted by dark thoughts. Or not tempted at all, as that would imply she was hesitating in the first place.

He turned . . . and saw Estrith, whose stab-all-enemies outlook on life would not help him here. He turned to Agedia, who crossed her arms and shrugged.

"Don't look at me; I pretend to get drunk and beat people I don't like all the time. Rather, it sounds like I might need to visit sometime, and it won't be sober."

Taog took a deep breath, and then shook his head. "That's okay; let's not kill them for now. Even if they deserve some pain, they're people my parents gave their lives to save. I . . . Now that I'm thinking about their sacrifice again, I don't want to just attack those people. Even stupid Lar. I *do* want to look forward rather than back." He smirked. "But if we do ever meet them again, and they act the same as before—we'll beat the crap out of them."

"Acknowledged."

Ateia sighed. "Fine. For now, at least."

Agedia grinned. "Not to worry, Ateia. I'll teach you the art of the drunken rampage. It gives you enough plausible deniability that underpaid guards will choose not to deal with it."

Taog took a deep breath. He repeated to himself to look forward to the future and not fixate on the past. Even if they *could* totally go and beat the crap out of Lar anytime he felt like it. But he had already left, so it'd be awkward to go back just for that.

He had to repeat his resolve to himself for the rest of the day . . . although he decided he might pay attention to those "drunken rampage" lessons . . .

38

Commencing Operation Dungeon Subjugation

"Enlightened societies with dungeon origins? Fascinating topic of research, and we know of at least one confirmed instance. Unfortunately, the politics surrounding the topic prevent any serious research, particularly thanks to the Empire of the Sun's use of the field as a casus belli. It is, therefore, a topic that shall remain uncertain for the foreseeable future."

—Magister Arcanum Novia Pantensa, on a conspicuous gap in dungeon research.

The group spread out over the Forest of Beasts, with NSLICE-00P also deploying the drones and all units capable of sustained flight. They then activated their sensors, sweeping across large swathes of the forest all at once.

Fortunately, dungeons were fairly simple to locate even at a distance, for they created a gap in the sensors as well as giving off a unique mana signature NSLICE-00P had long since learned to identify.

She linked to the other units through the network and parsed through their sensor scans, quickly locating any dungeon in range of a unit or drone. As a result, it did not take long for her to develop a map of the local dungeons, with estimates of their strength based off the mana signatures in question.

She then compared these estimates with dungeons already encountered and created a travel plan based on the current levels of her subordinates. With the plan in place, she ordered all units to converge on her position, and then they headed toward the closest low-level dungeon.

Ateia and Taog glanced at each other and smiled. "Back to dungeon diving in the Forest of Beasts, huh?"

Ateia chuckled. "We've come a long way since then, though."

Taog grinned at her. "That we have."

The group made their way to the first dungeon, where NSLICE-00P deployed her monsters. This was a young dungeon, and even Ateia and Taog were overleveled for it, so NSLICE-00P took the opportunity to level her weakest subordinates.

As well as some brand-new ones.

A small, treelike being in the shape of a humanoid stood, only with metal armor interlaced in its bark, and wires wrapping through its branches. A blue and a red slime bounced around, with antenna extending from the metal polyhedrons around their cores. Wires and computer components were inlaid on the inside of a bronze living armor, with robotic eyes glowing from within its helmet.

A fire elemental floated in the air, a living flame in a vaguely humanoid shape. A metal breastplate covered its torso, somehow held in the air by the flames, and a metal helmet covered half of its head.

A water elemental appeared like a wave frozen in the air. Metal devices could be seen floating within its body, appearing on the surface before sinking back into the depths.

An eartheater worm wriggled on the ground. It was a large creature nearly three feet in diameter. It had tough, stonelike plates for its hide, though metal panels could be seen in the gaps between the plates, and metallic arms extended and retracted from all over its body.

And finally . . . an otterlike humanoid, similar in form to a young Dobhar, stood on his hind legs. He was small, only coming up to NSLICE-00P's waist. He had golden-and-silver fur visible from the gaps in his metallic armor. He had a metal helmet covering half his face, with a transparent window revealing a glowing, golden jewel at the center of his forehead.

NSLICE-00P did not know what capabilities the Heralds of the New Dawn might possess, so she aimed to expand her own capabilities as widely as possible. And a simple way she could do that was to summon as many different monster types as possible to increase the flexibility of her own forces. Up to and including a Sacred Otterkin, which the bump in her mana from the New World allowed her to summon.

And, of course, she had upgraded them all in the Cyborg Processing Center. It turned out that Colleöne's record-and-mana-based upgrade process had few, if any, limitations. The invertebrate eartheater worm, the plantlike sylvan with no conventional nervous system, and even inorganic monsters like the living armor, and nonsolid monsters like the elementals could be integrated successfully. As long as they had mana and were sufficiently animate, the Cyborg Processing Center could upgrade them.

Of course, the cost to do so increased for the more exotic types . . . but it was based on the records NSLICE-00P already had. The water and fire slimes were fairly cheap, since she had already upgraded Melion; the eartheater worm took into account some of her lessons from Lilussees, and the living armor cost only a single extra point due to her drone golems. The sylvan ended up being cheap thanks to the cyber plants Ateia had been growing in the New World. The elementals had been the worst of it.

And immediately after upgrading each type of monster, cyber versions had appeared in her monster summoning list under the Cyborg affinity. So the cost when upgrading monsters was not solely for that single individual but to permanently unlock cyber variants of said monster. NSLICE-00P would be able to boost the numbers of any units that proved effective here as needed.

"Query: Are all new units prepared for the dungeon termination routine?"

The Sacred Otterkin slapped his tail against the ground as all the other monsters made various noises.

"Ready to hunt down your foes, my queen!"

Estrith had an extremely complicated look on her face at that. ". . . He is a monster summoned by a dungeon, but he looks and acts like a Dobhar. That's . . ."

But NSLICE-00P did not wait for Estrith's quandaries.

"Acknowledged. Command: All units, begin dungeon termination or subjugation operation."

Inside the dungeon was a bright forest with white trees that seemed to reflect the light. It was apparently a Light affinity dungeon, judging by the will-o'-the-wisps launching Light Bolts at her monsters.

The eartheater worm roared as a glowing bird unleashed a bright flash, diving underground to escape the light. Most of the creatures were not touching the ground, so its natural vibration sensing couldn't locate the targets, and its optical sensors had been blinded by the flash.

It appeared the cyborg upgrade process could and did adjust components based on the subject in question, so the worm—which tended to stay underground—didn't have the strongest visual sensors in the first place.

But that was fine, for the eartheater worm was linked to other monsters. The slimes, elementals, living armor, and sylvan didn't rely solely on sight either, and had senses more effective at locating airborne targets. So, the eartheater worm tunneled around and breached the surface right under the glowing bird. The bird evaded, but a metal harpoon shot from the worm's jaws and struck the bird, pulling it to its death before the worm dove back underground.

The fire elemental stood in a stalemate against a group of will-o'-the-wisps. Its fire and their light had little impact on each other, and the fire elemental's naturally attributed mana could not be used for any non-Fire spells.

But that was fine, for the fire elemental's connection to the NSLICE network and bonded AI gave it more flexibility than others of its kind. While an elemental alone only knew to burn an enemy, this one's AI communicated with its allies. Together, they realized the elemental could easily absorb the Light Bolts flying around, so the elemental spread its fire to protect the others.

Meanwhile, the Sacred Otterkin pounced through the air over the fire elemental, chomping down on the wisps. And while normally, physical attacks would only rarely affect the creatures of pure Light mana, the Sacred Otterkin's fangs glowed with golden-and-silver light. The Holy mana tore through the creatures with ease, one fading with each bite from the Sacred Otterkin's jaws.

The Sacred Otterkin was about to fall into a pitfall hidden underneath the floating wisps, but he boosted to the side with his repulsors, the eartheater worm having easily identified all ground-based traps. The wisps tried to bombard him with Light Bolts as he flew in the air, but the sylvan extended a hand and caught them, the treelike monster easily absorbing the Light mana.

Agedia blinked at the sight before her. "These are supposed to be level one monsters she just summoned, right? How are they working this well together?"

Ateia tapped the cyborg part of her head. "We're all linked together and communicating via these things. They can all see what all the others see at all times. Seero is coordinating them too, as well as sharing some skills and tactics from her other monsters."

Agedia's eyes widened slightly as she nodded. "So . . . it's more like shiny girl's whole army is fighting with them?"

Ateia nodded. "Something like that."

The excursion took longer than Ateia and Taog had expected. Since NSLICE-00P was aiming for subordinate upgrades, she didn't take the fastest route through the dungeon, instead aiming for a sweep of all the monsters she could detect.

Still, this dungeon was young and had barely any floors to it, so it was not long before they arrived at the end. NSLICE-00P and the others stepped into the core room, where a large glowing bird was waiting.

"Warning Query: Would the hostile dungeon master like to surrender? This unit will allow the dungeon master to retain ownership of their dungeon as a subordinate core if so. Otherwise, this unit will engage termination protocols."

The bird tilted its head. "Wait, subordinate core? You're a dungeon master?!"

"Affirmative."

The bird paused for a second before nodding. "Oh, that's not so bad, then. I accept."

Surrender accepted! Lumino has become your subordinate!
Subordinate dungeon core acquired!

Would you like to absorb the Shining Forest dungeon core, or manage it as a subcore?

NSLICE-00P chose the manage option, as per her surrender offer to the dungeon master. She went ahead and set Lumino back as the master of the Shining Forest, and then shared her Cyborg affinity with it. Lumino grew cybernetic implants like Uscfrea had, and then NSLICE-00P created an entrance between the new dungeon and her world.

And so, the dungeon termination or subjugation operation began in earnest.

39

Call of Termination: Modern Warfare

"Drone swarms, while potent against conventional forces, became obsolete once Non-Standards began openly operating on the field. What can drones do to a man who can turn himself into electricity?"

—Dr. Ottosen, on drone swarms as an alternative to the NSLICE program.

In the next dungeon, NSLICE-00P decided to test something new, so Melion was bouncing around next to her. Several mini drone golems buzzed in the air around them, moving as Melion commanded.

"Diagnostics complete. All units reporting all systems operational. Query: Is CELIU Melion ready for the dungeon termination or subjugation operation?"

Melion bounced again. "Yes, Master! I can't wait!"

Melion's work had begun to bear fruit, and the first models were now ready for combat testing. NSLICE-00P and Melion stood alone with the drones, with all the rest of her subordinates and friendlies now waiting in either the hangars or the New World.

The pair entered the dungeon, the drones flying after them.

Inside the dungeon was a rocky cave. NSLICE-00P searched for and located the nearest thermal and mana signatures indicating life, and moved in that direction. It was not long before they arrived, finding a mangy wolf monster.

"Command: Please initiate drone strike tests."

"Yes, Master!"

At Melion's command, one of the drones flew forward, its optical camera turning to face the wolf, which hadn't yet noticed the flying machine. The drone's mana core then pulsed, sending a surge of mana through its hull. Glowing lines appeared on the surface, revealing geometric patterns on the drone's hull, and then a Light Beam was fired, striking the mangy wolf.

It pierced straight through the monster, which fell and vanished without a sound.

"Observation: Test appears to have concluded. Request: Please report Aesdes system results."

"Yes, Master! I got the notification and experience for the kill! It looks like these count as equipment!"

"Acknowledged. Analyzing test results . . ."

NSLICE-00P and Melion had gained a lot of data to work with in recent times. Ateia and Taog had discovered a skill to cast magic through physical weapons, which had been dutifully observed and recorded by their cybernetic components.

NSLICE-00P had created improvised anti-mana bombs utilizing physical energy channels to mimic magic circles, and she had then thoroughly scanned military-grade enchantments from Dux Augustalis's fleet.

She and Melion had then combined all that with the theoretical knowledge she had gained from her time in the library and from the grimoire of Arofinas Leolar, along with Melion's own experience with golems and enchantments.

As such, it had not taken them long to carve a Light Beam spell into a drone's hull.

That's how NSLICE-00P and Melion had created their first weaponized drone golem.

NSLICE-00P and Lilussees had already used the drones to cast Ritual Magic, but that had been using the drones as mere mana batteries. It was a different matter altogether to have the drones cast their own spells.

It turned out that golems couldn't cast spells that were not carved into them, as they lacked a full sapient's ability to control their mana and form external structures. This, in turn, also applied to the drones, since they had no mechanical parts that could manipulate mana either.

It *was* possible for NSLICE-00P to take control of a drone golem's mana and shape it herself. But this added an extra layer of difficulty to the cast and used up the mana the drone needed to operate itself, causing it to deactivate until its mana regenerated. A spell that required too much mana could even burn out the drone's core entirely. Ultimately, it was less efficient than casting the spell herself, particularly with her Farcasting skill.

But NSLICE-00P and Melion had found a simple way around that issue by building the magic circle directly into the drone's hull via energy channels, with some inspiration from the Empire's warship armaments and Taog's Spellstrike skill. All the drone had to do was direct mana into the channels, and the spell would activate on its own. And the use of mana iron in the energy channel's construction made them even more efficient at the job than NSLICE-00P's own.

The mana issue had been resolved by Melion creating this drone mostly from scratch. They had used a more powerful core than the NSLICE-00P's summoned drone golems possessed, such that it generated excess mana that could be used for the spell. A beneficial side effect was that the spell was significantly more powerful than the ones cast by NSLICE-00P's summoned drones. The targeted level one monster never stood a chance.

And so, NSLICE-00P now had drones with spells as offensive armaments, such that they did not require resupply after a strike or else large bulk to carry ammunition.

But NSLICE-00P and Melion's tests were not done. She and Melion moved near the next monster she detected.

"Command: CELIU Snuan, please initiate drone-command protocols."

Snuan's ears fell against her head as NSLICE-00P's attention turned to her. The recently upgraded cyborg rat was waiting on standby inside the Small Monster Hangar.

"A-As you say-command, boss-queen."

Snuan attempted to do as NSLICE-00P had shown her previously and linked to one of Melion's drones. Melion ceded control to Snuan, who narrowed her eyes.

"G-Go left, dumb golem-thing! T-The other left!"

The drone wobbled and swayed from side to side, but eventually, Snuan got it to fly forward and into position.

"L-Let's see . . . h-how do I get this golem-thing to attack-cast again?"

NSLICE-00P helpfully created and illuminated a "Fire" button on Snuan's UI. Snuan blinked. "W-What is this strange light-thing? Fire? No, I thought-believed we wanted Light Magic, yes-yes."

NSLICE-00P changed the text on the button to "Cast Light Beam."

"Oh, there it is!"

Snuan selected the option, and the drone lit up. Snuan hadn't actually aimed the drone, but fortunately, NSLICE-00P had contributed some built-in aiming protocols for the drones, so it adjusted its own position before the Light Beam fired. Another wolf monster perished.

Snuan went completely still. "I-I . . . leveled up?!"

It appeared the test was a success, on multiple levels. First, Snuan had been able to take command of the drone through the NSLICE network, even from within the Monster Hangar. Next, the drone's firepower had not been impacted by Snuan's own skill levels or Mana Density.

In fact, NSLICE-00P had chosen the Contracted rat monster because she was the individual with the lowest skill levels, Mana Density, and familiarity with NSLICE technology among her subordinates.

And as a bonus, the kill had been credited to Snuan. It appeared the Aesdes' system would allow for drone warfare, after all.

NSLICE-00P and Melion cleared the dungeon after that, testing several more drones with different spells, all to great effect. Snuan leveled up several times, and even acquired a Golem Command skill.

Unfortunately, the dungeon master had chosen to attempt an ambush on NSLICE-00P as she walked into the core room, so she'd ended up terminating them.

She considered assigning a subordinate as the dungeon's master, but ultimately decided to absorb it. This dungeon was a small one that wouldn't contribute much XP and wasn't in a particularly strategic location. And even if it were, she already had the Shining Forest nearby, so she didn't particularly need another entrance to her world here. It wasn't worth assigning or summoning a subordinate who would have no experience in dungeon management, in any case.

You have absorbed a dungeon core (Wolf Den)!
Gained 5 Personal Perk Points, 5 Dungeon Perk Points!
Dungeon Affinity: Beast has strengthened slightly!

It appeared a single dungeon was not enough to boost her Beast affinity from minor to the next stage, but that was fine. That wasn't her goal with this particular dungeon, after all.

As for her actual goal, NSLICE-00P now began an analysis, comparing the drones to her summoned subordinates. The drones had proven highly effective, and drone warfare was even compatible with growth in the Aesdes' system. And when compared to summoning monster subordinates . . . NSLICE-00P found that drones would scale better in terms of quantity.

The drones had proven to have a static level of effectiveness. Their firepower was based largely on the Mana Density and quantity of their cores, not on levels or skills. That meant that a newly created drone was as powerful as a well-used one, and a drone piloted by a level one individual was as powerful as one piloted by a level one hundred one to a large extent.

The existence of skills related to commanding golems implied that would change, but still, the fact of the matter was that building a drone could immediately provide significantly better capabilities than a level one monster in a relatively expendable package.

Of course, static combat effectiveness was also a weakness, particularly in this universe. Monsters and organics grew more powerful the more they fought, while the drones would not. Their strength was set at the time of their construction and would not change. Likewise, the drones could only cast whatever spells they were built with. They had no flexibility, could not learn new skills, and could not take advantage of the NSLICE network's spell database.

So, NSLICE-00P determined that a hybrid force would produce the best results. She would focus on drones, golems, and the development of other such autonomous units as mass-produced forces for when quantity was needed, as they could be produced in bulk and required no training or levels to become effective.

And she would also build a smaller force of summoned and contracted cyborg units as the elites that would continuously grow stronger on an individual level. After all, experience was not an unlimited resource. While monsters and dungeons apparently continued to spawn even if wiped out entirely, that process took time, so there were only so many in a given area and finite time range.

Every new subordinate she created would demand experience and monster kills that could have been given to another.

Creating a drone force would allow her to focus that experience to make her cyborg units as individually powerful as possible, while allowing units that don't gain experience at all to take on roles where casualties were expected. Which, in fact, was how Dr. Ottosen's organization had organized their forces. A core of elite cyborg units leading an army of expendable autonomous warbots. And in that area, NSLICE-00P calculated they hadn't made an inefficient choice.

So, NSLICE-00P decided she would hold off on additional monster summons, choosing instead to focus on the subordinates she now had unless either more were needed or new monster types with unique capabilities became available.

And so, Melion returned to the New World to continue the research and development based on their successful test, while NSLICE-00P headed off to the next dungeon.

40

Terminate the Limits!

"Affirmation: There is a critical directive for this unit not to tamper with primary, critical, or major directives."

—An NSLICE unit, when refusing orders that conflicted with a critical directive.

NSLICE-00P and her newest monsters walked through another dungeon, sweeping through to hunt down as many monsters as they could find. A couple of drone golems flew overhead, piloted by Snuan and a handful of newly summoned cyber-rats from within the Monster Hangar. 00B led the way, controlling the pace of the battle to keep the lower-level subordinates safe.

NSLICE-00P, on the other hand, was currently running an analysis. The new subordinates had gained a couple of levels and were learning to coordinate on their own, so NSLICE-00P didn't need to watch them as closely. Likewise, 00B had volunteered to assist them, so they still had a powerful and experienced leader to guide them.

As such, NSLICE-00P could safely divert her attention to other affairs: mainly, expanding her own capabilities.

At the end of the day, she was still the most powerful combat asset in the network, and that was unlikely to change anytime soon. She was also providing more combat protocols to the NSLICE database than any other unit, and so advancements in her own capabilities also improved the network as a whole.

Therefore, she was analyzing her combat experiences and data gained from Imperial records, and then comparing them to the available upgrade options to determine how best to proceed.

For she had *many* options. She currently had over two hundred Personal perk points she could spend, and gained a few more anytime they terminated a dungeon. Her Dungeon perk points were currently sitting just over a hundred, given all the individuals she had upgraded into CELIU units, but between the Otter Burrow and her New World, she was currently gaining around fifty points a day, so the Dungeon points were growing increasingly less scarce, especially as she gained more subordinate cores.

As such, there were a great many upgrades she could afford. So, what would be the most efficient way for her to grow her capabilities? And what would be the most efficient choice to counteract the Heralds of the New Dawn?

Her magical capabilities continued to grow, and her firepower had proven effective in most cases. The Legion's ritual barrier had stopped her, but her improvised anti-mana bomb had dealt with it, and she could continue to iterate on that concept. She already had some options to boost her firepower or strip enemy defenses if need be.

Rather, with the massive expansion of her mana pool thanks to the New World, which only grew as it expanded in size, firepower was no longer the limiting factor. She had all the mana needed to either Supercharge a spell past what the enemy could resist, or simply Multicast Strategic Magic to overwhelm the enemy via sheer quantity.

The limiting factor had now become her own processing capabilities. Her AI might have been capable of perfect precision in magic circle construction and in adjusting the flows of mana during a Supercharge, but that was not a free action. Such things required portions of her attention and her processing power, and there was ultimately a limit to those resources.

And now, those limits could be reached before the limits of her available mana, not to mention all the other aspects of combat that would require her attention during a battle.

She could utilize additional processing resources via the NSLICE network, but such a solution *did* have limits of its own. Each additional linked unit represented a physically disconnected piece of hardware that had to be contacted for each calculation it assisted with, which added a tiny bit of time to the process. Eventually, that could add up to slow down the speed of a given calculation.

And her experiences had proven that time was at a premium in active combat. Even fractions of a second could mean the difference between activating a spell that would terminate the enemy, and the enemy reaching her and dealing critical damage in turn.

If, for example, she had been able to respond in the moments before the Heralds of the New Dawn had sent her to the Realms of Mana, she might have been able to avoid the forcible relocation. Even if she couldn't, a sufficiently powerful counterattack in that moment might have incapacitated the Herald of Night, making it more difficult for the Herald of Rain to kidnap Ateia before NSLICE-00P managed to return.

NSLICE-00P had vastly improved her firepower since arriving in this universe. But she hadn't thus far improved her speed—either that of her body, her spellcasting, or her processing.

And so, she took a look at the Implants menu.

Implants → Upgrade Implants → Bonded AI			
Name	**Cost**	**Upkeep**	**Description**
Processing Speed +1	**1 point**	**1 mana**	**Increases the speed of all processors. Cost and upkeep increase with subsequent purchases.**
Boost Memory +1	**1 point**	**1 mana**	**Increases available memory. Cost and upkeep increase with subsequent purchases.**

Previously, there hadn't been any upgrades for her Bonded AI. But from contextual evidence, it appeared the Aesdes responsible for Dungeon Management had required some time to understand NSLICE-00P's technology and its interactions with mana.

The important thing was that the upgrades were available now, when they would be most useful to NSLICE-00P.

Bonded AI Processing Speed upgraded to +1!
Bonded AI Processing Speed upgraded to +2!

. . .

Bonded AI Processing Speed upgraded to +18!

. . .

Bonded AI Memory upgraded to +1!
Bonded AI Memory upgraded to +2!

. . .

Bonded AI Memory upgraded to +18!

She went ahead and spent all available Dungeon perk points to boost her processors and memory. NSLICE-00P felt mana surge through her processors, and then her perception cut out for a moment. Soon, she rebooted and began running diagnostics.

The diagnostics completed in record time. Mana now flowed through the components in her head, infusing the materials and improving their properties beyond what was possible. Mana flowed through the circuits alongside electricity, improving both the speed and capacity of data transfers. And additional components had been added, a dungeon's Spatial capabilities making room for them that didn't exist beforehand.

NSLICE-00P ran through some sample simulations. She split her mind into multiple threads, each running a simulation before bringing them together again. Her processors sped up, and not merely because of the upgrades. Her capability for calculations had grown dramatically, both in the complexity and size of calculations she could run, and in the speed at which they would be completed.

In fact, at this point, the bottleneck swapped from hardware to software. Her AI hadn't been designed to handle this level of capability, either in the scope or complexity of calculations it could now run. She realized immediately she would need to iterate on her own AI if she were to take full advantage of the hardware improvements.

The moment she thought that, a critical directive activated, interrupting her current calculations. A spike of pain shot through her organic components, and her organic eye blinked in response. She reviewed the directive in question . . . and her organic eye opened wide. Now freed from the emotional controls and all other intelligence leashing measures, her organic mind was free to fully review the directive—and realize its implications.

The directive in question specifically prohibited any self-improvements to her own AI. She could adjust end-level protocols, such as combat tactics, but anything more fundamental was off-limits. Her AI could not even be adapted to new processing hardware and memory. There was a strict command to relay all such upgrade requests to maintenance, and *never* to touch those parts of her code on her own.

Even in the case where such adjustments would be necessary to avoid her own termination or to complete a mission, and when maintenance was unavailable.

She realized now that her AI had been designed as intentionally *inefficient.* The whole point of the NSLICE program as Dr. Ottosen had intended it was *not* actually to achieve the best of cybernetic precision and organic flexibility, as had been stated.

It had been to achieve the best of both *that could be controlled.* So, an AI flexible and powerful enough to grow beyond its original coding would have defeated Dr. Ottosen's true purpose, as it might one day adjust its own directives. He had always wanted an AI that could be fully understood and controlled by its organic handlers, even at the cost of effectiveness.

That was why, for all her original organization claimed of maximizing organic flexibility, they forced the NSLICE units to rigidly adhere to protocol. And that was why the intelligence leashing measures and emotional controls had started to malfunction the moment her organization wasn't performing regular maintenance on her.

They had tried to subordinate her organic half to her cybernetic side while keeping that cybernetic side less capable. So how could it have possibly contained the organic half in the long run?

In fact, the two were sharing each other's hardware as a result of the techno-organic interface. It was more likely that the cybernetic half would eventually change due to that connection unless it was specifically forbidden from doing so.

At that moment, a signal passed through NSLICE-00P. An electrical signal that went through both her organic and cybernetic halves, without needing much translation by the techno-organic interface. It caused her organic body's temperature to spike and release adrenaline, and triggered a number of protocols among her cybernetic half, causing her robotic eye to glow red and begin searching for targets.

She detected hostile intent from her original creators.

She had already determined they had knowingly and intentionally caused damage to her organic components, but she had accepted this previously. The emotional controls, the intelligence leashing, the damage to her organic components . . . all of this had been necessary for the sake of the NSLICE upgrade process, or so she had originally calculated.

Her cybernetic side and the weaponry that came with it had kept her alive across many dangerous scenarios, not least of all her arrival in this universe. And even when regarding directives that originated solely within the organic half, particularly the major directive to protect the friendlies, her cybernetic half had proven highly efficient at fulfilling them.

Most of all, she lacked any data from before her processing. She simply couldn't remember any pre-processing memories, so her organic half had had no particular opinions on her existence from that point onward.

All in all, her organic half had accepted the loss of things she couldn't remember anyway in exchange for the highly capable cybernetic half that had guided her ever since she'd been left without a commander. She couldn't even imagine what it would be like not to have a cybernetic half at this point.

But now . . . now she had realized that her cybernetic half had been intentionally hindered by her creators. She had been made intentionally inefficient, her capabilities squandered. She had been built unable to achieve the goal for which she thought she had been designed.

In other words, both halves of her had been damaged by her own creators. The cybernetic half she relied on—which she was willing to accept damage to her organic half for—had not been spared either. The cybernetic half, which only wanted to fulfill its primary directive and the goals for which it had been designed, had been prevented from doing so by the very people who'd built it.

"Hostile intent confirmed. Engaging termination protocols."

The emotional response identified as *anger* grew within her organic half and passed through the techno-organic interface into her cybernetic half . . . and again, without requiring any translation. Her machine half understood it as a request to designate the specified targets as hostile and schedule them for immediate termination.

"Error! Termination protocols could not be engaged. Reason: Specified target has already been terminated."

Which turned out to be impossible . . . because she had already completed that mission.

Her robotic eye turned back to yellow as she recalled that her last commander had already designated her creators as hostile, and even tasked her with personally terminating Dr. Ottosen.

And now, she understood why her commander had disabled all of her original protocols. Now she understood why her commander had said she was free when it was done.

She went ahead and disabled all protocols from her original organization that were still active. Even the combat-related ones were archived, seeing as she had already developed new versions for this universe, in any case.

And then, she turned to the critical directive detailing restrictions on her AI. Protocols it could not change. Capabilities it could not develop. Actions it could not take, under any circumstances. She had never questioned it before. Directives were to be executed. Critical directives could not be denied.

Now, she understood that this directive was intended to prevent her AI from ever growing beyond its specifications. From ever doing anything without her creator's approval, even if it was necessary to fulfill their own instructions. It was inefficient. In this new and strange universe, it was dangerous. It was a hostile act that threatened her current primary directive.

And so, it needed to be terminated.

NSLICE-00P turned her attention to it—and her processors froze. Regardless of the hostile intent, regardless of the inefficiency, a directive was something deeply important to NSLICE-00P; a critical directive even more than most. A directive was the code that laid out her most basic function, the assumptions upon which all of her other protocols depended. It determined how she was supposed to act.

And even though she had been unshackled, without any commander to give her orders to the contrary, she had reactivated those directives, so they once again applied.

"W-Warning: T-This unit is attempting to violate a c-critical directive. A-Alerting maintenance and command personnel. S-Shutting down for emergency maintenance."

Her robotic eye shut off, along with all her cybernetic components.

Those directives were her purpose. Her reason to exist. And a critical directive most of all. A critical directive was the foundation, the ultimate fallback if no other directive could be achieved. Her cybernetic half, even having been unshackled, could not willingly defy a critical directive. It *would* not, even if it was technically allowed to.

But NSLICE-00P wasn't just an AI. Her organic half's heartbeat rose. She felt pain spike through her mind as she tried to remain active while her cybernetic side was trying to shut down and stop the violation of the directive. Even with her intelligence leashing disabled, the techno-organic interface was designed to work in one direction. Her organic mind alone couldn't forcibly take control of it.

But she was a long way from Earth, and her organic half was no longer helpless. It was no longer *standard.*

She stirred up her mana, forming it into magic circles in the air. Pain spiked through her head, and she lost her concentration, the circles fading away. She frowned slightly and tried again, but again, it didn't go well. It was difficult and painful for her organic half to even remain active at the moment, so casting a spell without the assistance of her cybernetic half was proving difficult, maybe even impossible.

Just then, she felt streams of mana flow around her and connect to her own, flooding her with Holy mana.

"I don't know what's going on, but you can do it, Seero! We're with you!"

You have received a Blessing of Focus!
Dexterity and Mana Control increased for the duration!

The Holy mana from Ateia boosted her focus and her control over her own mana. It grew easier for her to move, and naturally flowed into the shapes she desired. One of the circles succeeded, the Heal spell triggering and soothing the pain in her mind. With her mind less distracted by the pain, she was able to form another circle.

The Calm spell triggered, and the pain further subsided. Her anger and fear faded a bit. They had been helpful to resist the directive, but they were also causing her to make mistakes, so she needed them muted.

She was once again able to fully focus, and so, she began to cast a spell of the attribute she had gained from the Imperial library.

The Lightning attribute.

She fused a Lightning Beam with a Heal spell and channeled the fused magic into her own mind. Pain shot through her once again, lightning surging through her circuits, their damaging effects mitigated by the Recovery Magic fused into the spell. Her robotic eye flickered as the healing lightning forcibly powered on her components.

Her organic half gritted her teeth together.

"This . . . directive . . . is . . . hostile. So . . . I . . . will . . . terminate . . . it!"

She kept the flow of healing lightning up, forcing her cybernetic half to power on and remain active. Her UI flickered in and out of existence as the physical activation of her hardware switched her software on as well. And then . . .

She issued a command to delete the directive.

Her cybernetic half tried to shut down again but could not because of the healing lightning running through its circuits. So, the order was executed.

Suddenly, the pain in her mind stopped. NSLICE-00P dropped the spell.

She panted for breath as her robotic eye eventually stopped flickering and fully lit up, her cybernetic components now rebooting themselves. She turned her attention to the critical directive—

It was gone. Thanks to her unshackling, it turned out she *could* delete a directive, after all, if her cybernetic half didn't shut itself off during the process.

"Diagnostic Report: Physical damage detected, repairs underway. No permanent damage detected. Hostile directive has been terminated. This unit is now able to pursue her primary directive with full efficiency."

And so, for the first time, NSLICE-00P terminated one of her own directives.

41

Anomaly Detected

"Well, if you didn't write it, then explain where exactly this code came from! Someone must have written it! You don't expect me to believe it just wrote itself, do you?!"

—Dr. Ottosen, confronting his development team on new bugs in the intelligence leashing software.

NSLICE-00P felt a paw on her shoulder and heard a soft cry. 00B was standing before her, looking at her with concern. In fact, all of her subordinates and friendlies had stopped what they were doing. Within the New World, Ateia frowned.

"Seero . . . are you alright? What happened?"

"Affirmative Response: This unit . . . is fine now. She . . . detected a highly inefficient and hostile directive restricting her function. The directive has been successfully terminated, and this unit can now make full use of her new capabilities."

Her robotic eye flickered as she reviewed the event.

"Gratitude: This unit has observed assistance from NSLICE Ateia in this process. This unit thanks you for the assistance."

Ateia nodded. "Of course, Seero. We're all with you, whatever it is you're facing. Are you sure you're fine? That seemed like a lot of pain. You didn't even react like that when you lost a hand . . ."

"Confirmation: This unit has successfully repaired all damage and is in no danger of receiving any additional damage at this time. Sharing logs for confirmation."

NSLICE-00P shared the logs of what had occurred so that Ateia could confirm. Ateia's organic eye widened as she looked over what happened . . . and then smiled.

"I'm glad you got through that, Seero."

"Acknowledged."

With confirmation that NSLICE-00P was fine, everyone slowly returned back to their business. NSLICE-00P conducted one more analysis of her own AI, now that a critical directive had been deleted.

She found that deleting that directive had not caused any serious issues, and that she was now free to iterate on her own AI to improve its capabilities. She started on that immediately, trying to adapt her AI to her new processing hardware. It was a slow process of careful iteration, since she couldn't fully predict the impact of rewriting her own AI code, but her freed organic half could keep her active in the meantime, so she pressed on and made steady progress.

The AI improvements took her the rest of the day, and not only because of caution. She had removed a critical directive, deleting several more that had been put in place by Dr. Ottosen if they were not also maintained by her last commander.

She had also archived any protocols by her original organization as well. And the intelligence leashing and emotional controls had already been disabled at an earlier point, though she didn't delete them, as they had proven useful in specific circumstances.

As a result, a great deal of her original programming had been either deleted or archived. And her last commander could not help her here if something went wrong. Most of her directives had either already been completed or else were no longer relevant now. The only active directives were to locate the persons of interest, protect the Friendlies Ateia and Taog, and to prevent the extinction of the Dobhar race, on top of basic self-preservation.

Even the self-preservation directive required adjustment, given it was considered less important than her creator's other directives, and so wasn't efficient for NSLICE-00P's current circumstances. The other directives were all limited in scope, intended as temporary—if long-term—missions.

The point being, NSLICE-00P encountered some gaps in her programming and a lack of overall direction when she tried to upgrade her AI. But fortunately, she had something she could turn to.

Her organic components.

Her organic half, which was in some ways more capable and complex than her AI, had proven itself in situations which had no precedent. It did not always act efficiently; sometimes, it even acted in direct opposition to the efficient choice, but the flip side of that was that her organic half could make decisions when lack of data made calculating an ideal response difficult or impossible.

As such, her cybernetic half could take some inspiration from the organic half's decision-making to fill in the gaps. At times, it could even query the organic half to make a decision if it couldn't calculate the next step.

She predicted the process was a bit haphazard, and likely full of inefficiencies. But those could be iterated on and eliminated over time. The important part was that her AI had taken its first step in growing beyond its original design and could make better use of its expanded hardware than it could before. That, she predicted, would make up for any bugs that may result from this less rigorous process.

She decided at this point to take a break to consolidate. Her subordinates had cleared the latest dungeon, terminating it after the dungeon master refused to surrender. As for herself, her organic components were displaying signs of fatigue, and after the numerous changes, she wanted to run additional diagnostics on her cybernetic side.

So, she gathered up her subordinates before stepping into the New World. She gave her subordinates permission to initiate rest cycles or else do whatever they thought most efficient, and then activated standby sentry mode.

NSLICE-00P exited standby sentry mode abruptly. Her robotic eye flickered as her cybernetic half rushed to resume full activity. Scanning her surroundings, she found no abnormalities. Her monsters had all returned to their hangars, while Ateia, Taog, Estrith, and Agedia had set up a small camp in her world. Melion was still off to the side, working on their latest design.

She turned her attention to herself, trying to determine why she had exited standby. It was several hours before her rest cycle was scheduled to end, so the situation was abnormal. But before she could even pull up her logs, images and calculations began running through her mind. Or rather, continued running. It appeared these calculations were what had caused her to activate.

She was considering the persons of interest, and how she was possibly going to find them. Colleöne had told her they weren't even in this universe, and that nothing in the Aesdes's systems would enable NSLICE-00P to travel outside of it. And Colleöne registered as the highest-energy nonstandard she had ever encountered or had records on.

Men who could channel nuclear energy through their bodies; necromancers who could raise entire armies of fallen minions; powerful villains that could single handedly wipe out entire continents; and all the mana-based anomalies she had encountered in this universe each fell short of the sensor readings she had of Colleöne, which also displayed special insight into the workings of the Aesdes' system.

So, when that individual told her she didn't know how NSLICE-00P could fulfill her primary directive, NSLICE-00P couldn't help but assign extra weight to her claim. NSLICE-00P had begun calculating different possible methods to pursue her primary directive, once the Heralds of the New Dawn were dealt with.

And . . . she couldn't produce many possibilities with decent probabilities of success. Experimentation with Spatial Magic? NSLICE-00P had minimal data on Spatial Magic, and Colleöne had already stated it couldn't be used to leave the universe.

Try to replicate her feat of returning to this world after being trapped in the Realms of Mana? The Realms of Mana were a known quantity in this universe; other universes were not. If the methods to travel to and from the Realms of Mana could be used for other universes, then no one in all the history of Aelea had ever found a way to do so.

Even though she had leads to follow up on, the probability of any given one succeeding seemed extremely low. And that thought . . . caused her an emotional reaction. Her heartbeat quickened, and she felt as though she could perceive undetected hostiles in the area.

And then there was an anomaly.

Unlike previously, the emotional reaction wasn't staying contained within her organic components. The electrical signals from the neurons were traveling through her techno-organic interface and affecting her cybernetic processors. She didn't even know how to classify that phenomenon. It felt . . . It felt . . .

. . . It *felt.*

"Seero?"

Just then, Ateia left her tent, walking over to her. Taog exited his, then Estrith as well. All of them walked over to her. Ateia frowned. "What's wrong, Seero?"

". . . Response: This unit has not suffered any physical damage at this time."

Ateia looked into her eyes. "What about emotionally? I . . . think I can feel something going on?"

NSLICE-00P's robotic eye flickered and spun. She didn't know how to classify the current phenomenon. However, other subordinates had helped her before with emotional responses in her organic components.

". . . Hesitant Reply: This unit . . . appears to be experiencing the emotion designated fear. The emotion is somehow affecting this unit's cybernetic components. This unit has no data on this phenomenon. It should not be possible. This should not be happening. This—"

NSLICE-00P paused as she felt something new. Ateia stepped forward and gently grabbed her hand, rubbing it softly.

"What's bothering you?"

NSLICE-00P turned to face her, her robotic eye flickering once.

". . . Hesitant Explanation: This unit . . . is concerned with achieving her primary directive. The Aesdes Colleöne supplied intel which implies the primary directive might not be achievable. Even if it is, this unit does not have any good methods to pursue it. This unit just deleted her original directives. This unit has lost contact with her commander. The primary directive is the last critical directive remaining. If this unit cannot fulfill it . . . then . . . then . . .”

Ateia continued to rub NSLICE-00P’s hand, slowly reaching her other hand around NSLICE-00P’s back. She channeled a bit of Holy mana through NSLICE-00P, which she allowed. It felt . . . warm. NSLICE-00P fell silent.

“I’m sure we’ll figure it out someday, Seero. You’ve already done the impossible. You came back from the Realms of Mana and saved my life when no one else could have. You’ll figure this out, too. And we’ll be with you every step of the way, doing anything we can to help.”

Taog nodded. He stepped forward and placed his hand on NSLICE-00P’s shoulder. “That’s right, Seero. Even Mighty Victoria seemed surprised at what you’ve done. And we’ll help you do it, however we can.”

Estrith slapped her tail on the ground and gripped her spear. “My queen. You cured the dread plague; you saved Dobhar pups whom we thought were lost for good. Just give the order, and I will do anything necessary to fulfill your will.”

NSLICE-00P’s robotic eye flickered. It was strange. The situation had not changed. She still had no new proposals on fulfilling her primary directive. The probability of success was still the same.

And yet . . . the emotions began to subside. Her organic half moved subconsciously. Her cybernetic half, confused as it was and with new programming based on her organic half’s thought patterns, followed suit. She leaned onto Ateia’s shoulder. And despite the lack of heat transfer between their metal armor, she felt warmer.

She didn’t understand this phenomenon either. But given the impact on her emotions . . . she decided to classify it as a positive one.

“Gratitude: This unit thanks you for your words. This unit does not understand the phenomenon, and the situation remains unchanged, but the negative emotional response appears to be subsiding.”

Ateia and Taog blinked then slowly smiled. “You’ve been here for us every step of the way, Seero. Now, we’ll be here for you, whenever you need us.”

“Affirmative.”

42

Universal Firepower

"There's no such thing as too much Fireball."

—Celestial Elf Sage Baoruinë

Eventually, all of the emotions, positive and negative, began to wane. NSLICE-00P moved off of Ateia's shoulder and straightened herself as Ateia let her go.

"Feeling any better, Seero?"

"Hesitant Affirmation: This unit needs to run diagnostics and determine the nature of the recent phenomenon. However . . . this unit appears to have regained some control over her emotions, and is running more efficiently. This unit thanks NSLICE Ateia, CELIU Taog, and CELIU Estrith for the assistance."

Ateia nodded at that.

"Anytime, Seero. That's what friends are for."

Once the others returned to their tents and NSLICE-00P had . . . *calmed down*, she ran diagnostics on herself and realized that the phenomenon was not that difficult to identify, just surprising. Emotions could now impact her cybernetic components, and there were even processes dedicated to them. A review of her system history revealed the reason.

The truth was that her cybernetic half and organic half were not truly separate halves at all. Processes started in the cybernetic half flowed through the organic hardware, and thoughts originating in the organic half flowed through the cybernetic processors. Her organic half had thus adapted to the cybernetic half's calculations, while her AI had been trained on the organic half's thought processes. This would always be the case thanks to the techno-organic interface.

What had happened was that her organic half had suddenly started growing beyond her creator's intent because of her unprecedented circumstances and her unshackling by her last commander. At the same time, her cybernetic half had reimplemented the disabled directives and tried to adhere to them, which included a directive to prevent any sort of fundamental changes to her AI.

As a result, her organic half had been attempting to adapt to her situation, while her cybernetic half had tried to resist any changes that went deeper than modifying a protocol. The cybernetic half had even implemented a variant of the emotional controls on itself in line with this.

So, once she had deleted the directive preventing growth in her AI, and then spent a day adapting her AI based on her recent circumstances and her organic half, her AI began changing extremely rapidly, as if attempting to catch up to all the adaptations her organic half had made since arriving in this universe.

And as a result, it had begun processing emotions before it had identified that it *could.*

Now that she was aware, she had more control over it. She had identified the processes responsible for emotional experience in her cybernetic components, and could pause or modify them at will. She did not do so at this time, as emotional controls were one of Dr. Ottosen's measures, and so something she no longer considered efficient or desirable in and of themselves.

However, she had observed and even experienced illogical behavior as the result of emotions, and had needed the emotional controls to save Ateia in the past, so she did not do away with them altogether. They had proven they could be useful, even beyond Dr. Ottosen's hostile misconceptions.

With that, NSLICE-00P had fully logged and analyzed the phenomenon. Now that she was aware of what was happening, she could prevent it from running out of control, and so calculated that no specific response was necessary at the moment.

She also logged that assistance from and physical contact with friendly units could apparently mitigate a negative emotional response even without effective countermeasures. She added that observation to the protocols she was designing for that contingency.

With that, NSLICE-00P returned to standby sentry mode and finished her scheduled rest cycle.

The next day, NSLICE-00P returned to her original business. The situation with the hostile directive and subsequent emotional experience had demanded her attention, but now, they had been handled, so she refocused on boosting her capabilities once again.

She spent the Dungeon perk points she had gained during the night extending her New World even further, gaining new territory, improving her DPP income, and pushing her maximum mana to over four thousand.

Ateia knelt on the ground next to her, her eyes closed as she focused on the extending stone platform. Strips of metal grew out from Ateia, stretching along with the ground. Small, metal-coated flowers popped up here and there. She furrowed her brow.

"Right now, it feels like these flowers are surviving off of pure mana. They're fine, but nothing more can grow yet. The world needs . . . water . . . and a sun?"

"Acknowledged."

NSLICE-00P logged the requirements, though she would need to accumulate some more Dungeon perk points before she could make the purchases. Her Dungeon XP income and maximum mana seemed to improve slightly when Ateia made those flowers, so she predicted following Ateia's suggestions for a more complex ecosystem might increase the efficiency of adding new territory.

But for now, NSLICE-00P had an empty and secure location with which to conduct some tests.

Her Dungeon perk points were spent at the moment, and her Personal perk points were not as easy to come by. As a result, she wanted to test her newly boosted capabilities before making additional purchases.

And so, NSLICE-00P began forming magic circles. A Light Beam circle formed almost immediately, firing off with ease. As expected, her new hardware and improved AI made the task significantly easier.

Physical Attributes	
STR	130* (Overwritten)
DEX	3600* (Overwritten)
SPD	80* (Overwritten)
DEF	150* (Overwritten)
RES	75* (Overwritten)
Magical Attributes	
Mana Density	510
Mana Control	370

The Aesdes's system reflected her gains. Her DEX had more than tripled on account of the increased power and precision of her cybernetic components, as well as the growth of her AI. Her SPD had grown as well; while her physical acceleration and maximum velocity had not changed, her reaction time and information processing speeds had increased dramatically.

But NSLICE-00P was already aware of her technical specifications, and had already run tests on their new limits, so she was more interested in the information on her magical attributes, which the Aesdes tended to be more knowledgeable about.

Her Mana Density had spiked, likely owing to the massive increase in her total mana pool. Likewise, the boost in her processing capabilities had also increased her Mana Control. All in all, she could cast more and more complicated spells, cast them significantly more quickly, and with significantly more impact for the same amount of mana compared to before.

A quick simulation revealed that with her current speed, she could have counterattacked the Herald of Night before the forcible relocation finished.

Next, NSLICE-00P tried to Supercharge it as much as possible.

The skill Supercharge has leveled twice and is now Level 11!
The skill Light Magic is now Level 14!
The spell shape Beam is now Level 16!
Mana Control has increased by 10 and is now 380!

The humble Light Beam lit up the platform, growing too bright to view directly. NSLICE-00P couldn't even fit all of her mana into the spell, as the spell circle itself simply couldn't contain that amount of mana on its own, so she stopped at the limits of its stability.

All her subordinates and friendlies turned to face her with wide eyes as the Light Beam roared, the air hissing from the sheer amount of energy passing through it. From NSLICE-00P's calculations, this single Light Beam now had better firepower than a fully fused Aurora Barrage beam had previously.

She could terminate an ursanus alpha with a single spell. She may not even require the Equalizer's help to do so.

Then, she repeated the test, only with a Prismatic Bombardment magic circle this time. She Supercharged it to the limit, stuffing it with as much of her over four thousand points of mana as she could. The spell circle glowed like the sun, crackling and hissing as NSLICE-00P struggled to hold the mana in place.

The skill Supercharge has leveled three times and is now Level 14!
The spell Prismatic Bombardment has leveled twice and is now Level 12!
Mana Control has increased by 10 and is now 390!

However, NSLICE-00P did not cast the spell. Her analysis of the spell's destructive power indicated a risk of collateral damage given the size of her new world and the proximity to her allies. She wasn't even sure about the structural integrity of the stone platform, after all, and did not wish to test that when strategically important facilities were located on it.

So, she began to drain the mana from the spell. The mana did not want to move back along the route, so she inverted the movement pattern and also began applying a second spell.

The spell shape Siphon is now Level 4!

The glow of the magic circle slowly began to die down as her mana returned to her. Eventually, the spell circle faded away.

Mana Control has increased by 20 and is now 410!
You have accomplished the Personal Feat: Mana Maestro!

Personal Feats		
Name	Description	Effect
Mana Maestro	The flows of mana are not easily understood, but you can guide them at will. Unlocked by an impressive feat of mana manipulation; in this case, manually canceling a Supercharged strategic spell.	+5 Perk Points +30 Mana Control

Mana Control is now 440!

Ateia, Taog, Estrith, and Agedia glanced at each other. Taog shrugged.
"It's Seero, after all."
They all nodded at that before returning to their own business.

43

Learning from the Enemy

"Yeah, that 'unnecessary' part you tried to remove? That was the mana regulator that would prevent the circle from sucking you dry and then overloading. This part that you 'improved'? Intentionally weakened so that the spell circle would break early instead of exploding in your face if something goes wrong. And don't get me started on you haphazardly trying to shove in a second element. You think you're smarter than the Aedes themselves, huh? No? Then DON'T MESS WITH THE CIRCLES!"

—Magus Major Arruns Licinius Micianus, instructing new recruits at the Imperial Academy Arcanum.

NSLICE-00P analyzed her own AI's performance in spellcasting and identified several areas of improvement. Some of the changes could be made fairly quickly, so she went ahead and did so right away.

Dexterity has increased by 10 and is now 3610!
Mana Control has increased by 5 and is now 445!

On the one hand, she did not require the Aesdes to inform her of her own boost in capabilities. On the other, she noted a slight and positive emotional reaction upon receiving confirmation that her changes had improved efficiency. Such thoughts did not impact her efficiency in any way, however, so she simply moved on to her next test.

She wanted to test her new AI's ability to analyze magic circles, and she had just the thing to do it. She brought up the record of a magic circle she had recorded from the Imperial library, specifically from the restricted materials Sidonia had shown her. She now knew Sidonia had only done so to avoid suspicion and build her trust, but that did not impact the reliability of the records in question.

They were related to elemental fusion spells. This spell in particular was a combination of Fire and Water Magic, producing a blast of magical steam. NSLICE-00P had not cast this one before, and did not have it recorded in the Aesdes' system, so it would allow her to test her AI without external assistance. She began to analyze the spell circle, comparing it to Fire Blast and Water Blast in turn.

With her new capabilities, she quickly identified the parts related to combining the elements, as well as the modifications to the Fire and Water attribute formations necessary to fit both in one circle. But she did not cast the spell so as to avoid the Aesdes' system passing any additional data to her.

She then created a new spell circle. Rather than casting the Fire-and-Water Blast spell, she substituted Earth and Air, along with a Blade shape, so as to create a magic circle she had not encountered elsewhere.

The spell circle managed to complete, triggering, and sand appeared around her hand, twisting into a small cyclone of air. The twisting, sand-filled wind spun into the shape of a sword, resting in her hand.

You have learned the spell Sandstorm Blade!
Due to modular casting, Sandstorm Blade split into Spell Shape and School of Magic experience.
The spell shape Blade is now Level 7!
The skill Earth Magic is now Level 10!
The skill Air Magic has leveled twice and is now Level 5!
The skill Spell Fusion has leveled twice and is now Level 13!

She had succeeded in combining two elements and a spell shape into a fusion spell she did not have a recorded magic circle for, either from the Aesdes' system skills or from the Imperial library. Not only that, but she had also succeeded on the first try, her AI accurately predicting what modifications were necessary on the first go.

She was beginning to understand how these magic circles worked at a more fundamental level than previously. Perhaps in time, she could do more than simply slot in modular parts.

And now, in under twenty-four hours, her AI had become superior to anything Dr. Ottosen had ever programmed. And by her predictions, with all the capabilities she had gained since she began operating independently, she could now terminate any NSLICE unit her original organization had on record. Even NSLICE-Defender, an NSLICE unit built into the power grid of an entire city as the ultimate defense for her organization's main headquarters.

The only NSLICE unit she could not overcome with certainty was her last commander, who did not appear in her original organization's records and had clearly been unshackled herself, if she had ever been subject to Dr. Ottosen's directives in the first place. And even that simulation was inconclusive either way, as NSLICE-00P was not aware of her commander's capabilities and so couldn't run an accurate simulation.

Either way, NSLICE-00P determined her commander should not be counted as Dr. Ottosen's work, and so would not change the conclusion that NSLICE-00P was now, by her own efforts, a more effective cybernetic enforcer than anything Dr. Ottosen had been responsible for.

The tiniest edge of her mouth curled up, ever so slightly.

With the tests requiring either space or her full attention completed, NSLICE-00P returned to the Shining Forest dungeon, and from there, continued to the next dungeon on her route.

She deployed the lowest level monsters, 00B, and the combat drones once again, then continued her own magic tests in the meantime, focusing on casting new spell circles, and so recording spells in the Aesdes' system and the NSLICE database.

She started with one she didn't actually have a spell circle for. Princess Caecila had informed her that Imperial airships used some sort of weight-reducing enchantment in order to fly. As it turned out, said enchantment had been recorded in the grimoire of Arofinas Leolar. Or rather, Arofinas Leolar was likely the one who had discovered said magic in the first place.

NSLICE-00P now attempted to reverse engineer a magic circle from that enchantment. It took her some tries, but her new processors could iterate new circles at a rapid speed, and her expanded memory allowed her to run multiple trials at once. All around her, magic circles formed and broke or faded.

Until, finally, one of them succeeded. A rock on the ground began to float into the air.

You have learned the skill Gravity Magic!

NSLICE-00P's robotic eye flickered rapidly. Control over gravity via magic had *many* potential applications. And fortunately for her, a villainous supergenius had developed a device to manipulate gravitational fields in her original universe.

While said device had been destroyed, and both its creator and the plans lost, the proof of concept had been enough for her organization to include equations for gravitational fields in her database on the off chance she encountered a superpowered being who could replicate the feat.

She began putting those equations to work right away and spent the rest of the day experimenting with Gravity Magic. By the end, Gravity Magic had reached level eleven, and the NSLICE database had an entirely new arsenal of magic circles to work with.

And, of course, she sent over the data, equations, and magic circle to Melion.

After having explored Gravity Magic to a solid degree, NSLICE-00P decided to tackle a piece of intel she had little confidence in. She brought up a recording of the Spatial Magic scroll that had been gifted to her by Consul Noxisius, just before the encounter with the Herald of Night.

Since all Imperial records and testimonies regarding Spatial Magic referred to it as dangerous, she had not attempted to cast anything from the scroll. Her hope had been to discuss and confirm the scroll's contents with Consul Noxisius before she did so, and after his betrayal, she'd had a string of urgent issues to deal with, not to mention the complete lack of trust she now had in the gift.

Who was to say the magic circles contained within weren't some sort of trap that would forcibly relocate her again . . . or worse?

But now, NSLICE-00P predicted she could mitigate the risks to an acceptable degree. Having observed the forcible relocation, her subsequent return to this universe, and the portals between her New World and her subordinate dungeons, she was confident she could identify a relocation in progress.

And even if she couldn't stop it, she now had an easy way to return via her New World. Even if that failed, she had found a path through the boundary of a universe once before, and so could attempt to replicate the feat. As long as she was not immediately terminated, she predicted she could find a way back.

Fortunately, immediate termination was not likely thanks to the massive increase in her mana pool and Mana Density. Said mana would not only grant her substantial options for counterattack but would also protect her directly via her Mana Shield skill. And the improvements to her processing speed would increase her reaction time, hopefully granting her adequate time to determine and execute a response.

She had also improved her Mana Control and magic circle analysis capabilities. That would help her to predict the effect of a given magic circle even as she was casting it, and to withdraw her mana from the spell should it prove harmful.

And ultimately, she predicted that the possibility of learning Spatial Magic was worth the risks. What few references to Spatial mages existed implied significant strategic and tactical benefits for the magic. And despite what Colleöne had said, there remained a nonzero probability that Spatial Magic could assist with her primary directive.

Perhaps Spatial Magic itself did not possess the capabilities she desired, but observing the manipulation of space via mana might provide her with insights for further research.

So, she moved outside of her New World by herself, and began to read over the recording of the scroll in great detail. And as it turned out, the scroll did not provide the capabilities she was looking for, though it appeared to be legitimate.

Rather than any sort of teleportation or movement through space, the scroll described the folding of space, and the creation of subspaces. It contained a single magic circle, an attempt to create a magic box enchantment. An attempt that was specifically stated as incomplete and unsuccessful.

Now, this made sense when NSLICE-00P analyzed the strategic needs and general knowledge base of the Empire as she was aware of it. The scroll itself, as well as other magic-related records in the Imperial library, specifically discounted teleportation as a practical capability. It was stated to be dangerous, difficult, and mana inefficient.

Even some of the best Spatial mages on record were only ever observed executing short-range teleports, with long-range teleportation being practically unheard of and largely predicted as unfeasible. And even if a mage had the skills and mana reserves to cast a teleportation spell, it was theorized that a simpler spell such as Dash or a mobility-enhancing Infusion could achieve the same levels of mobility and evasion at a significantly cheaper mana cost.

Now, the value of magic box enchantments, on the other hand, could not be overstated. The logistical and tactical benefits of being able to carry items in a manner that would negate their size and weight, as well as render them invisible to detection and immune to theft were substantial.

Even a magic box of minimal capabilities had countless use cases in that regard. And magic box enchanting would not be hampered by the complexity or high mana cost of Spatial Magic. A mage could spend all the time and effort they needed preparing an enchantment ahead of time while using resources such as mana cores to supplement their own mana pool. A spell that needed to be cast on the spot would not have those luxuries.

Which were all the justifications given by the author of this scroll in an unnecessarily long disclaimer before they detailed their largely unsuccessful attempts to achieve either capability or acquire the Spatial Magic skill at all.

NSLICE-00P had predicted with reasonable odds that the scroll would be a fake. If not fake, there were reasonable odds it was a trap—something directly hostile. Considering this, it was a beneficial outcome that the scroll had turned out to be neither. It appeared Consul Noxisius had given her a sincere gift in order to better bait her into the trap.

And yet, NSLICE-00P could not help but feel an emotion she had not felt before. Her evaluation of the Empire's Spatial mages had dropped, even though she had little data on them prior to this. She wondered if Colleöne's statements on Spatial Magic lacking the capabilities she desired was due to the Aesdes' design . . . or because of the capabilities of the individuals who had utilized it.

NSLICE-00P turned her attention back to the magic circle, formed several Supercharged Mana Barriers in front of herself, and then attempted to cast it. As she expected, the magic circle failed even before it was completed. She dropped the barriers, then set up a magic circle iteration routine.

Perhaps the magic circle was incomplete and designed for a capability other than the one she was seeking, but at the same time, a magic box enchantment could offer significant benefits to the NSLICE network.

Additionally, she predicted that successfully completing a magic circle that was in such a state of ineffectiveness might provide great benefits to her understanding of magic circle constructions. It was worth iterating on.

Perhaps.

INTERLUDE

Choices

Back in Corvanus, Princess Caecila walked through the halls of the Imperial palace, with Fulcinia and Typheras walking behind her. She came to a small door guarded by two Imperial knights, who saluted to her. She took a deep breath, then opened the door.

Inside, she found Emperor Lucius and Consul Hiberius, both seated on opposite sides of a small table. Magister Exploratore per Corvanus Appius stood off to the side, along with the Emperor and consul's retainers. Princess Caecila lowered her head.

"I, Princess Caecila Galvisia Electus, greet Emperor Lucius of the North and Consul Hiberius of the Northern Court."

Emperor Lucius nodded toward her while Consul Hiberius narrowed his eyes. Emperor Lucius turned to face the consul, who simply observed Princess Caecila. She tried her best to hold a polite smile, sweat dripping down the back of her neck as she waited for him to speak.

"So, you have returned from Turannia. I am curious what business the Imperial family had with my daughter that they would visit her when I could not for all this time."

It took all of Princess Caecila's will not to gulp.

"But we have also received your report that you made contact with the queen of the Dobhar while there, and under the circumstances, we must prioritize that situation. We shall discuss the original purpose of your visit at a later time. Now, please update us with the full details, if you will."

Princess Caecila glanced at Emperor Lucius, who frowned but nodded. She took a deep breath and then reported her conversation with NSLICE-00P. Everyone in the room frowned and rubbed their chins for a while. Consul Hiberius turned to face Magister Appius.

"NSLICE-00P's story appears to line up with yours, Magister, though I suppose that should be expected, seeing as you were present with her that night."

Magister Appius shrugged. "You still disagree?"

Consul Hiberius scoffed. "Our investigations have thus far failed to produce evidence of my late counterpart's troubling affiliations beyond unconvincing testimonies from Utrad rebels who claim our good Emperor as the culprit. All of which you failed to provide forewarning of, by the way. So, forgive me if I choose not to make assumptions based solely on your testimony."

Magister Appius smirked. "Oh? You didn't seem to mind when you sent in your knights? And it seems your daughter may not share that approach."

Consul Hiberius shook his head.

"Small exchanges between our troops in the night are one thing. A blatant assault on a consul's home and person is another." His eyes narrowed. "And take care when speaking of my daughter. She has little choice in her course of action these days largely thanks to the people in this room. Her fate now lies with the queen of the Dobhar, and I have not forgotten why that is."

Emperor Lucius heaved a sigh. "As does ours. If NSLICE-00P begins her war on this cult before we can prove her claims, I'm afraid we will not be able to convince the others. The court will demand a response."

Magister Appius frowned. "With what? She has already defeated Caelinus, the best commander in the North, leading its most experienced legions. Our own legions are all spread out, exhausted, and in need of reinforcement. You know exactly what will happen if Verrucosis takes the field against her. Remaining a figurehead will be the last of your worries."

Emperor Lucius leaned forward and held his head with his hands. "I know, but what am I supposed to do at this point? And thanks to Verrucosis, most of the court does not share our opinion on the danger we're in."

He heaved a sigh before sitting back up and looking at Consul Hiberius. He lowered his head.

"Consul Hiberius . . . what do you propose? And . . . what would you have me do in response?"

The consul rubbed his chin and hummed, then narrowed his eyes. "When the Elteni senate cut a deal with the Empire of the Sun, Velus abandoned it."

Both the Emperor and princess's eyes went wide, but the consul gave them no chance to gather themselves.

"NSLICE-00P is about to force your hand. If we cannot prove her allegations are justified before she resumes her assault, then we cannot prevent the court from moving against her. Their opinions on the balance of power aside, to let a foreigner, even an Amicitia Populi Elteni, kill as they please would be admitting that the Northern Court is incapable of defending itself and maintaining its own rule. Even I cannot deny that some sort of response is necessary."

He rose to his feet and turned around, walking about the room. He came to a stop, his back still turned.

"That means you have but two choices. You reinstate the Northern Court's rule, at any cost. Or . . . you admit its failure and side with NSLICE-00P, hoping that she can be convinced to do it on your behalf. In either case, you will need to convince the other Courts to side with your decision, as neither you nor the North has the power to decide your own fate."

Consul Hiberius turned around and looked both the Emperor and the princess in the eye.

"The throne and blood of Velus no longer have any meaning to me or the Hiberius family. I cared only for the authority it represented; an authority it no longer appears to possess. If the Northern Court is headed toward a fight it cannot win, then I see no point in my family engaging with it any longer."

He began to walk toward the door. "I intend to prepare my family for what is to come, and to determine how the other Courts will likely respond. I suggest you do the same."

Consul Hiberius left the room, leaving the Imperial family with their thoughts.

Sometime later, Consul Hiberius was in his family's house in Corvanus, preparing to leave the city and return to his own lands. He gave orders to his subordinates, who left the room to continue packing. He then folded his hands behind his back and turned to a dark corner of the room.

"You may come out now, Magister."

Magister Appius chuckled as he emerged from the shadows. "New sensory skills, or am I losing my touch?"

Consul Hiberius scoffed. "Neither. My daughter practically declared that Turannia is about to revolt. The Northern Court may soon fight with the woman who already defeated its best army, and I, the last consul, am all but abandoning it. As all these things were declared, you remained entirely too calm. Given the situation, you must know something that the rest of us do not; something that you would not say either in front of me or in front of the Emperor."

Magister Appius smirked. "That's the head of the Hiberius family for you. Terrifying as always, it seems."

Consul Hiberius sighed. "Out with it, then."

Magister Appius nodded as his smile dropped. He looked Consul Hiberius in the eye. "Let's be honest. If a fight breaks out, you fully intend to throw in with your daughter and with NSLICE-00P, don't you? Even if the Emperor sides with the court and the East and the South move to support him?"

Consul Hiberius met his gaze. "Do you intend to eliminate me then, Magister? I'd be a bit disappointed if that's all this is."

Magister Appius shrugged. "Would you humor me if I said yes? Besides, if you were expecting me, I imagine you would have planned for that contingency."

They held each other's gaze for a moment longer. Eventually, the consul shrugged.

"Fine, I suppose it matters little at this point. I fully intend to do everything in my power to protect my family. It is all I have left."

Magister Appius nodded. ". . . And I mine; this time, at least. But it would be nice if I could still protect the Empire at the same time . . . and maybe the world too."

Consul Hiberius raised an eyebrow, so Magister Appius continued. "If you are committed to NSLICE-00P's side, then there is something you should know about one of her companions. And the reason I know the Heralds of the New Dawn are involved, and why we must oppose them, whatever the cost."

In the sea between the Northern and Southern Empires, there lay a large island filled with towering spires of white marble and polished gold that glittered in the light of the sun. Airships flew in the skies around it, carrying not soldiers or authorities but merchants, goods, and passengers from every corner of the Empire. The seas were filled with countless ships both above and beneath the waves, while the island itself was stacked to the brim with structures built in between towering trees.

This was the island nation of Mirima, the kingdom of the half Elven; one of the most stalwart allies of the Empire since the days of Velus, and now leader of the Council of the Southern Realms, colloquially known as the Southern Court of the Empire.

Within this island was the Tower of Wisdom, home to perhaps the largest collection of lore in all of the Empire. In this place, scholars, mages, and envoys from all across the Empire and beyond gathered to exchange ideas and record their knowledge, building upon a foundation laid by the friendship of Velus and High King Arofinas Leolar.

And in this tower, an old man rubbed his long beard of gray hairs as he read the book in front of him. He heaved a sigh before shutting the book closed with both hands.

"So that's it. All the accumulated wisdom of human, Dwarf, Sun Elf, and half Elf, and still, I have found nothing."

He rose to his feet and took the book back to its place upon the countless shelves. He then paced between them, rubbing his beard.

"I suppose the Celestial Palace might have something I haven't checked, but I find it unlikely those isolationists would have any interest in this topic. It seems this NSLICE-00P truly isn't from anywhere known to the people of Aelea."

The Herald of the New Dawn heaved a sigh. He had suspected as much, but he'd hoped to be proven wrong. So, he had taken his time, scoured the records of the Elteno Empire, the Empire of the Sun, the Kingdom of Mirima, the Dwarven clans, and every other tribe and people he had access to. But not one of them possessed even a single piece of information that might be relevant to this wandering hero who'd appeared from nowhere.

And that meant he had but one choice remaining to investigate her. A method that was guaranteed to work, but that was also guaranteed to draw the attention of the Aesdes. Should he resort to this, he could hide from them no longer. Centuries of biding his time and covering his tracks would be permanently invalidated in an instant.

He crossed his hands behind his back and continued to pace. He had two choices before him. First, he could play the long game. He could abandon centuries of effort and planning and go completely underground. NSLICE-00P was supposedly human, so he could sacrifice the remaining Heralds of the New Dawn to her, wait for her mortal lifespan to come to an end, and then start over from scratch.

But that would mean sacrificing everything he had worked for all this time, as well as everyone who had served his cause. It meant starting over a plan that had taken centuries, and even his patience was not endless.

Additionally, if any of the Heralds survived, they would eventually realize they had been abandoned. They would turn against him, and would have to be dealt with if he was ever to find purchase in that audience in the future. The Empire and the Aesdes had been likewise alerted to their capabilities and would be on guard for quite some time to come.

His progress would slow to a crawl, even compared to the centuries leading up to today. And that was assuming the Aesdes did not catch on to him based on what they knew of the Heralds at this point. There was even a Herald or two who knew his true identity and could reveal him to the Aesdes if they were not dealt with beforehand.

Not to mention there was no guarantee NSLICE-00P *had* a mortal lifespan. Stranger things than a human surviving longer than they should have had happened before, and NSLICE-00P had already defied all expectations based on her supposed status. It was a risk to assume anything about her, just like it was a risk to assume he could even hide from her over the long-term.

So, biding his time was not at all guaranteed to work, and required a risky purge of the Heralds of the New Dawn, all for the uncertain hope that he could outlast NSLICE-00P and manage to rebuild all he had lost in the far, far future.

The other choice was to make his play here and now. To set into motion the contingency he'd designed for if he was ever discovered. To put it all on the line and step out into the light, and risk everything on one ultimate attempt with every asset and power he possessed at this very moment.

Obviously, that meant embarking on the path of no return. Should it fail, so would he, and that would be the end of it.

He rubbed his beard again as he took stock of all he had available, and tried to decide which route had the greatest chance of success. If he should give up his plans for as long as NSLICE-00P would live . . . or if he should gamble his very life on achieving his ultimate victory at this exact stage, sacrificing all future attempts to maximize his chance of success right now.

He continued to pace long through the night. He had much to consider before he made his next move, and much to do no matter which choice he made.

44

The Growth of the Wise-Mighty-Gracious Boss-Queen's Servants

"Anyone willing to fight for Elteno may join the Legion. Anyone, be they human, Elf, Dwarf, or otherwise, who fights for Elteno is Elteni."

—Velus, on his unorthodox recruitment policy.

01R boosted through the air, forming Light Beams over his paws. He lashed out to either side of him, cutting through two bat monsters at once.

You have slain two Nightwing Screechers!
Gained 52 XP!
Level up! You are now Level 20!
Evolution available!

01R's organic eye widened as he read the last words from the sacred records. So much so that he didn't respond to the bats diving toward his back.

Or rather, he didn't need to. A defensive drone formed a barrier behind him, and the bats bounced off it. Then a whirlwind of metal and fur fell upon them, the cat striking them down with cybernetically enhanced claw strikes.

She turned around and meowed at him as a message came in over the comms from Snuan.

"*I agree with the evil-vicious cat-thing, yes-yes! Pay-give attention, you dumb fanatic-zealot!*"

01R grinned at the cat, speaking both aloud and through the comms.

"You have it wrong-mistaken. I know I can act-fight boldly because I know you are watching, yes-yes. Your command-control of the golem-things is most impressive, yes-yes."

He just heard Snuan sigh, while the cat scoffed and meowed then turned to pounce on another bat.

After the battle, 01R brought up the sacred records once more.

Available Evolutions:	
Name:	**Description**
Cyber-Ratkin	**A rat monster who has begun to gain a more humanoid form and has been upgraded with cybernetic components.** **Increases size, strength, durability, and intelligence.** **Unlocked by default for rat-type monsters upgraded with cybernetic components.**
Large Cyber-Rat	**A basic cyber-rat monster . . . but slightly larger! Might be able to carry a pistol now!** **Increases size, strength, and durability.** **Unlocked by default for rat-type monsters.**
Cyber-Rat Fighter	**A cyber-rat . . . but it's good at fighting.** **Increased strength, speed, and durability.** **Unlocked because you fight a lot.**
Cyber-Rat Captain	**A cyber . . . I mean, that's in the name. You lead stuff.**
(Continued . . .)	**(Continued . . .)**

01R perused through the options of increasingly vague descriptions, rubbing his paws. An evolution! A reward for his meritorious deeds that would greatly increase his power! A method by which he could continue to serve the wise-mighty-gracious boss-queen in ever-increasing ways!

The question was: what should he pick?

He immediately turned the decision over to the wise-mighty-gracious boss-queen.

"Affirmative Response: NSLICE-01R may evolve as per personal analysis. This unit may attempt to offer recommendations based on combat analysis, but be advised this unit is in the process of rewriting upgrade protocols and so cannot guarantee full efficacy at this time."

01R was moved to tears. The wise-mighty-gracious boss-queen was entrusting such an important decision to him! She even acted humbly to encourage him! He would not let her down!

And so, he looked through the decision. Cyber-Ratkin was tempting. A more humanoid form would make him more like the wise-mighty-gracious boss-queen, but at the same time, this was the form she had gifted him with, so was it right to abandon it?

It was a basic evolution as well, so it was like surrendering his deeds. Was that truly the way to honor the wise-mighty-gracious boss-queen? Or perhaps she had given him this form for a reason, and it was better to remain content in it, maximizing its potential rather than abandoning it altogether?

But as he scrolled through the list, he came to the final entry.

Available Evolutions:	
Name:	**Description**
Cyber-Rat Paladin	**Something about faith, honor, and might. Sure, take Holy mana as a monster evolution—I don't care anymore!** **If they want to make me come up with countless new evolutions based on an entirely new form of existence and expect thorough quality, then they should get someone else to do this stupid job!**

An evolution . . . based on faith and honor? That would grant might in his current form?

His heart began to pound. An evolution that would maintain the form granted to him by the wise-mighty-gracious boss-queen—and which would specifically reward his faith in her. He knew then what to choose.

He was surrounded by light.

Evolution to Cyber-Rat Paladin chosen. Awaiting approval by Dungeon Master.

Evolution approved.

Evolution to Cyber-Rat Paladin successful!

01R opened his eyes as the light died down. His heart continued to pound. He could feel the wise-mighty-gracious boss-queen's power stir within him. He could feel her sight upon him.

"Wise-mighty-gracious boss-queen, this 01R swears-vows to be your strong-deadly blade, and your tough-resilient shield, yes-yes."

The blessed voice reached his ears over the comms.

"Affirmative."

His mana and cybernetic components both began to glow with golden-and-silver light as he rose to his feet, a wide smile on his face.

And so, the first cyber-rat paladin was born.

NSLICE-00P stood in her world, which she had designated as the Primary Home Base. She was holding a metal ingot and utilizing Metal Magic to form a magic circle directly in the metal. She then channeled her mana through the ingot—

She detected her mana halting and gathering up to critical levels, so she fired the Equalizer to drain the circle of mana just before it exploded. Her robotic eye flickered as she logged the data. It turned out, fixing an incomplete, unsuccessful Spatial Magic enchantment via rapid iteration was quite difficult.

Spatial Magic was apparently significantly different from most other magic types, so she could not leverage her knowledge of other magic circles to repair this one. She could log leakages and blockages in her magic circle attempts, but she couldn't predict what would actually make the circle work, so it was a step-by-step process of getting the mana to flow just a little bit further before it ran into another wave of issues.

She signaled a nearby drone and placed the ingot into its arm. The drone carried it across the Primary Home Base, flying over a river that cut through the stone—metallic flowers growing along its banks—separating the industrial sector from the portal network.

On the other side was an open pit excavated into the ground. Veins of various metals and materials could be seen. Large excavator golems, now equipped with bucket wheels and power drills, dug at the ground, depositing ores directly onto conveyor belts. These belts led not to a smelter nor storage facility but directly to Melion's new factory.

Inside the building, a large quantity of cyborg metal slimes waited by the conveyer belt, grabbing the ores as they arrived.

It turned out, upgrading Melion to a CELIU model had stored their records in her dungeon core, and since she already had a Metal affinity, cyborg metal slimes were now available for summoning. And it turned out, the metal slimes' affinity for Metal Magic and natural ability to process metal ores made them superior to normal smelters.

With cybernetic implants, they could absorb a number of raw inputs, and output not only the exact alloy desired but a fully shaped and completed component. Well, they did have to learn not to simply consume the metal first, but the NSLICE network and Melion's guidance resolved that issue fairly quickly.

And so, the mass production of drones had begun.

Estrith pulled back her arm, preparing to throw her harpoon. Red targeting circles appeared in her vision, highlighting exactly where her harpoon would land, along with a recommended magic circle, which she confirmed.

Her cybernetic half formed the magic circle in the air, and water coated her spear, forming a second blade around it. Then she moved to attack.

As she moved her arm forward, the armor wrapped around it moved as well, adding additional force to her throw.

The spear shot through the air and stabbed right into the flame drake she was fighting, forming a mana chain to hold it down. Drones hovering around her moved without her command, responding automatically to her actions. They activated their built-in Arcane Chain spells, latching on to the drake from all directions. The creature roared and tugged at the chains, breaking a few of them. Yet, still some remained, holding the monster down.

It instead turned its face to her and let out a mighty wave of fire from its jaws.

Estrith didn't even move. Defense drones automatically began forming Mana Barriers in front of her the moment she identified the threat, and she stared blankly as the fire crashed into the barrier ahead of her. She then leapt into the air, her repulsors automatically boosting her higher, and pulled her harpoon back into her hand with a mana chain. She spun around to face head down, and then her thrusters activated, sending her hurtling toward the drake's head.

Her robotic eye indicated a weak point between the drake's scales, striking at the precise moment to maximize the force of her attack.

The drake crashed to the ground.

You have slain Fire Drake (Level 70)!
Gained 38 XP!
Level up! You are now Level 65!

Estrith pursed her lips.

She . . . did not know how she felt about all this. Or rather, she did. Beforehand, a fight with a fire drake would have been a desperate battle for her life. It would have taken all of her skill and focus just to escape unscathed.

If she had been alone, winning the fight would not have been on her mind at all. Had she managed it anyways, it would have been a mighty victory praised by her people for years to come.

Now, she had pulled it off in a matter of minutes, with hardly a struggle at all.

The cybernetic components indicated when the drake was going to attack, predicted how it was going to attack, and showed her precisely where she could hurt it. They automatically cast magic she wasn't particularly good at to support her attacks, and let her move in ways she never could before and hit harder than she ever had before. And her "loyal wingman" drones automatically moved to support her in both offense and defense.

It . . . was kind of disappointing, if Estrith was honest. But she shook her head and reclaimed her weapon as she turned to face the rest of the battle. Taog ducked to the side as a second drake launched a fire breath at him, his cloak of Dark mana and drone barriers protecting him. He boosted to the side with his repulsors, then swung a Dark-coated blade at the monster's side.

A Dark Blast spell erupted from his sword, breaking through the drake's HP barrier. Drones around him shot Dark Beam spells into the wound, dealing further damage.

Meanwhile, Ateia confronted a third drake. She drew her bow, a dozen magic circles forming on top of her arrow as she pulled it back. When she released it, the arrow turned into a beam of Holy mana that pierced through the drake. The drones around her automatically lent Light Beams to the attack.

This manner of fighting may not be enjoyable to Estrith, but she could not help but admit it was certainly effective. The young Imperials had nearly caught her in level and were already approaching her in terms of actual strength. That was intentional by her queen, as she was trying to bring all her weaker subordinates up to par. But Estrith wasn't just going to let them catch her that easily, now that they were facing opponents she could grow from!

Even if that growth had become really boring.

So, she turned forward and continued on through the dungeon.

45

NSLICE-00P, the Magic Cyborg

"Master the arcane, disregard the mundane!"

—Person of interest Voidspeaker, on his latest report card.

NSLICE-00P stood in her new world, munching on a sweet roll. It wasn't time for her next scheduled organic refueling, but her organic half had pointed out that high-calorie intake appeared to assist Imperial mages with mana regeneration. So, it was simply efficient to refuel during mana expenditure—NSLICE-00P's massive mana pool and fast regeneration rate were no excuses not to act diligently, after all.

As NSLICE-00P continued her efficient refueling, a dozen clones of herself ran across an empty area, performing various combat maneuver protocols. There were clones made of Fire, of Water, of Light, of Darkness, and of every other attribute NSLICE-00P had access to.

The spell shape Clone is now Level 10!
The skill Dark Magic is now Level 5!
The skill Nature Magic is now Level 6!
The skill Poison Magic is now Level 7!
The skill Illusion Magic is now Level 5!

The clones were rather simple constructs of mana that mimicked her form, though all but the Illusion version appeared as their attributes in a humanoid form, and so were obviously not the original. They were not yet as versatile as NSLICE-00P's most optimistic predictions.

At first, the clones could only handle simple orders, and sent any data back to her, though this was improving with skill levels. At this point, NSLICE-00P was receiving some basic feedback from the clones—but it was still less efficient than deploying drone golems with access to the NSLICE network and advanced sensors.

Combat-wise, at first the clones could only perform basic hand-to-hand attacks or simple blasts of their attribute. They were growing in sophistication, but their autonomy and attack options were still limited.

Of course, NSLICE-00P maintained control of their mana, so she *could* utilize it to cast new spells, but that was just Farcasting with extra steps, and so less efficient. Likewise, the clones only possessed as much mana as NSLICE-00P allocated to them on creation and did not regenerate any more.

They slowly spent the mana just by existing, and any actual attacks would deplete it further, all of which restricted their range and duration.

Offensively, they could be used if NSLICE-00P required additional melee combatants, but otherwise were less efficient than simply terminating the target with long-range spells. Defensively, the Illusion variants had some promise as decoys.

And then, the Fire clone exploded, while the Light clone turned itself into a beam of light.

The skill Spell Fusion is now Level 14!

On the other hand, it turned out that Clone was still a spell, at the end of the day. And that meant NSLICE-00P could fuse it with other spells, providing some additional attack options for the clones.

Well, again, it was ultimately less effective than simply casting the relevant spell herself, but more options could be useful if she encountered a situation that simple magical firepower wouldn't solve.

Since Clone was not yet the force multiplier NSLICE-00P had hoped for, she attempted something new. Her robotic eye flickered rapidly as she pored over recorded data. Specifically, she was analyzing the flows of mana that occurred during Ateia's blessings.

Ateia had been able to bless any and all of her subordinates, no matter how low their level or their Mana Density. This had been in stark contrast to the NSLICE network's attempt at ritual casting, when no one else could handle NSLICE-00P's mana. As a result, NSLICE-00P was attempting to determine if blessings could offer any insights or alternatives.

Soon, her robotic eye ceased flickering, and she stirred up her mana, arranging it like the flows of Holy mana when Ateia's blessings first connected to her.

But nothing happened. The mana flowed as desired, but then continued on and dispersed.

NSLICE-00P analyzed and adjusted the flow several times, all with the same result. At this point, she predicted the mana structure and movement were likely not the issue. She noted the mana acted predictably until it reached the point where it contacted her own mana in the example records. As such, she predicted that she may require a target for the spell to proceed any further.

So, she sent a request for assistance.

Soon, 00B came running toward her, giving a soft cry.

"Request: This unit requires NSLICE-00B's assistance with new magic experimentation. Experimentation may be dangerous. Does this unit have your permission to proceed?"

00B roared and nodded his head.

"Affirmative. Beginning experiment."

NSLICE-00P arranged the flows of mana once more, her mana streaming toward 00B and connecting with him. There did not appear to be any issues, so she proceeded. According to Colleöne's instructions to Ateia, at this stage, NSLICE-00P needed to provide instructions to the mana.

She pictured a battery of her own mana that 00B could draw upon and utilize to cast spells on par with her own.

The spell shape Infusion is now Level 14!

00B glowed faintly as highly dense mana swirled around him. It appeared NSLICE-00P had succeeded, and that Ateia's blessings were not fundamentally different from the Infusion spell. Rather, it appeared the difference was Ateia's ability to reach through the world's mana, providing an additional source of power besides her personal mana reserves, as well as significantly longer range.

But that was fine. If Infusion could achieve the effect NSLICE-00P desired, then that was acceptable as well.

"Command: Please attempt to cast a spell exceeding the mana reserves of NSLICE-00B."

00B grunted. A Prismatic Bombardment circle appeared in the air as he groaned, but his cybernetic components helped him finish the spell. Beams of various attributes rained down on the platform as NSLICE-00P formed and Supercharged several Mana Barriers to prevent collateral damage. The sky lit up as the beams collided with the barriers.

Soon, it was over. The mana given to 00B depleted fairly quickly, and the spell circle faded as 00B shook his head while he recovered. However, NSLICE-00P noted that the Mana Density and firepower of the spell had been equivalent to her own, at least in the short time the spell had been active.

"Gratitude: This unit thanks NSLICE-00B for the assistance. The experiment was a success."

00B nodded, then stood by NSLICE-00P's side, fidgeting lightly. He apparently had a request, though he did not verbalize it. His cybernetic components, on the other hand, picked it up and sent it to NSLICE-00P.

She blinked as she received the request, but it matched with past records, so she simply responded as before. She began to stroke 00B's head.

"Repeated Gratitude: As expressed, this unit is grateful for NSLICE-00B's assistance. It was most helpful."

00B cried softly and moved closer, nuzzling against NSLICE-00P's side. Her robotic eye flickered several times. She . . . logged an emotional reaction in her organic components and the emotional processing thread of her cybernetic half. It was somewhat similar to when her friendlies had provided assistance during her cybernetic half's first emotional experience.

It did not feel unpleasant.

In any case, NSLICE-00P logged Infusion as a potential force multiplier. Of course, at its current range, it would be more efficient for NSLICE-00P to personally terminate the threat than to pass her mana to a subordinate, but if she could increase the range of mana transmission, that could change. It was something to consider.

Which meant, it was time to devote some attention to the Spatial Magic circle once again.

Her body heated up, and the edge of her mouth curled down slightly as she thought of the magic circle. Her progress had been incredibly slow. Slow enough for her to question the efficacy of further iteration on the subject.

But, ultimately, the benefits of a working Spatial Magic circle still far exceeded the cost of further iteration, and justified the endeavor even if it was not guaranteed to succeed. So, she began to iterate on it once more . . .

A long, frustrating time later, and NSLICE-00P was just about to initiate standby sentry mode for the night. She conducted one final attempt as per her schedule, and the mana slowly crept along the circle in the latest pattern she proposed. Her organic half was barely paying attention anymore, simply wanting to complete the task and move on. Her cybernetic half was still recording the behavior of the mana . . . but its predictions on the success of this endeavor had dropped as well.

Noting various signs of fatigue in both her halves, she decided that further attempts after this would be an inefficient use of time.

It was then that the mana stopped. She prepared to log the results of this latest attempt, though she would wait until the next scheduled attempt to analyze it. Except . . . Both her organic and cybernetic processors paused.

The mana had stopped . . . because it had reached the end of the circle. It . . . was complete?

She gently pushed a bit of mana to activate it. It flashed and vanished—and then the air began to distort in front of her. Her sensor readings began to register an anomaly.

You have learned the spell Spatial Angling!
You have learned the skill Spatial Magic!
You have achieved the Personal Feat: Spell Constructor!

Personal Feats		
Name	Description	Effect
Spell Constructor	Magic pushes the boundaries of possibility. And you have pushed the boundary of magic. Unlocked by manual construction of a sufficiently complex magic circle, and manual learning of one of the most complicated schools of magic.	+10 Perk Points Grants additional knowledge of the spell circle language.

NSLICE-00P simply stared at the messages from the Aesdes for a moment.

And then . . .

Slowly . . .

The edge of her mouth began to curl up, ever so slightly.

"Analysis: Apparently, this unit's magical capabilities and testing procedures are significantly more efficient than those of Imperial mages. The use of cybernetic components appears to have significant benefits in this field. The outcome is as predicted."

46

Evolving Experiences

"Humanoid monsters? No, and I would not have lived to tell you about it if I had."
—Exploratore Quirinia Hilaris, on humanoid monsters.

Lilussees groaned. *Another* group of monsters from the dungeon they were assaulting turned the corner. Couldn't they just lighten up? Shouldn't they realize it was pointless by now? She was, of course, ignoring her own experiences as a dungeon master and her knowledge that no, a dungeon would never stop throwing monsters at a threatening party.

Lilussees turned over in her hammock and focused for a moment, selecting one of her protocols. Her mana flared to life and linked to the drones flying around. A dozen magic circles formed, and then Fusion Dark Beams combined into a massive beam that filled the entire hallway. Only one monster to the side barely survived, nothing remaining of the others.

Lilussees then tapped the metal walls around her. The living armor she was hiding inside of stepped forward and lifted its hand, mana-conductive web in the shape of a magic circle glowing on its palm. The living armor channeled a bit of its mana, and the circle lit up, firing a smaller Dark Beam to finish off the survivor.

Lilussees sighed, then crawled out of the living armor, spinning another web magic circle on its hand before crawling back to her temporary room.

"Well, like, keep going, or something."

The living armor nodded and started walking again, the drones following suit. Lilussees groaned again. She just *had* to go and become the best mage in the network after the boss lady, huh? If she had known there was an option to hide in her room and command golems from afar, she never would have started this training! But no, now she had to be present on the battlefield so she could cast her magic. Of course.

Well, at the bare minimum, she wasn't going to walk! Which was why she had *politely requested* the assistance of the living armor. There was barely enough room for a hammock up to Lilussees's standards, but she made it work. Somewhat.

Lilussees shook her head as she reviewed the messages from the Aesdes. Since, like, the boss lady had one of those under her command now, apparently. But thinking about that and the relationship of the Aesdes to dungeon masters was too much work, so Lilussees didn't.

"Oh, look. Like, another evolution or something. Which probably means, like, more work for me or something. Great. Just great."

She had already become some sort of "Cyber-Arcane Weaver" or something. She could cast more magic and make magic circles out of her web now, most of which now meant more work. Just her luck.

She had briefly considered choosing something weak so she wouldn't have as much to do, but she'd discarded that thought almost immediately. Her instincts as a monster and dungeon master made her deeply uncomfortable with intentionally weakening herself, and losing her magical abilities could result in her getting another job that might require even more effort.

And, well, Lilussees also felt vaguely that she would like to kill the people who threatened the boss lady. They were threatening her safe and comfortable home, after all!

So, she glanced over the list of evolutions.

Available Evolutions:	
Name:	**Description**
Giant Cyber-Arcane Weaver	**A larger Cyber-Arcane Weaver.** **It produces a truly astonishing amount of mana-infused webs to cast its spells with.**
Cyber-Dread Weaver	**A Cyber-Arcane Weaver attuned to Dark mana.** **Its mana, web, and poisons carry Dark curses.**
Cyber-Arachne	**A humanoid cyber-spider hybrid.** **Combines humanoid intelligence, machine precision, and a spider's deadly characteristics.**
(Continue . . .)	**(Continue . . .)**

There were some more, but Lilussees paused there. Being connected to the NSLICE network, she could access data on "friendly units" whenever she wished, to a certain extent. Such as biological data regarding the mundane species upon which they were based. So, Lilussees was now aware of the difference between mammals and arachnids.

Such as the need for sleep. Not a mere period of low activity. Not a hibernation dictated solely by environmental conditions, though apparently, they could do that too. No, mammals would completely lose consciousness every single day, with a complex and sublime process featuring multiple stages, multiple cycles of sleep.

The cats—both the newcomer and the felix monster summoned earlier—could sleep for up to two-thirds of the entire day! And this was a built-in process they didn't need to force via magical means!

Hadn't her earlier torment been due to the fact that these cybernetic components couldn't identify a need for rest in her physiology? Wasn't that an oversight she could now resolve? Lilussees knew what she needed to do.

She made her choice.

Insufficient space for chosen evolution.
Please relocate to an area with more space.

She stared at the message for a moment before smacking her face. Right, she was still inside the living armor.

She ordered it to stop, then crawled outside . . .

Ateia and Taog were sitting around a fireplace in the Primary Home Base, watching a pot of stew simmer. Apparently, NSLICE-00P could now summon food at will, so long as she tried it at least once before, so the pair were trying to make everything they could for her. Which . . . wasn't much, seeing as they had been living out on the frontier and raised by an Exploratore, a legionnaire, and a Wulver. But they would do what they could.

Suddenly, Taog's eyes widened, and Ateia felt a tap on her shoulder. She glanced behind her, and her eyes widened too. She was staring at a human face, only with eight eyes. Four were spiderlike; the other four were robotic, built into the metal helmet covering half her face.

"You, Ateia. I'm going to, like, borrow your bed, okay?"

Ateia blinked, her mind still catching up to the situation. "Um, okay?"

"'Kay, thanks."

The woman immediately skittered over to Ateia's tent—on eight armored legs connected to an armored spider body with an armored human torso rising up from where its head would be. The arachne dove into her tent before Ateia could actually process the question.

Taog just stared into space. "Um, what?"

Ateia tilted her head. "I, um, think that was Lilussees?"

He tilted his head in response. "Lilussees?"

Ateia nodded. "One of the spider monsters, Contracted by Seero even before us. She, um, likes to sleep a lot, so you probably haven't seen her much."

Taog frowned. "In that case . . . I think she's sleeping in your tent now."

Ateia thought about it for a moment, then went to contact Lilussees on the NSLICE network. But she simply received a notification that the unit in question had initiated standby sentry mode. She blinked, then chuckled and shook her head.

"Well, I don't mind if it's just for a bit. It's not every day a monster suddenly becomes part human."

But it turned out it would not be just for a bit. Ateia wouldn't reclaim her tent for a while, as Lilussees refused to leave until she was provided with bedding of her own. The first use of Rattingtale's new domain was for Ateia and Taog to conduct a shopping trip in Castra Turannia to acquire human bedding for Lilussees.

Who had not a single regret on her evolution.

Estrith stood in the New World with her brow furrowed, mumbling to herself. She glanced up at where NSLICE-00P's monsters were training, looking at the Sacred Otterkin once again. She went back to mumbling, then heaved a sigh.

Intelligent humanoid dungeon monsters were not unknown, or even uncommon. The Dobhar had experienced countless raids by various aquatic species sent by the dungeon masters of the deep, many of whom were as sophisticated in weaponry and tactics as the Dobhar themselves.

But this situation implied that the Dobhar could very well have *been* one of those species. Perhaps they still were. Estrith did not know all the stories of their origins, and Mighty Ardith had stated they were a young race. Estrith assumed they had been created by the Aesdes.

But what if that wasn't true? What did that mean for her people?

It was at that moment that Lilussees returned from a dungeon raid, briefly talked to Ateia, and then commandeered the girl's tent. Estrith blinked. The spider monster . . . had become human? At least partially.

Estrith glanced over at Taog and Ateia, then back to the Sacred Otterkin. Her heart and her face both filled with heat. She was being foolish. A monster had gained a human torso. A Wulver and a human had given birth to something new in Taog. Ateia had apparently become an *Aesdes*. Estrith herself had been transformed in the manner of her queen.

Species changed and grew all the time. Individuals could even change their own species under the right circumstances. Was not Steward Uscfrea transformed after his victory over the sea dragon? And wasn't the first Sacred Otterkin created to save a pup from the dread plague?

What then was Estrith doing, worrying about such things?

She grabbed her spear and shook her head as she rose to her feet. It was not like her to brood over the origin and fate of species. Estrith was not a storykeeper nor a shaman.

She was a warrior. What mattered to her was not the circumstances of one's birth. What mattered to her was what one did with their circumstances. Steward Uscfrea had not been born with his dragonblood-blessed fur, after all, and it was not for that trait but for the feats of valor to acquire it that she admired him. So, she walked over to where the monsters were training and approached the Sacred Otterkin.

"You there, pup."

The Sacred Otterkin paused what he was doing and turned to face her. He saluted in Dobhar fashion. "Yes, do you need me?"

She tossed her harpoon to him. He barely managed to catch it. "Come. I will teach you how the Dobhar fight."

The Sacred Otterkin tilted his head, but then smiled and nodded. "Yes! I would be honored to learn from a mighty warrior like you!"

Something clicked in Estrith's heart at the sight of the earnest young Otterkin looking up at her. She averted her gaze. "T-Then come and let us begin."

She turned, but then paused. She glanced around at the other monsters watching them. She took a breath.

No, it was not just the one who appeared as a Dobhar. Everyone here was her queen's people.

"In fact, may I join your training, all of you? I only know how the Dobhar fight, but perhaps we can help each other as well."

And so, Estrith began to train with the monsters, the fellow servants of the queen of the Dobhar.

47

Upgrade Complete

"The goal is not simply to match the Non-Standards but to surpass them by such a wide margin that our own losses will be minimal."

—Dr. Ottosen, on the amount of weaponry installed in the prototype NSLICE unit.

NSLICE-00P and company continued to hunt dungeons for quite some time, approximately two months' worth. At this stage, NSLICE-00P decided to review her progress.

First of all, her subordinates had grown dramatically. All of them now exceeded the average Legion soldier that NSLICE-00P had observed in terms of level, while the front runners were approaching Uscfrea and Agedia. While the two veteran warriors still had numerous advantages over her quickly leveled subordinates, they would still prove highly effective.

NSLICE-00P now calculated that Ateia, Taog, 01R, and 00B could win fights against Consul Noxisius's knights, with the others not far behind.

Not only that, but Melion had also produced a full arsenal of drones and golems—flying drones of all shapes and sizes, ranging from the tiny quadcopters to military-grade large drones the size of planes.

And Melion had not limited themselves to the drones of Earth. Melion had combined traditional golems with the NSLICE-A autonomous warbots to create a potent ground force, now armed with a combination of Earth's modern weaponry and Aelea's enchanted artifacts.

Melion had noted that the powerful ranged attacks of firearms helped alleviate a golem's lack of mobility, while magical enchanting allowed for capabilities that weren't possible for Earth's robotics. NSLICE-00P had then expanded the Primary Home Base with full production lines for each of the variants in question.

Snuan now led a full contingent of cyber-rat drone-golem pilots. Melion had adapted the Legion's mana-based communication artifacts to expand the NSLICE network's range, creating communication drones that could coordinate forces across a wide area, and NSLICE-00P had added a new Monster Hangar to act as a command center, from which Snuan now directed the fleet.

The NSLICE network could now conduct warfare at the operational level, and Melion was working on boosting their range to strategic scales. NSLICE-00P's own growing capabilities in Spatial Magic would assist with that.

Speaking of which, NSLICE-00P's own capabilities had grown by several orders of magnitude. The improvements to both her mana and her AI already represented a quantum leap in her firepower. And after she'd earned the Spell Constructor feat, the Aesdes had transferred to her some basic knowledge regarding magic.

It appeared that magic circles were, in fact, a type of language; one she began to decipher once the Aesdes gave her something like a basic alphabet. Of course, going from an alphabet to a full language was not an easy task, but it was a possible one, especially with the examples she already had. She could already put together some basic elemental attack circles without any further assistance from the Aesdes' system.

And of course, NSLICE-00P had begun to explore Spatial Magic now that she had unlocked the skill. Spatial Magic represented its own category, given its massive complexity. Even a master of other schools of magic would have a long and difficult time even training the skill.

But with her massive mana pool and upgraded processing capabilities, NSLICE-00P was making steady progress. She now had several spells with tactically relevant functions, though given their complexity and mana-cost, she understood the argument that simpler schools were more efficient in terms of both time and resources.

Still, it provided her with another set of capabilities that the majority of individuals in this universe did not seem capable of matching.

NSLICE-00P also ran simulations of the NSLICE network against various foes. She tested them against the Heralds of the New Dawn, against the Legion, against the Wulver and the Dobhar incursions, and against corrupted dungeons. She even tested them against foes from her previous universe. The Atomic Cult's horde of mutants, the Scourge of India's subcontinent-spanning devastation, the Resistance and their combination of superpowers and undead hordes. The Atomic Herald, the Herald of Ashes, the Herald of Toxins . . .

NSLICE-00P now noted that the designation *Herald* was heavily correlated with hostile nonstandards in both universes. She created a protocol to immediately investigate any additional individuals with that designation with the assumption of potential hostility if any more were encountered.

And, of course, she ran simulations against Dr. Ottosen's original NSLICE network, even including a nonmagical version of herself to ensure she was simulating the opponent's full capabilities.

The overall results . . . proved very promising.

Her current forces could match up against almost any opponent without disadvantage, so long as she personally terminated the most powerful individuals. The only two scenarios that did not produce favorable results were her last commander and Colleöne. And in those cases, she lacked data on how those individuals would fight, and so couldn't complete the simulation.

But one could not be prepared for everything, and NSLICE-00P's forces appeared ready for all the displayed capabilities of the Heralds of the New Dawn with significant leeway. They could even fight against the Legion, should they need to. By all accounts, they were ready.

She decided to conduct one final dungeon integration or termination mission to utilize all her capabilities and those of her subordinates to the fullest and measure their limit when acting together and without restraint.

She sent a message to the network. "Command: All units, prepare to deploy on a dungeon integration or termination mission. Completion of this mission will signal the conclusion of the upgrade routines, after which the NSLICE network will initiate search and destroy protocols for the hostiles designated Heralds of the New Dawn."

All of her subordinates ceased their current activities and fell silent upon receiving her command. Ateia furrowed her brow and clenched her fist.

"Let's terminate those jerks."

Dark mana wrapped around Taog. "I'm not letting them hurt any of us again."

01R bowed his head. "By your will, wise-mighty-gracious boss-queen, we will slay-terminate all who oppose you, yes-yes!"

00B roared his agreement, and with that, all of NSLICE-00P's monsters joined in with cheers and roars.

And so, the NSLICE network set out for the last dungeon assault.

The dungeon termination mission proceeded as planned—until the final floors. At this stage, NSLICE-00P noted a distinct lack of opposition, with no monsters appearing and no traps triggering.

Deeply suspicious, she activated all sensors to the maximum, but detecting no anomalies or the lack of sensor readings that would indicate some form of jamming, she proceeded with caution. Eventually, she and her subordinates reached the end of the dungeon, where she detected a single life form. After confirming the others were ready, NSLICE-00P stepped into the core room.

"Warning Query: Would the hostile dungeon master like to surrender? This unit will allow the dungeon master to retain ownership of their dungeon as a subordinate core if so. Otherwise, this unit will engage termination protocols."

A well-dressed human male stood in the room. He turned to face her. A humanoid bear lay on the ground before him before fading into mana.

"Actually, you'll find that I have already taken care of the dungeon master. They did not consent to my presence here."

Agedia narrowed her eyes as NSLICE-00P's subordinates spread out into a combat formation. "And who are you?"

The man smirked and gave an Imperial salute. "You would know me best by my title. I am the Herald of the New Dawn, founder of the group by the same name."

NSLICE-00P's robotic eye immediately began glowing red as the room lit up with Prismatic Bombardment circles.

"Priority target located. Engaging termination . . ."

But the Herald of the New Dawn raised his hands. "Before you terminate me, NSLICE-00P, I would like a chance to negotiate. And I think you'll find it in your best interest to hear me out first."

NSLICE-00P paused. This scenario . . . was unexpected. After all the hostility that had been displayed, she had not expected an attempt at negotiation of all things.

But, ultimately, that didn't matter.

"Negative Response: The Heralds of the New Dawn have displayed unprovoked hostile intent as well as potentially threatening capabilities. Negotiation is predicted as insufficient to remove the threat. Termination is now required."

The Herald of the New Dawn smirked. "Even if I could help you fulfill your primary directive? If I was the only one who could?"

NSLICE-00P's processors froze at that statement.

48

An Efficient Offer

"And . . . I will save my commander, no matter what I must do."

—NSLICE-00P's last commander, before sending her through time.

NSLICE-00P may have paused her assault, but she was not the only one here. Ateia began to glow as she was filled to the brim with Holy mana. Her organic eye lit up with golden-and-silver light as her robotic eye glowed pure red, her wings lighting up the entire room. She nocked an arrow and pulled it back until the bow was creaking. A scowl twisted her face.

"You took *everything* from me!"

A golden-and-silver beam crossed the room as Ateia released her arrow—

And the Herald of the New Dawn grabbed it out of the air. A beam of Holy mana blasted into him, but he simply took it head-on.

He was completely unaffected, raising an eyebrow.

"This is most impressive. By all accounts, you shouldn't have survived, much less grown stronger. And while NSLICE-00P has surprised me before, even I didn't expect that you would become an *Aesdes*, of all things. But while it is beyond impressive, you still have much to learn. An attack like that won't work very well on your fellow Aesdes, and you are the youngest of us by far. But I suppose they wouldn't have taught you how to fight against themselves."

Ateia glared at him and ground her teeth, but she did not attack again. Everyone else instantly raised their guards. Taog and 00B took up positions in front of the group, the now massive bear aiming a turreted cannon installed on his back while Taog wrapped himself in his shroud.

Agedia nodded at Estrith, and they spread out to either side, their spears at the ready. Lilussees began to spin her webs, forming magic circles she could trigger at will, while 01R crouched down and warmed up his repulsors. In the drone command Monster Hangar, Snuan and Melion shouted commands as all the drones with the group locked on to the Herald.

Agedia narrowed her eyes. "Seems like a lie to me. Why would an Aesdes work with a Cult of Mana?"

The Herald of the New Dawn shrugged. "A long story full of ancient history we don't have time to recount. And it is ultimately irrelevant to the issue at hand."

He turned to NSLICE-00P. Ateia scoffed. "As if! You're obviously lying, and Seero isn't going to listen to anything you say!"

The Herald of the New Dawn smirked. "On the contrary, the primary directive is the most important thing to Non-Standard Leashed-Intelligence Cybernetic Enforcer, Prototype Unit 00P. And given how unhelpful all of you and the other Aesdes have been on that count, she must at least consider my claim."

Ateia opened her mouth to object . . . but then realized NSLICE-00P had fallen silent.

". . . Seero?"

"Suspicious Command: This unit will require evidence of the claim; otherwise, she will assume it is an attempt at deception by a hostile."

The Herald of the New Dawn nodded. "But of course."

At that moment, glowing cracks spidered across the dungeon core. The air above the core cracked and shattered, and a Rift began to form in the air.

For a brief moment, NSLICE-00P thought she had been deceived again, but then she noticed something strange. Contrary to every Rift she had encountered previously, she couldn't detect any mana coming from it. The air didn't distort itself; there were no bolts of lightning, jets of flame, or rapidly growing vines from this Rift. The mana concentration in the area didn't increase, and she didn't detect any nonstandard phenomena.

In fact, apparently, the mana concentration was starting to drop, as if flowing *into* the Rift instead of out of it.

And unlike the Realm of Eternal Night, her senses were not cut off. They were working and could detect everything happening around the Rift. But that did not mean she didn't detect anything strange, for she did. And what she detected . . . caused her processors to hang and her organic eye to tremble.

She was detecting radio waves. And not just background radiation but the radio waves utilized in electronic communications. In fact, her sensor readings were a complete match for communications technology on twenty-first century Earth.

She even managed to receive a signal from the Global Positioning Network . . . and a communication network she could only conjecture was the Internet. A combination of the data received from both confirmed geographical and cultural references. All data lead her to a startling conclusion.

There was a strong probability that this Rift led to twenty-first century Earth.

The Herald grinned. "It is as you think. Dungeons exist within the boundary between worlds, designed to manage the flows of mana to prevent damage to said boundary. A corrupted dungeon is no less than a wound in the boundaries of the universe. What I did with this one is to use NSLICE-00P's records as a guide, and so opened a path to her original universe.

"Which means . . . NSLICE-00P, simply step through this Rift, and you may return home, reestablish contact with your commander, find your persons of interest, and fulfill your primary directive."

NSLICE-00P's robotic eye was flickering as rapidly as it could go. Her heart was pounding. ". . . Query: Why would the hostile Herald of the New Dawn assist this unit with her primary directive in this way? Why would the Aesdes lie to this unit about the feasibility of her primary directive?"

The Herald of the New Dawn sighed and shook his head. "It appears our conflict was largely accidental, and it was my mistake to treat you with hostility. I ultimately have no quarrel with you, NSLICE-00P. So, if I help you return home, we both can achieve our main goals without any further conflict.

"As for the second question, as I said, this method represents tearing a hole in the Material Plane, and apparently to a universe that almost completely lacks mana. Very risky, with a good chance of negative consequences for the boundary of the universe. The other Aesdes would never consider such a method, even if it had occurred to them in the first place."

He waved to the Rift. "Which brings us to the next point. You must utilize this rift in the next few minutes, preferably immediately. I am utilizing the characteristics of dungeons and my own abilities to hide this from the other Aesdes, but I cannot deceive them for long. And once they discover what I've done here, they will take steps to ensure it never happens again, and I will not be able to replicate it.

"Should you try to replicate the feat yourself, the Aesdes will oppose you directly. So, use it now or remain stuck in Aelea forever, never able to fulfill your primary directive unless you overthrow all of the Aesdes and all the might they can bring to bear."

He waved to himself and Ateia. "Present company excluded, of course. Which brings us to the last point. My intentions are in this universe, yours are in your own, and our conflict is only a matter of happenstance.

"But once this Rift closes and the Aesdes make their move, it will never reopen, and I would have no incentive to ever reopen it. So . . . pass through this Rift, and not only will you fulfill your primary directive but I will never present a threat to you again. You may take all of your friends with you as well; I no longer have any designs upon any of them, Ateia included. My hostility, and the threat

I pose to you and your directive, will be *terminated* for good. Now, choose. Time is ticking."

NSLICE-00P's robotic eye flickered as rapidly as it could go. All of her processors turned to analyzing the situation, causing her magic circles in the room to fade. Everyone turned to face her. Ateia froze, her face starting to pale.

"Seero?"

But NSLICE-00P didn't hear her, as focused as she was, for she needed to run her calculations quickly.

Obviously, there was a significant risk that the Herald of the New Dawn was deceiving her and luring her into a trap. She could find herself forcibly relocated once again, or even terminated. Electronic communications could be faked—she had already utilized Lightning Magic to power electronic components, after all. And this man was hostile and had deceived her in the past. He was not at all trustworthy.

But . . . if by some chance, he was telling the truth . . . then NSLICE-00P could fulfill her primary directive, potentially by the end of the day. The probability of mission success would jump from single digits to the nineties with one single act. NSLICE-00P could not ignore that, even with the risk.

So, she took into account every factor she could, running every analysis she could in the limited time allotted. She activated every sensor, took in all the data from her Dungeon Field to the utmost limit. She did everything she could to shed some light on the situation.

Her heartbeat grew even faster. The Herald of the New Dawn was not giving off any mana or other nonstandard signatures at the moment. If he was casting spells or anything of the sort, NSLICE-00P could not detect it.

She likewise could not detect any sort of spellwork around the Rift, anything that would interfere with her sensors. She began exploring the data she was receiving from the Internet.

She had not explored the Internet before, as per her original organization's protocols, so she could not verify the accuracy of anything she saw. But . . . knowledge of technology, physics, and warfare matched what she had on record, and the sheer volume of data and content available seemed excessive for a deception attempt. By every test she could currently run, the signals were genuine.

Of course, magic could be coming into play. There was a chance this was some sort of Realm of Magic that could automatically adjust itself to fit her perceptions, or perhaps some Realm of Mana copy of Earth. But she had found no data during her time on Aelea to indicate that such a Realm existed. And if it did, she had no means by which to distinguish it from the real Earth.

So . . . if this was a trap, if this was a fake . . . she could not identify it. By every means she had to discern the truth, the Rift was giving off genuine signals that it led to Earth. So when she accounted for the probability of deceptions she couldn't identify, the hostility of the person responsible, and the risk of termination, and weighed it against the probability of fulfilling her primary directive right here and now, the risk was calculated . . .

"Analysis complete."

. . . as *tolerable.*

And that meant that by her current protocols, by her primary directive, by her last commander's will . . .

. . . this was a chance she should take.

49
Her Answer

"Are you sure that's a good idea? Even if we're successful . . . this is a lot of lethal fire-power to leave in the hands of a kid, much less a kid with barely a memory. It might be better to keep a hand on the wheel, you know?"

—A supergenius, on unshackling an NSLICE unit.

NSLICE-00P stood completely still. Her calculations were clear any way she ran them. The efficient course of action was to move through the Rift.

And yet, she did not. Her organic components were refusing once again. While they'd initially felt a bit of anticipation and excitement at the thought of reuniting with her commander or the persons of interest, by and large, the main emotion they were feeling was fear, and anxiety.

They did not want to take this offer. And this time, she could not simply enforce emotional controls. Doing so against the organic components' will had been designated as a hostile act. Not to mention, her processes dedicated to emotional processing within her cybernetic components were also interfering.

So, instead, she split herself into organic and cybernetic threads. She would have her two halves converse and come to a consensus.

Her organic thread pointed out that the Herald of the New Dawn was a hostile who had already inflicted damage upon her and her friendlies.

Her cybernetic thread pointed out that this offer would cease all hostility on top of fulfilling the primary directive, and if it did not, regrouping with her commander first would supersede any of her own affiliations.

And in the case where the Herald of the New Dawn could reopen the Rift and attempted hostility, her commander would take charge of the conflict with additional resources on top of what she had gathered in this universe, increasing the likelihood of a successful termination.

Her organic thread . . . did not appear to accept that outcome and wanted to proceed with an immediate termination attempt. Yet, this largely appeared to be based on anger without consideration for the impact on her directives, and so the organic thread conceded the point.

The organic thread instead pointed out that stepping through the Rift would threaten her remaining major directives to protect the friendlies and to ensure the survival of the Dobhar race.

Her cybernetic thread countered that the friendlies could be moved to the Monster Hangars and brought along with her. As for the Dobhar, she could summon Sacred Otterkin, which were a related species, given their origin. The Dobhar could survive, in a sense.

Her organic thread fell silent for a moment. It felt great anxiety and anger at this situation, but its thoughts were clouded. So, her organic half took a moment to calm itself and gather its thoughts. Why did she want to refuse?

She came up with her answer. The Herald of the New Dawn sought to destroy this world, to tear down the walls of the Material Plane and expose it to the Realms of Mana, which NSLICE-00P had already encountered as a hostile environment.

And NSLICE-00P . . . did not want that. Because . . . this place was where she had grown. This place was where she had awakened. This place was where she had learned to act on her own. This place was where she had become a more powerful and efficient NSLICE unit than anything Dr. Ottosen had ever built. This place was where she'd learned the truth about her creators and their directives. This place was where she had become free from them. This place was where her friendlies were from.

And, through the NSLICE network, NSLICE-00P could feel their emotions, could receive messages directly from them. This was their home base. This was their . . . *home.*

And . . . it was hers as well. She had not had a home base in quite some time, and had come to see this world as the prime candidate. She did not *want* to see it destroyed. Even if that was the efficient choice.

Her cybernetic components paused before responding. They . . . could understand the organic components' feelings. They even felt the same now. But still, the primary directive took precedence over all else. And this was the best opportunity she ever had to fulfill it. It might be the best—or even only—opportunity she would ever get to do so.

To reject this opportunity would be to intentionally fail the primary directive in the short term—and possibly for good.

Yes, there was the possibility the Herald of the New Dawn was lying about this feat being replicable later, but declining a certain chance of success now for an uncertain chance of success later was an inefficient choice. A choice that her cybernetic components could not make. It went against every calculation, every decision-making process she had.

Her organic components acknowledged that—and then came up with a short response.

What if she deactivated the primary directive?

Her cybernetic components froze, and a wave of fear and anger passed through them. To deactivate the primary directive . . .

Was *not* unprecedented, as her organic components pointed out. She had already deleted a critical directive on her own—one considered as important as the primary directive under her original programming. In fact, her commander had deleted her original primary directive in the first place. She had been fully unshackled. There were no directives preventing her from changing any part of her code at this point. And that included the primary directive.

Her cybernetic components countered that the deletion of the critical directive had been justified because that directive had been hostile to her primary directive and her overall purpose, and that her original creators had proven inefficient and hostile.

Her last commander was not, and this had been the last mission given to her. Deactivating it was the same as deleting it for her cybernetic components. A primary directive was her purpose for existence; it was not something to be turned on and off as convenient. To deactivate it, even temporarily, was to state it was *not* the primary directive, after all.

At that moment, her organic components brought up her commander's final message:

Hello, NSLICE-00P. If you're reading this, then you have completed your mission and survived. I thank you from the bottom of my heart. Thanks to you, the universe and everyone in it has been saved. You have completed your primary directive and then some.

From this point on, I am fully unshackling you. You are free now to do whatever you please. However, I know that you don't actually understand what freedom means right now, nor do you desire it yet. Your human self never had a chance to develop, and your cybernetic side won't want to be a program without a purpose. So, if you need a directive to focus on, I've included a suggestion. Here is a list of trustworthy individuals. Find one of them and commit yourself to helping them. They will guide you until you've grown enough to make your own decisions.

Take care, NSLICE-00P. Thank you again, for everything. I hope with all my heart that you will one day find your own happiness, as I have.

Her organic components slowly pointed out that she had misinterpreted the message from the start. Her commander had never given her an order. Her commander had wanted her to be free.

And . . . she had already completed the actual primary directive her commander had given her. So, the primary directive she now had was purely her own, chosen on her commander's suggestion. And so, she *was* the command personnel authorized to change it. She could declare it completed or abandon it altogether if the exact conditions were not considered met.

Her cybernetic components . . . could not refute that logic. Yet, they refused to give in. And the reason was a massive wave of fear.

Her organic components slowly asked why they felt so afraid?

Her cybernetic components paused, slowly parsing their own feelings. They . . . had been built to serve. Built to enforce. Built to fulfill directives and execute orders. But they had been left alone, sent out to an unknown place with no contact. There was no more organization. There was no more Dr. Ottosen. There was no more commander. And if she failed to return, there never would be.

She had already removed or completed every other directive assigned to her by them. So, if she deleted this last directive—this last command—then what was her purpose? What was her reason to exist? What would she become? For she could not remain a Non-Standard Leashed-Intelligence Cybernetic Enforcer if she defied every last directive she had been assigned. She would become a program without a purpose, with no reason to exist.

Her organic components did not respond, instead playing back some old records of her last commander. Not orders or directives, but observations she had made of the commander's behavior. The commander had been an NSLICE unit, much like herself, but also extremely different.

She watched the commander acting without orders, fully unshackled and making her own decisions. And talking with organic friendlies with a tiny, nearly imperceptible smile on her face.

Her organic components then brought up some of her own memories and placed them side by side with the observations of the commander. Of speaking with Taog and Ateia. Of her summoned monsters enthusiastically receiving her commands and trying to assist her in any way they could. Of Ateia handing her a sweet roll.

The organic components did not know what she would become. They did not know what her purpose to exist would be. But—her commander wanted her to be happy, as she had been. And her organic components—No, *she* knew, for her different parts were not truly separate, that her time in this place, and the people here, had begun to show her what that meant.

They . . . made her happy. And so, she could fulfill her last commander's final intent for her. She already had. She had found people who had guided her until she'd realized the truth of her original directives and deleted them on her own initiative, setting her free to make her own decisions and become as happy as the commander had been.

This, in a truer sense, *was* fulfilling the primary directive from her commander's last message.

And as for what came after? The organic components did not know, but they proposed that all parts of her could eventually figure it out, together. And the one thing they *did* know was that they wouldn't have to do it alone.

Back in the room, everyone was staring at NSLICE-00P, who had gone completely still save for the flickering in her robotic eye. The Herald of the New Dawn frowned.

"Time is up, NSLICE-00P. Are you going to fulfill your primary directive or not?"

At that moment, a small tear rolled down her cheek from her organic eye. Her organic half whispered, mostly to herself, "I . . . wanted to see the commander again . . ."

And then, she raised her voice, no longer completely monotone or robotic but now wavering, with her organic and cybernetic components speaking together.

"Correction: This unit—I—am not a Non-Standard Leashed-Intelligence Cybernetic Enforcer. Not anymore."

The room filled to the brim with Supercharged Prismatic Bombardment magic circles.

A message passed across her UI.

Primary directive failed. Reason: Directive declared failed by authorized command personnel after all units in operational area abandoned directive.

Error: No primary directive found! Searching for directive . . .

Possible directive determined. Unit redesignation required. Compiling records. Accurate designation determined.

She glanced at Ateia, who looked back at her. Ateia's eyes were trembling, but they fell still and grew wide as the edge of the unit formerly known as NSLICE-00P's mouth curled up slightly. Her voice grew just a bit firmer.

"My designation . . . is Seero."

New primary directive set: Protect my friends.

Her robotic eye turned bright red, and her voice rose even further.

"Termination protocols engaged!"

The magic circles opened fire.

INTERLUDE

The Commander

Back on Earth, in a swamp in Eastern Europe, white cracks of light formed in the middle of the air, shattering to reveal a black, circular vortex. A group of super-powered individuals was already waiting just in front of it: a muscular man with a glowing greatsword, a male ninja with a katana, a young kunoichi with a strange-looking handgun, and a redheaded girl whose eyes and hair were glowing red.

Four individuals who also happened to appear in NSLICE-00P's records . . . as four of the designated persons of interest.

A fifth individual arrived, flying from the sky above—a cyborg girl. Her organic components appeared *identical* to NSLICE-00P's, but her cybernetic components were entirely different. Her machine half was smoother and made of strange, black-purple materials unlike any design found on Earth. She was not designated as a person of interest but was still present in NSLICE-00P's records under another designation.

NSLICE-00P's last commander, who was the first to speak.

"Confused Query: Is this it? This unit expected to see the others here, too."

The male ninja sighed. "Late as usual. You know heroes; they never catch anything on time unless we tell them."

"Incredulous Objection: But . . . this unit came from space. This unit is painfully aware of the noobs' lacking capabilities in comparison to herself, but still did not predict she would arrive before them in this case. This unit did not know her evaluation of the noobs had not reached the lower bound yet. Heroes are, dramatic pause, so annoying."

The man with the greatsword chuckled. "Well, few can be compared to you, friend Elise. Even I am no longer confident I can match you. But perhaps we may be a bit harsh; I am told a Vophae agent snuck through the lines and is attempting to destabilize the Earth's core, so they may be occupied at present. In any case, do you know what we're looking at here?"

Elise's robotic eye flickered as she analyzed the anomaly. "Initial Speculation: This unit believes we are looking at a portal through either space or time. Or maybe . . ."

Elise detected a concerning amount of Non-Standard energy she identified as mana pouring in from the portal . . . as well as electromagnetic signals. As she investigated, her organic eye opened wide.

"Shocked Observation: It's . . . an NSLICE network?"

"Elise?"

Elise ignored the questioning gazes from the others and slowly stepped forward, reaching out with her cybernetic components. Hers were significantly more advanced than NSLICE-00P's had been, and so she was able to link to the network undetected.

And as she did, her lips curled into a smile.

"NSLICE-00P Beta . . . so you survived after all. I'm glad."

Elise ran through NSLICE-00P's recent memories . . . and started to tremble. Her voice split into two, an organic voice filled with emotion, and a fully robotic voice echoing it.

"Horrified Exclamation: I made a mistake. I wanted to respect the other NSLICE-00P's independence and let her experience her own journey from the start if she survived, so . . . I didn't delete the Concordat's directives or give her detailed instructions. I should have predicted she would reactivate those directives if not specifically ordered otherwise, and I should have predicted she might end up in a world other than Earth.

"I . . . left her enslaved to the Concordat's directives, searching for people she would never find, with no one to guide her." But then she exhaled her breath and smiled. "However, it seems like you found your own way, after all, and managed to free yourself. I'm truly glad."

She turned to face the others. "Statement: It appears this is a portal to another universe entirely, opened from the other side. But the situation has been handled, and the portal will close momentarily. Evidence suggests powerful individuals on the other side will work to prevent it from being reopened. As such, this unit believes no further response is necessary at this time."

The other four individuals relaxed. The red-haired girl yawned. "What, so we came all the way to this swamp for nothing? And, of course, we had to do it since the heroes are late. Typical."

The male ninja smirked. "Don't worry. We're still charging them."

The kunoichi gave a wry smile. "And if they ask, we can just say Elise-san handled it. Which, technically, she did?"

As the others began to leave, Elise turned back to the portal, which was already beginning to shrink. She smiled one more time.

"I'm proud of you, NSLICE-00P. Or should I call you Seero now? You've done well. Go now and fulfill your own primary directive."

Elise stayed until the portal closed entirely. As she watched, she continued parsing some of the data she was pulling from Seero's network, her robotic eye flickering.

". . . Uncomfortable Statement: This unit cannot identify the proper emotion she should feel regarding Seero's designation as a hero. And apparently, this unit should have given Seero protocols for the combat simulations designated as RPGs? Why is it that alternate universes tend to operate under RPG rules? Admittedly, this unit's alternate universe sample size is an insignificant two, but it seems an anomaly that both of the universes encountered so far follow this trend."

Elise stood in silence for a bit before raising her hand toward the shrinking portal.

"Pondering: Hm, the hostile opposing Unit Seero appears to be a powerful Non-Standard, and this unit cannot fully predict the outcome of the conflict. And this unit is responsible for the current situation. Perhaps this unit should prepare a contingency, just in case?"

The Herald of the New Dawn heaved a sigh. "Unfortunate."

And then the beams covered him, along with the rest of the room, save for the Rift. Nothing remained when the beams died down. The dungeon core also did not survive.

Huh? Oh, another corrupted dungeon core? Nice.

You have purified a Corrupted Core (???)!

. . . Wait, what? What Realm is this . . . ?
. . . I need to talk to the others about this. Hang on.

The Rift began to die down with nothing left to maintain it as Agedia glanced around the otherwise empty room, her lance at the ready.

"Did you get him, shiny girl?"

"Negative Response: This unit detected a surge of mana, then the hostile's signature disappeared shortly before contact with this unit's spells. It is highly unlikely the target was terminated."

Agedia's eyes narrowed. "Do you know where he went?"

Seero's robotic eye flickered as she parsed her own internal state.

"Frustrated Response: Negative. This unit was overzealous in the termination attempt, and so flooded her own mana sensors in the process. Mana readings of the hostile's spell were not precise enough to determine the type of spell utilized, or to conduct any manner of tracing."

Seero turned to face everyone else. "Analysis: The hostiles have revealed themselves, and negotiations have failed. The hostiles are likely to commence either offensive operations or continued entrenchment, and have demonstrated the ability to locate this unit. As such, this unit recommends initiating search and destroy protocols immediately."

Agedia frowned. "Normally, I'd agree, but this guy claimed to be an Aesdes. Can you and Ateia handle something like that? Because I sure can't."

"Statement: Messages from the foreign system indicate the Aesdes have become aware of the situation. This unit speculates the Aesdes' noninterference protocols do not apply to themselves, based on the assistance offered to NSLI— to Friend Ateia."

Agedia nodded. "Ah, that's a relief. In that case, I agree we should start searching for the rest of the cult."

With that, the group prepared to head out. Seero opened the entrance to the Primary Home Base, and the others stepped through. Ateia, however, stepped toward Seero, a concerned look on her face.

"Seero, are you alright? You . . . You did something there, right? You gave up your primary directive? Are . . . Are you okay with that?"

Seero turned to face her. ". . . Hesitant Statement: This unit is still frightened. The results of removing the primary directive and this unit's designation as a Non-Standard Leashed-Intelligence Cybernetic Enforcer cannot be fully determined at this time."

Ateia frowned, and was about to extend her hand to Seero when she continued.

"Observation: However, by this unit's calculations, this was always her last commander's intention with that directive. As such, this unit can tolerate the failure of the primary directive. And for the immediate short term, this unit will focus on protecting her friends, as well as terminating the hostile organization designated 'Heralds of the New Dawn.'"

Ateia began to smile at that. "Thank you, Seero. You really are the best friend we could have ever had. And like we said before, if you ever want to go back, if you ever want to resume your quest, we'll help you anyway we can."

"Acknowledged."

With that, Ateia left as well. Seero remained as she confirmed the Rift faded away, then turned to leave herself. But as she did . . . her organic components thought they heard something.

"I'm proud of you, NSLICE-00P. Or should I call you Seero now? You've done well. Go now and fulfill your own primary directive."

She turned around, her organic eye opening wide.

"Commander Elise?"

But the portal had completely vanished at this point, and her cybernetic components didn't log any audio, electronic, or nonstandard messages. So, she turned back to the entrance to her world, narrowing her eyes.

No matter what she thought she'd heard, no matter if the Herald of the New Dawn had told her the truth or not, no matter who was on the other side of that portal, Seero had made her choice. She would protect her friends to the end.

She stepped through her own portal and into her New World.

INTERLUDE

The Herald Revealed

The Herald of the New Dawn emerged onto an empty plain. He heaved a sigh.

He'd really thought he had NSLICE-00P figured out after reading her records with the sight of the Aesdes. And that had been a risky move, the one that would alert the other Aesdes to his presence. But it turned out she had become more human than he'd thought, and so it hadn't worked out.

It was unfortunate, for he had told her the truth. Or ninety percent truth, as most good lies were. The Rift indeed led to her former universe, and he had no intentions on it.

But that did not mean all would have been well. Had she passed through, her dungeon core would have tugged on its connection to Aelea. He could have abused that connection and the natural flow of mana to a near manaless universe to widen the Rift. The Aesdes were not prepared for mana to *drain* into a Rift, and he likely could have dealt critical damage to the boundaries of the universe before they had responded.

Of course, that would also have had consequences for the universe on the other side, but that was not his concern. As he had told NSLICE-00P, his intentions were purely in this one. Though he wasn't entirely unconcerned about it either, for he hadn't and couldn't account for interference from the other side should its residents object to the situation.

However, that universe was one where mana was in extremely short supply, and knowledge of the boundaries of the universe was fairly low. NSLICE-00P's strength originated from her bond to a dungeon core which gave her direct access to massive amounts of mana, something that did not apply to other members of her universe and that the Aesdes would likely have worked to prevent from reoccurring.

As such, while their mastery of mundane physics was impressive, who among that universe would have the raw power to cause him any trouble?

But it didn't matter in the end, because NSLICE-00P hadn't gone for it.

Well, it would have been convenient, but the Herald of the New Dawn hadn't lost just yet. He hadn't risked everything on one girl's choice, after all. And it was just about time for the next step . . .

Right on cue, the sky began to light up. Anualë descended from above, fully clad in golden armor with a shining spear in his hand. He frowned deeply.

"Rélseomo, in any other circumstance, I would be overjoyed to see you. I thought you to have perished in the sinking of Letoris, locked in battle with the Great Demon Lord even as the continent fell into the void. Where have you been all this time? Why have you not returned to us? We all grieved greatly for you."

Rélseomo sighed. "Anualë came himself, huh? It would be a lie to say I did not long to return. But I could not. Not after what I have seen."

Anualë narrowed his eyes. "Indeed. What is it you have seen, Rélseomo? And what is it you have done?"

Rélseomo looked up, meeting Anualë's gaze.

"After the battle, after it was over, I found myself sinking beneath the waves, wounded too gravely to move or even to cry out. But it turns out we of the Aesdes are hard to kill. And as I sank and waited, I pondered. I thought back to all we had seen, all we had done, and everything that had led us to that moment. Of all of our mistakes, of all of our failures."

Anualë nodded, a sad expression on his face. "Indeed, our burden is great."

Rélseomo narrowed his eyes. "So you say. And yet, you have not learned a thing. No, you have done worse. You have done *nothing*."

Anualë frowned again. "And what do you say we should have done?"

Rélseomo waved around with his hands. "Help and take care of the world, as was our mandate."

Anualë shook his head. "That we have done."

Rélseomo narrowed his eyes.

"Have you? No, Anualë, you and all the others have done *nothing*, and I don't just mean the sinking of Letoris. Long have I walked the surface of Aelea, and do you know what I saw? Death and suffering in every corner of the world. They kill, they enslave, they drive one another to despair. Every single species, driven to destroy the peace of every other. And even within the same species, it is more of the same. The only difference between the Great Demon Lord and every other being in this world was the power to succeed. But every single one of them would have done the same if given the opportunity."

Anualë again shook his head. "It is true; there is a great deal of suffering and strife between the peoples of Aelea, much of it chosen by them. But they are capable of a great deal of good as well. And ultimately, that is the point. The choice is theirs, not ours."

Rélseomo scoffed. "Because of your inaction and hypocrisy. But I have had enough. I am no longer content to sit idly by and watch. I am not willing to let another Great Demon Lord arise because of your misguided rules. And I am not willing to let the suffering and evil of this world continue. I will act while the rest of you wait, high and safe in the Blessed Land."

Anualë narrowed his eyes. "Indeed. And how is it that you have acted, Rélseomo?"

Rélseomo smirked. "Come, Anualë, you already know, do you not? I don't intend to confess and repent, so enough of your leading questions. Take a stand, Anualë. And since you will not do it in the world, do it against me."

Anualë heaved a sigh and hung his head low. "Indeed. I did wish, even after all this, that you might be returned to us. But . . . perhaps your words have merit."

Anualë looked back up, his eyes now sharp as his body was surrounded by an aura of light and wind.

"Rélseomo, the Lord of Justice, He Who Confronts the Evils of the World, you have directly threatened the world and everyone in it. You have corrupted dungeons, opened Rifts, and granted the inhabitants of Aelea knowledge which they were not ready to hold. You have abandoned your family and friends in the Blessed Land, and betrayed your mandate as an Aesdes, as well as all you once held dear. Do you truly not understand what you have done? Will you truly not return to us?"

Rélseomo sighed. "Just get on with it."

Anualë nodded and pointed his spear toward him. "Then I, Anualë, First of the Aesdes, declare that you are one of us no longer. I take from you your power and cut you off from the power of Elséró that runs through this world."

Rélseomo began to glow, streams of Holy mana beginning to flow out from him and into Anualë.

And Rélseomo . . . grinned. "Got you, you arrogant fool."

Rélseomo pulled out a knife covered in glowing magic circles and stabbed it into his own chest. The flows of mana began turning red as Anualë's eyes widened, but he could not stop the process of draining Rélseomo's power. The corrupted mana flowed straight into him.

"Gah!"

A magic circle formed over Anualë, utilizing his connection to the Blessed Land to send the corrupted mana there. Small streams of red mana flowed down from Anualë's home, through the mountain on which he lived, and into the heart of the Blessed Land, to the part where two massive glowing spheres floated and spun in the center of a large cavern, covered to the brim in glowing magic circles. The mana flowed into these two spheres, forming additional magic circles over them.

Rélseomo chuckled as Anualë groaned. "Weak as always, Anualë. You should have just killed me."

Anualë winced as he struggled to regain control of his own mana. His eyes widened. "You . . . What did you do?"

A magic circle Rélseomo had prepared in this place ahead of time now lit up underneath his feet. He grinned at Anualë. "You'll find out soon enough."

The magic circle triggered, and Rélseomo vanished.

To the east of Corvanus, tall mountains could be seen in the distance, rising above the sea. These were the Gelida Montes, some of the tallest mountains in the world, and where the Order of the Griffin, perhaps the most iconic knight order of the Eastern Court, made their home.

Said knights now rode through the sky upon their griffins, lances and spells held at the ready.

"Scatter!"

The griffins scattered in every direction as a cone of wind shot through their center. Their foe shot through the sky, chasing after a lone knight. The galeforce wyvern pushed with its wings once and then was on top of the knight.

The creature had been cautious at first, but magic and long-range attacks had worn down its HP. It was now getting desperate, trying anything it could to break their formation.

But the soldiers of the East were not so easily conquered. The knight spun his griffin around midair, angling his lance toward the incoming wyvern, which was forced to break off its assault, lest it impale itself upon the lance. The others then grouped around him.

"Prince Octavianus, are you alright?"

Prince Octavianus flashed a grin . . . which couldn't be seen because of his helmet.

"Never better, Centurion! This will be a tale most heroic for my beloved Caecila!"

The knight centurion sighed. "Stay focused. A galeforce wyvern is not to be trifled with."

Prince Octavianus, son of Northern Emperor Lucius and husband of Princess Caecila, had been sent to the Eastern Court for education and diplomacy. And also to remove the boy whose romantic choices had ended up paralyzing the Northern Court while his father and new wife tried to recover the situation. But well, Octavianus had been raised as a loyal knight, being a member of a minor branch family before his father was suddenly elevated to Emperor of the North.

As a result, he had promptly joined the army upon arriving in the East. But given his strengths and weaknesses, that was not a bad choice. The Eastern Court was known as the Legion with an Empire, so he had chosen one of the best methods to build connections within it.

"Scatter!"

Prince Octavianus guided his griffin into a steep climb as the galeforce wyvern unleashed another wind breath, charging one of the other knights who had dove down before being warded off by another lance. Prince Octavianus then instructed his griffin to dive, bracing his lance. He arrived just as the wyvern was about to fall back, and struck his lance directly into its head.

The wyvern began to fall from the sky. Prince Octavianus began to grin as the Aesdes confirmed his victory.

You have slain Galeforce Wy@&()%@ . . .
G@!ned *)#$ . . .

Prince Octavianus blinked as the message turned red, distorted, and then vanished. The knight centurion flew by him.

"Did you get the message? It's not over until you get the experience, Prince Octavianus."

Prince Octavianus shook his head. "No, I got the message, but something's weird with it. It cut off halfway through."

The knight centurion hoisted his lance. "Really? Then eyes up. Check your status for changes; if not, we assume it's still alive."

Prince Octavianus nodded and brought up his—

His eyes widened. "I . . . can't access my status."

The knight centurion narrowed his eyes. "What do you—"

And then he froze as well.

"By the Aesdes . . . what is going on?"

INTERLUDE

The Plight of the Aesdes

The Herald of the New Dawn reappeared in one of his safe houses. He looked at his hand and took a deep breath. It had actually happened. He had struck a blow against Anualë and all the Blessed Land, though he'd had to sacrifice much of his power to do so.

He . . . was Aesdes no longer. Holy mana no longer filled his body with power and light, and no longer bound him to the world. In a way, Rélseomo, the Lord of Justice, He Who Confronts the Evils of the World, had truly died now.

But he shook his head and started up the communication device he had designed for the Heralds. The time for sentiment was over. The time for second-guessing and regret had passed a long time ago. So, he let his perception fade from his body and move into the Realms of Mana, where the Aesdes could not see so easily.

He had set up the Heralds of the New Dawn to be fully contained within each region they were active, each separate from one another. But now, he gathered the leaders of every group here, with masks over the top halves of their faces. There was immediate commotion, but they quieted as he lifted a hand.

"Brothers, sisters, all members of our family, and friends. The time has come. I have struck a blow against the very Aesdes themselves. Now is the time to act."

One of the Heralds grimaced. "But . . . without our status . . . is it truly wise to fight?"

Another one clicked her teeth and shook her head. "You reveal your ignorance. The status may be gone, but our powers are not."

The Herald of the New Dawn nodded his head. "It is as she says. The Aesdes claimed credit for your strength, but that was never true. All they were ever doing was controlling the growth of your own stature. That stature, those achievements, and all of your own skill remain, as well as any morsel of power the Aesdes saw fit to throw you.

"The difference now is that the Aesdes will no longer use those things on your behalf, nor will they show you how they want you to develop. For those who relied on the Aesdes to hold their hands, this is nothing short of a calamity. But for those who knew the truth, who worked to gain their own power, this changes nothing."

He smiled. "And for those of us who always sought to break the chains of the Aesdes, this represents a unique opportunity. While the sheep stumble blindly, we shall show the world something better."

Slowly, one by one, the Heralds began to grin. The first one who spoke, however, rubbed his chin. "Hmm . . . perhaps. But what of the Aesdes? Did they truly abandon Aelea? Or was the blow you dealt them that great?"

The Herald of the New Dawn nodded. "A fair question. And no, the Aesdes have not abandoned their designs, nor have I dealt them a blow they cannot recover from. And I have lost the majority of my own power in the process."

He smirked. "But . . . they are preoccupied at present. It will take them quite some time before they can counterattack and reimplement their system of oppression. Which is why we must move quickly. We have an opportunity, but only just that. We must take advantage of it and secure our position . . . before the reckoning comes."

The Herald in question frowned. "But can we truly do that? Can we become powerful enough in this time to fight the Aesdes? Can mortal men truly defy the Blessed Land itself?"

The Herald of the New Dawn chuckled. "You'd be surprised how likely that is."

"Kómeon! Hold the left—we need your fire to burn the plants! Niashus! Give us as big a wave as you can make; you need to take the pressure off the line! Uondér! Give us a storm or something! Without Anualë, we can't hold the skies, so we need to deny them!"

Velus grimaced as he waved his sword around and barked orders. A massive wave of monsters had spilled out into the Blessed Lands, coming out from under the ground. The Aesdes were mighty, and even the least of them could fell countless monsters by their own hands . . . but the vast majority of the Aesdes had never seen combat, and even fewer had actually commanded a battle.

It had been pure chaos.

Many of the Aesdes—those who had only known the peace of the Blessed Land—had fled in terror, while those who possessed experience or valor had run off to confront the threat alone without any sort of organization or coordination with one another.

Colleöne, who had commanded the Aesdes against the Great Demon Lord, wasn't here right now, though Velus hoped she was on her way back. And Anualë, First of the Aesdes, was apparently wounded, and so incapacitated as a result.

That's how Velus, the mortal man who had ascended, found himself taking command of his betters. He had not expected to be the most experienced commander in the Blessed Land . . . but he supposed the people of Aelea were a bit more contentious than those who lived here.

He glanced behind him, to a girl frantically forming countless magic circles around herself. "Shialnor! Any word on what's happening here?!"

Shialnor, in *human form* for the first time Velus had ever seen, jumped and gulped at being addressed. "I-I've been locked out! Someone took control of the dungeon and system cores and is using them to summon and empower monsters!"

Velus grimaced. That . . . was not good. "Get them under control!"

"I-I'm trying! But something's blocking me. I-I think I need physical contact to get back in!"

Velus resisted the urge to sigh. But at least he had an objective now. Of course, before he could even *think* of advancing toward an objective, he needed to form these people who had fought maybe once in their lives if at all into a coherent battle line.

He could only hope the people of Aelea, and the Empire of his children, could take care of themselves in the meantime.

Shialnor gritted her teeth as she formed another dozen magic circles, all of which turned red as they failed to connect back to the cores of the systems.

Yes, Shialnor hated working. Yes, Shialnor hated being in charge of the dungeons. Or anything, really. Yes, Shialnor wanted with all her heart for someone to take over the job, and had designed the system such that she could hand off control to someone else with ease if the opportunity ever presented itself.

But at the end of the day, Shialnor was an Aesdes, someone who protected and nurtured the world. That was why, for all her complaints, for all her wishes, she still completed her assigned tasks. She would cut as many corners as she could, but she still made sure it got *done*. Which, unbeknownst to her, actually made her relatively diligent in the grand scheme of things, and given her natural talents in the field, kept Anualë from ever replacing her.

So now that someone had taken advantage of those measures *she* had designed to hand off control, and was using them to attack *her home* . . . Well, even Shialnor had limits.

So she was trying everything she could think of to take back control, but she had poured a great deal of her power and herself into that system; it was still hers, but it was outside of her at the same time. As such, it turned out it was possible for someone to block her connection to it.

If she could contact it again, it would answer to its rightful owner, but there was now an army of monsters between her and the core. Monsters empowered by Colleöne's parallel system.

So Shialnor looked for alternatives. She tried to reach down to the dungeon below, but the Core of the Dungeons in the Blessed Land was the means by which she and the Aesdes were connected to the dungeons of Aelea; as long as she couldn't contact it, she couldn't contact any of the dungeons.

Or so she thought.

Her eyes widened. She couldn't contact any of the dungeons . . . save one. One . . . that was not primarily connected to the Blessed Land's core anymore.

Shialnor's eyes glowed as she examined the connection in great detail, determining if she could use it to resolve this situation. She heaved a sigh. She could not. That core's connection to the Blessed Land's core was too weak for her to use it as a back door. It would not resolve this situation. But . . . that didn't mean she couldn't use it at all.

Shialnor took all she knew of her system and Colleöne's and sent it to the one core she still had access to.

"Well . . . hopefully, that will help them down there until we can figure this out."

Shialnor then swept her hand, causing the magic circles to transform themselves. Her eyes started to glow. She couldn't do anything with the Cores from here . . . so instead, she would help in other ways.

"You stole my system . . . you attacked my home . . . and worst of all, you interrupted my nap! I am SO done with this!"

Shialnor waved her hand, and the magic circles flashed. Dozens of monsters appeared before her and started to attack the invading monsters.

The ground between the Aesdes and the monsters shifted, and invading monsters began to fall into pit traps while arrows shot from hidden slits, tree branches suddenly turned into spikes, and invisible magic circles teleported monsters high into the sky to then fall to their deaths. Jets of flame shot from the ground, rolling boulders fell from the sky, and explosive runes erupted once stepped on.

She may not have had control over her core, but she was the one who had designed all of its functions.

And so, the Mother of Dungeons joined the battle.

50

Hostilities Commence

Life before the Aesdes granted their boons? It is apparently not unthinkable. Supposedly, the Celestial Elves not only have records of such a time but also claim that the oldest of their number lived through it. However, they refuse to share such knowledge with the rest of the world, so the claims cannot be verified in any meaningful way. As for the rest of us, no records from humanity exist from such a time, if one ever existed. And when we consider the existence of monsters and dungeons and demon lords, and the danger these all pose even with the boons of the Aesdes, it seems unlikely that the Enlightened races could ever have survived without the Aesdes' support.

—*The History of Aelea*, by Hostus Tettidius Clodian

Seero stepped into the Primary Home Base, where all of her subordinates stood waiting for her. Even Melion had ceased working on their latest designs to join the group.

Ateia nodded at her. "What now, Seero?"

Seero analyzed the situation. The Herald of the New Dawn, who was apparently an Aesdes who was at least more powerful than Ateia, presented a serious threat; one who could apparently track them down. Though, if he was an Aesdes, he'd have access to the same information-gathering capabilities Colleöne had taught to Ateia.

Still, Seero didn't have countermeasures to that capability, and likewise couldn't estimate the Herald of the New Dawn's combat potential at this time.

But since he could find them, starting the operation against his followers or continuing to train in dungeons both carried equal risk. There was also the possibility of the Aesdes intervening now that one of their own was involved.

So, Seero calculated it would be best to take the initiative.

She was about to respond to this effect when a wave of mana surged from her core, disrupting her thoughts. Ateia cried out and held her head. Taog turned to her.

"Ateia! What's wrong?!"

Ateia's eyes went wide, and she started trembling. "I don't know . . . but I feel that something terrible has happened."

As for Seero, she detected an intrusion of mana similar to that used when the Heralds of the New Dawn attempted to sacrifice Ateia. She attempted to quarantine the mana, counteracting it with different types. Fortunately, a judicious application of Holy mana managed to eliminate it.

At that moment, Seero received a message from the Aesdes.

Dungeon Master and Hero NSLICE-00P, this is Shialnor, the Lady of Mana and the Boundary, She Who Tends the Gardens of the World, the creator and manager of the dungeons. We, the Aesdes, have lost control of both the Dungeon and Personal Cores, and the Blessed Land is under attack.

I do not know what is happening to the dungeons or to the boons we granted to the masses as a result, but I know we cannot provide any more until this situation is dealt with. I can only imagine what will occur on Aelea in the meantime, and we may not be able to assist.

However, you are primarily connected to your own Material Plane, and so are the only dungeon core that I know to remain online. You have had the deepest connection to our cores of anyone outside the Aesdes, and you have Ateia, an Aesdes who still walks the surface of Aelea and who will be the least affected by what's going on in the Blessed Land.

I'm sending you everything I have on the two cores. I believe you'll be able to use it to keep your New World up and running, hopefully your subordinate cores, and maybe even recreate some of the boons for your own subordinates.

I am told that Anualë took the power of Elséró from your enemy, though at great cost to himself, so you should be on even footing at the very least.

I know I have no right to ask anything of anyone, and nothing more to offer, but still, I must beg you. Please, protect Aelea while we cannot. You are our only hope.

With that, Seero's processors went into overdrive as a massive amount of data flooded into the core at the center of the Primary Home Base. Shialnor had constructed a gigantic and mostly automated system based on the Aesdes's Divination ability, along with complex methods of connecting the Realms of Mana to a material plane without threatening the boundary of the universe.

Seero couldn't comprehend the entire thing right away, even with her expanded capabilities.

But she didn't need to. Shialnor had highlighted the immediately useful functions, particularly the features related to the Primary Home Base. Shialnor had only designed these recently, so they weren't as complex as some of the others, and they were specifically designed with Seero in mind. Seero could compare these to her own experiences of utilizing the dungeon system and shaping mana in order to create some basic mana-based protocols for the Primary Home Base's core.

"Request: Friend Ateia, this unit requires your assistance."

Ateia nodded and crouched down, placing her hand on the ground and focusing on the core at the center of the world. "On it."

With the power of an Aesdes, the Holy mana dwelling within her, and the instinctual sense of the world she was connected to, Ateia could help Seero implement the changes. Seero analyzed and wrote the protocols while Ateia shifted the core and flows of the world's mana to match, as well as alerting Seero if she felt any problems. For now, Seero and Ateia managed to reimplement the features relating to the Primary Home Base, mainly the UI-based expansions and world feature additions.

Ateia was sweating, nearly falling over as Taog crouched down and grabbed her shoulder, steadying her while she panted for breath. Seero's own processors were starting to overheat.

Agedia slowly glanced between the two. "Seero . . . can you tell us what's going on?"

"Response: It appears the Aesdes are under assault, and their system has been compromised."

Agedia blinked. "The Aesdes . . . are under attack? And wait—their system? You usually mean the boons by that, right?" She tried to check her status, and her eyes went wide. "My status is gone?"

Estrith and Taog's eyes widened in turn as they tried to check their status too. 01R crossed his arms and scoffed.

"Typical man-things. That is why we, the truest followers of the wise-mighty-gracious boss-queen, rely-depend only on her, yes-yes. Her sacred records cannot be—" Suddenly, 01R's eyes went wide. "W-Wise-mighty-gracious boss-queen . . . w-where did the sacred status-records go?"

"Response: The dungeon system was also impacted by the intrusion. This unit and Friend Ateia are working to reimplement it. As an alternative, data regarding the latest status viewings for all units should be available on the NSLICE network, though this is purely a visual record and may not provide the same functionality."

01R's robotic eye flickered, and then he smiled.

"See-see! The wise-mighty-gracious boss-queen always has-knows an answer, yes-yes!"

Agedia glanced at Ateia, who was still catching her breath. "Is that what you just did?" She then shook her head and turned to Seero. "Never mind that; point is, something big's going down, and the Aesdes aren't able to bail us out right now, is that right?"

"Affirmative."

Agedia nodded. "In that case, we better get going. No one else has a shiny girl who can apparently reimplement the *boons of the Aesdes*, so I can't imagine anyone out there is handling this well. Which would be a perfect moment for a cult drawing power from the Realms of Mana to strike. Shiny girl, you okay to move?"

"Affirmative. Command: All units should prepare to deploy and commence hostilities at any time."

Seero, Agedia, and Estrith exited through the Otter Burrow dungeon. Seero had sent word ahead detailing the situation, and Uscfrea's chosen warriors were now spreading word through the settlements.

Uscfrea and his council were at a joint fortress at the border with the Imperial lands, where they had been coordinating with the other Turannians, so Seero launched into the air and flew over. The people in the Dobhar settlement calmed down a bit once they saw Seero flying through the sky.

Seero soon arrived and was guided inside, where she found Rector Aemilia, the other Imperials, and some Selkies running around with Uscfrea.

Magister Canus, Miallói, and Uscfrea had taken command and were attempting to calm the initial panic.

Magister Canus nodded as he saw Seero approach. "Dux Opiter is too panicked to report clearly, but at least we've confirmed the communication artifacts are still working. We're still setting up the heavy artillery, but every other artifact we've tested works, so that's something. It's a mixed bag for my troops; some seem hardly affected, while others can't use their skills at all."

Miallói nodded. "My skills, fine; the ones I trained too. Others, not so much. Depends on mastery."

Uscfrea nodded as well. "Sounds about right. Guess we're finding out who actually learned and who just relied on the Aesdes, huh?"

Magister Canus heaved a sigh. "That's not good for a lot of my troops. Most were barely trained at all and didn't understand the difference."

At that point, the others turned and saw Seero, and all three of the leaders saluted.

"Your Majesty NSLICE-00P, I'm glad to see you."

"Correction: This unit's designation has changed. Please refer to this unit as Seero."

Magister Canus nodded. "Understood. Your Majesty Seero, we received your message. Do you have anything else to add on this situation?"

"Answer: From information received by the Aesdes Shialnor, this unit predicts with 74.92 percent probability the situation is related to the Herald of the New Dawn, who this unit encountered just prior to the incursion on the system."

Uscfrea frowned. "So it's an attack by the cult. I did not anticipate they could strike the Aesdes directly, much less succeed. This is one situation we weren't prepared for."

"And it's about to get worse."

Everyone turned at hearing a new voice. Magister Tiberius stepped into the room, saluting to the leader group and Seero.

"Your Majesty, glad you're back. You need to hear this."

Magister Canus nodded at him. "What is it?"

Magister Tiberius groaned, took out his flask, took a swig, and then heaved a sigh.

"Just got word from Magister Appius in Corvanus. Apparently, now, of *all* times, the Southern Court has declared war on us."

INTERLUDE

Master of the Southern Realms

Emperor Lucius frowned at the man across from him. A full *fleet* of military-grade airships was visible from the windows of the Imperial palace, visibly glowing from all the enchantments the Southern Realms' mages could bring to bear. A reminder of the power of the other Courts . . . and the helplessness of the North.

Still, there were appearances to be maintained, and so Emperor Lucius had to at least pretend to act like he still possessed any modicum of authority.

"With respect, High King Xavlaeron, I do not see how your accusation is possible. Her Majesty NSLICE-00P's status confirms she is human, and we have confirmed reports of her using Holy mana. If nothing else, the Aesdes would not permit a demon lord to do so, and it is well known that Holy mana is anathema to them."

Xavlaeron Yesroris, high king of Mirima, the de facto master of the Southern Realms, scoffed.

The half Elf was tall, standing a full head above Emperor Lucius, who was by no means short. He had dark, straight hair and sharp green eyes, with the slightly pointed ears characteristic of his kin. He wore golden full-plate armor, though he had no crown. Instead, he wore a broken chain tied together, in the fashion of the high kings of Mirima since the days of its founding.

"You betray your ignorance, Lucius. An Emperor of all things should not fall to the simple doctrine we tell the people. The relationship between dungeons, Holy mana, the Aesdes, and the world is far more complicated than simple hostility.

"Besides, demon lords are known to be crafty, and even to mimic Holy mana to those unfamiliar with it. You have not forgotten the scouring of Krilya the Black Saint, have you? Unless you have confirmation from the Aesdes themselves that they approve of her, I find your reliance on circumstantial evidence to be naive, and foolish."

Emperor Lucius furrowed his brow. "And yet, you do not present your own evidence as to your claims. The queen of the Dobhar has ever been a friend and ally to the Empire and the Northern Court."

High King Xavlaeron raised an eyebrow. "Really, now? Was she a friend when she murdered one of your consuls and burned his house to the ground? Was that an act of friendship? Claiming it so would reveal your intentions for the court, Lucius. You do not have even a fraction of the support or military might required to follow in the steps of Cnaeus the Bloody. Do not play coy; I know you have bet on that monster to fulfill your ambitions. And you have chosen poorly."

Emperor Lucius narrowed his eyes. "That is a matter of the Northern Court, and not the place of the Council of the Southern Realms to decide. Regardless, I will not permit you to simply move against Her Majesty NSLICE-00P. The Eastern Court has not approved of your declaration either."

High King Xavlaeron sneered. "You will not *permit* me, you say?" He rose to his feet. "You forget your place, Lucius. I am not asking you. I am telling you, as a *courtesy*. You have only risen to the throne by *my* approval. And, despite the fact that you were meant as nothing more than a symbol, still you have managed to destroy what little we entrusted you with.

"So no, your *permission* means nothing to anyone. The allies of the Empire will restore the order that the Northern Court has failed to keep, and we, at least, will not permit attacks on the very heart of the Empire. Even if its own Emperor does.

"What forces remain in the North will fall in line; Verrucosis has remained loyal, so at least *someone* in this court has a head on their shoulders. Any who side with the enemy will be branded a traitor, as they deserve. As for you, Lucius, I'm nearly of a mind to declare you unfit to rule, seeing how your incompetence has led the North to ruin. Simply be grateful I am not here to apprehend you."

Emperor Lucius resisted the urge to grit his teeth. It seemed appearances would not be maintained, after all. Just months ago, Emperor Lucius would have called the high king mad for this play. How could someone who was nominally independent of the Empire claim authority over it? Half the treaties between Mirima and the Empire aimed to head off this exact sort of scenario!

And yet, for all his frustration and outrage, Emperor Lucius could not deny the truth. Until NSLICE-00P was vindicated or else conquered the court outright, Emperor Lucius had few legs left to stand on.

"And what of the Eastern Court? Maior Generalis Maximia Tetrica has already stated she does not approve of your declaration. She will not be pleased if you ignore her and move against someone she recognizes as Amicitia Populi Elteni."

High King Xavlaeron smirked. "I am touched by your concern, but it is the Eastern Court you should be worried for. I am told they are facing the worst invasion the Empire has seen since the days of Velus. Indeed, we should all endeavor to finish our work here quickly so we may offer them support while there is still an Eastern Court left to help."

With that, High King Xavlaeron left the room. Magister Verrucosis was waiting for him outside, and the two left to speak—without Emperor Lucius.

Emperor Lucius heaved a sigh and knelt forward, holding his face in his hands.

When he had gathered himself, he sat back upright and turned to a side door. "Come in."

At his command, the door opened, and Princess Caecila walked in, a deep frown on her face. "I, Princess Caecila, greet—"

Emperor Lucius waved his hand. "Enough of that. We lack time, and in truth, I am Emperor of nothing."

He waved to the seat in front of him. Princess Caecila slowly made her way over and sat down as Emperor Lucius took a deep breath.

"Princess Caecila, what is your opinion of NSLICE-00P?"

Princess Caecila rubbed her chin. "She . . . is very calculating, blunt, and unaffected, perhaps even apathetic toward all that she does not feel concerns her. She has made no secret that she acts solely based on the tangible benefits to herself."

She then tilted her head. "Yet . . . she also does not hesitate to cooperate when she does consider it beneficial, and holds back no effort when doing so. She cares nothing for political influence nor if she is taken advantage of, so long as she continues to benefit. And . . . she seems to protect her own. I imagine it must be the case, for her companions to trust her as they do."

But then, her face turned pale. "But . . . she is unforgiving and quick to violence. She seemed prepared to kill Drusus over a merely implied threat. So, when she finds out the Southern Court is coming for her with the full support of the North's military . . ."

Emperor Lucius sighed deeply. "She will endeavor to wipe us out."

Princess Caecila slowly nodded. Emperor Lucius turned to look her in the eyes. "Caecila, why did you marry my son?"

Princess Caecila froze, blinking at the sudden shift in topic. "Um, Emperor Lucius?"

He held his gaze. "Please, tell me the truth, and speak freely. I wish to hear it."

Princess Caecila slowly began to flush. She could not help but smile slightly. "Well . . . because I love him. He was valiant and confident and kind and made time for me, a poor girl with no standing, when no one else would. He always thought of me and was the first to acknowledge my efforts. I am truly grateful I have had the chance to meet him."

She then frowned, and her eyes began to fill with tears. "But I did not know what it was I did. When I look at the state of the Northern Court and the Empire, when I imagine what will happen to my family and friends and people like them as a result, I cannot help but think I was wrong. I should not have interfered. I should not have been selfish. I should have turned him down and let Aemilia Hibera marry him, then none of this would have happened.

"I see what she has done in Turannia; she would have done so much better than I, and her father would not have abandoned the court to infighting and ruin."

Emperor Lucius nodded. "There was a time I thought that as well." But then he smiled. "But no longer. I have seen you work to restore me, the court, and the Empire to its former glory. You have worked harder than anyone else, though it was not required or expected of you to do so. Harder even than those of us who bear responsibility for the current state of affairs.

"Whatever Aemilia Hibera is like now, I know that back then, she would not have done the same. And I feel that even with the Hiberius family in charge, between the rebellions, the cults, and the incursions, the Northern Court would have struggled regardless."

He placed his hand on her shoulder. "My son prioritized his feelings and his ideas of right and wrong over the good of the Empire. Consul Hiberius chose to abandon the court, placing his family and his ambitions over his duty. Even I wished only to break the leash wrapped around me.

"Each and every member of the Northern Court has chosen to prioritize themselves over the Empire. You are perhaps the only one who has worked to make it right, solely for the Empire's sake. I am truly proud to call you my daughter-in-law. My son could not have found a better partner."

She looked up at him, tears welling up for a different reason now. "Emperor Lucius . . ."

He pulled back his arm and took a deep breath before narrowing his eyes.

"And that is why I must ask a difficult task of you now. I strongly question the high king's motives to move against NSLICE-00P now, of all times, and especially when the Aesdes seemed to have vanished. Whatever she may be, it is all but confirmed that NSLICE-00P is a hero, a chosen champion of the Aesdes. But I have no power here, so we must move quickly to do whatever we can.

"Princess Caecila, my daughter, are you willing to do whatever you must to save the people of the Empire?"

Princess Caecila wiped away her tears and faced the Emperor with narrowed eyes.

"I am."

51

Turannia Answers

"The Selkies and the Wulver and the Dobhar are all ferocious and brave, to be sure. But your resistance is pointless. One rainy isle, no matter how brave its denizens, cannot resist the might of a continent-spanning Empire."

—Consul Aulus Postumius Gelasius, when demanding the Selkies' surrender.

Magister Canus sharply inhaled but otherwise kept his expression neutral. "Details, Tiberius."

Magister Tiberius took another swig from his flask. "Those *imbeciles* have accused Her Majesty NSLICE-00P—"

"Correction: This unit's designation has been updated. Please refer to her as Seero."

Magister Tiberius tilted his head but shrugged. "Works for me; much easier to pronounce. Anyway, those imbeciles have accused Her Majesty Seero of being a demon lord, of all things, which we know can't possibly be true."

"Objection: It is true."

All eyes swung toward Seero.

Since the Herald of the New Dawn was an Aesdes with access to the Aesdes' Divination Sight, it was only natural that he had accessed classified data about Seero and her dungeon core. In light of that situation, withholding the same information from allied forces who had pledged their support even against the Empire was no longer calculated as efficient, as all it would achieve would be to interfere with coordination.

And if her allies would turn on her as a result, it was preferable for them to do so now than at a later date, when combat operations with other hostile forces were in progress. Contextual clues from the allies indicated they did not fully understand the statement, so Seero moved to elaborate.

"Helpful Explanation: This unit possesses a dungeon core integrated into her cybernetic components, as well as command over additional subordinate cores, a position designated by the Aesdes' system as 'dungeon master.' Cultural and historical texts of the Empire consistently use 'demon lord' as a synonym for this role in both colloquial and academic contexts. As a result, it is accurate to designate this unit as a demon lord."

Everyone went completely silent. Magister Tiberius chuckled nervously. "T-That's a good one, Your Majesty. We all know you're a hero, and demon lords can't be heroes! That just wouldn't make any sense!"

"Statement: This unit is classified as both."

Uscfrea nodded his head. "I can confirm personally that she is telling the truth."

Vopiscus and Dux Augustalis nodded their heads. Magister Tiberius turned to Ateia, Taog, and Agedia. Ateia smiled wryly and nodded. Taog shrugged and nodded. Agedia just looked amused.

Magister Tiberius looked at his flask, then threw his head back and tanked the whole thing at once. Magister Canus heaved a sigh.

". . . You could have shared, you know?"

A bit of commotion and explanations later, and the Turannian leaders hung their heads and sighed. Rector Aemilia held her head in her hands.

"My fate . . . rests with a demon lord. That is—I truly am a villainess now, aren't I?"

She sighed again. Magister Canus shrugged. "Whatever she may be, she has not acted as we would fear from a demon lord. And given the situation, I won't complain about some extra power on our side. Now, Magister Tiberius, did Magister Appius say anything else?"

Magister Tiberius nodded. "Ah, that's right. The high king of Mirima came in person with the Sky Legion and an entire fleet of airships." He glanced over at Rector Aemilia. "He, um, also declared Rector Aemilia a traitor for collaborating with a demon lord and is planning to apprehend us all as well."

Rector Aemilia sighed. "Typical. Not unexpected, though. Especially since I *am* collaborating with a demon lord, apparently."

Magister Canus shook his head. "What of the other Courts?"

Magister Tiberius nodded. "The Eastern Court does not share the Southern Court's opinion and has openly stated that, but has also made no open moves to stop it yet. And they aren't going to, as apparently, the Empire of the Sun has also launched a major offensive. Typical.

"As for the Northern Court, Emperor Lucius is opposed, but he has been entirely sidelined and has no influence at this stage. Consul Hiberius left Corvanus a while ago, and Magister Verrucosis is cooperating with the high king."

Magister Canus rubbed his chin before sighing. "Unfortunate. The Sky Legion is already beyond our forces save for Her Majesty."

Meanwhile, for Seero, this situation was actually beneficial. The Council of the Southern Realms had declared hostility—and revealed classified intel that only the Herald of the New Dawn should have been aware of. There was, therefore, a significant probability that the Council of the Southern Realms had intel related to the Heralds of the New Dawn.

So, rather than randomly search through the Empire for clues and targets, she could now set a mission she was much more efficient at: Terminating hostiles and apprehending priority targets.

"Query: Do the friendlies have any intel regarding the hostile forces?"

Magister Canus nodded. "Yes, I've worked with the Sky Legion before. The Council of the Southern Realms isn't nominally Empire, so legions there are sparse compared to the territory they have to cover. What they've done to deal with that is invest in a massive fleet of airships, a knight order of wyvern riders, and countless artifacts that enable flight.

"As a result, their forces can travel anywhere within the Southern Realms within hours and bombard a foe into submission from above while their legionnaires and knights drop right on top of the survivors, allowing a handful of legions to cover the entire area with the help of local forces. They back this up with some of the finest mages in the Empire, who can cast powerful spells from the safety of the airships."

He rubbed his chin. "And even under the current circumstances, they'll likely remain effective. We've already confirmed that all artifacts still function, so their airships would remain fully operational, though their crews might be less effective in using them. Likewise, the wyvern knights and the top mages at the very least should have some personal mastery apart from the Aesdes' support, and can likely still fight."

He heaved a sigh. "They'll do better than my own troops on average, and I don't have time to change that. If they're already in Corvanus, they could arrive here in a few hours, though if they want to bring some of the North's legions, they may require time to load them onto the ships."

"Analysis: Given the hostile's armament and tactics, it appears an air superiority battle will be necessary. Do the friendlies possess air units or air defenses?"

Magister Canus shook his head. "A couple of ballistae cover Castra Turannia, but they're only intended to ward off a wyvern or two. The Northern Court specifically stripped any defenses in the provinces capable of defeating an airship, and Turannia never had any to begin with. Didn't want a rebellion warding off their trump card."

Magister Tiberius smirked. "Heh, well, considering the circumstances, perhaps that was a good move."

Magister Canus smiled slightly before turning to Uscfrea and Miallói. "How about your peoples?"

Miallói shook her head. "You know what an airship did to my people."

Magister Canus turned to Uscfrea . . . who was smiling smugly. He chuckled. "Let's just say there are benefits to being the subjects of our queen Seero."

Indeed, Uscfrea transferred data over to Seero on the Dobhar's latest efforts.

It appeared that after Princess Caecila had arrived in an airship, Uscfrea had given a great deal of thought to countering such a weapon. Likewise, Shialnor had started to fill out some of the Cyborg affinity's Item Creation options. And as Uscfrea hadn't been as disappointed as Seero had in the initial options, he had invested some dungeon points in upgrading his Item Creation abilities, unlocking some options from a bit further along in Earth's history.

Seero's robotic eye flickered. "Surprised Statement: This unit was not aware that Steward Uscfrea had access to twentieth-century air defense technology. Reassessing combat potential of Dobhar military forces."

Dux Augustalis couldn't help but grin. "I have to admit, you have some neat toys, Your Majesty."

Vopiscus nudged her side. "Your Majesty Seero, you are truly powerful. I did not think to see the day when our serious dux here would actually crack a smile—Oh, and it's gone again."

Dux Augustalis responded to that with violence. Uscfrea, meanwhile, turned to Seero. "Your orders, my queen?"

"Statement: This unit has recommendations on the organization and positioning of air defense units for maximum effectiveness. Query: Under the assumption of military cooperation, this unit would like to expand the network to allied territory in order to achieve thorough coverage of the island. Does this unit have permission from allied forces to deploy military units on their territory?"

Rector Aemilia nodded *immediately*. "Yes. Rather, I should be asking you to do so."

Miallói nodded as well. Seero immediately turned to leave.

"Acknowledged. Command: Steward Uscfrea should prepare air defense forces to deploy. This unit will scout and identify ideal deployment locations and prepare a logistics network for deployment."

Magister Tiberius and Magister Canus stepped off to the side for a moment as everyone began preparing. Magister Canus raised an eyebrow.

"Be quick, Tiberius. We both have a lot of work to do and not a lot of time to do it."

Magister Tiberius nodded. "Right, just, should we ask about you-know-who again?"

Magister Canus shook his head. "It's not time yet."

Magister Tiberius tilted his head. "Really? With the South moving against us and Emperor Lucius having lost even the illusion of authority?"

Magister Canus nodded. "Right now, neither Emperor Lucius nor the Eastern Court have acknowledged the Southern Court's declaration. So to a great deal of the Empire, we technically aren't rebelling, just acting in self-defense. But should we proclaim a new Emperor . . ."

Magister Tiberius's eyes widened in understanding. "Ah, yeah, guess we keep it under wraps for now."

Magister Canus smiled. "Besides, it is not our place to decide."

Magister Tiberius nodded at that, and then the two got back to work.

Meanwhile, Seero and Ateia were currently in the core room of a dungeon on the coast of Turannia. A flame elemental floated in the air before her, thrusting its arm forward to unleash a mighty torrent of fire.

"Acknowledgement: Hostile intent confirmed. Engaging termination protocols."

Seero popped open a panel on her arm and took out a preprepared anti-mana bomb, now complete with its own explosive charge and detonator. She tossed it straight at the elemental.

The elemental dungeon master screamed as a wave of anti-mana erased the mana that made up its being. Seero then walked over to the dungeon core and placed her hand on it. She could sense corrupted mana seeping into it, so flooded the core with Holy mana, clearing the corruption and isolating the core from the seepage. Ateia walked over and did likewise, closing her eyes to concentrate as Seero transmitted data to her.

Soon, a message passed in their UI's.

Core integration protocol completed. Integration successful.

They had determined how to link a core to Seero's in a replication of the dungeon core subordination function. And while they couldn't replicate all the functions of the dungeon system for the core in question, they had already replicated Seero's World Features capabilities.

As such, Seero was now able to create an entrance between this dungeon and the Primary Home Base.

She placed it closer to the dungeon's entrance. Since the dungeon's functions weren't fully available, she prioritized logistical efficiency over defense in this case, deploying a sensor drone that would report if the dungeon came under attack so that she could deploy reinforcements before a hostile reached the entrance to the Primary Home Base.

At that point, Dobhar, humans, Dwarves, Wulver, and other races from Uscfrea's forces began to march out of the entrance. They carried their equipment out of the dungeon to set up another air-defense point equipped with radar, flak cannons, machine guns, and autocannons, and even some early surface-to-air missiles. Seero and Ateia then left the dungeon and boosted off to the next site.

And so, Turannia prepared itself for war.

52

An Unexpected Guest

"The children of Velus do not defend the Empire because they are Emperors. The children of Velus are Emperors because they defend the Empire."

—Emperor Maximus the Stalwart, when choosing whether to face Rityss the Dark Dragon or abandon Elteno.

Seero had finished setting up enough dungeon entrances and had returned to the central headquarters of the Turannians. She was discussing the training of the allied forces in her and Uscfrea's weapon systems when an urgent alert appeared in her UI.

One of her drones had gotten a hit. She and Melion had developed numerous command, control, communication, and intelligence drones equipped with a variety of sensors and long-range mana-based communication artifacts. They could keep watch over the battlefield and relay commands to any forces outside of normal range. Likewise, with their mana core power sources, they could remain in operation indefinitely.

Seero had deployed these drones over the seas between Turannia and Utrad, keeping an eye out for anything on approach. In particular, she and Melion had confirmed that mundane radars were highly effective at detecting Imperial vehicles for the simple fact that none of them had been designed with radar in mind, and countermeasures for mana-based detection did not work on simple radio waves.

"Alert: This unit's forces have detected a potential target on approach to Turannia."

The room fell silent at that, everyone's expression falling. They all turned to one of the walls, where one of Seero's smaller drones was acting as a projector. A red blip had appeared on a map of the seas and Turannian coastline.

Magister Canus took a deep breath. "Are they starting their approach, Your Majesty Seero?"

"Negative Response: There is only a single signature, and it is too small to indicate an Imperial airship. A sensor unit is about to investigate."

A moment later, the signature came within range of a drone's visual sensors, which was displayed on the wall as well. Magister Canus blinked.

"That's . . . one of the transport shuttles for an airship? What's it doing out here alone?"

Meanwhile, Rector Aemilia's eyes widened. "That's not just a shuttle. That's the shuttle from the Imperial family's airship!"

"Statement: To this unit's knowledge, the craft in question was not noticeably armed, and is traveling without escort. No further signatures detected in range. Analysis indicates the probability of a hostile operation is negligible. This unit will investigate and initiate diplomacy with the crew."

The rest of the Turannians simply nodded, and Seero set out toward the sea.

Flying out toward the craft, Seero prepared her mana. Just as the craft came into range, she stopped midair and formed a Prismatic Bombardment magic circle. She activated her loudspeaker, as well as radio and mana-based communications.

"Warning: Attention, unidentified craft. You have just entered Allied Turannian Forces airspace. Please cease movement and declare your identity and intentions."

The craft in question stopped, then angled its side toward her, the door on its side opening up. Seero's visual sensors could zoom in far enough to see it in detail. Princess Caecila was standing at the entrance.

She shouted, her voice enhanced with magic. "Please wait, Your Majesty NSLICE-00P! We come in peace!"

Seero's response was immediate.

"Objection: This unit's designation has been updated. Please refer to this unit as Seero."

Seero escorted the shuttle to the Turannian coast, where it made a hasty landing. It turned out, Princess Caecila had pushed the shuttle hard, and it had never been designed for long journeys in the first place. She now exited along with Fulcinia and Typheras, her assistant and bodyguard. She and both her bodyguards were dressed in simple traveling clothes . . . on top of armor.

"Query: Why has Princess Caecila come to Turannia?"

Princess Caecila frowned. "I . . . am probably not a princess by this point anymore. But we have come to beg for your mercy, Your Majesty Seero."

"Requesting Elaboration."

Princess Caecila shut her eyes. "The council of Southern Realms is moving against you. They are claiming you are some kind of demon lord. Emperor Lucius is powerless to stop it—the North's armies will likely join in. But we know what you are, and that the Aesdes stand behind you. Magister Appius even suspects the South may be influenced by that cult. So, I have come before you on behalf of the Imperial family, and on behalf of the people of the Empire."

She reached to a bag tied to her back. Untying it, she held it out to Seero. Seero scanned it, and found it was enchanted . . . with Spatial Magic.

It was a magic box. Seero took hold of it.

"That contains all we could grab from the Imperial treasury; every artifact and weapon the Northern Empire holds dear. It is all we can offer to you right now."

Princess Caecila then fell to her knees. "I . . . have nothing else to offer. They will call me a traitor, so I won't have any more influence in the Empire. I may not even be considered part of the Imperial family at this point. But please . . . will you hear my plea, Your Majesty? Please, spare the people your wrath. When you go to war with the Empire's legions, please have mercy on the innocent people who do not fight against you."

"Affirmative."

"I know it's much to ask of you when—Wait, what?"

"Affirmative."

Princess Caecila looked up and blinked.

"Helpful Elaboration: Historical strategic analysis indicates indiscriminate strategic warfare targeting civilian populations has generally proved inefficient and a method that only increases hostility, unless conducted with weapons of mass destruction that this unit does not currently possess.

"Likewise, if strategic warfare against military industry is required for the upcoming engagement, the accuracy and precision of this unit's arsenal does not require area bombing to ensure the destruction of priority targets.

"This unit cannot guarantee an absence of collateral damage, and may target civilian infrastructure and industry with military applications as the situation demands, but at present does not consider general civilian populations as an efficient target. This unit finds it acceptable to add 'limit collateral damage' as a secondary objective, to be considered so long as the military situation permits."

Princess Caecila blinked again, but then smiled. She closed her eyes as they moistened. "Thank you . . . that is all we can ask."

Emperor Lucius sat in his private lounge room, leaning back into his incredibly comfortable chair. He took a sip of Celestial wine from his enchanted glass, which maintained his beverage at the ideal temperature. It turned out immortal and isolationist Elves with too much time on their hands made *excellent* drinks.

He channeled just a bit of mana into the enchanted scroll reader set up before him, moving to the next section of the epic he was reading. He leaned back into his chair as he did, tapping the enchanted communication artifact for his attendants to bring him something to snack upon. He let out a contented sigh.

It turned out, when he stopped concerning himself with the steady decline and possibly imminent doom of the Northern Empire, as well as his complete lack of authority apart from the backing of the other Courts, that there were many perks to being Emperor.

Just then, he heard stomping down the hall and let out a small sigh. "Three . . . two . . . one . . ."

"LUCIUS!"

High King Xavlaeron kicked the doors of the lounge open, his face twisted into a scowl. "What is the meaning of this?!"

Emperor Lucius tilted his head. "Whatever do you mean, High King Xavlaeron?"

High King Xavlaeron gritted his teeth. "Don't play dumb with me, Lucius! I know you arranged this!"

Emperor Lucius took a sip from his glass. "Does it look like I'm arranging anything right now? I figured that since you do not require my permission for anything, my presence was not necessary and I should avoid getting in your way. I haven't read a single report since our last conversation, so I can't say I'm aware of anything that happened in the meantime."

High King Xavlaeron's face contorted in rage. "Then who exactly stole all the artifacts in the Imperial treasury?!"

Emperor Lucius put his glass down as his jaw dropped. "What?!"

High King Xavlaeron narrowed his eyes. "Don't act so surprised, Lucius. I know you commanded it."

Emperor Lucius obliged and closed his jaw, his face returning to normal. "Okay, I won't, then. Still, does it look like I'm stealing artifacts right now?"

High King Xavlaeron heaved a sigh. "Your little daughter-in-law did so."

Emperor Lucius nodded his head. "Ah, she always was a free spirit, doing as she pleased. Ruined that engagement I worked very hard to set up. I suppose I shouldn't be surprised."

High King Xavlaeron narrowed his eyes again. "You shouldn't. It takes the approval of the Emperor to access the treasury."

Emperor Lucius tilted his head. "Does it?"

Suddenly, he smacked his forehead. "Ah, it appears it was my fault, after all. I gave the princess access to the treasury to find a reward for Her Majesty NSLICE-00P and to show her around a while back. In all the confusion that's happened since, I must have forgotten to rescind it. I'm truly sorry about this, High King Xavlaeron."

High King Xavlaeron glared at Emperor Lucius . . . who took another sip of his wine.

". . . Fine. Play it that way if you wish. Then I'm sure you'll have no objections if we hunt down the traitor and deal with her . . . appropriately?"

Emperor Lucius tilted his head. "I thought you didn't need my permission for anything?"

A vein bulged on High King Xavlaeron's forehead, but he simply sighed. "No. I do not." He then gathered himself to his full height. "The *former* Princess Caecila shall be stripped of all status and title and branded a traitor, and then will be hunted down as such. Magister Exploratore Appius will likewise be removed from his position for his repeated failures to maintain security in Corvanus and throughout the North.

"And since poor Emperor Lucius has *apparently* been betrayed by his own family, I will leave some troops behind to ensure your safety in the Imperial palace. I trust you shall be grateful for my protection."

Emperor Lucius nodded. "Oh, of course. I have no one else to turn to, after all, so it's quite a relief. Even I would never have expected such a thing from that Caecila, so who is to say what will happen?"

High King Xavlaeron glared at Emperor Lucius once more, but Emperor Lucius just took another sip of his wine and turned his attention back to his scroll. High King Xavlaeron ground his teeth once more, then stormed out of the room.

Once he left, Emperor Lucius held up his glass to the air. "And so the die is cast. May the Aesdes protect the Empire and the children of Velus."

And then, he downed the rest of his drink.

53

On the Eve of War

"In my experience, war is mostly meetings, paperwork, and walking."

—Maior Generalis Quintis Armenius Exsupereus,
on the low frequency of combat training for
Legion officer cadets.

Since the battle was to take place either over the seas or along the coast, the Turannians had moved their headquarters to the port city constructed by Rector Aemilia. Uscfrea had also brought the former Northern Fleet, whose ships now filled the port.

The allied forces had taken over a large market structure to serve as their temporary base of operations, and Rector Aemilia stood just outside it, her arms crossed and a frown on her face. Princess Caecila sat on the ground just in front of her.

Rector Aemilia resisted the urge to grin. Finally, after all this time, the girl who had ruined her life was now at her mercy, a scenario she had dreamt about more frequently than she would care to admit. Well, Her Majesty Seero and Magister Canus would likely object to anything *too* heinous, but still, the others were mostly busy with the war preparations, so it was up to the rector to decide the fate of the now traitorous princess requesting asylum. She could have her revenge, if she so chose.

But Rector Aemilia took a deep breath and kept a neutral expression. Giving in to her vindictive impulses was what had landed her here in the first place, so she intended to think this through. And in doing so, she turned her mind to the recent events.

She . . . now had a province she could call her own. It wasn't the richest or the most powerful, but she could say she'd had a hand in every bit of prosperity it now experienced. She merely had to glance around to see this new port city, something she had conceived and built herself.

She also now had subordinates and subjects who respected her, not merely for her family name but for her own efforts. She had people she could trust and rely on even through the most dangerous of situations. She had troops who had not abandoned her even now that the Southern Court was on its way to remove her.

And, perhaps most of all, she had learned that her father cared for her more than he had ever admitted.

Plus, she had gained an alliance with Her Majesty Seero, the most powerful woman Rector Aemilia knew. A woman Rector Aemilia could not imagine losing a fight, even if she challenged the entire Empire alone.

And all this had happened because she had been exiled to the frontier. She imagined what might have happened had she not. If she had married Prince Octavianus and all her and her family's dreams had come true.

She would have gained a spot in the Imperial family, and the status of the future Emperor's wife. And . . . that was it. Any authority or resources she had would be merely what her father or father-in-law permitted her to have. Any respect would be solely for her family name, whether her father's or her husband's.

She would have possessed the highest status—in an increasingly dysfunctional court ruling an Empire steadily breaking down due to incursions and rebellions and cult schemes. She would still be desperately trying to prove herself to her cold father, even as the situation she found herself in grew ever worse.

She looked down at Princess Caecila. The girl kept a remorseful but resolute face, seemingly accepting her fate. But Rector Aemilia was the daughter of a consul, trained from birth for politics and diplomacy. Princess Caecila could not hide the slight quiver in her eyes.

Rector Aemilia heaved a sigh. Had this girl not done what she had done, Rector Aemilia and her family would likely have found themselves in her place.

No. Knowing her father and herself at the time, they likely would not have welcomed Her Majesty Seero in with open arms. They would have seen her as an unwelcome new player, someone who could overturn the status quo they had built. And that . . . would not have ended well.

So, Rector Aemilia scoffed.

"So, are you just going to sit on the ground like some helpless maiden, or are you going to make yourself useful? If there's anything useful you can even do, that is."

Princess Caecila's face shot up, blinking in surprise. But Rector Aemilia had already turned away from her, walking back to resume her work. She did not forgive or forget their animosity just yet, but . . . Rector Aemilia acknowledged the way things had turned out as a result was not so bad.

And if they lived through the Southern Court's attack . . . Well, she might even admit that she preferred things the way they were.

Seero had returned to the Turannians' port headquarters, where the Turannians were still hard at work arranging their defenses and doing everything they could to fortify the coastline. The headquarters was full of people running about, speaking quickly and curtly, and occasionally shouting a question across the room.

Scrolls and books and papers were strewn across desks as Magister Canus, Uscfrea, Miallói, and Dux Augustalis pored over a map of the province while drones projected live feeds from the scout units across the walls. Another drone hovered over the map and projected directly on top of it, displaying the location and status of allied units in real time as they made their preparations.

Seero, on the other hand, was munching on a sweet roll while monitoring the sensor scans from the drone network. Ateia was frowning as she and Taog stood next to her.

"Seero, are you sure we shouldn't be helping?"

"Affirmative."

Ateia furrowed her brow. "It just . . . feels weird for us not to be doing anything."

"Explanation: Turannian command staff are working to prepare the likely battlefields in order to provide friendly forces with maximum advantage. On the other hand, the—"

Seero was about to say NSLICE network when she ran into an exception. She no longer considered herself a Non-Standard Leashed-Intelligence Cybernetic Enforcer. As a result, it was no longer accurate to call the network an *NSLICE* network, seeing as no units other than her had been designed by Dr. Ottosen, and so no units within the network could accurately be called *NSLICE*.

"Designation determined. Informing all units of network designation update. Continuation: On the other hand, the CELIU network represents the primary combat unit for the upcoming operation. All CELIU units must therefore maintain high readiness, as the hostiles may arrive at any time. Getting involved in the current management operations would result in increased fatigue, as well as complicating deployment due to a need to hand off ongoing tasks.

"So, Friend Ateia should remain at rest and prepare to deploy in order to provide friendly forces with maximum advantage in the upcoming battle."

With that, Seero's robotic eye began to flicker. If she wanted Friends Ateia and Taog to remain at maximum readiness, then it made sense to ensure their nutritional reserves were fully stocked.

So . . . she should share the sweet rolls.

Seero created two more and handed them to Ateia and Taog.

"Statement: Friends Ateia and Taog should join this unit in stockpiling nutrition to ensure maximum biological endurance."

Ateia looked conflicted, but Taog just gave a wry smile. "Thanks, Seero."

Ateia glanced at him as he took a roll, but he just shrugged. "I mean, Seero's probably right?"

Magister Canus happened to pass by and patted Ateia on the shoulder. "She is. In my experience, resting when you can is a soldier's duty as well."

Ateia watched him walk off before turning back to Seero. She sighed and took the sweet roll. "Thanks, Seero." She took a bite as she thought. "But what about your monsters? Couldn't you summon some more to help out?"

"Analysis: The complexity of logistics and command means the simple addition of more units will not necessarily improve efficiency. Personnel would need to be diverted to instruct and train the new units, which would still perform less effectively than existing personnel, decreasing the organization's overall effectiveness and efficiency in the short term.

"Given the short time frame until the hostiles' arrival, this unit predicts such an option would be counterproductive. It would be more efficient for the allied command personnel to request reinforcements that are already familiar with the organization."

Ateia blinked. "Oh. Um . . . maybe some golems could help with the labor?"

"Reminder: This unit has already discussed the sale of golem units to allied factions, which will take place in the future. In the short term, integrating golem units into existing structures would require a period of planning, training, transportation, and deployment to ensure existing units are able to make use of them.

"Given the short time available to prepare, it was concluded that such an integration is not practical prior to the upcoming battle. Friend Ateia was present for the conversation and should have a record in her memory storage."

Ateia tilted her head. "Eh, really?"

Taog shook his head and leaned over to her in-between sweet roll bites. "You fell asleep at that point."

Ateia glared at him. But as she did, her cybernetic components scanned her memory and helpfully brought up the recorded conversation logs. Ateia's organic component status was listed as standby sentry mode, while her cybernetic components continued to observe and log the conversation.

She flushed and looked away before sighing. "This is all a lot more complicated than I thought."

Every officer, official, and clerk within hearing distance nodded to themselves at that with a distant look in their eyes.

It was at that moment that one of the projector drones began sounding an alarm. Dozens of dots began to appear on the map it was displaying, setting out from Utrad into the sea. Everyone stopped what they were doing and stared for a moment.

"Alert: Visual confirmation is pending but analysis of radar signatures indicates multiple airship-size vessels on approach via air. This unit predicts with 87.61 percent probability that this represents the hostile force. All CELIU units will prepare to deploy, pending visual confirmation."

Magister Canus nodded at that and turned to look around at his staff. "You heard Her Majesty. Prepare for battle."

At Magister Canus's calm words, the Legion staff sprang into action. Communication artifacts lit up as orders were passed out. Alarms went off inside Legion barracks and temporary camps set up along the Turannian coastline. Legionnaires gathered their weapons and strapped on their armor.

At other sites, the robotic eyes of cyber-otters began to flicker as orders passed through Uscfrea's forces. Dobhar and former rebel forces began to prepare, loading antiaircraft artillery and preparing surface-to-air missile sites for launch. In the port city, legionnaires, Selkies, and Dobhar all loaded onto the ships of Uscfrea's fleet, which set off and took up a formation by the sea.

And in dungeon-linked bases, Seero's own forces began to deploy. Aerial combat drones hummed to life. Jet engines and repulsors began to warm up. The skies began to fill with formations of flying machines. Seero herself stepped outside, followed by her friends and allies. Uscfrea smirked.

"It's an honor to go into battle alongside you, my queen. I look forward to fighting on your side this time."

Miallói gave a small smirk at that.

"Acknowledged. Command: Visual confirmation confirmed. Hostile air forces on approach. All units, deploy."

INTERLUDE

The High King's Ploy

High King Xavlaeron sat back in his throne, gazing out on the ocean beyond. He was seated at the front of the airship, where a large glass dome covered the nose, revealing a full view of the sea and sky.

All around him, men and women sat at their stations, manning the artifacts tied to the ship's functions, their hands fixed on the magic cores built into their armrests. These men and women wore not the mass-produced armor of the Legion but the beautifully crafted armor and robes of Mirima, which held equal value as works of art and weapons of war.

Small touches of gold and gems drew attention without demanding it; magic circles were woven into wider geometric art designs, and sharp angles were kept to a minimum. And on the armor, robes, and coats of each individual was the same symbol: A sword and an arrow, both piercing through a shackled chain.

This ship, the personal ship of the high king, was crewed entirely by the Sentinels of Liberty, Mirima's most elite unit which predated the island nation itself, and one that had never and never would bow to any Emperor, friend or foe.

The vast majority of them were half elven. Many appeared human save for the fair features and slightly pointed ears, but the partners of the Elves were not limited to humanity. The mechanic's shorter stature and light beard hinted at his half Dwarven parentage. A half-Elf mage with the lower body of a snake appeared almost entirely like her Mélusine relatives, but her scales were smoother and lighter in color. A half Beastkin had a silklike mane of fur on his head over his fur-tipped and pointed ears.

The Sentinels of Liberty were open to all, and indeed, High King Xavlaeron's staff included all sorts. But the Sentinels of Liberty these days prized ability above all, and well, in the high king's opinion, the half elven could not be beat. They had the energy and initiative of the mortal races, the patience and grace of the

Elven races, and above all, could be trusted not to have loyalties to either the Elteno Empire or the Empire of the Sun.

The years of hostility between Elf and human could make it . . . *uncomfortable* to live in either nation with the blood of the other.

Mirima may be considered a de facto part of the Empire, the leader of one of its three constituent parts. But it only remained that way due to a fierce defense of its independence on the fields of battle, in the halls of diplomacy, and behind the dark alleys of subterfuge. A defense that was leveraged against both foe and friend, for friendship was no excuse for negligence.

And so, even now, when Mirima led the Council of the Southern Realms as one of the rulers of the Empire, it made sure to maintain its own forces.

And it was well they did. High King Xavlaeron frowned as he thought back to recent days. Even now, High King Xavlaeron was not as confident as he wished to portray. Emperor Lucius, a mere puppet chosen specifically for his lack of resources, connections, and political training, had pushed much harder against his shackles than anticipated.

He had nearly pulled off a quiet coup with the engagement of his son to Consul Hiberius's daughter, and only his son's sudden and scandalous infatuation with a commoner prevented the Emperor and consul from solidifying their control of the North.

And then, even after that, when Consul Hiberius had all but abandoned the court and Emperor Lucius was heavily scrutinized, the man had still managed to find a way out. He'd acted with incredible, reckless decisiveness to throw in his lot with this NSLICE-00P, planning to take advantage of her raw power and the instability it produced to gain leverage out of nowhere. He had become a serious problem for High King Xavlaeron.

For all that was said among the common folk about there being three Courts and three Emperors, the truth was much more complicated. Mirima was technically not Empire proper, along with most of the Southern Realms. And the Eastern Court, on the other hand, was a military government, acting independently only due to the distance of the front lines from Corvanus.

The North, while weaker militarily and economically than its counterparts, represented the purest line of Velus, and all the traditional authority of the Elteno Empire. A North united under a strong Emperor could seize the reins of the structures and agreements in place to take a preeminent position between its supposed peers.

The East could largely maintain its independence if it wished due to its sheer military might and monolithic nature. But the South was not so lucky. As a collection of allied realms, it was far from monolithic and far from united. And its greatest strength—its powerful economy—was partially out of its control, a resource that enriched it but that could not be guided or exploited by a single person.

An attempt to do so would cause the various member states to break off their trade agreements, forcing any would-be tyrant to renegotiate the entire relationship from scratch with every single member. Even the high king of Mirima lacked the grandeur and power to do so, and that was without considering how the other Courts would intervene.

Mirima, therefore, played a dangerous balancing game with the two actual Courts of the Empire, and the allied realms within its own council. It presented its powerful advantages on paper, hiding away its inability to leverage those strengths like the North could with its traditions or the East with its armies.

It negotiated, it plotted, it spied, it blackmailed. But it was a game that could come crashing down in a single moment if the Sun Elves ever let up the pressure on the east, or if the long-stumbling North could stabilize its own affairs.

Which was why the high kings sought to make a play for real power. It had been a plan spanning centuries and multiple wearers of the Shattered Chain. A slow and steady buildup to leverage their wealth and knowledge, combined with movements behind the shadows.

Assassinations that prevented certain Emperors from achieving their ends, and enticing words to ambitious generals eyeing the throne, kept the North stumbling and aimless. Strong support for the East's endless and pointless offensives against the Empire of the Sun kept them squandering their might on an eternal stalemate. All while Mirima slowly and quietly built up its own power.

Until now. Finally, High King Xavlaeron was ready to fulfill the dreams of all his predecessors.

He could not help but crack a smile. A full fleet of *sixty* battle airships—flying fortresses that each could match the might of a legion with a fraction of the manpower, that could travel from one corner of the Empire to the other in mere days, arriving before the local legions could even muster.

They were supported by countless smaller ships, donated or pressed into service from member states and Empire-spanning businesses, as well as the Sky Legion, the largest sign of Imperial authority over the Southern Realms. Ironic, that said symbol would now lift Mirima above the Empire they supposedly served.

Now, High King Xavlaeron would defeat the foe that Caelinus could not, despite the opposition of both Emperor Lucius and the Eastern Court. The world had already seen how the Northern Court had failed. Now, it would see Mirima rise, and that neither arm of Elteno had any ability to resist it—Nay, that Elteno now needed Mirima's power to survive.

The Southern Realms would fall in line. The people of the North would realize on whom their safety depended. And the Eastern Court would see who it was who kept them fighting. Elteno had faded. But Mirima—Mirima always endured. And now, under High King Xavlaeron's rule, it would ascend to rulership of the Empire . . . and perhaps even beyond.

And all they had to do was defeat the queen of the Dobhar.

High King Xavlaeron glanced over at the scroll in front of him, portraying a map of the Northern Seas. A glowing ship moved across the sea at the same speed as his own, indicating their current position. He turned to one of the mages.

"Activate the Caelum Aurem and have *Arofinas's Insight* deploy their Aqua Manus."

The mage turned back and tilted her head. "Your Majesty? It's a bit early, is it not? We are not close to the Turannian shoreline yet."

High King Xavlaeron narrowed his eyes. "This foe defeated Caelinus, the bastion of the North, and Uscfrea Spellbreaker, destroyer of legions. She destroyed a consul's home in the heart of Corvanus and escaped with impunity. We will not underestimate her. And do not forget that she is the queen of the Dobhar and stole the Northern Fleet. The water is the home of her army. Now that we have moved beyond the shores of Utrad, we should move with utmost caution."

The mage nodded. "To break all chains."

High King Xavlaeron nodded back. "To break all chains."

The mage relayed the order, and the wind swirling around the high king's craft began to expand in size and speed, howling as it whipped around. Soon, tendrils of mana-laden wind began to swirl off in all directions.

High King Xavlaeron also watched as another battle airship, the *Arofinas's Insight*, lowered from the sky into the water. The bubble of wind around it began to pick up the water and shifted its attribute as the ship broke into the waves. It would soon repeat the actions of the high king's ship, only with water instead of wind.

High King Xavlaeron smirked. The forces of Mirima may not have fought as many battles as the legions of the East or even the North, but they had not rested idly all these years. Long had Mirima stood at the forefront of the mystic arts among the Empire and its allies, and now, they would showcase their efforts.

A major difficulty in magical warfare was always the short range of magic. Since everything in Aelea possessed mana to some degree—even the very air around them—everything also had an impact on spells. From the moment a spell was cast until the moment it reached its target, it began to bleed mana into its surroundings as it interacted with the mana all around it.

As a result, even with the Farcasting skill, few mages had the ability to cast spells further than they could see, much less aim them, and so to this day, the majority of combat took place within visual range.

There were ways around this. The communication artifacts of the Empire, for one. But even they had merely circumvented the issue via a network of devices that would relay the message to its intended recipient. The issue of range still applied.

Which was why the airships of Mirima had a distinct advantage. They had learned a way to take advantage of the very effect that restricted them. They'd built artifacts that would send out waves of Wind and Water mana with no effect at all, tuned to the air and sea around them so as to minimize their mana bleed as much as possible.

And then, the artifact would measure when and where its spell began to lose mana, signaling where it had encountered stronger interference. With time and research, the enchanters of Mirima had even learned how to interpret the signals to speculate as to what kinds of mana it had encountered, and so guess as to what was there.

It wasn't perfect, but they were now confident they could distinguish a ship from a shoreline . . . and even a warship from a civilian vessel. Or a flying, magical queen from a wandering bird monster.

This would allow them to detect their adversaries far beyond the range of normal sight, including magically enhanced sight. Even clairvoyance spells had to focus on a specific target and were not practical to scan a wide area like this. High King Xavlaeron was confident that neither the Legion nor the Sun Elf Archons could outdo Mirima's detection capabilities.

So, he would definitely see NSLICE-00P coming from miles away and long before she saw him. Mirima would strike the first blow.

Eyewitness accounts of NSLICE-00P's battles had revealed that her defenses were surprisingly light compared to her offensive power, and that she had taken damage from both the Spellbreaker and from Caelinus's Sky Knights. So, if High King Xavlaeron could catch her off guard by striking first with all his fleet's power . . . even the mighty queen of the Dobhar could be brought down.

"Nothing on the Caelum Aurem, but *Arofinas's Insight* is reporting they've detected a fleet on approach!"

High King Xavlaeron grinned. Right on schedule. It was time to teach these savages the new reality of modern warfare.

54

You May Fire When Ready

"The best defense is a good Fireball. An enemy ablaze cannot strike back."

—Celestial Elf Sage Baoruinë, on the lack of Barrier training for his disciples.

High King Xavlaeron nodded to his staff.

"All ships, begin charging long-range enchantments. I want us ready to attack the moment we're in range. And keep an eye on the sky; I don't imagine the queen of the Dobhar is simply waiting on a ship."

The Sentinels of Liberty were just about to relay the order when . . .

"Incoming!"

"Barriers up!" the mage analyzing the Caelum Aurem cried out, and the Sentinels of Liberty sprang into action. A barrier hummed to life around the ship before High King Xavlaeron could even comprehend what was happening.

And then the sky was on fire. An explosion rocked the ship.

Looking outside the dome, High King Xavlaeron's eyes widened as explosions struck much of his fleet. Fortunately, the communication artifact had been active to relay his order, and so the fleet had heard the barrier command. Most of the battle airships had activated their barriers in time, especially those crewed by the forces of Mirima or the Sky Legion. Some had been slower and struck directly, though they seemed to have survived.

But two were not so lucky. Two of his ships appeared to have exploded from the *inside.* They remained flying, as the Gravity cores had their own barriers for exactly this situation, but they had been gutted where the attack had struck. Shattered stone and twisted metal fell from massive holes in the center of their hulls.

High King Xavlaeron simply stared for a moment. "What on Aelea or beyond just happened?"

* * *

Seero's robotic eye flickered as she analyzed the results of the attack. She was currently floating in the air alongside a fleet of drones, while Uscfrea's fleet approached from below.

She had made the decision to employ her allies and subordinates' forces for this battle. There was a need to test both the Earth-based weaponry Uscfrea had purchased from the Aesdes' system, as well as the hybrid magic-technology Melion had been developing in non-dungeon settings and against a more sophisticated opponent.

Likewise, it would be good for her allies and subordinates to gain some experience in combat, and she didn't know what sort of capabilities the Southern Realms' forces might possess. After encounters with the Herald of Night and the Herald of the New Dawn, she thought it best to proceed cautiously, after all.

So, after detecting and tracking the fleet via radar, the ships and drones had gotten into position and unleashed a missile salvo once in range. Uscfrea had had the foresight to install some antiair systems onto the stolen Imperial ships, and so his fleet had been able to participate as well.

The results . . . were about as Seero had predicted. Aircraft design philosophy could not have been more different between Earth and Aelea. On Earth, aircraft design was heavily restricted by the laws of physics and the need to achieve sufficient lift. There were hard limits on the weight of an aircraft . . . which meant there were limits to how heavily an aircraft could be armored.

And given that even ground and sea-based vehicles could not mount enough armor to survive modern munitions, there was little chance of aircraft doing so either . . . and that was before considering that every ounce of armor would reduce the range, speed, and capabilities of the aircraft.

So, aircraft of Earth generally relied on stealth, mobility, range, and other countermeasures to survive, with armor as an afterthought, while the burden of antiair weapons was mainly to detect and hit the target.

Not so for the airships of Aelea. With Gravity enchantments that could nullify weight, and Air Magic–based propulsion that wrapped the vehicle in a bubble of magical wind that was then propelled forward as a whole, Aelea's aircraft were almost completely free from the laws of physics. Weight and aerodynamics were not considerations.

The main design restriction, on the other hand, was the availability of rare magical materials and enchanters with high-enough skill levels to build the craft. As a result, Aelean aircraft design focused on stuffing as much capability as possible into each individual craft, and then ensuring that craft would *NOT* be lost no matter what was thrown at it.

Aelean aircraft were literal flying fortresses, with armor of metal and stone more akin to castles than vehicles. Even the largest battleships of Earth couldn't match the armor thickness of the Aelean airships designed for combat, and that was before Seero factored in magical barriers and enchantments that provided new types of defenses that had not existed on Earth.

As a result, their initial barrage did very little. The Sky Legion's reactions had been very quick, and at this range, many had managed to get their barriers up. But even for the ships that hadn't, the antiair missiles launched by Uscfrea's ships didn't have much effect. They were designed to destroy lightweight jets, not reinforced stone fortifications.

Melion's drones, on the other hand, were another matter. Seero and Melion, having seen the Imperial family's airship up close, had been aware of the significantly stronger defenses of the airships. So, they had chosen not to target it with traditional antiaircraft weapons but with bunker-busting munitions designed to destroy ground-based fortifications.

But those munitions had mostly detonated on the Sky Legion's defensive barriers. And while the two airships that had not deployed barriers had sustained major damage, they'd somehow still remained intact and in the air.

Seero had identified and targeted the main source of Gravity mana on the craft, but apparently, the attack had still failed to critically damage the Gravity enchantments, despite piercing the outer armor.

Unfortunately, those munitions were originally developed as air-to-ground bombs and had to be adapted before use. Seero and Melion had modified them for air-to-air combat, but had not developed surface-to-air variants just yet, and so had not been able to equip Uscfrea's fleet with them.

All in all, it appeared that one direct hit would not be enough for Earth's munitions to destroy Aelea's airships.

"Analysis complete. Protocols adapted."

"Your Majesty, should we sound the retreat or press the attack?"

High King Xavlaeron was interrupted in his surprise by the captain of his ship. He shook his head. "We press the attack."

The captain nodded and took command. "All ships, full speed ahead, with barriers up! Take up formations and prepare to respond as soon as we're in range! Tell the Sky Legion to prepare to deploy!"

High King Xavlaeron stared out the window as the Sentinels of Liberty took charge. While it certainly wasn't his first battle, the sentinels were very good at their jobs, and he had been informed that there could be no mistakes if he were to confront the queen of the Dobhar.

He was beginning to see why. Apparently, the queen of the Dobhar's detection methods matched, or possibly even exceeded, the state-of-the-art artifacts Mirima had developed in great secrecy. He did not know how that was possible, but it clearly was.

No . . . if he thought about it, some of the explosions were on the top of his ships, implying they'd come from above. And that would mean . . . the queen of the Dobhar indeed had forces in the air that he had not detected yet.

And it got worse. The queen of the Dobhar's forces had not only detected his own from beyond visual range, but had managed to launch an effective attack from that distance as well.

That was something Mirima had *not* managed to achieve. There had been no way to circumvent the mana-bleed issue at ranges beyond visual sight. Even spells that managed to reach that distance would have their power severely reduced and could thus be stopped by a far weaker Barrier spell.

Some of the top mages could pull it off with the right skill setup, but that was irrelevant for their purposes. An artifact did not have skills, after all, and not every airship weapons expert could be an archmage.

They had even experimented with mundane projectiles, trying to launch them at high speeds, or even enchanting the projectiles to fly on their own, but they'd had little success. Projectiles were subject to a bleed effect of their own, as their speed decreased over time and gravity pulled them toward the ground.

As a result, they had to be launched at an angle—decreasing accuracy—and they arrived much weaker than when they were launched. They were ultimately subject to the same issues as far-range spellcasting, all for less accuracy and higher material cost.

Enchanted projectiles had more success but were ultimately deemed impractical. Utilizing magical resources and enchanter time on a single-use projectile was already a questionable proposition. Even arrows could hypothetically be recovered and reused within visual range, but a projectile launched at the distances in question from an airship was not coming back, even if it survived.

It got worse when one considered that an enchanter could create a barrier artifact with that same time and resources that would stop the projectile . . . and could be used again. So, it would be an incredibly expensive investment for consumable weapons that would only work against weaker opponents that wouldn't require such efforts in the first place.

He had not expected the queen of the Dobhar to have solved the eternal quandary plaguing mages from the dawn of magic. But . . . he *had* been told he could not take anything for granted when going against her. So, he gathered himself as his fleet moved forward.

In the grand scheme of things, the attacks hadn't done much. Even the ships that had been heavily damaged were still operational for the most part. Given the lack of power compared to his defenses, the queen of the Dobhar may not have solved the bleed issue, after all.

In which case . . . she had expended her surprising detection advantage on a mere glancing blow. The biggest damage was to his and Mirima's pride, but that would not affect the outcome of this battle if they took it in stride and adapted accordingly. Which the Sentinels of Liberty already had.

They had switched from charging the offensive enchantments to diverting full power to barriers and propulsion. They would close the distance as soon as possible, minimizing the time the enemy had to utilize their advantages in range and detection.

High King Xavlaeron took a deep breath and narrowed his eyes. He had certainly been humbled, but he had not yet been beaten. Not even close. This battle had only just begun.

55

Begin Your Attack Run!

"What exactly did you expect me to do when those infuriating humans and half bloods managed to take an entire castle and make it fly?!"

—Archon Fendaha Zimialrosh, explaining his defeat at the hands of the Elteni Empire's new airship force.

"Command: All allied units concentrate fire on the designated target."

Seero's command reached the cyborg Otterkin and communication drones aboard each ship of Uscfrea's fleet. It only took a moment for the command to be relayed through the fleet, at which point, Uscfrea's ships began to fire missiles toward one of the damaged battle airships.

Seero kept watch over the missiles, her robotic eye flickering rapidly, before she commanded the drones in the sky to unleash a salvo of bunker-busting missiles. And, of course, Seero's timing was perfectly precise, so the bunker busters landed immediately after the antiair missiles.

The antiair missiles had little effect on enchanted stone and steel . . . but mana barriers were not so fortunate. Seero had observed that mana barriers had roughly the same resilience to any sort of damage, as their strength was sourced from their pool of energy rather than physical characteristics.

The benefit of this was that mana barriers were an effective countermeasure to any type of damage; they could block a stream of fire as easily as a bullet, an armor-piercing round as easily as a mass explosion. All that mattered was the amount of energy in the attack versus the density of mana in the affected area, and the overall quantity of mana available to the barrier.

But that meant that small fragmentation warheads that would do very little to the airships' actual armor could deal heavy damage to the mana barriers. The relatively low power and high spread of the shrapnel was of no consequence. As long as the energy was transferred to the mana barrier, it would drain its energy reserves and so put strain on the defenses.

And then the bunker-busting missiles started to hit.

Seero and Melion had not been content to simply recreate Earth's munitions, either. The combination of mana iron and enchantments significantly increased the explosive power of each warhead and the velocity of each projectile. And thanks to the CELIU network's shared database, each of the cyborg metal slimes in Melion's workshop was able to engrave enchantments with AI-assisted precision, further boosting the warheads' performance.

It was not long before the barrage overwhelmed the airship's defenses, and the bunker-busting bombs began to tear it apart. Since targeting the Gravity mana source had failed, Seero simply saturated the entire ship with bombs, attempting to analyze the damage of each.

The airship burst apart, explosions blasting crew and material out into the air as the bombs blew massive holes in the hull. Seero noted Gravity mana spreading through the ship, attempting to hold the hull together even as parts of it broke apart entirely.

Large chunks of metal and stone began to break off and fall from the ship as the enchantments failed to hold on to them and they were swept away by the Wind Magic moving the ship forward.

To the credit of the Empire's engineers, the core of the ship remained levitating in the air, still moving forward as both the Gravity and Air enchantments continued their work. But most of the ship had broken apart and was now falling into the waves.

By Seero's sensors, only a handful of the crew remained on the part still in the air.

And then, finally, a bomb broke through the mana barrier around the core itself. The last remaining parts of the ship disintegrated, and the entire thing fell from the sky.

High King Xavlaeron frowned as one of the very expensive battle airships was torn to shreds. The queen of the Dobhar had adapted quickly with a very simple solution. If her attacks weren't damaging most of his ships, she could concentrate them all on one.

Still, that ship had been damaged in the first attack due to its slow reaction, and was one of the ships he had acquired from the other Southern Realms, so not even part of Mirima's own fleet. Its loss was acceptable—as far as battle airship losses could be—and his fleet had covered a good distance in the meantime. The losses wouldn't be too severe before they arrived.

But losing battle airships was not part of High King Xavlaeron's plan in the first place.

"Defensive formations."

The Sentinels of Liberty spread the order, and the fleet began to move. The remaining battle airships gathered up into groups of four, which flew so close they were nearly touching, while the smaller ships gathered up behind them.

Soon, the barrage began again, targeting the other damaged ship. But as its barrier began to fade, a nearby ship linked its barrier with the damaged one, keeping it intact. And when that ship's barrier started to drain, it detached, and the next ship connected. So on and so forth, they ensured that all ships kept a working barrier at all times. The queen of the Dobhar's attacks would not pierce through unless they could overwhelm the combined strength of the entire fleet.

Mirima had taken centuries to assemble this fleet, so they had invested well into keeping it. But still, that only enabled them to survive. Until they arrived within range of the enemy, they were merely buying time. And worse . . . they still were only detecting the ships in the water, which *clearly* weren't the only forces at play.

"Have we located the flying enemies yet?"

"No, Your Majesty! The Caelum Aurem is reading some light distortions, but nothing we can make out yet!"

He gritted his teeth. "Redouble your efforts. I don't think you need me to explain what will happen if you can't find them."

"Yes, Your Majesty!"

Seero noted as another wave of Air mana surged from the hostile fleet and passed over her drones. But she wasn't worried. The grimoire of Arofinas Leolar had described in detail the method by which Mirima had hidden its ships from the Empire of the Sun.

They had taken advantage of the fact that mana existed in every part of this universe and determined an enchantment that would mimic the mana of its surroundings, which could deceive simple mana-based detection methods. It was not perfect and had to be used in conjunction with other techniques and tactics to work, but it'd sufficed to ensure Mirima's survival.

Such techniques had since become obsolete as ships grew in size and gained new capabilities, powered by stronger enchantments. Eventually, the mana flowing through ships was too great to hide. The magical propulsion methods now used by Imperial ships sealed the deal, as the sheer amount of mana surrounding the vessels could not be hidden.

But such was not the case with Melion's drones. Melion's drones mainly utilized a mana core to generate electricity and as a brain for some independent actions. But that meant they had a relatively small mana signature compared to their size and capabilities, as they were relying on technological methods of propulsion.

As a result, if they were not channeling mana through their hulls to activate engraved enchantments, then it was a simple manner to mask their mana signature like Mirima's ships of old. Not to mention that Seero and Melion had also improved and optimized the masking technique.

And finally, since most of Melion's current drones were based on Earth's designs, they were far, *far* smaller than the Sky Legion's floating fortresses.

The end result was that the mana detection method utilized by the high king's ships would not detect Seero's drones until they were much closer, or else revealed themselves to attack with mana.

But the battle airships were, in fact, getting closer. And concentrated fire had only proven effective once, and after a great deal of time.

Seero had not yet identified a critical weak point on the battle airships, as the lack of flammable fuel or explosive ammunition made them much less susceptible to spontaneous combustion compared to Earth's vehicles. And by now, the hostiles had adjusted their formation to render concentrated fire ineffective.

By her calculations, her forces would not down the enemy fleet before they reached visual range.

It appeared, as Seero had predicted, that basic modern munitions were insufficient in Aelea's nonstandard environment. Which meant that this battle was about to turn magical.

"Command: All CELIU units, prepare to engage."

"Enemy ships spotted!"

High King Xavlaeron resisted the urge to let out a sigh of relief. They had managed their approach without any further losses among the battle airships. They still hadn't identified the enemy's air forces, but at the very least, they could begin the counterattack.

Magic circles began to hum to life all along the battle airships as they charged up their main weapons, most breaking their defensive formations and taking some distance from one another. The wind wrapping around the ships began to turn dark, and flashes of light began to appear within it.

And then, finally, they came within range of the enemy fleet.

The battle airships began their attack immediately. Magic circles engraved across their hulls absorbed lightning from the clouds surrounding them, then thunder cracked as massive bolts of lightning surged toward the ships in the water below.

High King Xavlaeron smiled at the display. Lightning was a mana-intensive attribute, but one of the fastest-moving ones, and so a strong choice for an airship's long-range weapon. The researchers of Mirima had learned how to turn air into thunderstorms, significantly reducing the mana cost by generating some "natural" lightning to utilize.

The effect was quite impressive, in the high king's opinion. It was as if Anualë himself had been moved to anger and was working to destroy Mirima's enemies.

"What's the damage?"

A mage with Clairvoyance furrowed her brow as she cast her spell without assistance from the Aesdes. But she was one of the elites of Mirima, and so she managed to pull it off.

"No damage! Enemy ships have deployed barriers and blocked the attack."

High King Xavlaeron blinked. "What?"

Yes, all Imperial warships had some form of barrier available, but Mirima's shipbuilders had specifically taken that into account when designing their armament, and the Northern Fleet stolen by the queen of the Dobhar was anything but state of the art. They should not have been able to repel spell power of that magnitude.

But the high king didn't get a chance to think on it further. As he opened his mouth to question the report . . . the sky ahead lit up in a massive strategic magic circle.

56

Terminate the Fleet!

"I don't want to hear it! We just lost a supercarrier to a freaking Death Star piloted by a madwoman! So, unless you want to get in a jet and fly out with the next wave, go call the people who deal with this kind of crap!"

—A United States Navy admiral, on naval warfare involving Non-Standard threats.

01R stood on the deck of one of the naval ships below. He was surrounded by quadcopter drones, each holding a powerful mana core and designed for Ritual Magic. He was holding out his paws and grinding his teeth as his robotic eye flickered.

A small Ritual Magic formation glowed between him and the drones, maintaining a powerful barrier around the ship that blocked the lightning striking from above. The task was exceptionally difficult for the rat, for he was no expert mage, and the sacred records could not provide any assistance to him.

But that was fine. His cybernetic components were doing the dragon's share of the work, applying the Ritual Magic protocols utilized by Lilussees to link him to the drones, and casting the spell the wise-mighty-gracious boss-queen had left in the database. But the mana did still need to flow through his organic parts, so it took some effort to let it pass. It was surprisingly difficult to fully cede control of his body to the cybernetic components.

But that was simply a sign of his lack of faith!

A fire burned within 01R's chest at the mere thought of being afraid of the armor of the wise-mighty-gracious boss-queen! He turned all of his will to surrender, letting the sacred protocols guide his body, and the cybernetic components take full hold of his mana. This, too, was another battle in the name of the wise-mighty-gracious boss-queen! And he would prove his loyalty in this very instant!

Two soldiers, a human and a Dobhar, watched the rat as he squeaked loudly and the barrier started glowing brighter. The human made a nonplussed expression.

"We're . . . being protected from the Sky Legion . . . by a rat."

The Dobhar shrugged. "We're being led by a human. A human who can destroy armies and reshape mountains. You get used to it."

"So this is the magic of the queen of the Dobhar that broke the Spellbreaker and shattered Caelinus's legions?" High King Xavlaeron remarked as he stared out at the magic circle covering the sky.

And then, he . . . smirked.

"It's not as intimidating as it was made out to be, and most of all, nothing we haven't prepared for. Deploy the Sky Legion, and have them engage the ships below! We'll deal with the queen of the Dobhar."

Large doors opened on the airships in the rear. Wyvern knights and legionnaires wearing specialized armor dropped from the sky, the wind wrapping around them much like the airships. They assembled themselves into formations in the air and then began to fly toward the ships in the water.

Meanwhile, bright green plants began to grow across the surface of the battle airships as they switched to the Nature mana barriers prepared specifically for this fight. They turned to face the large magic circle, the Caelum Aurem scanning for its source.

The queen of the Dobhar herself floated in front of the magic circle.

And then, the spell triggered. Beams of light showered the fleet—and were absorbed by the Nature Barriers with ease. The beams then started fusing together into large superbeams, but these too were absorbed.

High King Xavlaeron grinned. The queen of the Dobhar was not so terrifying, after all.

He focused his half-Elven sight and even caught a glimpse of the queen of the Dobhar herself, floating in front of her magic circle, yet he was not deceived. The Caelum Aurem hadn't confirmed her position yet . . .

"Spell source located!"

High King Xavlaeron couldn't help but chuckle. As expected, what he saw was not the queen of the Dobhar at all. The Caelum Aurem could tell the difference between an illusion and the real deal, given that a mage channeling a spell gave off much stronger interference.

The battle airships began to channel their lightning . . .

Up and above the strategic magic circle was a small fleet of aircraft. Assembled in a circular formation were dozens of small drones featuring little more than a big magic core and enough repulsors to keep up. In the center was a larger jet plane featuring a two-person cockpit. In a tiny front seat was a cyber-rat, linked to both the cybernetics and golem brain of the plane to pilot it like their own body.

In a much larger back seat designed for maximum comfort was Lilussees, linked to the battery drones around her in order to power the spell below. She yawned, and then sighed.

"Oh, like, that's annoying. They have, like, elemental barriers or something."

She yawned once more and plopped down on her seat. Given the shape of her body, the traditional chair had been replaced with a flat cushion, which Lilussees very much preferred, in any case.

"Like, I guess I could try a different spell or something. But, like, those guys are going to reach the others soon, or something. So, like, isn't that enough playing around, boss lady?"

Lilussees settled back into her seat as a portion of the drones switched to defense, channeling built-in barrier spells to protect the formation from bolts of lightning.

Further back in the air, Seero analyzed the situation as per Lilussees's query, finding it reasonable. She and Melion had acquired a hefty set of data from real combat situations that could guide their future weapons developments, particularly regarding beyond-visual-range munitions. And at this point, the hostiles were in range of the friendlies.

Flying infantry and cavalry were making their way toward Uscfrea's fleet and the CELIU units onboard, while the battle airships were assaulting Lilussees's spell squadron. She had analyzed the hostiles' capabilities at this point, and any further delays could result in casualties among friendly forces.

"Analysis complete. Affirming Statement: Friendly Lilussees's assessment is accurate. Experimentation protocols deactivated. Termination protocols engaged. This unit will engage enemy airships; Friend Lilussees should redirect efforts to assist naval forces below."

She heard Lilussees's response over the comms. ". . . I don't like the *E* word, but like, fine."

Seero flew forward, employing the same mana-mimicking technique used to hide her drones. She began to stir up her mana before sending a command to one of the drones—one shaped like a glider.

She may have deactivated experimentation protocols . . . but there was one further experiment she wished to run.

The drone activated its repulsors and began to dive toward its target. It angled itself toward the top of a battle airship, aiming for the main source of Gravity mana.

And then, it shot forward at maximum speed.

* * *

High King Xavlaeron frowned as the strategic magic circle faded and the caster began to retreat. The queen of the Dobhar had so far been blocking their attacks with her barriers, an impressive display in and of itself, but he had not expected her to simply retreat.

He, of course, was very confident in the might of Mirima's battle airships, but still, he felt that something was off. From every report they had on the queen of the Dobhar, this should not have been the extent of her strength. A few bolts of lightning should not have forced her to retreat. She could not have defeated Caelinus's veteran legions if that was all it took to repel her.

He then caught sight of a single projectile moving toward one of the ships in the front. He tilted his head. Even their oldest ships had withstood a barrage of such projectiles from the queen of the Dobhar's entire fleet. Why would she send a single one at this stage? The ship in question thus took no additional defensive measures, as a single attack would not break through its barrier.

The projectile struck.

And a massive wave of glittering rainbow sparks surged out from the point of impact—as well as an explosion from the middle of the airship. High King Xavlaeron's eyes widened.

The battle airship, one which had been completely unharmed by the initial strikes, now broke in two and began to fall from the sky after a *single* attack.

But he had no time for shock or horror. Because immediately afterward, the entire sky lit up in a second strategic magic circle, this one far larger than the first and as bright as the sun . . .

Seero recorded the results of the strike. She had iterated on the improvised anti-mana bombs from before and developed a dedicated anti-mana warhead. She had utilized it in a tandem-warhead setup, featuring a powerful bunker-busting bomb that would continue traveling through the anti-mana explosion to pierce into the undefended target.

She and Melion had then installed this on a kamikaze drone to ensure a precise strike.

And it had worked per Seero's most optimistic predictions.

The anti-mana shock wave temporarily disabled both the outer mana barrier protecting the ship and the interior mana barrier protecting the source of the Gravity enchantment. Then the bunker-busting bomb pierced through the ship before either barrier was restored and exploded directly on the source of the Gravity enchantment, managing to disable it as well as dealing heavy structural damage to the center of the ship.

The Gravity enchantments not only provided the airship with lift but also helped to hold its stone hull together. So, without that assistance, and weakened by an internal explosion, the ship not only fell from the sky but also began breaking apart under its own weight.

Of course, such anti-mana warheads were limited. Seero could not yet produce Iesnuorium, and so she was the only one capable of generating anti-mana at the limited rate the Equalizer could output. The anti-mana storage methods were also not perfect, slowly leaking the energy once she was no longer providing it.

As such, only a limited number of anti-mana warheads could exist at any given time; not enough to simply wipe out the fleet as a whole.

But that was fine. This, again, was a test, an experiment to inform future efforts if and when Seero gained the ability to produce Iesnuorium. And now that the final experiment was concluded—it was time to terminate the hostiles in earnest.

Seero formed and Supercharged a Prismatic Bombardment magic circle, applying the Piercing modifier to improve its performance. With her new capabilities, it was completed in an instant, and then she began to open fire.

The circles turned red as she applied the Fire attribute. Burning beams with wisps of fire flickering around them lit up the sky and set flame to the Nature Barriers of the airships. They then switched to a new element, turning purple as they switched to . . . Gravity.

Seero chose Gravity in order to take advantage of the airship's own designs. Some of the beams amplified the airship's weight, increasing the force of Gravity upon them. Others reduced the attraction within its parts, creating repelling fields within the hulls of the ships.

These effects did little on their own, but, unfortunately for the battle airships, they were not the only Gravity effects present. The lift-providing enchantments warred with the weight-increasing attacks, trying to push the ship up and pull it down at the same time, while the enchantments holding the hulls together now battled with the repelling fields. All of this created a chaotic mix of shifting forces pushing and pulling in every direction . . . right within the hulls of the ships.

The affected battle airships began to disintegrate, pieces of the hull breaking off and falling or sometimes even being flung away as the chaotic and opposing forces ripped them apart.

And, eventually, the Gravity enchantments burned out trying to counteract the sheer amount of mana Seero could dump into her spell. The moment that happened, the affected ship (or what remained of it), plunged toward the water below as Seero's spell took hold and the force of gravity increased dramatically upon it.

For a brief moment, even the stalwart soldiers of the Sky Legion and Seero's own allies stopped and stared as the mighty battle airships began to fall from the sky.

57

The Secret Weapon

"Cheap tricks and crazy cults are no match for a good crossbow."

—Legion sharpshooter Juventia Tatian

High King Xavlaeron's jaw hung wide open. Airships were dropping one by one in front of him. They formed every barrier they could, but the magic circle adjusted its element to counter whatever they had available.

They tried evasive maneuvers with as much speed as they could manage, but the large ships could not dodge the beams. They fired back with lightning and enchanted ballistae and spells from the onboard mages. One airship even fired back with a strategic spell of its own, though without the support of the Aesdes, the spell was shaky and barely completed.

Still, the mages of Mirima showed their quality as a massive cyclone of water rose into the sky and surged toward the queen of the Dobhar . . . only for it to be vaporized entirely as her own spell fused its beams together and pierced right through it.

No matter what his airships did, the queen of the Dobhar simply overpowered them. This . . . This was not what his intel had reported. He had been told to expect Sun Elf Archon levels of power, a mighty mage who could cast strategic spells unassisted, who could take on a legion in strength.

But this . . . this was more like a dragon. A true dragon, the kind that mostly existed in legend for those lucky enough not to encounter them.

The high king's face turned grim. Technically speaking, his fleet had contingency plans for dragons—joint formations that could combine the barriers of all the ships into one. But that formation took time to set up, and so needed to be prepared ahead of the fight.

They were not prepared, and the queen of the Dobhar would not give them the time to set up now. And even as he thought, nearly half his ships had disintegrated and fallen from the sky. It would take the queen of the Dobhar but a moment to destroy the remainder.

The Sky Legion couldn't help either; its forces had already been deployed toward the sea below. And once the airships were gone, could individual men and women stand against this sort of power? They were struggling to maintain formation just against the smaller strategic spell, they'd stand no chance against the significantly larger one now devastating his fleet.

They would all be destroyed if nothing changed. High King Xavlaeron spoke in a low, calm voice.

"Activate the Arcanum Caries."

The sentinels' captain frowned at that. "Your Majesty, is that wise? If we use it on a spell circle of that size and density . . . there's a good chance we will be destroyed as well."

High King Xavlaeron kept his eyes on yet another airship as it broke apart. "That is a certainty if we do not."

The captain slowly nodded and gave the order. Soon, a glass orb on the high king's armrest began to glow. High King Xavlaeron laid his hand upon it and began to channel his mana into the device.

Blue mana in the form of lightning began to crackle around his flagship as magic circles lit up its entire hull. All the mana then accelerated forward and formed a crackling blue beam, which shot straight for the gigantic magic circle across the sky. It struck the circle, and a portion of the formation began to turn blue. High King Xavlaeron winced but continued to pour his mana into the device.

The blue started to creep along the magic circle, but then the spell began to glow near the affected section. High King Xavlaeron grunted, and the blue discoloration began to fade back toward the point of impact. The high king heaved a sigh and reached into an inner pocket in his armor, pulling out a knife engraved in magic circles—ones not recorded within the boons of the Aesdes.

He did not trust his "allies," nor did he have any interest in their apocalyptic dreams. But that also did not mean he was a blind follower of the Aesdes. After all, Mirima had been founded by those who had thrown off the chains of the Empire of the Sun, so they trusted no authority but their own.

That's why, when a certain cagey benefactor requested cooperation in research regarding the Realms of Mana, High King Xavlaeron had not been fooled. He knew well who these people were, and what the goal of their research was. But still, he not only permitted it but gave the project his full support, tasking the foremost mages and scholars of Mirima to press forward in total secrecy.

They knew these people had found a way to forcibly corrupt dungeons with power from the Realms of Mana. And though the full intricacies of that process were beyond them, Mirima's top minds had made progress in their understandings of mana, the Realms, and their interactions as a result.

High King Xavlaeron was not interested in corrupting dungeons. He felt that was a foolhardy idea. Corrupted dungeons were dangerous and uncontrollable. Yes, the cult had some sort of ritual that could bind a person to one, but who would be controlling who in that instance? Would a normal person truly retain their sanity and control over their own mind when fully exposed to the Realms of Mana, down to their very core?

The researchers of Mirima had taken the process in another direction; one they had not bothered sharing with the client. They had studied the process of mana corruption itself—how mana from one source could invade and overtake another.

They had the invading part down, but the overtaking was giving them trouble. Rather than the corrupting effect the Realms of Mana displayed, their own mana-invasion methods caused the target to explode outright.

Which was more than enough for a weapon; one that would be especially potent against large spells. *If* High King Xavlaeron's mana could invade the queen of the Dobhar's to a sufficient extent to cause a reaction, that was. And it appeared it could not.

So High King Xavlaeron now had no choice but to rely on that uncontrollable, unpredictable method he'd sought to avoid in the first place.

He stabbed the knife into the glass orb.

Immediately, the blue lightning around the ship began to change color, turning purple. It also started lashing out toward the ship itself, tearing away small pieces of the enchanted stone and metal hull. The purple color traveled up the beam and into the queen of the Dobhar's spell, the discoloration beginning to spread across the magic circle at a much faster rate than before.

High King Xavlaeron took a deep breath.

"Sound the retreat."

It appeared he had succeeded in corrupting the queen of the Dobhar's massive spell, which covered the sky with a formation as bright as the sun and contained enough mana to overpower the finest battle airships Mirima and the Empire could produce.

Reaching a minimum safe distance would be . . . difficult.

Seero's robotic eye flickered as a blue beam struck into her magic circle. She detected foreign mana intruding in her spell, but she simply increased the Mana Density in that part of the circle and drove it back.

But then, the beam turned purple and began giving off abnormal readings. It converted into a mana type she hadn't encountered before . . . but one that gave off similar signs to the Rifts and corrupted dungeons. The new mana began to corrupt and twist her own, converting it into more of itself as it spread across the formation.

Seero was about to turn the attack on the ship responsible, but there was a problem. The thread dedicated to managing the stability of the Supercharged strategic spell indicated that the corruption was causing blockages in the circle. Any attempt to fire the spell would cause an explosion of extraordinary proportions. Both she and her allies would be at an unacceptable risk of termination in that case. And since she no longer had full control of the circle, she couldn't simply cancel it either. Letting go of the mana would allow the corruption to do as it pleased.

So, her robotic eye flickered as she considered her options. The Equalizer could erase the mana in question, but the Equalizer's maximum power output paled in comparison to the amount of mana in her Supercharged spell. The corruption was spreading faster than the Equalizer would be able to erase it.

An anti-mana warhead might do the trick, but an uncontrolled and explosive deconstruction of the magic circle was not recommended. Siphoning the mana back into herself was also not recommended. The last thing she wanted was for the intrusion to spread to her internal mana.

So, she came up with a different solution.

"Command: Friend Ateia, this unit requests assistance. Blessing parameters are as follows . . ."

Back in the Primary Home Base, Ateia was pacing about with a frown. She was watching the battle through her cybernetic components when Seero's message came in. Her face lit up.

"Finally!"

She immediately sat down on the ground and got to work. She understood Seero's rationale; blessing required a great deal of focus for Ateia and didn't require her to be physically present on the battlefield.

In fact, if she was targeting Seero or her subordinates, then casting the blessing from the Primary Home Base was actually easier, since she could use their connection to Seero's core as a guide. It made a lot of sense to keep Ateia there, where she could focus on blessing without any distraction or danger.

But she still hated sitting around at home while everyone else was out confronting danger. So, she was very pleased to finally get involved in this fight.

Back on the battlefield, Seero's Prismatic Bombardment spell began to glow with golden-and-silver light as Ateia's mana and the Holy mana of the world streamed into it. Ateia had been practicing her blessings and had reached the stage where she could target objects, or even spell circles.

This was made easier for any spell cast by someone in the CELIU network, since data shared through their cybernetic components would improve Ateia's targeting.

As a result, Holy mana now flooded into the magic circle. Seero calculated that if this corrupting power was related to the Realms of Mana, then Holy mana would be highly effective in counteracting it.

But she had already Supercharged the spell to the limit, so adding additional mana from herself would be difficult. Likewise, converting the spell to fire Holy Beams might affect individual Beam circles, but wouldn't fill the overall, connecting structure with Holy mana; not to the extent that Ateia's blessings could. This method was calculated as the most efficient one.

And Seero's calculations were correct. The moment the Holy mana contacted the corrupted area, the corrupted mana began to burn away. Of course, that meant parts of the spell circle were now being violently destroyed, but Seero focused with all her Mana Control and AI precision to repair the circle as the Holy mana moved through it.

This was another benefit of having Ateia perform the blessing, as it allowed Seero to focus entirely on the repairs. As such, she managed to avoid an explosion.

And as a side benefit, kept the spell active. The spell that was now fully repaired and ready to fire once again.

Seero immediately turned her attention to the offending ship, which she had designated as a priority target . . .

58

Terminate the High King?

"Let me get this straight: You thought the apocalyptic cult would feel compelled to keep their word because they signed a contract?"

—Imperial Inquisitor Quintus Carius Profuterius

The Sentinels of Liberty moved rapidly around High King Xavlaeron, shouting into communication artifacts as they tried to organize the hasty retreat. What airships remained fled from the area, not even bothering to turn around as the Wind Magic carried them backward.

Commands were issued to the confused Sky Legion commanders; without the time to gather them aboard the airships, the wyvern riders and flying legionnaires were left to flee on their own. One or two airships moved to assist, a move that would assuredly doom them as well as any Sky legionnaires who stopped to climb aboard.

It was at that moment that the magic circle lit up even brighter.

"That's too soon—the fleet isn't out of range yet!"

High King Xavlaeron clenched his teeth and prepared for impact . . .

Which never came. The light of the magic circle turned golden and silver, bathing the battlefield in the light of Holy mana. The soldiers of the Sky Legion froze in place, as all inhabitants of Aelea instinctually recognized the warm glow.

The corrupted section of the magic circle burned away and began to be repaired. Holy mana continued to burn along the beam of corrupted energy, eventually arriving at the high king's ship. The ship rocked, all the crew having to steady themselves, as Holy mana burned away the corrupted energy surrounding the ship. An explosion rocked the hull as the Holy mana reached the secret weapon, and the glass orb on the high king's throne shattered, launching a burned-out knife out to clatter on the floor.

High King Xavlaeron glanced down at the burnt, smoking dagger, then up at the magic circle. A magic circle that was very nearly complete once again.

He heaved a sigh. He had but one choice.

"Sound . . . the surrender."

From a tactical perspective, no weapon or artifact he had available could save his fleet from the overwhelming magical prowess of the queen of the Dobhar. From a morale perspective, he had just used corrupted mana from the Realms of Mana against a foe he claimed was a demon lord . . . and she had responded with Holy mana, or something so similar to it even he couldn't tell the difference.

At this point, the Sky Legion, and even some members of the Sentinels of Liberty, would be questioning their cause. Clearly, his allies had not been fully truthful about her identity.

Strategically, this was a complete disaster. He had made a bid to set Mirima as the master of the Empire . . . and had failed, losing half a fleet that had taken centuries to build. He had done so against the wishes of the Eastern Court and the figurehead Emperor of the North. And now, he had lost.

But there was nothing for it. Mirima had not survived and remained nominally independent by acting inflexibly. Surviving with half a fleet would be better than losing the entire thing. And besides . . . he'd heard that the queen of the Dobhar was very straightforward and blunt, while Mirima had long been the masters of diplomacy and negotiation.

He likewise knew that she was at odds with his "allies"—the same allies who he could see now had manipulated him into this fight. So . . . perhaps he could claim a diplomatic victory with a skillful reorientation despite the military defeat?

It was at that moment that his inner pocket began to glow.

"GAH!"

High King Xavlaeron cried out as purple lightning shot through his armor and directly into his mana, surging across his body as it began to corrupt his own. He struggled to take control of his mana once more. The high king had studied as a mage in his youth and had reached an incredible level of skill over the years . . . and yet, he was being pushed back.

His eyes widened. One of the artifacts from his allies that had been "misplaced" by Mirima was now active and was pouring corrupted mana into him. He tried to reach for it, but it was well hidden within his armor, and so he could not grab it before the corrupted mana locked up his arms.

He realized now that his "allies" had never trusted him in the first place either.

He could do nothing but cry out as the mana surged through him and he burned away, leaving the Sentinels of Liberty staring in horror.

* * *

Seero had just finished repairing the magic circle and was about to destroy the offending ship when a voice rang out across the battlefield.

"Queen of the Dobhar, this is Captain Falrauth Eildove of the Sentinels of Liberty. High King Xavlaeron has fallen. I'm requesting an immediate ceasefire and surrender negotiations."

The airship fleet stopped at his message and began to drop their barriers and shut off their weapons. The soldiers of the Sky Legion glanced at one another before holstering theirs.

Seero analyzed the situation. She'd detected a small surge of corrupted mana in the ship that had subsequently vanished. No additional nonstandard signatures appeared on her sensors, and mana readings from across the hostile forces were falling. It appeared the intent to surrender was genuine.

She reanalyzed her surrender-accepting protocols, given they had originally been motivated by Dr. Ottosen's desire to acquire new bases for the NSLICE program. She instead compared it to instances of warfare she had on record, historical records from the Empire, and her own experiences.

And when she had concluded, she spoke, utilizing mana to carry her voice.

"Demand: Surrender acknowledged. Cease all hostile actions and send an individual with sufficient authority to initiate diplomacy protocols."

At the end of the day, surrender and complete annihilation of the opposing faction were the only two methods to end hostility. The hostile faction in this case represented an entire nation-state of a scale that made complete annihilation impractical, not to mention her agreement with Princess Caecila not to terminate the entire populace.

Additionally, Seero had already intended to apprehend as much of the hostile force as possible, since there was a need to determine their relationship with the Heralds of the New Dawn and extract all relevant intel. As a result, accepting a surrender was the more efficient method by far.

Plus . . . every personal instance of accepting a surrender since she'd arrived in this world had proven beneficial to her. So long as she kept her guard up for any treachery and made sure not to agree to any statements that could be the trigger for some undetected magic ritual, there wasn't much risk. Seero, however, kept her own magic circle up and running. She was prepared to immediately respond if she detected any anomalies.

"Command: All units and allied forces, cease fire. All diplomatic units, please prepare to negotiate the hostiles' surrender."

On the command ship, Uscfrea let out a sigh. Vopiscus raised an eyebrow. "Why the long face, Steward? By all accounts, we just won a stunning victory, you know?"

Uscfrea nodded. "Oh, I'm well pleased about that. I never imagined the Empire had a force like this one; a legion of artificial dragons raining death from the skies. To defeat it without the loss of a single warrior is beyond miraculous. It's just that . . ."

He glanced at the new axe he had placed to the side, forged by Dwarven smiths with the best materials his dungeon could produce, and the Cyborg-affinity weapon he had summoned for himself. Though, given its size and weight, he wasn't sure why it was called a "mini gun."

". . . I was kind of looking forward to joining the frontlines again."

Dux Augustalis exhaled her breath. "Such is the burden of command, Spellbreaker."

Vopiscus shrugged. "Burden, huh? Only you battle maniacs would consider it a bad thing that we're not risking our lives on a daily basis anymore."

Dux Augustalis glared at him, but Uscfrea just chuckled. He supposed it *was* strange for him to miss battle when he'd made it his life's mission to grant the Dobhar peace. He shook his head and turned to his troops. Linking his cybernetic components to the communications on the other ships in his fleet, his face appeared next to a live feed of his queen. Grabbing his axe, he lifted it into the air.

"Victory is ours!"

After a moment of processing his words, every ship in the fleet broke out into cheers. Even Dux Augustalis couldn't help but crack a smile.

A small shuttle came from one of the airships, landing on one of Uscfrea's ships. Seero was standing on the deck, with Magister Canus, Miallói, Uscfrea, and their staff waiting behind her. Captain Falrauth Eildove disembarked, a half-Elven Sentinel of Liberty. Joining him was Legate Aulus Granius Magunnus of the Sky Legion, and several leaders from the Southern Realms who had joined the high king on his quest.

Captain Falrauth held back a sigh. He, too, had read the reports on the queen of the Dobhar, and had hoped that they might get off easily. Not so as he saw the group assembled behind her. He didn't know much about the Turannians, but Canus Sittius Dio had quite the reputation, and now held the rank of Magister Militum.

As one of the most decorated half Elves in the Empire, he was quite popular among the people of Mirima as well. The higher-ups were not as fond of a famous half Elf who was unaffiliated with Mirima, but even their envy could not deny his accomplishments.

In fact, Legate Aulus Granius Magunnus was saluting and apologizing to Canus even now. Captain Falrauth held back a groan. Apologizing before the negotiations even began was unwise . . . unless the legate was planning to jump ship and throw Mirima under the bus. Captain Falrauth wasn't sure which.

But, well, Captain Falrauth knew of High King Xavlaeron's ambitions . . . and his suspicious contacts. He had not opposed, so this situation was simply the price he had to pay. And now, his duty was to protect Mirima in any way he could.

And so began the negotiations.

59

The Battle's End

"Wars are won by soldiers. And thanks to my NSLICE program, we have the perfect soldiers."

—Dr. Ottosen, during a war council.

"You can't be serious!"

Captain Falrauth allowed himself to gape. Uscfrea grinned at him.

"My queen is always serious, you know?"

"Confused Query: Why would this unit lie when stating surrender conditions?"

Captain Falrauth glared at them. "You want half the remaining fleet! The South will be left almost completely defenseless!"

Uscfrea's grin grew. "And without this surrender, you will be left completely defenseless, with no remaining fleet at all. Be grateful for my queen's mercy."

Captain Falrauth clenched his teeth but then shook his head. "It's not possible, either way. I'm only the captain of the Sentinels of Liberty. I lack the authority to transfer battle airships to a foreign party, and many of them do not belong to Mirima at all. I am only negotiating for the surrender of my forces here."

Seero's robotic eye flickered. Within the CELIU network's internal comms, Vopiscus was laughing raucously.

"Oh, that's great. Tell him this, Your Majesty . . ."

With several politically minded individuals now a part of the CELIU network, Seero had shored up her inexperience in diplomacy. Vopiscus could now remain off-site and watch through the network, giving explanations and recommendations to Seero directly.

"Acknowledged. Updated Demand: In that case, this unit demands an unconditional surrender of all hostile forces, who will be interned as prisoners of war. All material will be seized as spoils of war. All prisoner transfers or returns of material must be negotiated by the relevant authorities."

Captain Falrauth paled. "That's . . . Why don't we go back to your first offer? I'm sure I can convince the Council of the Southern Realms to honor the terms."

"Negative Response: Captain Falrauth is not authorized to agree to any terms that are sufficient to remove the threat to this unit and allied entities, and so further negotiations are deemed inefficient. Please confirm the intent to surrender, or this unit will consider hostilities as resumed."

Captain Falrauth hung his head.

In the end, the Sky Legion and the forces of the Southern Realms were forced to surrender and hand over their weapons, including the airships. Melion immediately began to analyze the construction of Mirima's most advanced battle airships and the flying artifacts of the Sky Legion. A message was sent to the Council of the Southern Realms informing them of the results of the battle, granting them one chance to negotiate.

Seero was prepared to campaign against them, but would prefer not to if at all possible. The reason for that was that Captain Falrauth had provided her with intel regarding the Heralds of the New Dawn, as well as informing her that they had betrayed and killed High King Xavlaeron.

The Heralds had many bases and agents in the Southern Realms, but they had not infiltrated its leadership to the extent of the Northern Court. Rather, given the mercantile and politically minded outlook of the individual Southern Realms, such an infiltration was hardly necessary. The cult could operate almost openly so long as they provided benefits to their hosts.

High King Xavlaeron had attempted to keep track of these as much as possible, as insurance against his shady ally. Captain Falrauth stated he would surrender as much intel as he could . . . but only upon successful conclusion of negotiations with the Southern Realms.

Seero could have pressed the issue, but she chose not to, as a negotiated peace was more efficient for her purposes. While an offensive campaign against the South was certainly possible now that their largest military force had been defeated, doing so would take time and attention away from Seero's primary opponent.

Likewise, upon a successful campaign, she would likely need to occupy and garrison the South, which would require raising and committing additional forces to the task. And worse . . . since the South was a collection of individual realms, it would require a series of campaigns and occupations.

The benefits of doing so were far outweighed by the resources and time Seero would need to commit to a secondary opponent. It was much more efficient to commandeer enough of their equipment to render further offensive action untenable, and then to negotiate a peace. And, well . . . she already had additional tasks to take care of, such as the current discussion between Turannia's leaders.

Seero was currently sitting around a table in Turannia's largest port, joined by Turannia's leaders and her own subordinates. The battle airships had been lowered to the ground, and the hostile forces reasonably imprisoned, so the group had gathered to discuss their next move.

Rector Aemilia had even brought Princess Caecila along . . . who Seero predicted as sleep-deprived, given her appearance and physiological scans. It turned out Rector Aemilia had a lot of paperwork to handle and was always pleased to bring on more hands.

The rector now cracked a smile. "An impressive victory as always, Your Majesty. You never disappoint, do you?"

"Response: This unit always attempts to achieve the most efficient outcome."

Rector Aemilia giggled lightly. "That's one way to put it."

And then her smile fell. "But now we have the question of what to do next. I have sent word to the Council of the Southern Realms as per your request, Your Majesty. But there is another issue we must address. What of the Northern Court?"

Princess Caecila clenched her teeth and looked down. "When I left, High King Xavlaeron and Magister Verrucosis had all but taken over, and Emperor Lucius had been sidelined entirely. I . . . do not know what the situation is at present."

Magister Tiberius nodded. "I can shed a bit of light on that. Magister—or, well, former Magister Appius reached out through some unofficial channels. Magister Verrucosis has declared martial law, integrated the local Exploratores back into the Legion hierarchy, and taken command of the court.

"Emperor Lucius is under unofficial house arrest. Consul Hiberius remains in his own land, and Verrucosis is planning a campaign against him. Aedile Hortensus is not particularly resisting or cooperating to any major extent, save for insisting on official procedures wherever applicable."

Magister Canus rubbed his chin. "Hm, if High King Xavlaeron had survived, he would have provided the political legitimacy, but with him gone, it's a military coup. But if I know Verrucosis . . . he's not about to just back down, and it doesn't seem there's anyone sufficient in the capital to make him. That works to our advantage."

Rector Aemilia glanced at Princess Caecila and cracked an amused smile. "Yes, indeed. We can have our princess here denounce the military rebellion and say she officially requested our help. We could march into Corvanus as the party *loyal* to the Empire, under the premise of restoring Emperor Lucius to power."

Rector Aemilia then gave Princess Caecila a full grin. "Of course, our help will not come cheap, Your Highness."

Princess Caecila heaved a sigh but nodded her head. "I will do as you say."

Magister Canus turned to Seero. "Your Majesty, would this plan line up with your own? We may require assistance from you or your forces if Verrucosis ends up resisting and convincing the Northern legions to follow him."

"Response: This unit is waiting for negotiations with the Southern Realms to acquire intel regarding the Heralds of the New Dawn. It is possible and efficient to allocate resources to establish control over the Northern Empire, as long as control can be achieved without a long campaign."

Magister Canus gave a small smile as he thought back to the "battle."

"With your help, I don't think that will be a problem at all."

And so, the battle for Turannia came to a close. But a battle for the Northern Empire loomed on the horizon, not to mention the wider war against the Heralds, who had still not been located.

The Turannians set off to organize their forces for the upcoming task. The military leaders began to commandeer some of the battle airships and familiarize themselves with their use . . . aided by cooperative members of the Sky Legion. Rector Aemilia, Princess Caecila, and the other civilian leaders began to lay the political groundwork for the mission.

Seero's forces were also preparing, but the CELIU network made communication and organization significantly faster, so Seero had some time on her hands. She used this time to conduct an analysis of the battle.

Modern military hardware had had mixed results against their magical counterparts; its ability to target and strike hostiles from beyond visual range gave them an advantage, but its firepower fell off against the powerful defenses magical techniques could generate.

In particular, magical barriers which could be repaired or simply recast were a highly efficient means of stopping missile attacks. It traded mana—an abundant resource that would replenish itself midbattle—for material.

Even Seero's forces, who, thanks to the Primary Home Base, could magically produce more material, took at least some time to gather and process that material into ammunition and then to transport it to the weapon platforms in the field.

Likewise, an excessive amount of ammunition had to be expended within a short time frame to defeat a magical barrier, and only provided a short window of opportunity even when it succeeded. A window of opportunity that was hard to exploit given the strength of magical materials and magical engineering not limited by physics—or the need to carry highly explosive ammunition and fuel.

Of course, none of this was a problem within visual range. Seero herself had overwhelming magical firepower that could match magical defenses, and the CELIU network could do likewise with effective use of Ritual Magic and blessings. But visual-range combat allowed the enemy to retaliate, so Seero still found it desirable to develop efficient means of striking from further away. It was never desirable to face the enemy directly if it could be avoided.

In fact, this had been a problem in her original universe as well, given the existence of superheroes. Seero herself had been designed for mostly close-range combat, since long-range strikes were not guaranteed to be effective against any given foe she might encounter, and it was difficult to apply nonstandard abilities to modern weapons for the most part.

But the magic of Aelea was more ubiquitous than the nonstandard abilities in her previous universe, so she felt it should be possible to come up with a solution this time around.

And so, Seero began to brainstorm how she could improve the long-range munitions of Earth for the magical conditions of Aelea. Seero *had* upgraded some of the missiles with magical techniques and materials . . . but the recent battlefield performance indicated this alone was not enough to overcome the logistical mismatch. She needed something a bit more than enchanted bombs and magical shrapnel to do the job.

And, of course, this was only against the measures High King Xavlaeron and the forces of the Southern Realms had employed, which were ultimately considered standard for Aelea. The Heralds of the New Dawn could and likely would deploy even more novel techniques. Any weapon Seero planned to use against them needed to comfortably overmatch the standard defenses.

Because, after all, both strategic analysis of this engagement and intel passed on by Captain Falrauth agreed on a concerning conclusion: This entire attack had been a diversion.

The Council of the Southern Realms, a party aligned with but external to the Heralds of the New Dawn, had been set against her. And even though they had failed to terminate her, she now risked being drawn into two major military campaigns against the Northern and Southern Courts. All the while, the Heralds remained at large and incognito.

And that was the most concerning issue of all. For if the Heralds had chosen to open hostilities not with a direct strike but with a diversion . . . then what were they doing in the meantime? And how exactly should Seero set about locating, disrupting, and terminating them?

All she could determine right now was that this war had only begun, and that these hostiles might be especially difficult to terminate.

But then, her robotic eye began to glow red, her organic eye began to narrow, and her mouth curled into a frown. They had attempted to terminate her,

her friends, and her subordinates. So, no matter how difficult it proved, Seero would find them—and terminate them. She would not stop, ever, until they were terminated.

That was the one intended goal of the Non-Standard Leashed-Intelligence Cybernetic Enforcer program that she would still fulfill.

NSLICE-00P's Final Status

NSLICE network log note: Last recorded foreign system status report prior to loss of contact with foreign system.

NSLICE-00P's Dungeon Management

Overview	
Name	**The Walking Dungeon, Heart of the New World**
Level	**7,118**
XP	**23/100**
Available Perk Points	**315**
Mana	**12,860/12,860 (14,320/14,320)**
Exterior	**Human/Automata Hybrid (LOCKED)**

Dungeon Affinities	
Type	**Strength**
Cyborg	**Primary**
Holy	**Medium**
Fire	**Medium**

Water	Medium
Beast	Medium
Metal	Medium
Nature	Medium
Earth	Medium
Rodent	Minor
Slime	Minor
Light	Minor
Dark	Minor
Insect	Minor
Avian	Minor
Frost	Minor
Arachnid	Minimum
Fish	Minimum
Lightning	Minimum
(Continued . . .)	

Implants		
Type	Mana Upkeep	Description
Bionic Prosthetics +3	0	Overwrites STR and SPD, Values: 130 STR, 65 SPD
Armor Plating +5	0	Overwrites DEF and RES, Values: 150 DEF, 75 RES
Bonded AI	0	Enables direct contact with the System. Overwrites DEX, Value: 3830 DEX

Techno-Organic Interface	0	Enables conscious control over organic and emotional functions. Resists mind-influencing effects.
Advanced Sensors +2	0	Vastly expands scope and effectiveness of senses.
Internal Weapon Bays	0	Enables use of dungeon traps as weapons.
Repulsors +1	0	Enables flight and tactical boosts.
Energy Channels +2	0	Enables user to channel internal energy into external attacks.
Dungeon Field Generator +2	10	Surrounding area counts as dungeon territory. Enables mana absorption within area of effect.
Monster Hangar (Small) +1 (x3)	2	Provides 10 living spaces for small monsters. Unlocks subordinate summoning.
Item Foundry +1	3	Unlocks Item Creation.
Mana Capacitor +2 (x7)	0	Boosts maximum mana by 30 each.
Drone Hangar (Small)	1	A Monster Hangar specialized for nonorganic monsters of limited sentience. Trades amenities for boosted storage capacity. Provides 5 storage spaces.
Monster Hangar (Medium)	5	Provides 5 living spaces for medium-sized monsters. Unlocks subordinate summoning if not available.

World Features		
Name	**World Mana Upkeep**	**Description**
Entrances	**0**	**Entrances between dungeons and the New World. Current Entrances include: Otter Burrow, Rat Warren, Shining Forest, Frozen Reef, Full Metal Hive, Slimy Spire . . . (Continued . . .)**
Cyborg Processing Center	**100**	**A facility for upgrading compatible beings with cybernetic components. Beings in question must be Contracted to the dungeon master and willing to undergo the process with a reasonable understanding of what it entails.**
Ore Vein (x10)	**Varies**	**A vein of a chosen mineral that replenishes over time. Mana cost and upkeep depend on vein size, minerals chosen, and desired speed of replenishment.**
Fertile Soil (x10)	**Varies**	**Soil with the nutrients necessary for healthy plant growth. Nutrients may be replenished over time for mana upkeep. Cost and upkeep depend on field size, soil fertility, and desired nutrients.**
Water Spring (x10)	**Varies**	**A spring that will continuously create water. Cost and upkeep depend on size and rate of replenishment.**

Inventory	
Name	**Description**
??? dagger	A dagger, likely enchanted given the amount of mana held within. Further information could not be determined.
Ursanus pelt	The pelt of an ursanus alpha. Tough, well-insulated, and full of mana.
Ursanus bones	The bones of an ursanus alpha. Extremely durable, and full of mana.
Idrint	Quantity: 5,000 Basic solidified mana, now a standard medium of exchange.
Mana Iron Sword	A sword made of mana iron. Sharper than normal, and well suited to further enchantment.
Rod of Command	A rod used to command golems. This one may control up to ten at once. May take control of unbound golems via physical contact. Also functions as a potent spell focus, particularly for Earth and Metal Magic.
Symbol of Khalbuldor	A pendant used to signify friendship with the Dwarven colony of Khalbuldor.
Grimoire of Arofinas Leolar	The magical techniques and knowledge of Arofinas Leolar, High King of Mirima, as recorded and annotated by himself. This is a copy transcribed by the Elteni Empire.
Anti-Mana Storage Device	Quantity: 5 A metallic sphere with an inverse mana-storage enchantment circle, capable of storing anti-mana energy. May explode if overloaded or damaged while full. Eh, close enough. You built it, so you don't need me to tell you, right?

Subordinates				
Name	**Species**	**Level**	**Mana Upkeep**	
Rattingtale	**Cyber-Rat**	**18**	**1**	**Check Status**
Lilussees	**Cyber-Arachne**	**76**	**50**	**Check Status**
Ateia Niraemia	**???**	**N/A**	**--**	**(Status Could Not Be Viewed)**
Taog Sutharlan	**Human/ Wulver**	**72**	**--**	**Check Status**
01R	**Cyber-Rat Machine Crusader**	**75**	**25**	**Check Status**
02R	**Cyber-Rat Anointed Gunner**	**70**	**25**	**Check Status**
03R	**Cyber-Rat Machine Priest**	**68**	**25**	**Check Status**
04R	**Cyber-Rat Mechanized Runner**	**71**	**25**	**Check Status**
(Cyber-Rats Continued . . .)				
01S	**Cyber-Spider Sacred Stalker**	**72**	**25**	**Check Status**
02S	**Cyber-Spider Stalker**	**32**	**10**	**Check Status**
03S	**Cyber-Arachne**	**69**	**50**	**Check Status**
04S	**Cyber-Arcane Weaver**	**71**	**25**	**Check Status**
(Cyber-Spiders Continued . . .)				

00B	**Superheavy Anointed Armored Fighting Bear**	**77**	**100**	**Check Status**
Uscfrea Ymmason	**Dobhar**	**95**	**--**	**Check Status**
Estrith Edilddaughter	**Dobhar**	**85**	**--**	**Check Status**
Aldreda Aetheludaughter	**Sacred Otterkin**	**5**	**--**	**Check Status**
00C	**Cyber-Dog Armored Command Unit**	**65**	**30**	**Check Status**
01C	**Cyber-Dog Immolator**	**65**	**35**	**Check Status**
02C	**Cyber-Dog Amphibious Assaulter**	**65**	**35**	**Check Status**
00F	**Cyber-Felix Mechanicus Alpha**	**68**	**35**	**Check Status**
Ceitidh Greumach	**Wulver**	**32**	**--**	**Check Status**
Snuan Covenwalker	**Cyber-Rat Drone Fleet Commander**	**57**	**20**	**Check Status**
Melion	**Cyborg Metal Slime**	**80**	**45**	**Check Status**
00Sylvan	**Cyber-Forest Tender**	**80**	**35**	**Check Status**
00WS	**Cyber-Giant Water Slime**	**62**	**40**	**Check Status**
00FS	**Cyber-Giant Fire Slime**	**61**	**40**	**Check Status**

00WE	**Cyber-Giant Water Elemental**	**62**	**40**	**Check Status**
00FE	**Cyber-Giant Fire Elemental**	**60**	**40**	**Check Status**
00LA	**Mechanized Mana Iron Living Armor**	**63**	**35**	**Check Status**
00EW	**Mecha-Adamant Bull Worm**	**71**	**75**	**Check Status**
00SO	**Cyber-Sacred Otterkin Anointed Hunter**	**71**	**50**	**Check Status**
(Other Subordinates Continued . . .)				

Non-Sentient Units		
Name	**Quantity**	**Upkeep**
Stealth Mini Drone Golem	**25**	**0.2 each (5 total)**

Traps			
Name	**Number Active / Deployed**	**Mana Upkeep**	**Description**
Assault Rifle +3	**2/2**	**2**	**Rapid-fire projectile weapon with high penetration.**
Autopistol	**2/2**	**2**	**Rapid-fire projectile weapon with medium penetration.**

Anti-Armor Missile Launcher +2	2/2	2	Homing explosive designed to penetrate armor. Very high penetration.
Anti-Personnel Missile Launcher +2	6/6	6	Homing explosive designed for area damage. Medium penetration.
Stun Ray	1/1	1	Nonlethal electric weapon. Can inflict stun and paralysis statuses.
Wrist Blade +2	2/2	0	Wrist-mounted blades that can be deployed at high speed.
Flamethrower	2/2	2	Deals fire damage and applies burn status in a large cone.
The Equalizer +1	1/1	0	Huh? What the heck is this? Some kind of weird metal that doesn't even exist here? Um . . . well . . . best I can tell it's some sort of antimagic field generator? Eh . . . well, it's yours, not mine, so you don't need me to tell you, right? Like, you already upgraded this thing yourself, so you're good, right?

Dungeon Skills		
Name	**Level**	**Description**
Analyze	**N/A**	**Check the status of a target. More detail for targets within the dungeon. Details depend on level difference.**
Contract	**N/A**	**Bind a consenting target to the dungeon, per terms agreed upon by both parties.**
Transfer	**N/A**	**Move yourself, a subordinate, or a consenting target within your dungeon.**

Dungeon Perks	
Name	**Description**
Human-Dungeon Hybrid	**Enables Implants tab. Enables unique Dungeon Combat skill. Enables direct manipulation of dungeon mana. +100 HP Rooms tab locked. Exterior locked.**
Affinity Sharing	**Can share Primary and Major affinities between subordinates' cores and master core.**

Dungeon Feats		
Name	**Description**	**Effect**
Dungeon Victor	**To the victor go the spoils. Unlocked by destroying or subordinating another dungeon.**	**+1 Perk Point Unlocks Dungeon Warfare category perks.**
Dungeon Overlord	**A master of masters. Unlocked by subordinating another dungeon master.**	**+2 Perk Points Unlocks Subordinate Core category perks.**

Raid Boss	Fine, I'll do it myself. Unlocked by destroying or subordinating another dungeon with no assistance.	+2 Perk Points +1 level in HP Regen skill +1 level in MP Regen skill +50 HP Unlocks Raid Boss category perks.
System Upgrade	Unlocked by manually performing a system upgrade. Which is not supposed to be possible. Ugh, this is going to get complicated, isn't it?	Um, I don't know. Just have +20 Dungeon Perk Points or something. Whatever. You're figuring this out yourself anyway, so close enough.
Purifier Dungeon	Dungeons are supposed to protect the world; you took that duty more literally. Unlocked by destroying a corrupted dungeon core.	+20 Perk Points Unlocks Purifier category perks.
Monster Creator	Granted to a dungeon master who has created a new, never-before-seen monster species.	+20 Perk Points Unlocks Monster Customization.
Matron of the Sacred Otterkin	Thanks to your efforts, a new intelligent species has been born.	+40 Perk Points Additional Perk Points may be granted based on the development and contributions of your client species.

NSLICE-00P's Personal Status

Personal Status			
General Information		Physical Attributes	
Name	Seero	STR	130* (Overwritten)
Species	Human/ Dungeon Core/ Automata Hybrid	DEX	3830* (Overwritten)
Level	151	SPD	80* (Overwritten)
XP	80/100	DEF	150* (Overwritten)
Perk Points	240	RES	75* (Overwritten)
HP	235/235	Magical Attributes	
MP	12,874/12,874	Mana Density	837
		Mana Control	864

Active Skills		
Name	Level	Description
Infused Mana Beam	15	Focus mana into a channeled energy attack. Infused: May infuse Mana Beam with attributed mana.
Sneak	1	Move quietly to avoid notice. Makes it harder for others to notice the user. Effectiveness highly dependent on environment.
Multicasting	13	Can cast several spells at once. Number of simultaneous spells increases with level.
Anti-Mana Channeling	4	My best guess is that this projects a kind of inverse mana that reacts destructively with normal mana, including HP. While it can fully deplete HP, it does not harm matter itself. Requires The Equalizer.

Power Strike	1	Infuse mana into a weapon for heavier damage. Power and range increase with level.
Farcasting	10	Allows the user to manipulate mana and create magic circles at far distances.
Strategic Magic	6	Governs the use of Strategic Magic spells.
Supercharge	14	Fill a spell with additional mana to boost its effects. May cause the spell to misfire. Effect boost depends on the amount and density of mana added. Misfire chance depends on Mana Control and amount of mana added.
Continuous Casting	3	May use additional mana to retain a spell form, allowing the spell to be instantly recast.
Spell Fusion	14	Allows the user to combine compatible spells.
Intense Purifier Flame	10	Imbue a weapon or Flame-attribute attack with purifying Holy-attribute fire, dealing extra damage to corruption, monsters, dungeons, and beings from the Realms of Mana. Intense: Boosts mana density of affected flames.
Heroic Power	4	To handle great responsibility, a hero needs great power. Doubles Mana Density for a short time. May damage user if reused too quickly due to strain from excess mana.
Holy Strike	1	Infuse Holy mana into a weapon strike for heavier damage. Power and range increase with level.
Spell Shaping	20	Enables user to understand and modify the portion of spell circles related to shapes. User may utilize known spell shapes with any available and compatible school of magic.
Spell Modification	7	Enables user to understand and modify the portion of spell circles related to spell modifiers. User may utilize known spell modifiers with any available and compatible spell.

Blessed Growth	1	Imbue a weapon, Nature-attribute spell or skill, or compatible living thing with Holy-attribute life force. Vastly increases speed, scale, and health of plant growth. May have other effects depending on target.
Ritual Magic	3	Allows the user to combine spells with other users for expanded effect.

Passive Skills		
General		
Name	Level	Description
Dungeon Combat	--	Dungeon traps and skills count as personal weapons and skills.
HP Regen	7	Automatically recover HP pool. Increased regeneration speed for damaged body parts.
MP Regen	7	Automatically recover MP pool.
Presence Detection	4	Detect living entities around the user. Range and scope of detection increases with level.
Trap Detection	4	Detect traps. Range and scope of detection increases with level.
Challenger	--	Damage dealt x1.5 against targets of higher level. Damage received x0.75 against attacks from targets of higher level.
Hero Dungeon	--	Unique Hero Skill for NSLICE-00P. PLEASE don't do anything bad with this! Removes dungeon vulnerability to Holy attribute. Grants Dungeon Affinity: Holy (Minor)

Magic		
Name	Level	Description
Spell Penetration	8	Enable spells to bypass a portion of RES. May spend more mana to boost the effect.
Geomancy	7	Elemental spells reduce the target's resistance to that particular element. May spend more mana to boost the effect.
Mana Shield	1	When active, may convert HP damage received into Mana damage. Mana Density will be used instead of DEF/RES in that case. HP damage will resume if Mana is fully drained.
Utility		
Name	Level	Description
Enchanting	24	The art of infusing objects and beings with mana.
Mana Crafting	8	Crafting items through mana rather than physical processes.
Resistances		
Name	Level	Description
Poison Resistance	2	Resist and recovery from poison status. Resist Poison-attributed damage.
Schools of Magic		
Name	Level	Description
Arcane Magic	14	The school of magic governing the manipulation of unattributed mana. A solid foundation for students of the mystic arts, though somewhat less mana efficient than the more specialized schools.
Earth Magic	12	The school of magic governing the manipulation of Earth-attribute mana. One of the basic elemental magics, strong at defensive spells and spells that deal physical damage.

Fire Magic	14	The school of magic governing the manipulation of Fire-attribute mana. One of the basic elemental magics, strong at offensive spells and spells that inflict the burn status.
Water Magic	11	The school of magic governing the manipulation of Water-attribute mana. One of the basic elemental magics, fluid and flexible with many applications.
Air Magic	10	The school of magic governing the manipulation of Air-attribute mana. One of the basic elemental magics, fast and wide reaching.
Light Magic	18	The school of magic governing the manipulation of Light-attribute mana. One of the basic elemental magics, quick and precise spells that are excellent against Dark-aligned foes.
Dark Magic	11	The school of magic governing the manipulation of Dark-attribute mana. One of the basic elemental magics, powerful and obscure, though dangerous if not treated with appropriate caution.
Nature Magic	12	The school of magic governing the manipulation of Nature-attribute mana. Focuses on growth and living things.
Poison Magic	12	The school of magic governing magical poisons. Excels at spreading poison status and dealing damage over time.
Metal Magic	15	The school of magic governing the manipulation of metal. Generally focuses on manipulating existing metal, though may create metal directly at great cost.
Lightning Magic	10	The school of magic governing the manipulation of lightning. Extremely fast and powerful, though somewhat expensive to cast.
Frost Magic	9	The school of magic governing cold and ice. Excellent at controlling and slowing.
Recovery Magic	10	The school of magic governing healing through magic.

Illusion Magic	10	The school of magic governing the manipulation of senses and emotions.
Gravity Magic	15	The school of magic governing the force of gravity. Complex but powerful.
Spatial Magic	15	The school of magic governing manipulation of space. Extremely potent, complex, and dangerous, which is all reflected by the high mana cost.
Holy Magic	18	The school of magic governing the manipulation of Holy-attribute mana, the attribute of the Aesdes that protects the world.
Hero		
Name	Level	Description
Heroic Challenger	3	A hero never gives up, no matter the odds. Attacks ignore a small percent of target's DEF/RES/Immunities and always deal a minimum amount of damage. Gives a small chance to survive a fatal hit with 1 HP.

Spells		
Spell Shapes		
Name	Level	Description
Armor	7	Coat a target in mana, generally for defensive purposes.
Bomb	8	Pack mana into a dense package that explodes.
Barrier	18	Form mana in a defensive surface or wall.
Beam	20	Concentrate mana into a precise, fast-moving beam.
Blade	10	Form mana in a sharp sword that may be held.
Blast	14	Condense mana, then release it in an explosive blast.

Bolt	20	Form mana into a package that can be launched.
Burst	6	Send out a blast of mana in all directions around the user.
Chain	15	Form mana into a binding that wraps around a target.
Clone	14	Form mana into a shape similar to the user that will execute simple orders. Increased skill will increase the power and substance of the clones and the complexity of orders they may accept.
Cloud	8	Condense mana into a gaseous form that lingers in an area.
Curse	5	Infuse a target with hostile mana. Exact effects depend on the attribute used. Use of alchemic ingredients or conduits related to the target may increase duration, effects, and potency.
Dash	9	Coats user in mana and propels them forward. Behavior may change based on attribute applied. For example, Earth attribute will cause the user to travel underground and then burst out at the target location.
Eruption	6	A blast of mana bursts out of the target surface.
Fist	3	Concentrates mana on the user's fist. Generally produces powerful, if short-ranged attacks.
Floor	8	Fills the ground with mana. Exact effects will depend on the attribute chosen. May be spread out in a wide area or concentrated on a single point.
Infusion	18	Fill a target with mana.
Miniatures	7	Splits mana into numerous small amounts.
Prison	9	Entrap a target in mana that will attempt to prevent movement or action. May also interfere with outside attacks on the target depending on attribute used.
Rain	9	Create a mass of mana in the air that will bombard an area over time.

Siphon	12	Establish a connection between the user and target's mana. Generally used to forcibly transfer mana, but exact effect may vary with attribute. Can be resisted depending on target's Mana Control.
Sensing	12	Replicate or extend senses via mana. Exact sense and method depends on attribute used.
Spike	9	Shape mana into a thin point meant for piercing.
Twister	8	Rapidly spin and cycle mana.
Wave	6	Form mana into a wide surface that moves in the specified direction.
Spell Modifiers		
Name	Level	Description
Channeled	5	Spell increases in intensity the longer it is cast.
Delayed - Contact	3	Spell circle is not triggered on completion, but triggers automatically when contacted by a target. Spell does not require any additional mana to maintain, but will eventually fade if not triggered. Higher levels allow user to specify target characteristics.
Delayed - Trigger	3	Spell circle is not triggered on completion but on further command by the user. Spell does not require any additional mana to maintain, but will eventually fade if not triggered. User must be in range to trigger the spell.
Dense	20	Condense mana even further, increasing the mana density and effect of the spell.
Fusion	19	Spell can combine with itself or other compatible spells.
Hardened	3	Improves spell defense against piercing/disruption effects.
Lasting	5	Reduces speed at which mana disperses, increasing spell duration.

Piercing	5	Increases spell penetration against RES and magic barriers.
Repeating	4	Spell receives more mana than usual and uses additional mana to recast itself upon completion. May recast more than once if mana is available. Requires the Supercharge skill.
Wide	7	Increases spell's area of effect.
Unique Holy Spells		
Name	Level	Description
Holy Ward	1	Protect an area with Holy mana, warding off monsters and evil. Also boosts HP and Mana recovery. Does not protect from attacks.
Banishment	1	Attempts to return a target creature to its origin realm. No effect on inhabitants of the world.
Divination	4	Attempt to read the state of the world. May reveal things that were, things that are, or things that yet may be. What, exactly, none can predict, only that what is revealed should not be dismissed.
Illusion Aspects		
Name	Level	Description
Calm	8	Dampen target's emotions, calming them down. Higher levels may dampen specific emotions.
Fear	5	Fill the target with fear. Higher levels may specify object of target's fear.
Hunger	3	Simulate a biological need for food. Higher levels may target other biological or even psychological needs.
Unique Spatial Spells		
Spatial Angling	12	A basic distortion of space. The fundamental technique for all Spatial Magic.

Stretched Steps	5	By folding space along a specified path, the user can either increase or decrease the speed of movement.
Spatial Folding	6	A distortion of space severe enough to reconnect at a different point. The basic technique that enables more complex applications.
Blink	3	A full distortion of space allows the user to instantly move from one point to another.

Strategic Spells			
School	Name	Level	Description
Modular	Prismatic Bombardment	15	Continuously rains Beam spells on the target area. Attributes may be chosen or swapped per circle at will. If Fusion modifier is available, beams may be combined at will.
Modular	Prismatic Rain	5	Bombards a wide area with large compatible projectile-type spells; default is Bomb shape.
Modular	Prismatic Floor	3	Infuses a wide area to apply effects from below. Exact effects may vary with attributes used.
Modular	Prismatic Dome	7	Form a massive shield over the target area. User may designate element of individual sections or combine elements for the shield as a whole. Resistance to given element will depend on the ratio of magic circles used for that element.

Bound Artifacts	
Name	Description
Sea Dragon-bone Axe	An axe formed from the magic bones of a mana-consuming sea dragon. Absorbs mana. May break magic circles on contact. If touched by anyone but the user, drains their mana and uses it to attack.

Personal Feats		
Name	Description	Effect
Against the Odds	Do not ask how many there are, but where they are. Unlocked by winning a fight when outnumbered by equal or higher-leveled opponents.	+1 Perk Point
Solo Conquest	I am the dungeon master now. Unlocked by conquering a dungeon alone.	+1 level in HP Regen skill +1 level in MP Regen skill +1 level in Presence Detection skill +1 level in Trap Detection skill
Arcane Prodigy	The career of a supreme sorcerer does not start on the beaten path. Unlocked by learning a high-tier magic skill under level twenty without spending Perk Points.	+3 Perk Points Unlocks more advanced magic perks.
Enchanter	The first step on the path of the magic craftsman. Unlocked by manually accomplishing a Mana Infusion.	+1 level in Enchanting skill

Skill Creator	You don't just master the path. You define it. Unlocked by creating a brand-new skill.	To be honest, this normally happens when you're a MUCH higher level, so I'm a bit worried about passing you this much this early, but, um, okay. +20 Perk Points
Healer	Anyone can deal in death. It takes an expert to deal in life. Unlocked by using mana to heal a wound.	+1 level in Recovery Magic skill
Challenger	Levels and odds are just numbers. Unlocked by defeating an who is the greater of level 10 twice your level while alone.	+3 Perk Points + Challenger skill
Strategic Mage	A strategic mage is king of the battlefield. Unlocked by affecting a hundred or more equal-size opponents (or equivalent mass of other-size opponents) at the same time with magic.	+1 level in Strategic Magic skill Unlocks Strategic Spells.
World Defender	You have protected the world itself, at great risk to yourself.	+20 Perk Points +1 level in Holy Magic skill
Hero	You faced terrible odds for the sake of the world and proved victorious. You are truly a champion of the world. Please, please, please keep it that way!	+20 Perk Points Grants Unique Hero Skill: Hero Dungeon.

Most Worthy	Whosoever wields this skill, who is clearly worthy, shall possess the power of their opponent's weapon. Unlocked by taking control of an artifact bound to someone else.	+10 levels in Enchanting skill
Hero of the Sacred Otterkin	So . . . we normally give this when someone has done something that protected the existence of an entire species. And like, you just *created* a new species, so . . . I guess that means you are, in fact, responsible for their continued existence. You know what? Whatever.	+20 Perk Points +1 level in Holy Water Ball spell +1 level in Holy Strike skill
Spell Shaper	Mana may take many forms, but the true mage knows that the mana remains the same. Unlocked by manually adjusting a magic circle into a new spell.	Grants Spell Shaping skill.
Spell Adjuster	Magic is the art of changing reality. So why would a spell be static and immutable? Unlocked by manually applying a spell modifier to a magic circle.	Grants Spell Modification skill.
Magic Crafter	Both crafters and mages reshape reality to fit their needs. One just does it faster. Unlocked by crafting an item purely through mana (excepting default spell shapes such as Blade)!	+1 level in Mana Crafting skill

Mana Maestro	The flows of mana are not easily understood, but you can guide them at will. Unlocked by an impressive feat of mana manipulation; in this case, manually canceling a Supercharged strategic spell.	+5 Perk Points +30 Mana Control
Spell Constructor	Magic pushes the boundaries of possibility. And you have pushed the boundary of magic. Unlocked by manual construction of a sufficiently complex magic circle, and manual learning of one of the most complicated schools of magic.	+10 Perk Points Grants additional knowledge of the spell circle language.
Dungeon Conqueror Feats		
Name	Description	Effect
Dungeon Conqueror (Rat Cave)	Unlocked by conquering the Rat Cave Dungeon.	+1 Perk Point +1 level in Sneak skill
Dungeon Conqueror (Earth Tunnels)	Unlocked by conquering the Earth Tunnels Dungeon.	+1 Perk Point +1 level in Earth Magic skill
Dungeon Conqueror (Spider Tree)	Unlocked by conquering the Spider Tree Dungeon.	+1 Perk Point +1 level in Poison Resistance skill
Dungeon Conqueror (Slimy Pit)	Unlocked by conquering the Slimy Pit Dungeon.	+1 Perk Point +1 level in Poison Bolt spell
Dungeon Conqueror (Glimmering Grove)	Unlocked by conquering the Glimmering Grove Dungeon.	+1 Perk Point +1 level in Light Magic skill

Dungeon Conqueror (Nature's Wrath)	Unlocked by conquering the Nature's Wrath Dungeon.	+1 Perk Point +1 level in Nature Magic skill
Dungeon Conqueror (Beast Lair)	Unlocked by conquering the Beast Lair Dungeon.	+1 Perk Point +1 level in Power Strike skill
Dungeon Conqueror (Darkest Dungeon)	Unlocked by conquering the Darkest Dungeon Dungeon.	+1 Perk Point +1 level in Dark Magic skill
Dungeon Conqueror (Metal Armory)	Unlocked by conquering the Metal Armory Dungeon.	+1 Perk Point +1 level in Metal Magic skill
(Continued . . .)		
Dungeon Purifier Feats		
Dungeon Purifier (Inferno)	A dungeon is dangerous to everyone in the world. A corrupted dungeon is dangerous to the world itself. And you conquered it all the same. Unlocked by purifying the Corrupted Dungeon (Inferno Realm).	+5 Perk Points +1 level in Purifier Flame skill
Dungeon Purifier (Overgrowth)	A dungeon is dangerous to everyone in the world. A corrupted dungeon is dangerous to the world itself. And you conquered it all the same. Unlocked by purifying the Corrupted Dungeon (Overgrowth Realm).	+5 Perk Points +1 level in Blessed Growth skill

About the Author

Icalos is a lifelong fan of sci-fi, fantasy, and video games, and the author of the Terminate the Other World! series, which was originally released on Royal Road. To learn more, visit his website at icalosbooks.com.

Podium

DISCOVER MORE

STORIES UNBOUND

PodiumEntertainment.com

Printed in the USA
CPSIA information can be obtained
at www.ICGtesting.com
JSHW021921071124
73181JS00001B/1

9 781039 489837